SOMETIMES NUCLEAR WEAPONS DON'T
HAVE TO BE DETONATED TO CAUSE DISASTER

HAWTHORN'S HILL

SOMETIMES NUCLEAR WEAPONS DON'T
HAVE TO BE DETONATED TO CAUSE DISASTER

HAWTHORN'S HILL

MEREO
CIRENCESTER

Mereo Books

1A The Wool Market Dyer Street Cirencester Gloucestershire GL7 2PR
An imprint of Memoirs Publishing www.mereobooks.com

Hawthorn's Hill: 978-1-86151-304-5

First published in Great Britain in 2015
by Mereo Books, an imprint of Memoirs Publishing

The address for Memoirs Publishing Group Limited can be found at
www.memoirspublishing.com

The Memoirs Publishing Group Ltd Reg. No. 7834348

The Memoirs Publishing Group supports both The Forest Stewardship Council® (FSC®) and
the PEFC® leading international forest-certification organisations. Our books carrying both the
FSC label and the PEFC® and are printed on FSC®-certified paper. FSC® is the only
forest-certification scheme supported by the leading environmental organisations including
Greenpeace. Our paper procurement policy can be found at
www.memoirspublishing.com/environment

Cover design: Ray Lipscombe

Typeset in 11/14pt Bembo
by Wiltshire Associates Publisher Services Ltd. Printed and bound in Great Britain by
Printondemand-Worldwide, Peterborough PE2 6XD

To Susan, who put up with my ramblings

CHAPTER ONE

Lieutenant Colonel Frederick Zawutu, 'Mutti' in the local patois, used his regimental forage cap to wipe the dust-caked sweat from his brow and leaped from the Command Land Rover outside the old Government building. His paler-skinned adjutant, Captain de Lancy, followed. The two men walked delicately over a scattering of broken masonry towards a gaping hole in the stuccoed wall a few paces in front of them.

Just then there came a sharp report from behind and simultaneously a bullet flicked Zawutu's left epaulette. It ripped off the badge-emblazoned button and left a frayed remnant of epaulette flapping loosely on a few tenuous threads. Zawutu flinched at the missile's passing and jerked his head away from the pressure wave that indented his cheek like a ghostly puff of breath.

"Christ!" he exclaimed incongruously, for he was a Muslim. But almost before the word was out, the deflected high-velocity, steel-jacketed round spun and slammed into the concrete wall immediately in front of the two officers and sprayed out a cone of jagged-edged masonry chips in a deadly arc. The Colonel and de Lancy reacted too late to protect themselves. De Lancy, slightly behind, was partially shielded and received only superficial cuts about the face. Zawutu took the brunt of it. One razor-sharp segment with enough velocity to penetrate a plank sliced open his left cheek like a zip. Instinctively he clamped a hand to the injury and swung round to face the incoming fire, in anticipation of another shot.

"No!" screamed de Lancy, grabbing the Colonel's arm.

"Leave me," Zawutu ordered, pulling away. "The bastard's up there somewhere." He indicated the flat face of the building opposite. "And I want him."

The escort, a platoon from Zawutu's own 2nd Eshanti Regiment, deployed rapidly and began working its way towards the entrance of the building. The Subaltern in command gave a hand signal and the leading section rushed the shrapnel-scarred doorway under cover of rapid fire from the other two sections of the platoon.

Zawutu, standing like a statue, assessed the target building with a soldier's eye. The only possible firing position, taking into account the bullet's trajectory, was behind one of the first floor windows. He called out to the subaltern "Up there" and pointed. De Lancy, worried for his own safety as well as that of his commanding officer, took another grip on the Colonel's sleeve.

"Gently," Zawutu said sternly, brushing off the urgent hand for a second time. "We must not be seen to be afraid."

A moment later a short, sharp burst of automatic fire from inside the building preceded the sudden and ungainly despatch of a body through the window Zawutu had indicated. A doll-like shape crashed to the ground only yards away and lay broken where it fell. A pool of deep red began to form around the head.

Zawutu sniffed. "Gotcha," he said, and waved his thanks to the platoon commander. He then turned to de Lancy. "Suicidal idiot," he said of the sniper. "Now we can go in." He kicked aside heaps of assorted rubble, creating dust spirals about his feet as he ducked through the ragged hole and straightened. He paused to pull a handkerchief from his pocket and press it to the spouting gash in his cheek. "Let's go" he ordered de Lancy, and advanced into the cavernous entrance hall.

A profound sense of triumph lent comfort to the heat of the afternoon. The stickiness of layers of sweat and grime, and now the blood which was already leaking from the soaked handkerchief and running freely down his face, seemed as nothing compared with what he had achieved this day. He halted in the centre of the atrium and dabbed again with the sodden handkerchief in a futile attempt to stem the flow. His heart raced still, but he was fit and it would soon settle.

The square hallway, deeply coated with the detritus of years of neglect, surrounded him. Fresh footprints trailed across the floor and each print revealed a small island of speckled marble which shone dully in the suppressed light. Towards the rear of the hall a pair of curved, ornately-banistered staircases ascended in two sweeping arcs to the floor above. He eyed their Victorian splendour and reflected that it had taken three days of genocidal bloodletting to make it possible for him to enter here and enjoy the inside of this colonial masterpiece. This one-time centre of colonial government held a strange fascination for him, always had, ever since his father had brought him here as a boy. He felt it again now and smiled in anticipation of stewardship.

The coup had succeeded beyond all expectation, but he was angry nevertheless. Brigadier Mgabi, the deposed President, could have prevented much of the bloodshed if he had not hung on to power for so long. The outcome had been inevitable from the morning of the second day. Capitulation then would have saved many lives, most of them from Mgabi's own tribe, the Ushkuu. But on this glorious day, why worry about such things? He wrung out the handkerchief, leaving a spattering of blood on the marble floor, and held it once more to his cheek.

"I am the new President of Zawanda" he said, as much to himself as to de Lancy. "Did you believe it could ever be?"

"It was ordained, sir," de Lancy replied unctuously.

Zawutu smiled at that and marched to the foot of the stairs, hands on hips. "Very well. Let us see what we have inherited."

De Lancy hesitated. "Shouldn't we wait until the building has been cleared, sir?"

"Nonsense," said Zawutu reassuringly. He pointed to the many confused footprints in the dust. "Major Moi is here somewhere, with a large force. He will have made it safe."

But not safe enough, thought de Lancy, glancing at Zawutu's bloodstained face and tentatively fingering his own where it had been grazed by slivers of flying concrete.

Zawutu glanced up into the towering atrium, at the magnificent stained-glass dome which allowed fragile beams of multi-coloured light to flicker in the mote-filled atmosphere like strings of excited glow worms. He felt proud to be here, in this place, like this.

"No parliament has sat here for twenty-four years since the first military coup of '75," he said to the ceiling, fascinated by the constantly-changing mix of colours way above his head. "The three presidents since then preferred to run the country from the Ministry of Defence offices on Ruanda Street. Did you know that? It's more defensible, you see, and they needed it to be, by God. Just look around you, see the neglect. I intend to change all that. I shall refurbish this wonderful place and rule from here." He lowered his head and glanced at his adjutant, slightly embarrassed at his own posturing.

De Lancy seemed to jerk his mind back from a distance. "I'm sorry, sir. I was just thinking about the troubles, the tribal wars," he said sombrely. "I was a young boy at the time of the first coup and I can still see the piles of bodies lying in the streets. I have seen it again today, though not so bad. It's amazing there are any warriors left in the two tribes." He hesitated at his boldness. "It was the first Ushkuu President after the British left who started this chain reaction, wasn't it? Used the army on the Eshanti?"

Zawutu nodded. "Impatience and greed were at the bottom of it. But the cycle stops here. Far better to make new friends of old enemies."

"Culture, sir. Tribal culture," de Lancy said. "The Eshanti and the Ushkuu have been at each other's throats for as long as time."

"But it doesn't always have to be like that," Zawutu replied curtly, for he had expected agreement. He wrung out the handkerchief, once again dripping blood on the ground. De Lancy sensibly held his tongue.

"The worst always occurs immediately after a coup," Zawutu went on. "When the winners take revenge on the losers. Ushkuu slaughter Eshanti, then Eshanti butcher the Ushkuu. It's madness, and I intend to stop it."

De Lancy said nothing. He still believed that the tribes were a law unto themselves, and whilst he hoped Zawutu would succeed in breaking the inexorable circle of death, he feared he might not.

Zawutu strode up three stairs, then came back down again, restless, uncertain what to do next. He could hardly believe his luck. A Lieutenant Colonel with only three year's seniority in rank, President! But then perhaps it was not so remarkable after all, for hadn't all those senior to him either already held the post or been too afraid to take it? It had simply been his turn.

Mgabi's regime had run its course. It had emulated the pattern of the previous two military juntas; once their Swiss bank accounts had reached a satisfactory level a sort of diplomatic fatigue set in, the labour of governing becoming too much of a chore. Better then to give way to a new contender and slip away with the spoils to some civilised country where a rich man was appreciated and the tap water safe to drink.

Zawutu smiled to himself at the irony. "This way, I think," he said to de Lancy, breaking the reflective mood with a shake of the head. Together they entered what had been the robing room and Zawutu gazed around the walls at the hooks and the lockers that had held nothing in them for those long years. The low placing of the hooks amused him. He had forgotten just how tall he himself was. Five feet eleven was unusually tall for a Zawandan. He had none of the rotundness that comes with a native diet heavy in carbohydrates. Some of his features were also atypical; the lips not so heavy, the whites of the eyes not so pigmented. In every other respect though, his appearance was true to the Zawandan mould. A round, cherubic face, a smile like a searchlight and woolly black hair tight to the skull. It was a handsome face even by Western standards, friendly, with a hint of good humour around the eyes and corners of the mouth, not to be mistaken for softness. Those who had erred in that respect had quickly come to regret it.

He cocked his head to one side at the sound of footsteps approaching, and smiled as his Regimental 2nd in Command, Major Josi Moi, bounced into the room with the gait of an Eshanti long distance tracker, rolling on heel and toe.

"Josi," Zawutu said ebulliently, stepping forward and embracing his junior officer. "We did it!"

Moi eased himself away. Such intimacy between males was not the way of the tribes. Even on such a glorious day as this, Mutti should remember his upbringing and curb these English habits. He nodded and flexed his lips into what passed for a smile. There was no softness there. Fat and squat like most of his tribe, Moi had bulging, heavily-pigmented eyes which looked everywhere but at you. His lips were thick and pendulous and he had the same skull cap type crinkly hair as his new President. He carried himself loosely, like an overweight athlete, and had the surly look of a man given to bouts of temper and violence; a man to be avoided if possible.

"Yes, Mutti," he said from a safe distance. "And we must quickly consolidate your victory. What's happened to your face?"

Zawutu dabbed repeatedly at the wound with the blood-sodden handkerchief. "It's nothing. Just a scratch."

"It needs attention" Moi said. He turned to de Lancy. "Find the Medical Officer."

Zawutu shook his head and de Lancy paused. "All in good time. First I want a shower in the Presidential Palace bathroom. The doctor can visit me there. After that we will consolidate. No one is going anywhere we can't find them. Patience, Josi."

Moi made no argument. He merely waved de Lancy out. "Check that it's secure out there," he ordered, then stood aside to let Zawutu pass. Zawutu emerged through the hole into brilliant sunlight and glanced around him. He again congratulated the young escort commander on his skill at disposing of the sniper, told Moi to get the hole fixed, then climbed aboard the command Land Rover.

"To the Palace," Moi instructed a delighted Lieutenant as he swung himself up into the cab of the leading truck.

★ ★ ★

On arrival Moi clicked his tongue in annoyance. The Palace servants, all seventy of them, knowing the form when a change of government is imminent, had fled. "Stupid cattle!" he exclaimed angrily. "They were Itulu tribe. They had nothing to fear from us."

Zawutu spoke softly but firmly. "Today is not a day for anger, Josi. They'll come back in a day or two, there's to be no recriminations or punishments. You can't blame the poor fools. Remember the cruelty that took place here the last two times? And anyway, they're not needed for a simple shower. Oh, and see if you can find a drink. The electricity is still on, so the refrigerators should be working. A long cool something for me and bring it to the Presidential bathroom."

Half way up the left hand sweep of a twin flight of stairs which mirrored exactly those in the Government building, Zawutu paused and called down, "I've changed my mind. Bring whisky if there is any. Bring the whole bloody bottle, I feel good."

Moi paused, then remembered that the boss did not take his religion so far as to deny himself alcohol. "Yes sir" he answered.

The bathroom referred to was an old-fashioned Victorian affair. It looked sad and neglected. Sand had penetrated here too and laid a gritty patina over everything. The heavy porcelain was badly chipped, the fitments rusty and broken and loose tiles leaned drunkenly from the walls.

Zawutu sighed. "The whole bloody country is the same," he muttered in exasperation as he turned on the shower taps and watched a dribble of rusty water emerge to drip sorrowfully into the bath and trace a revolting brown stain all the way to the plug hole. It had obviously been like this for a very long time.

He swore again and tried the bath taps. After a rumble from the pipes and a spurt or two of discoloured, gritty liquid, a steady flow of almost clean water built up and began to steam. There was actually a plug as well.

The new President undressed and lowered himself into the iron bath. An old jar of congealed bath salts, the cap removed and the whole jar submerged under water, produced a satisfying quantity of bubbles, which he swished backwards and forwards energetically. Suds soon overflowed onto the bathroom floor, but he ignored them.

"The whole place needs redecorating anyway," he announced to his distorted reflection in the patchily de-silvered mirror that somehow still clung to the wall opposite the bath.

He grunted pleasurably. After fighting a war, small though it had been in world terms, it was a delight to find himself concerned with matters of light and colour and furnishings. "I think I'll bring in an expert," he said to the mirror. "Someone from Europe."

He had just committed this idea to mind when Moi appeared carrying a laden tray.

"Have you brought bottled water?" Zawutu questioned anxiously. "No one should drink the poison that comes from these taps."

Moi held up a bottle of imported spring water. "But we won't need it," he said as he filled two capacious glasses to their rims with neat whisky. "This is a celebration."

Moi handed a glass to Zawutu, then seated himself gingerly on the enamel rim of the toilet bowl. The seat and lid had disappeared long ago, and the flush, judging by the encrusted condition of what remained, must have failed at about the same time, but Moi took no notice of the filth. He swallowed a large measure of whisky and spoke. "You should appear on television and let the people know you are their new President" he said.

Zawutu slapped his hand on the water in an angry gesture. More suds splashed over and Moi hastily jerked his feet out of harm's way. "No" Zawutu barked. "Only second raters do that. In civilised countries a change of leadership is announced routinely as a normal item on the news, and that's how it will be done here. See to it."

Moi nodded, calmly accepting the rebuke. "And what of the Ushkuu?"

"Leave them alone!" Zawutu said with considerable force. "Talk with their leaders. I want them pacified, not enraged. You understand me?"

Moi nodded again, but kept his eyes downcast to conceal a sudden flare of disappointment. The Ushkuu were the traditional enemies of the Eshanti. Culling the opposition tribe had always been the prerogative of a new President, and Moi had been looking forward to taking part in, if not leading, the bloody event. He suppressed his feelings with difficulty and managed to control his reply.

"We believe Brigadier Mgabi has fled to Kenya and most of his ministers with him. The Ushkuu have few leaders left. They will be flexible once we have made a few examples."

The word 'examples' rang a cautionary note in Zawutu's brain. He glanced sharply at the figure perched on the toilet rim. "No violence, Josi. Hear me. Just remember, I need peace, not continuous guerrilla warfare."

Moi raised his glass in salutation. "I shall do as you say, Mutti." The porcelain rim was cutting into his buttocks now and he stood up to massage the offended parts. He needed to get out of here anyway, before Mutti could place any more curbs on him.

"Should I gather all commanding officers and staff together?" he said as an excuse for leaving. "You will want to thank them and talk of the future?"

Zawutu opened his mouth to reply, but at that moment the Regimental Medical Officer walked in. Zawutu pointed to the ragged tear in his cheek, now surrounded with dried blood. "Sew this up" he commanded.

"Let me take a look" the MO replied calmly.

Zawutu ignored him. "Yes. Assemble all available officers down to the rank of Major," he said, turning back to Moi. "I'll be there as soon as this is done."

★ ★ ★

"Now what about this Zawandan business, Henry?" the PM asked his Foreign and Commonwealth Secretary, speaking over his shoulder from his position gazing out of one of the tall, rectangular Georgian windows of his private study at Number 10 Downing Street. He had called in Henry Beauchamp as soon as news of the military uprising in Zawanda had reached him.

Beauchamp, debonair as always in his dark grey Savile Row suit and Guards tie, short and stocky against the PM's six feet one inch, frowned as was his habit before answering questions. He stood half a room's width away from the Prime Minister, thighs not quite in contact with the edge of a magnificent circular table which formed a centrepiece to the room. He stared at the Prime Minister's back, thinking that he needed a haircut. Then he brought his mind back to the question.

"Lieutenant Colonel Zawutu will undoubtedly be the next President," he replied. "Fortunately he's not a bad chap by all accounts. A distinct improvement on Brigadier Mgabi certainly, and more popular with the army, which in itself is a miracle for that godforsaken place."

"Hmm" The PM said cautiously. He turned from observing a squirrel scamper across the lawn. "How these wild creatures survive in the city I'll never know," he said, to Beauchamp's mystification, then went on, "We've had little or no protest from Zawutu's immediate neighbours, nor, indeed, from the UN. Charles Pritchard spoke to me on the phone from New York only an hour ago to reassure me on that point. It seems everyone who matters will be glad to see the back of this Mgabi fellow. My guess is that Zawutu will be tolerated until he proves himself one way or the other. Is that the way you read the situation?"

He walked round his desk towards the centre table, halting diametrically across from his Foreign Secretary. Beauchamp was immediately and irrationally tempted to bend forward and rest his fingertips on the table's edge, but desisted in case he should defile the immaculately-polished surface. Instead he interlaced them, held them at chest height, then released them and let them fall to his sides. The need to make these small movements in the presence of the PM had become annoyingly compulsive ever since that luminary had once grumbled at him not to fidget. Beauchamp clenched his fists to his sides and pondered for the umpteenth time how such a plebeian Prime Minister - the man didn't even ride, let alone to hounds - could engender such a degree of nervousness in him. With an almost invisible, self-admonitory shake of the head he replied to the PM's question.

"It's very early days, Prime Minister. The event itself will probably pass with little turbulence. Many single-party African states will keep mum about it in case the notion of rebellion should infect their own people, whilst others will genuinely be pleased to see an end to oppression in Zawanda. I just hesitate about the aftermath. You know how these tribal nations operate. Success for Zawutu is synonymous with success for the Eshanti tribe. That in turn shuts off the money tap to the Ushkuu and foments old jealousies and hatreds. In the past, elements of the tribe loyal to the new regime have been allowed to indulge in what can only be described as genocidal culls. Whether Zawutu will resort to that sort of thing we don't know. He is more civilised than most of his predecessors, which is good. He has a second class honours degree in Political Science from Cambridge and one and a half years at Sandhurst, which should have smoothed out some of the rough edges, but one can't be sure with these people. They have a habit of reverting to type terribly easily. It's a matter of wait and see, I'm afraid."

The PM shrugged. This wasn't a terribly important event in today's world, he reasoned, particularly when set against such horrors as the civil war in Bosnia or the starving millions in West Africa, but it merited a response at least. Zawanda was, after all, a member of the British Commonwealth and the House would expect a statement.

"You're probably right," he said. "It isn't as if it's likely to spread or anything like that. Zawanda can only be about the size of Ireland, which for Africa is minuscule. But as nominal leader of the Commonwealth, Britain must be seen to be doing something about it. Not that we had much success in damping down the last three coups, nor even tried very hard, to be honest."

His regretful tone now changed to a more optimistic one. "But perhaps we can influence matters better this time by recognising the new regime immediately Zawutu's position is secure. Maybe offer token financial assistance to repair any structural damage with strings. There must be no culling of the Ushkuu."

Beauchamp nodded and used his right hand in a habitual movement to smooth down his close grey hair. "We'll have to be pretty quick off the mark," he pointed out. "Most tribal retribution takes place towards the end of a coup and during the first few days following. And even if Zawutu is against it, the Eshanti might run amuck before he can stop them. It's a gamble, Prime Minister, but we'll certainly do our best."

The PM then gave a smile, his first of the meeting. He tended not to smile too much at those already on board, but the odd grin kept the troops happy, he found. He therefore allowed Beauchamp the pleasure of a full, regularly-polished spread.

"One can't do more, Henry," he replied. "And in any event, as I say, Zawanda is too small a country for this coup to affect Britain one way or the other. Just try and smooth things through. Talk to Zawutu. Get his commitment to the Commonwealth and use it to control any excesses."

Beauchamp resented the patronising tone, though he should have been used to it. Socially the two were miles apart and the best Henry had ever been able to say of his party leader, in private and among his own cronies of course, was that Masters was *almost* a gentleman. Notwithstanding that, he replied courteously: "Yes, Prime Minister." He had, of course, recognised the valedictory nature of the rare Prime Ministerial smile and made his excuses.

"Oh and draft me a few cutting remarks to throw at the opposition. They're bound to blame us," the PM added, just as Beauchamp was about to close the door.

★ ★ ★

In countries across the world, the change of leadership in Zawanda was not considered a problem. Nevertheless, most, including the big ones ran routine checks on the new President on the basis that it is always prudent to learn as much as one can about a man who might be capable of springing a few unpleasant surprises.

In London they had it all on file anyway. The relevant department pulled it out, dusted it off and found it more interesting than they'd expected. Zawutu, it seemed, had talked a lot about his ambitions during his stints at Cambridge and Sandhurst, remarks assiduously recorded on account of his being considered minor aristocracy in his own country and therefore of passing interest to those with a watching brief over Commonwealth comings and goings. Since then his career had been followed with rather less interest, no more detailed than a minute or two on the file or a situation paper added by the then High Commissioner, a post no longer extant, having been axed years before for economic reasons. Nevertheless, the sum of the information collected had over the years built into an adequate picture of the man.

The father, an Eshanti chieftain, had, so the file informed, been a strong influence on the boy until an Ushkuu army sergeant had cut the old man down following the coup of 75. Zawutu had been preparing to enter manhood at the time and the trauma of losing his parent and ceremonial mentor had left a scar which, according to the history, had remained stubbornly with him. He had not sought revenge as tribal culture demanded an attitude which caused his own people to wonder about him. Then, as he matured, his frequent utterances on the subject of peaceful tribal co-existence were secretly laughed at in the villages and derided as ridiculous, except, that is, for a few minor chieftains who silently agreed with him.

In the UK, these same unpopular views found sympathy with his fellow students and cadets, and even higher up the system, where they were contrasted with the repressive policies of the then President and found refreshingly liberal; perhaps dangerously so for him when he returned to Zawanda, some thought.

The more solid facts in the file concerned his schooling at a Catholic mission, even though he was Muslim born; an overseas place at Cambridge University, contiguous with one of Zawanda's precious Sandhurst vacancies, all of which in their way invested him with a level of tutelage and western civilising influences which were rare in his country.

Promotions and the military oath of allegiance quite naturally muted the anarchical outbursts of his youth, though rumour had it that he still held strong views on the issue of tribal integration as a means of furthering Zawanda's development.

These simple facts and assumptions were reasonably well documented. However, the scrutineers found it odd that there was virtually nothing on file about his private life. He hadn't married; there had been a few girlfriends at Cambridge and one or two during his Sandhurst days, but other than that he had shown no serious interest in the opposite sex. There was no record of mistresses or girlfriends in Zawanda, where it was usual for Eshanti warriors to take one young girl after another to prove their manhood. The incongruity struck a discordant note at the Africa desk, but in the absence of a psychological analysis the profile was routinely updated as comprehensively as the various agencies could manage, collated and committed to computer by MI6, who flagged it for regular review. London then sat back to await the long term outcome of Zawutu's inevitable rise to power.

★ ★ ★

Once he had administered the local anaesthetic and inserted a row of fifteen stitches into Zawutu's cheek, the doctor jabbed in a shot of anti-tetanus serum and began re packing his medical haversack. "Ten days, sir," he said when asked about removing the stitches. "And the dressing should be changed every day. Shall I send you a nurse?"

Zawutu shook his head. "I'm sure we can manage. Thank you doctor."

The bathwater had cooled by now, but Zawutu lay there fingering his cheek. It felt dead and awkward as he stretched his jaw to test how much movement remained. "Bloody thing!" he muttered. To take his mind off it he began recalling the day Zawanda had received independence from colonial rule. It seemed appropriate just now when another new start was upon them. What a grand day it had been. Everyone had said so. There had been bands and flags and speeches, ceremonies of departure as British troops withdrew and native battalions assumed responsibility; and there was anxiety lest a larger neighbour should take advantage and invade. But still, it had been a grand day. There had even been fireworks.

His happy smile faded. It was also true, he pointed out to himself, that Zawanda had enjoyed nothing like it since. One dictator after another had bled the country dry. The British might have been domineering and autocratic, he reminded himself, but at least they were fair. They had been happy days, as he remembered them, and now he would bring them back for his people.

He shook his head clear of remembrances and stood to let the suds drain from his hard, well-muscled frame. He waited a moment, then stepped out and wrapped himself in a large towel.

In the bedroom a fresh uniform had been laid out. Moi must have sent to the barracks for it. He smiled at his friend's thoughtfulness.

As he dressed, his mind once more roved back over some of the key events which had brought him here. His days in the tribal village, the death of his father, his time in England. Cambridge. Sandhurst. The joy he had felt at moving straight from the repression of Zawanda into a society where speaking one's mind was encouraged, debate routine and criticism unpunished. He paused to smile and remember. Then a dark cloud seemed to pass across his face as he remembered too well. It had angered him then, and some of that anger returned now. Drinking in a Cambridge pub with an Australian and two British fellow undergraduates one evening during his second year, the talk had turned to a discussion about the old British Empire, or rather its dismemberment. He could hear it now, the cut and thrust. Erudite stuff. The terrorist campaigns of Kenya, Aden and Cyprus, the horrors of the India – Pakistan division, explored in intense debate. Should Britain have continued attempts to hold on to its colonial territories by force? "Perhaps," the Australian had said. "Look at the misery there is in Africa today compared with what it was like under colonial rule."

It was then that a naive, proud young Zawutu, finding himself marginalised by his lack of historical learning, interrupted. Africa, he knew about. It had been a clumsy moment and he felt the blood rush to his cheeks even now as he recalled the embarrassing moment when he had blurted out proudly: "Zawanda was smart enough to negotiate its own independence. There was no fighting,"

"Balls!" Peter Clements had exploded. "Britain gave it away with far too much haste, if you ask me." Then, seeing the pain on Zawutu's face, he had added more gently, "Don't you honestly know what happened?"

Zawutu had shaken his head in bewilderment. "I know we asked for independence within the Commonwealth," he had said, a little uncertain now that another version seemed imminent. Clements had seemed reluctant to disenchant him. He recalled as clearly as if it had happened only yesterday the look on Clements' face and the way his own stomach had clenched painfully as he waited and watched.

Peter had shaken his head to dissuade the others, he remembered, but the other Brit, Richard Granby, specific and direct, as seemed to be the way with science undergraduates, had ignored the warning and spoken up.

"No Freddie. In 1974 when Wilson came to power, it was during the miners' strike, if that sort of news reached you in Africa, and the economy wasn't too good here. The armed forces were being trimmed viciously, jobs were being lost willy nilly and overseas commitments cut to the bone. Zawanda fell early victim to that policy. Callaghan proposed independence and your people jumped at it, too hastily as it turned out."

He hadn't believed what he was hearing. Granby had made it sound as if Zawanda had been stupid to accept what now seemed to have been a devious political act. All the time he, Zawutu, had believed unquestioningly in the application and negotiation theory. Then, when Clements, in an attempt to extract the sting from Granby's innocent remarks, had picked up the story, the anger had begun.

"Dickie isn't quite correct," he said emolliently. "My father spent a lot of time in Africa, and he's always insisted that independence was thrust upon Zawanda against its will. Your country wasn't ready for self-rule. It hadn't the experienced politicians, no infrastructure to speak of and it relied on a single product economy - copper. It couldn't survive as a democracy, I remember him saying that, and that Britain should have been more understanding."

He had looked at Zawutu and realised with dismay that he had only made things worse.

"That's nonsense," Zawutu had demurred loudly, his tribal blood boiling. People nearby had looked round, startled by the raised voice, but Zawutu had ignored them. "We were ready. We did have the leaders. How do you think the tribes were organised? We had layers of management right up to Paramount Chieftains."

Granby, unrepentant, butted in again. "I'm sorry, Freddie, but that isn't good enough. Britain cast you off like a sinking ship that was threatening to take the lifeboat with it. The proof that you were incapable of ruling yourselves came in – seventy five, was it? Your first military coup? What was his name, your Minister of Defence who became President?"

"Kumba," Zawutu contributed bitterly, glaring at Granby malevolently.

"Kumba, that's right. Sounds as if you knew him?"

Zawutu wrenched his thoughts back to the present, glad to be rid of the shameful episode. Kumba. Yes I knew him, he muttered to himself, and it all came flooding back. His childhood village, the Ushkuu sergeant, the blood, his father's murder there among the grit and dung of the cattle corral; and the village was burned anyway. Telling it in that Cambridge pub had been a sort of catharsis prompted by the name Kumba. It had been excruciatingly painful even without revealing the worst part, the attempted rape of his sister, prevented at the cost of his mother's submission to the sickening, sexual brutality of the same murderous Ushkuu sergeant who had hacked his father to death. Such intimate knowledge was not something an Eshanti warrior could share.

He remembered again that day in Cambridge "God, I'm sorry," Clements had said gently. "We had no idea." He had flashed another cautionary glance at Granby. Zawutu smiled now, recalling his reply. "I am a man now," he said proudly, waving down their commiserations. "My revenge came when

19

the Eshanti General, N'Bata, knocked Kumba off his perch as a result of the '78 coup. That bastard Kumba was hacked down with a machete just like my father. His blood ran hot and swift over the floor of the Presidential Palace and he died screaming. I know, I was there. I helped. It happened just before I came here to Cambridge."

He remembered with a grim smile how his companions had gone suddenly very quiet at that point and Granby had turned pale. He glanced now at his reflection in the dressing table mirror and saw a little of what they must have seen, and he felt again the ghostly touch of his ancestors.

Back in the present, he considered what he had learned over his pint that day. Of the treachery of the British, the casual, heartless way they had abandoned an unprepared Zawanda. 'Perfidious Albion' - he had read it somewhere, in a history book, and believed it with all his heart. In their haste to rid themselves of the tiny financial burden Zawanda must have represented to the British, they had left behind only one working copper mine and, typically, a mixed tribal administration that was doomed to failure. He knew that now, but at the time he had felt proud of belonging to a free nation. He glanced again into the mirror. He would, he promised his reflection, make Zawanda proud again.

He fastened his regimental stable belt, adjusted his forage cap to dead centre of his forehead and made for the staircase, at the foot of which stood Moi in company with Captain de Lancy. De Lancy sprang to attention, saluted and at the same time eyed the plaster on Zawutu's cheek. He'd had it seen to, thank God.

Zawutu glanced down. In the strong afternoon light his adjutant's fairness of complexion stood out against the ebony of Moi's features, a contrast he had not noticed quite so starkly before. "You might almost be mistaken for an Englishman with a holiday tan," he said laughingly, which brought a flush to de Lancy's cheeks and embarrassed Zawutu as well. It was innocent remarks like that which had long given de Lancy cause to hate his genes. He blamed his father for the light complexion and his Eshanti mother for being foolish enough to go with an Englishman. The resultant dilution of tribal blood meant he would never be fully accepted by the tribes, where purity of race was almost a religion.

After a painful childhood he had found refuge in the Army, where good school results and a sharp intellect had compensated for lack of pigmentation. The three pips he now carried on his shoulders gave him authority of rank, but not the respect he could have demanded as a full blood. He knew how tenuous a hold he had on his future. Without the Army he would be relegated to the bottom of life's pile, an untouchable in a nation over-consciously proud of tribal history, heritage and blood lines. Eshanti women alone could not pass Eshanti blood on to their offspring, that was a matter of tribal fact. Survival, therefore, required absolute loyalty, blind obedience and flexibility of principles.

In Zawutu he had found a champion. A reasonable man, a man he could cling to and grow with, a man bereft of tribal bias.

"The city closed up tight?" Zawutu asked as he stepped from the bottom tread.

"Yes sir. Radio and television on normal programming, banks and post offices open, shutters coming down in the souks, police patrolling the streets and the city regiments confined to barracks as ordered, sir."

"And no Ushkuu may leave the city," Moi added significantly.

"And the dead?" Zawutu asked, relegating the Ushkuu, and Moi's obsession with them, until later.

"Removed for burial," de Lancy confirmed, and glanced questioningly at Moi.

"There's trouble brewing in the villages," Moi said flatly. "We have just been informed that groups of young Eshanti warriors are on the rampage."

"How bad is it?" Zawutu asked sharply.

"I can't say," Moi replied. "But 2nd Regiment is onto it. I'll let you know the form as soon as they've completed their sweep."

"2nd regiment? Who authorised their use?" Zawutu asked, his voice rising in alarm.

"I did," Moi replied blandly. "I didn't think that as President you would want to retain command of the regiment, so as the senior regimental officer remaining, and your Chief of Staff, I gave the order. I hope that's all right? It was urgent."

De Lancy added his concurrence. Crossing Moi was not a sensible thing for a half-caste like him to do, and, anyway, tackling the tribal situation had truly been urgent. Zawutu must see that.

"Very well then" Zawutu said, grim faced. "Keep me informed. And remember what I said earlier. No tribal cull. I want this pinched off before it develops. Now, let's join the other officers."

★ ★ ★

2nd Eshanti Regiment had spread itself out across the plains in platoon Groups, their orders from Major Moi deliberately vague and victim to as many interpretations as there were platoons on the ground. But given that this was an Eshanti regiment in Ushkuu territory, under the command of a young Major, third in command, the outcome was clearly predictable. Wherever platoon commanders came across trouble in progress, instead of separating the belligerents as was Zawutu's understanding, they stood back and let the raiding Eshanti warriors get on with it. Then, inevitably and with accelerating momentum, discipline among the troops began to evaporate as they hankered to join in the fun. Individual soldiers and soon whole sections began to exploit the situation and their young Eshanti officers did nothing to prevent it. Blood lust, fuelled by a natural desire to revenge the atrocities visited upon the Eshanti in past times, spurred them on. Wholesale slaughter stained the land with Ushkuu blood as things got badly out of hand. The inexperienced acting CO panicked and lost what little grip he had. His even more junior company commanders attempted to rein in their platoons, but communications were poor, radios outranged, militating against any hope of regaining quick control. By the evening of the second day following Zawutu's elevation to the Presidency, the countryside stank of fire and death and in the Eshanti villages warriors rejoiced.

The 2nd's temporary CO, reduced to a gibbering mess, abandoned his short-lived command and ran for the border into self-imposed exile, leaving the Regiment, killing frenzy spent, sated with blood and shame, to straggle miserably back to barracks under its now senior Major, Simba, a major of only one year's seniority but of considerably more backbone than the one who had deserted them. He clamped a confinement order on the whole barracks, retired to his quarters and lay on his bed to await the inevitable summons.

Zawutu would be furious and heads would roll – literally. Would his be one of them? He tried hard to control the trembling.

A delighted Moi kept the news from the President until the job was done. On the morning of the third day he decided to inform Zawutu of what had happened. He entered the Palace study to find Zawutu seated behind the old mahogany desk that had occupied this study since the British had first furnished it in 1896. The pictures on the walls, of ships and game animals and portraits of important Englishmen, were fading now.

★ ★ ★

Moi helped himself to a chair, and eyes downcast, showing false concern, began by asking if Zawutu had heard.

Zawutu shook his head. "Heard what?"

"About 2nd regiment."

Zawutu heard warning bells. "No. Tell me."

Moi glanced up to gauge the President's mood and turned his eyes away. Go carefully, he warned himself. In a muted voice he described what had transpired in the Ushkuu villages, playing the whole thing down as an unfortunate misunderstanding, exacerbated by the incompetence of the Regiment's officers.

"The CO disobeyed orders," he lied.

"And where is the CO now?" Zawutu enquired, dangerously calm. "Who did you appoint to command?"

"The senior major after me," he replied. "Major Eshambo. He's gone, the coward. Skipped across the border, by all accounts."

"So he cannot speak for himself. What about the acting 2ic?"

"Major Simba. He's in New London Barracks with the Regiment, sir."

"Tell me again what happened," Zawutu said, his tone unchanged.

Moi's account, a dissembled concoction of half-truths, enjoyed an uninterrupted hearing until Zawutu, unable to contain himself further, let fly his fury.

"Stand up!" he yelled, his spittle spraying Moi. "I told you there were to be no reprisals. No killings. Are you deaf or what? You deployed the regiment, you gave it its orders, you are responsible. Frankly, I don't believe you couldn't have prevented this tragedy."

Moi threw up his hands. "Mutti!" he pleaded.

"Don't interrupt!" Zawutu shot back. "My orders were clear. And now, because of your bungling, we have a situation the whole world will soon know about and condemn. I wanted a clean start, and you've fucked it up."

Moi hung his head and muttered, "My orders to Eshambo were clear, the man must have gone mad, got everything wrong."

"No. You got everything wrong!" Zawutu spat at him. "I delegated the responsibility to you and you made a balls of it. No tribal vengeance, I said. It's you who are mad." He stood and paced the room. "It's a mess, a bloody awful mess. What will the world think of President Zawutu now?"

Then his mood mellowed for a moment. He smiled grimly, his tribal genes momentarily on display, "But the bloody Ushkuu deserved it," he mumbled to himself.

Moi relaxed a little, but resisted the temptation to be drawn. Instead he played it safe. "I regret what has happened, Mutti. But it wasn't my fault. As for world opinion, it will soon pass."

Zawutu stiffened. "But it will be remembered. There is no excuse. The 2nd must be disciplined. It is imperative that those outside Zawanda see it done. Dismiss Simba - he can be reinstated after the fuss dies down - and select one Company Commander to be executed - no, too extreme. A court martial, then an appeal, and an execution only as a last resort. Strip the regiment of its colours and its battle honours."

Moi looked up. "What battle honours?"

"Yes. It will look and sound good and it's something the British will understand. The fact that there are no battle honours to remove is immaterial just now."

Moi nodded, relieved that his devious part in what had transpired had been overtaken in damage limitation. On the basis of that he felt bold enough to venture a suggestion; one he hoped might lighten the mood.

"A good excuse for a grand parade when you present new colours in a month or two," he said, his smile as crooked and insincere as always.

"Perhaps," Zawutu said with a wry grin. It was difficult to be angry with Josi for long. "But for now, see that my wishes are executed. And properly this time."

"I will see to it, Mutti."

The President gazed hard at Moi for a long time, holding him stiffly at attention. "Perhaps I should find out more about this affair. Things may not be quite as you make them out to be."

Moi shook his head, but looked worried. "No, Mutti, please," was all he said; an admission of sorts.

"Don't worry Josi," Zawutu went on. "I don't have the time. But hear me. No more acting independently. From now on you do as I say, no more and no less. Do you understand?"

"Yes sir," Moi replied humbly. Presidency was a concept he had difficulty with. In his mind, the man chastising him was still his Commanding Officer and friend. These were the only relationships he fully understood. Later, when he discovered what Presidents did, how they behaved, and essentially, what powers they had over life and death, perhaps things would change. But for now, stick with what you know, he cautioned himself.

★ ★ ★

CHAPTER TWO

The Zawandan Cabinet, such as it was, had been hastily constructed from Eshantis who were due patronage for their support during the coup. The portfolios of Interior, Trade and Defence were held by these men, whilst Zawutu held on to Foreign Affairs and Treasury; and for very good reasons, not least of which was that corruption in these posts had been rife. Only one office had gone to an Ushkuu, Tribal Affairs. Under the circumstances it could have gone to no other. With the Ushkuu tribe in almost open revolt over the recent massacre, only one of their own could possibly have filled the post, but even he did not entirely enjoy the trust of the Ushkuu chieftains. "He's one of them," was the criticism heard in the villages. His name was Balindi, a retired army officer who believed it better to fight the cause from within than oppose the new regime from without.

Moi was offered, and enthusiastically accepted, the Interior Ministry portfolio, old loyalties weighing more than common sense in the appointment. Zawutu had considered but dismissed the opportunity for mischief presented by the juxtaposition of Moi and Balindi. He believed he could control Moi's excesses. Moi thought otherwise.

Meetings were kept to a minimum during the rehabilitation

of the Civil Service, a lasting legacy of British rule. Sadly, many of the senior ranks had turned dishonest under the tutelage of corrupt ministers, but Zawutu knew who they were and had unceremoniously removed them from office. Thus, following a spate of promotions, old-style bureaucracy gradually took hold and soon a replacement driving licence again took six months to obtain, as in British days. Routine administration settled into its various ruts, and despite its clogging nature was left more or less untroubled by management. Ministers had more important matters to contend with under Zawutu's constant prodding.

Zawutu himself struggled with an almost empty exchequer. His predecessor had absconded with the bulk of the family silver, overlooking in his haste the aid payment which came in during the coup. Another was due this month. But even with these arrivals, bills still exceeded income by a substantial amount.

Zawutu surveyed the latest Treasury report with a hollow feeling. Zawanda, the documents told him, could not even meet its loans interest, let alone improve on essentials like sewerage, clean water, housing and so on. He ran an eye over the figures. From what he could see no government since the British had attempted to balance the budget, despite the presence in the interior of healthy volume-rich copper deposits. The only fully developed open cast mine, he noted, had once been highly profitable; the others, under development by the British before they left, had never been brought into production in the years since. The last British manager had departed long ago. Could he entice foreign experts back, he wondered?

He searched the report for encouragement, but the reading only depressed him further. No expatriate had worked in Zawanda since 1979, when the said last Brit had departed in the still of night across the border into Angola, prompted by the murder of an Ushkuu foreman for doing no more than sack an Eshanti labourer of proven acquisitive habits.

Zawutu brushed the depressing report aside, stood up and began pacing the room from wall to wall, halting finally before the portrait of the Queen.

"Fuck it!" he exclaimed to her. "If I can't create more wealth, generate more income, levy higher taxes, the country's buggered." He realised that continuous shortages would simply act as a wasting disease on the country. "You can see that, can't you, ma'am?" His master plan for one nation, rich, healthy and educated, looked like going down the tube.

"It's a bloody mess, your Majesty" he said. The Queen remained aloof from his vulgarities, and said nothing.

He was prompted to turn away from the portrait by a discreet tap at the door and the entry of Balindi. He felt foolish, realising that he might have been observed.

"Yes?" he said rather sharply.

"Good afternoon, sir" Balindi said. Zawutu could tell by his tone of voice that he carried bad news. He sighed deeply.

"Good morning, my friend. What is it now?"

The Minister for Tribal Affairs shrugged as he dragged a chair up to Zawutu's desk and sat on it. Turned sixty, his crinkly hair had gone grey, but the rest of him belied his age. Smooth cheeked and bright of eye, he studied the print of the Queen on the wall behind Zawutu before he spoke, wondering what it was about the portrait that had held the President's attention so intensely.

"Minister Moi is not being as even handed as he should be," he began, looking down from the picture. "I have many complaints from Ushkuu chiefs who say that he is engaging in positive discrimination against them." He eschewed the word 'provocation' in case it got to Moi's ears; he was secretly frightened of the Minister of the Interior.

Zawutu frowned at the mention of Josi's name. "Surely they're exaggerating," he suggested, but Balindi was inflamed beyond simple consolation.

"This is no good, sir" he said heatedly.

"Have you spoken with Major Moi?" Zawutu then enquired helpfully. He already knew the sort of answer he would receive.

Balindi shook his head violently. "Who can speak sensibly with him? Certainly not an Ushkuu. I would be afraid to interfere."

Zawutu sighed again. Josi was no more than a simple tribesman with a veneer of sophistication glued on at Sandhurst, a veneer that had begun to crack the moment he got home. Half an education, academic and military, instilled into a native candidate the Academy could not refuse or fail had made him into an unstable character. He knew all that, yet still believed he could rely on his long tribal friendship with Moi to engender loyalty and obedience. But if what Balindi had said was true, Moi had learned nothing from the 2nd Regiment debacle. For Allah's sake, he was no longer just a field officer in the army but a minister, and must be made to act accordingly.

"I'll speak with him," he assured Balindi. And by all the Gods he meant to. "I feel sure Major Moi would not deliberately incite trouble."

Balindi left, unimpressed and clearly unhappy. Zawutu walked to the door with him and gave him a smile and a handshake that cost a lot to do well under the circumstances.

"Leave it with me," he said to Balindi's back.

* * *

Back at his desk, he reached for the intercom to summon Josi, but somehow the Treasury report had shuffled its way back into the centre of the desk and the sight of it made him withdraw his extended forefinger. He'd deal with Moi later. "This bloody lot, too," he said aloud, thrusting the report aside. He leaned back in his chair and placed his hands behind his neck. At least, he reflected less gloomily, Britain had recognised the new government. Pity about the bridging loans, though, hastily withdrawn when news of the Ushkuu massacre had reached London.

A dark cloud the shape of Moi's face rose in his mind. "I'll sort him out once and for all," he promised himself, but then he smiled, remembering the scrapes they'd got into as children and young men together. Maybe the bridging loans could be resurrected on promises of good behaviour, he reasoned, switching back to what really mattered. "The things one has to do for one's country," he remarked to HMS *Andromeda*, which was thrusting its way through the waves on the opposite wall.

★ ★ ★

In and about the city of New London, building workers were well into repairing the damage wrought by the coup. Materials had been bought on tick from Gabon and Zaire, but the bills would be coming in soon and Zawutu wanted to pay them without delay. Good relations with his immediate neighbours were essential to his plans for Zawanda.

He had thought it through. It was vital that he should bring the copper mines back into production, even accepting losses at first so that he could demonstrate industrial potential to the outside world and tempt expert expatriate management back into the country; possibly on loan under the auspices of the UN or the World Bank. An aid now, pay later scheme would do nicely, he concluded. He could offer eventual self-sufficiency as an offset, with every probability of reducing aid requirements in the medium term and eliminating them altogether further out. He saw himself as an international player and Zawanda a country, small but to be reckoned with.

He sat exhausted at the end of a long day spent grappling

with economics that were as good as dead in the water. He moved from his desk to a deep, lavishly embroidered but grubby easy chair on a covered balcony facing the rear of the Palace. How soon, he wondered, until his grand canvas received even the first watery dabs of paint?

The shutters were thrown back and the calm of this typical Zawandan evening seemed to penetrate his soul as he looked out across the plains towards the dying sun hovering above an horizon of scrub and elephant grass. It was a sight he never tired of. This was the Zawanda he had loved as a child, the Zawanda his father had patiently unrolled before his eyes, had taught him to understand and cherish, a form of beauty he was determined to perpetuate. Sometimes he felt physically wedded to this land by a depth of spirit he could not explain. His pride swelled at the plans he had for this 'Heart of Africa', as his father had described it to him on an evening just such as this, man and boy trekking home from a trip into the bush. He couldn't remember what the trip had been about, but that magic moment and those magic words had remained with him, a sweet memory of the father he had lost.

In the embrace of honeyed nostalgia, a tap on the screen separating the balcony from the room itself hardly registered. He heard it on the edge of consciousness.

"Yes? Who's there?" he muttered impatiently, reluctant to drag his mind away from the happy memories of his boyhood.

"It's me," said Moi as he slipped round the screen's edge and occupied the other chair, uninvited. Zawutu looked across at him and saw mischievous eyes and a childishly petulant lower lip. How could he get angry with this product of tribal indoctrination? The things they'd shared as boys and men together, memories that were precious. He nodded at his old friend, leaned back in his chair and returned his gaze to the fading horizon.

It had been some time since the two men had found time to relax together, and Moi must have been as fatigued as his President, for he sat quietly looking beyond the balcony rail through vacant eyes with an occasional glance towards Mutti as he waited for the contemplative mood to pass.

"A whisky for me, I think," Zawutu said suddenly, surprising Moi out of his lethargy. "You'll have one too?"

Moi leaned across and rang the brass bell that stood on the glass-topped wicker table between them. In response a small, bent old man , wrinkled with great age, shuffled in, dragging his bare feet over the carpet, once of top quality but now threadbare. Dressed in blue trousers and white monkey jacket, but without shirt, tie or shoes, he smiled at Zawutu, displaying a mouth coloured by the berries the old men chewed, a mild narcotic of no proven danger. Gaps showed where teeth had long fallen out or been removed, but that took nothing from the dignity of the face. This old man had been a highly-respected warrior in his time.

Moi spoke to him. The old man switched his gaze and a cloud seemed to pass across his features, unnoticed by either Zawutu or Moi.

"Yes, sir?" the old man said, reconstituting the gappy smile.

"Two whiskies. Ice and water," Moi said in reply.

The old man bowed his head, turned and walked away.

"Why does he not wear the proper clothes?" Moi asked as soon as the elder was out of sight.

Zawutu laughed. "He's from our old village. He knew my father. Do you not recognise him?"

"Yes I do. It's old Mumbi, but why the funny dress?" Moi insisted.

"Well, when I sent for him I told him to see the housekeeper about his uniform. The idiot gave old Mumbi two pairs of trousers and two jackets, expecting the old boy to furnish the rest. But Mumbi wears a tribal skirt in the village and has never worn anything else, so he put on only what he was given and I haven't had the heart to tell him otherwise."

An amusing anecdote to most people, but to Moi it seemed an admission of weakness. A President should correct an old native who did the wrong thing. Mutti had always been so meticulous about such matters, and the change was worrying.

Mumbi came with the drinks and left, and the sun sank lower.

"How is your family?" Zawutu enquired.

"Well."

"Are you moving them to the city?"

Moi looked away coyly. "No. I'm too busy and they are happier where they are."

"Aaah!" said Zawutu with a knowing nod. "Now that you are important, you are not thinking of taking another wife, are you?"

Moi shook his head vehemently. "When Mohammed, peace be upon Him, decreed that a man may take five wives, He left us with a heavy burden. One is bad enough. Mine is anyway." he said, laughing heartily in his barking style. Zawutu joined in.

"What about you?" Moi enquired when his laughter had subsided. "It's past time."

Zawutu shook his head. With his own marriage years spent mostly in England and no father to arrange a bride for him he had remained a bachelor, and now, at thirty five, he had more or less settled for that. It had crossed his mind that he might need a hostess once the Palace was up and running, but she needn't be a wife. It wasn't that he disliked women or was particularly celibate; he just hadn't met anyone he felt that way about.

"Well, the old women are talking." Moi mimicked the high, complaining voice of an elderly tribal female: "'He should have been married years ago.' Even your mother is worried about you."

"I won't be driven into an arranged marriage," Zawutu said firmly.

"Sometimes they work very well," Moi pointed out, accurately.

"Maybe, but not for Presidents." Zawutu responded with a disarming smile. "Now where's the other half?"

Mumbi was rung for and given the order, leaving the two men to their silence. Moi had got the message, that Zawutu didn't want to discuss it further. In fact Zawutu was thinking about the damage old crone gossip might do his reputation.

The lights came on in the room, energised by Mumbi as he returned with the drinks.

"Thank you, Mumbi. You may take the rest of the evening off," Zawutu told him. "We can manage."

It was now black outside, with no lights to be seen from the outland facing balcony. The room lights, bright and enticing, were attracting insects in their droves and to remain in the open was becoming increasingly uncomfortable.

"I think we'd better go inside," Zawutu said as he struck at another insistent mosquito. Moi followed and closed the shutters behind him.

"I feel like having a woman," Moi muttered to himself, and was ready to make his excuses for the remark when Zawutu thumped him in the chest and said loudly, "And so do I."

Moi looked hard to see if the President was serious, then, satisfied, rang the intercom.

"de Lancy," said the answering voice.

"Moi. Come in."

Now Chief of Palace Security, de Lancy came at the double. "Yes, Mr President?" he said breathlessly upon seeing Zawutu. He clicked his heels as he came to a halt inside the room, pleased he had remembered the American form of address recently adopted by Zawutu.

Moi spoke brusquely, "Bring two Ushkuu maidens, virgins both of them, and young, very young, to the ante room off the President's sleeping quarters."

de Lancy looked from one man to the other, unsure. This wouldn't be the first time for Moi, but he had never pimped for the President before. Indeed, rumour had it that he would never need to, not for maidens anyway.

Zawutu nodded at him. "Do as Major Moi commands," he said.

De Lancy pulled himself together, enormously pleased that the rumours about his idol were untrue. "At once, sir," he said, and swivelled away, closing the door silently behind him.

"Get the champagne out, then," Zawutu prompted, slipping easily into the spirit of the occasion. "Half a dozen bottles at least. See you in the ante room."

It had been a while and he was feeling a bit like a teenager about to enjoy his first woman. He drank the last of his whisky and sauntered from the study, fingering a nascent erection through the pocket of his trousers.

The dressing room, or ante room as Moi called it military style, had retained much of its early splendour. Thick piled burgundy carpeting covered the floor wall to wall. Elaborate light brackets, all scrolls and curlicues, were positioned around the walls, each topped by a wafer-thin glass globe bearing hand-painted pictures of local animal life. Three deeply-cushioned settees, and as many easy chairs, upholstered to match the carpet, were arranged in an arc facing a false cast-iron fireplace. Various expensive-looking tables and ornaments seemed scattered about the room at random. The wardrobes, for this was a dressing room, were cleverly concealed as wall panels, ornately decorated in gold leaf scrolls, many adorned with paintings and prints of high-bosomed Victorian ladies. Double oak bedroom doors occupied a large proportion of the rear wall opposite the shuttered window.

Into this grand surround strolled Zawutu, followed almost at once by Moi and Mumbi.

"Sorry about this, Mumbi," Zawutu said when he saw the old man. "But you really can go to your bed now."

Mumbi sighed and nodded. "This man will not get up again tonight," he said, staring hard at Moi.

Moi frowned. "Go to bed old man, and stop complaining."

Mumbi left and Moi cracked open a bottle of champagne. He handed a fizzing glassful to the President. "Here's to a good fuck," he said.

Zawutu grinned. "And may there be many more." He raised the glass to his lips and drank deeply.

* * *

The second bottle was half empty by the time Captain de Lancy returned ushering two young native girls before him. He pushed them into the room and quickly retired. The girls, physically mature as women soon are in central Africa, stood in silence, heads bowed, one of them whimpering, the other holding her hand, comforting her.

"Sisters?" Moi asked, walking over to them and squeezing the already heavy breasts of the taller one as he would feel a fruit for ripeness. "Well?" he demanded, pinching one of the girl's nipples through her single shift with a twisting motion of his thumb and forefinger. The girl yelped, but dared not pull away. The younger girl's whimpering at once increased in volume and her shoulders began to shake.

Moi turned to Zawutu. "Which one do you prefer, Mr President?" he asked, pushing both girls forward.

Zawutu, high on alcohol and low on inhibition, fondled both girls' breasts. "This one," he said, placing his arm around the taller of the two and walking her through the oak doors into the bedroom. As he closed the door he heard a loud slap and Moi's exclamation, "Shut up snivelling!" Then the tearing of cloth.

Fired up with whisky and champagne, Zawutu had no time for preliminaries. Hurriedly he closed the door, lifted the girl's shift over her head, pushed her down onto the bed, then stood back and ran his eyes over her as if she were a prize cow at market. He saw dark, glistening skin on a beautifully moulded frame. Firm young breasts rose and fell rapidly, accelerated by fear. Her mound was faintly shadowed with body hair, and her long thighs were pinched tight together. Wildly stimulated, he tore off his clothes and stood there.

"Look at me," he commanded.

The girl opened her eyes and stared at his bulging phallus, mesmerised with terror. She had once accidentally spied her eldest brother's unformed penis full up, but never a grown man's until now, and this one was big and threatening.

Her lips moved in a silent "No!" as Zawutu leaned down, spread her legs wide and lunged at her. There followed an unholy duet of Zawutu's bull-like roar and her scream of agony as he thrust into her dry vagina and took her virginity. The loss of her childhood came brutally, with much pain and no love, not as she had imagined it would be when the time came.

It was soon over and he stood, leaving his child victim curled in a foetal position on the bed sobbing, one hand covering her eyes, the other gripped between her thighs as if nursing her pain. In the relative silence Zawutu could hear ugly animal-like sounds filtering through from next door and tried to ignore them.

He shook the girl by the shoulder. "Are you all right?" he asked gruffly.

She sat up bravely, chin resting on her chest, and nodded her head as best she could. An Ushkuu maiden did not show fear in the presence of an Eshanti.

"What's your name?"

She mumbled something.

"Speak up" Zawutu said his voice more gentle than before. "I don't bite."

"Uudi," she said, louder.

"And how old are you, Uudi?"

"I'm fourteen years."

In Zawanda fourteen was marriageable age, and Zawutu at once felt more comfortable with himself. "Look, there's a shower through there" he said. "Do you want to use it?"

She nodded again, more animated this time. "But I don't know how to work it," she confessed sorrowfully.

"Come with me," Zawutu said, and taking her by the hand he led her to the bathroom, leaving behind on the bedcover a dark stain where the girl had lain. She walked awkwardly half a pace behind, staring at the blood on her hand, and once again the tears ran freely.

He ignored it. She wasn't really hurt, he knew that. He drew the shower curtain across the bath, turned on the newly-installed shower unit and stepped under the jet. The girl's sniffing sounds subsided now and she giggled excitedly as he pulled her in after him. She laughed and cavorted like the child she was as she experienced her first artificially-warmed running shower; in her father's house the water ran only as warm as the sun could make it.

Zawutu smiled. Taking the soap, he lathered her shoulders and down to her buttocks, then turned her round and did the same for her front, lingering over her full breasts. He reflected sadly on how short a time they would be like this. In a few years they would be stretched and flabby with the stresses and strains of childbearing.

Uudi giggled shyly at his touch and kept her eyes averted, but the more Zawutu stroked her, the more he wanted her. The compulsion to have her again grew and grew until, with a snort, he took firm hold of her buttocks and raised her up. Her arms flew around his neck in panic, and as her thighs reached his waist he pulled them up and coaxed her legs round his hips, where she locked them quite naturally at the ankles. Zawutu lowered her gently onto his re-engorged penis and she winced just once and pressed her face hard into his shoulder as he thrust deeper.

The water thrashed down upon Zawutu's head and back as he held her. The breath rushed out of her body with each inward stroke, creating a regular, synchronised whimpering sound, and she clung to him all the harder. The pain was not as bad as the first time, but he filled her until she thought she must explode. Then gradually it became easier, and her attempts to give with the strokes turned to passive acceptance, then participation.

Zawutu felt the change at the same time as he sensed his climaxes begin. He thrust deeper and harder, then finished with a long-drawn-out sigh, maintaining the motion for a moment or two.

Suddenly the girl shuddered and dug her fingers into his neck in a violent, climactic spasm. She pulled her head away and looked into his face with wide-eyed astonishment. With an understanding smile, Zawutu held her firmly, then lowered her gently from him. "Good, eh?"

She giggled shyly.

"Come. Get dry," he instructed, wrapping a large bath towel round her shoulders and patting it here and there. Then he lifted her from the bath and stepped out himself. "Better get dressed," he said more harshly than he had intended, suddenly confused at what had occurred here with this child. A peasant girl and an Ushkuu at that. What was it about her that attracted him so? Maybe the way she had carried herself throughout her ordeal? But these thoughts were no more than fleeting. She was pretty and could be trained. Perhaps he'd keep her as his 'courtesan', a word he had picked up from a book on history. 'Mistress' sounded somehow dirty, which was not the way of Presidents.

The noises from next door had ceased, so Zawutu drew on a pair of uniform shorts, placed his arm around Uudi and walked her to the door, which he threw open for her. She took a pace and suddenly froze in a pose Zawutu had seen many times before in villages after a tribal raid. He had seen it in mothers gazing upon their dead children, in women looking at mutilated husbands, in men discovering their women raped and damaged. He pushed past her.

Moi stood zipping up his flies, a satisfied grin on his face. At his feet lay Uudi's sister, deathly still, ominously so, until Zawutu detected the faint rise and fall of her naked shoulders. She lay prone, legs apart, buttocks and upper thighs wet with blood. Moi followed Zawutu's gaze and laughed. "She fainted with pleasure," he said.

Zawutu turned to Uudi. "See to your sister," he commanded loudly, waking her from her trance like state. Then turning back to Moi, face set in rage, he pointed his finger at the outer door. "You. Get de Lancy. Now."

Moi's laughter died in his throat. "She's all right," he began resentfully. "I may have been a bit rough, but she's only an Ushkuu. Tight-arsed like all of them."

"Enough," Zawutu bellowed. "Do as I command, or you will regret this."

Moi's self-assurance buckled under Zawutu's fiery tongue and he hurried out of the room, calling de Lancy's name as he went.

"Is she all right?" Zawutu enquired, kneeling.

Uudi was cradling the younger girl's head. She looked up, tears streamed down her face. "She is waking up," she sobbed. "But she is hurt badly."

Zawutu nodded. He could see that. He jerked to his feet to meet de Lancy as he burst through the door.

"Mr President?" de Lancy barked, keeping his eyes averted

from the group on the floor. Moi had mentioned the President's mood.

"Get this girl a doctor" Zawutu commanded. "Do it now and stay with her until you can report back to me that she has been treated and is comfortable. I shall also want to know whether she will recover fully. Is that clear?"

de Lancy clicked his heels and said it was.

"Well do it at once, damn you! And take this girl." He eased Uudi to her feet. "Feed her and give her clean clothes. She will stay with her sister here in the servant's quarters until the doctor is satisfied that they are fit enough to leave, both of them."

de Lancy crossed hastily to where Uudi held her sister. "Here." he said, leaning down. "Give me her arm."

Between them they raised up the injured girl so that de Lancy could lift her into his arms. He turned and walked from the room as gently as he could, Uudi alongside, holding her sister's hand and crooning to her.

Moi came in through the doorway without so much as a glance at the group as it passed. Zawutu, shocked more by Moi's indifference than the injuries themselves – he had seen worse after a full platoon rape – turned and helped himself to a large brandy from a cabinet that stood against the wall beside the fireplace. In his fury he deliberately kept his back turned to Moi. He knew the man hated the Ushkuu, but deliberately to harm a young maiden was going too far. He would not tolerate such behaviour in a Minister of his government.

Moi shuffled to a halt to stare in consternation at his President's rigid, prohibiting back. He found himself shifting from foot to foot in a great cloud of uncertainty.

"Ushkuu, Mutti. Only an Ushkuu, and she isn't dead," he pleaded from behind.

"Damn you, Josi." Zawutu spat venomously, spinning round to face the object of his fury. "The Ushkuu are mad enough with me as it is without you injuring one of their young girls. A bit of harmless fun, rogering a maiden, that's OK, but deliberately damaging her, that's another matter. You will do everything you can to reduce the impact this is bound to have on my position. You will buy her new clothes and give her money when she leaves, and for Allah's sake and your own send her away happy." He held up a cautionary hand as Moi went to speak. "You will do as I say," he said, his tone brooking no argument. "Even to settling it amicably with the girl's family if need be, Ushkuu or not."

Moi hung his head in shame as was expected, but beneath the facade there flickered a fierce indignation. He could not understand what he had done wrong. Inflicting pain upon Ushkuu should be a matter for congratulation, not censure. He eyed his President warily through upturned eyes. "Of course, Mutti," he said, feigning contrition, but had to ask: "But why?"

"Just do it, Josi," Zawutu said wearily. "Now get cleaned up and join me in my study."

Moi nodded and headed for Zawutu's bathroom.

"Not in there!" Zawutu said, his voice like a whip. "Use the one down the corridor."

He suddenly realised that he must curb Moi's automatic presumption of intimacy and put some distance between them if he were to control the man's excesses. At the same time he recognised the need for at least one trusty thug on the team, and this one was at least the devil he knew.

In his study, sobered by events, Zawutu poured himself a whisky and settled into one of the deep-seated club chairs left over by the British administration. His problems, he reflected, apart from Moi and money, were gradually diminishing in both quantity and magnitude. The Palace servants had crept back in twos and threes and were running the place well enough for now. He had contacted a French interior designer, as the British hadn't the necessary flair for what he wanted. The army was in the process of integrating; Ushkuu, Eshanti and the lesser tribes such as the Itulu were remustering into mixed regiments. New recruits were posted to where they were most needed, no longer streamed into tribally-orientated formations as before. What few schools there were were full, and his policy of universal education awaited only more trained teachers. A new teacher's training establishment would take care of that as soon as he had the necessary funds to pay for it.

"That is the dilemma," he told himself. "How to pay for it all?" The state coffers were down to their last few millions and such aid as had been supplied would not service the nation's debt, let alone the reforms he had in mind. His brow creased as he struggled with this conundrum. Then a knock on the door heralded Moi's arrival.

Zawutu sighed with exasperation as Moi sauntered in without seeking permission. "Sit," Zawutu ordered peremptorily. Seeing Moi's crestfallen expression, he added, "No, get a drink, then sit."

Soon they were sipping contentedly from their glasses, the events of an hour ago relegated to memory, driven there by the threat of national insolvency, but not completely forgotten. Moi quickly relaxed in the company of an obviously more placid Zawutu and the conversation turned to village anecdotes, tales of extreme youth and what life had been like in those days. They recounted tales of raids and rapes and mayhem carried out in company with other young men from their village, and laughed together.

"They were good days," Zawutu said, drying the laughter tears from his cheeks.

"Yes, Mutti. But how things have changed," Moi replied.

Zawutu ignored the hidden meaning. "Money. The country needs money, lots of it," he injected, suddenly serious.

Mutti's anger had been too recent to risk flippancy, so Moi

too became as serious as was within his capability. "The mines will soon be producing," he offered.

"But not soon enough, and then only at a fraction of what the country needs."

"What else can we do then?" Moi asked, shaking his head. It all seemed simple enough to him, dig out more of it and sell it, but unfortunately the laws of supply and demand were not within the grasp of his untutored brain. The price/volume relationship would always remain an insurmountable obstacle to him. He sat, face creased in thought, pondering the argument and wondering why Mutti was blind to the obvious.

Zawutu added: "No. What we want is a way to squeeze more aid out of Britain, and anyone else we can con into it. Diplomatic persuasion isn't the answer. Who will listen to mere tribal chiefs? It would be like a gnat arguing with an elephant. We need something big, a splash, something grand enough to make countries sit up and take notice."

Moi grinned. This was more like it. "Kidnap a prime minister," he suggested, as if abducting eminent politicians were an everyday event. "Threaten an assassination."

"Not quite, Josi" Zawutu said seriously in reply. Josi's ideas might not be very bright, but he was thinking. "Both schemes would be too difficult and too risky. No. What we need is a threat big enough to frighten everybody into coughing up some cash without risk to us."

"Use the army," Moi then proffered, still urging violence as a solution.

Zawutu brushed this aside. "They may be British trained, but against the legions of the West?" he shook his head regretfully.

"Mmmm!" Moi grunted. "War, then," he announced proudly.

"We'll declare war on Gabon. Wherever there is war the rich

nations rush in with lots of money. All we need is a serious threat of war. Just crank up the border dispute by deploying the army in attack formation."

Zawutu opened his mouth to laugh, then changed his mind. The idea was not as crazy as it sounded.

"Maybe," he said. "But first we'll try more conventional means. Let's see if we can't get more aid from the UK, ask the UN and the World Bank to help, approach foreign banks." Then as an afterthought he added, "Our neighbours too. They might be willing to lend a hand."

Moi nodded, but he was unconvinced. Fighting for what you wanted made more sense to him, but he had to tread carefully. "It's been a rough day. Let's call it a night, shall we?" Zawutu said. He stood, forcing Moi to do likewise. He watched his Interior Minister leave the room and reflected on his warlike suggestion. He reminded himself to replace the weapons and ammunition used during the coup.

Zawutu waited until Moi's footsteps had receded, then he too left the room and headed for the servant's quarters, where he ran into Mumbi sitting on the attap roofed terrace of the long house in which he lived. The only light came from within, and it took Mumbi a minute to recognise through rheumy eyes who it was who had arrived in such a hurry. Then he struggled to his feet. "Mutti, is it you?"

"Sit, old man," Zawutu said, waving Mumbi back into the worn cane chair. "Would you know where they have put the young Ushkuu girls?"

Mumbi sat and rocked the chair back onto its two creaky back legs.

"Girls?" he queried, between puffs on an old, carved wooden pipe. "I did see some girls with two name. If this old head is right you will find them in the next hut."

Zawutu smiled at the native nickname for de Lancy, thanked the old man and hurried on. The next hut, the twin of Mumbi's, stood at right angles. Zawutu reached it in a few strides.

"de Lancy," he called as he stepped up onto the terrace. "de Lancy, where the devil are you?"

A door opened further along, letting loose a yellow beam of light, into which de Lancy stepped.

"Are the girls inside?" Zawutu asked, brushing past the suddenly rigid captain, who was quivering at full attention. The younger girl lay on a bed, naked from the waist down. A man was bending over her.

"You," Zawutu said. "Are you the doctor? How is this girl?"

The man spoke without looking round, disgust ringing in every word: "You should be ashamed," he began angrily.

"No!" Uudi cried from the shadows at the head of the bed. "This man did not do this. It was another man." She came forward and stood between the doctor and Zawutu, as if to guard the very man who had so recently raped her.

"It's all right, child," Zawutu said. "The doctor doesn't know who I am."

The doctor had not paused once in his work, but now he glanced round. "I'm sorry, your honour. You were in the shadows."

He turned back to his task, more important than chatting with Presidents, and continued in language obviously intended to shock.

"This child has been torn front and back. Her cervix is damaged and there was much bleeding, which I have now controlled. I am repairing her anus, which suffered the worst trauma. After that I will sew up her vagina and move her to a hospital. She needs round-the-clock nursing in case of further haemorrhage, which is quite possible with these injuries. She's a lucky young girl. If this had happened in her village she would probably have bled to death. Here, at least we can put her back together."

Zawutu did not flinch. "Will she be all right in the end? Do you know?" Uudi sobbed loudly at that and Zawutu placed a comforting arm around her.

"I should think so," the doctor said. "Although the damage is extensive it isn't irreversible, so I'd say yes, she will be sexually normal."

"See," Zawutu said to Uudi. "She'll be fine. Then to the doctor, "Can we not hire nurses to look after her here? I would rather she stayed at the Palace until she is well enough to go home. Her sister will stay with her."

"Well, I suppose it can be arranged. Yes, all right."

The doctor's mood was more agreeable now as he transferred his ministrations to the girl's vagina. "Not as bad as I'd thought," he muttered as he threaded another suture.

Zawutu thanked him. The last thing he wanted was for this story to leak out. The two hospitals in New London were not the most secure establishments in that regard. Even keeping the girls here held a faint risk of the Ushkuu causing trouble over the affair, and he wanted to avoid that at all costs. He traced the action taken so far; was it sufficient? Then it occurred to him that if the child's recovery were to take any length of time, something would have to be done about pacifying her family. He turned to Uudi.

"It's very late. Won't your parents be worried?"

Uudi shrugged. "We were visiting friends," she said.

"Perhaps you should go to your village and say that your sister is staying with them overnight. It would be bad for your Mutter to know the truth."

Uudi shrugged again. "It is a walk of many hours to my village and I am tired."

He toyed with sending her in one of the palace cars, but thought better of it. Arriving in a luxury car would look suspicious. "Tomorrow then," he said. "I shall send you in a taxi. Tell Mutter that your friend's father paid. Can you do that?"

"Oh yes," she replied.

"Very well then. I'll drop by tomorrow to see how your sister is." With that he turned and left the room.

Outside, de Lancy got to his feet. "Is everything to your satisfaction, Mr President, sir?"

"You have done well," Zawutu told him. "Tomorrow I want you to arrange for the elder girl to be taken to her village in a taxi, then brought back here after she has spent a short time with her family. I don't want her left there."

"Very good, sir."

"See the doctor away then get some sleep," Zawutu told him.

As he walked back to his quarters he fumed at the predicament Moi had dropped him in. And to hell with him! From now on the bugger could handle his own messes, and Allah help him if he implicated his President. The slightest Ushkuu retaliation for this would bring down a shower of elephant shit on Josi Moi, he promised himself grimly.

★ ★ ★

With the two girls safely out of circulation inside the Palace grounds Zawutu felt more comfortable, and as an added bonus Uudi would now be available on demand. He hadn't broached the subject of consent, as he had no need to. She would obey the President and probably feel honoured; her family too. But something about her made him want to do this right, to talk rather than take. He would not do it just yet, not until the sister was safely up and around. Then he would speak with Uudi, and, hopefully, enjoy her again.

The younger girl was well on the way to full recovery and there had been no Ushkuu reaction so far. Uudi had been to her father's house and returned, and with a bit of luck the whole miserable affair might well now be behind them. But luck was not a commodity he was enjoying too much of these days.

CHAPTER THREE

The President stared at the sheaf of papers before him. The Queen gazed out across the room from the wall behind as if to keep an eye on HMS *Andromeda*, but she could do nothing for Zawutu. He had sat hunched over his ornate Victorian desk, having hardly slept for a week in anticipation of a good result from his widespread begging letters. And here they were – the replies.

The UN was sympathetic, but excused itself; we do not dispense aid in cash form, try the World Bank, it said. The World Bank suggested the Japanese, who suggested the Germans, who, speaking for themselves, and the European Union as well apparently, wondered if the Commonwealth might help, but Britain had already said no. He would have tried the Scandinavians next, but word of his difficulties had spread like lightning across the World's financial markets and he could almost hear the thunder of bank vaults being slammed and locked against him. He rested his head in his hands and swore a whole catalogue of Eshanti oaths. Britain is responsible, he told himself. They promised aid and reneged on it. They must help me now. Desperate words.

The call to Beauchamp took several hours to come through and when it did, Zawutu snatched up the phone, calmed himself and put on his most persuasive voice. "Ah, Minister, about this aid business," he began.

Beauchamp cut him off without ceremony. "Sorry Freddie."

Zawutu bridled at the familiarity, but in this case need was greater than pride, so he held his tongue.

"We are reviewing our aid budget," Beauchamp went on in a supercilious voice. "Particularly that element which applies to the Commonwealth,"

"But will that mean more aid?" Zawutu asked, fighting down the temptation to tell the man to stop waffling and come out with it.

"It would be wrong of me to prejudge the outcome of the committee's deliberations," Beauchamp replied in politico speak. "It could go either way, but there remains, of course, the matter of the Ushkuu."

"Well, thank you," Zawutu said, his face burning with the effort to remain civil. "I've explained what happened there, but perhaps you'll let me know the committee decision in due course."

"Of course, Freddie, but as I say: it could go either way."

Zawutu recognised a polite refusal when he heard it and slammed the phone down angrily onto its cradle. "Get me some tea," he barked into the intercom at his secretary. "Oh, and see if you can locate Major Moi. I'd like to see him in about half an hour."

Frustrated beyond reason, Zawutu's Eshanti genes overrode all else and he thought only of revenge. He sat there imagining the sensual pleasure it would give him to hack out Beauchamp's oily tongue with a blunt knife and make him swallow it whole. But by the time Moi appeared, he had regained some of his balance.

"Sit," he ordered.

Moi, unsure of what this was about, seated himself in the

chair nearest the desk and waited. The stupid secretary had not said why the President wanted to see him, claiming he didn't know, the lying pig. He hated not knowing beforehand. Foreknowledge can be vital.

Zawutu rose from his seat and began to pace. After two circuits he halted in front of Moi, who by this time had started to sweat and fidget from the tension.

"Maybe it's time to try your way," he said gruffly.

Moi blinked, taken aback, unprepared, flustered. "My way, Mutti?" he repeated. He was angry at having to ask. He swore he'd kill that bloody secretary.

"Yes, Josi. I've discovered it's the only way we'll get any help."

Moi understood now. "And you want me to organise something?" His pulse beat a tattoo of exhilaration.

"Well, not just yet." Zawutu came back disappointingly. His anger had cooled and reason told him it made no sense for little Zawanda to play the blackmail game. He had neither the political muscle nor the military strength to make a threat of violence look realistic.

"Perhaps I can frighten them into coughing up another way," he said thoughtfully. "Paint a picture of an Africa deep in debt, of a whole black continent plagued with famine, starvation and dying infants. They will have seen those BBC TV documentaries of Somalia, Ethiopia and the Sudan. Imagine the same over the whole face of Africa, I shall tell them. Describe in graphic detail what failure to act now could cost them in the long term. Point out that it will be no use them wringing their hands yet again when it is too late. How much better to adopt a policy of prevention now. They can't ignore us, Josi. The world is one habitat."

Moi looked blank. What was he doing here if all Mutti wanted was to talk about it again? For a sublime moment the

President had seemed to see sense and had come near to sanctioning physical violence. He hesitated, then blurted out: "Force of words never won anything, Mutti. Force of arms is what makes people jump."

"Yes, my friend, but words first. In the world of politics words have power; power to embarrass, to persuade, to threaten. Leave me to work with words. You stick to preparing the army and security forces."

"For what, Mutti?"

"To keep us in power until I can get what we need. The Ushkuu are unhappy still, the Itulu are ready to join them and the Eshanti are grumbling among themselves. I don't want the tribes at each other's throats. It will only make Beauchamp even more resistant."

Moi grinned his twisted grin. "I shall keep them occupied," he assured his President.

"Very well," Zawutu said, "But remember. No letting things get out of hand." It was a timely reference to the Ushkuu massacre and what it had already cost Zawanda. The young Ushkuu maiden had fully recovered and gone home with a tale of having stayed with friends in another village. Carefully tutored in her story by Uudi, there had been no escape of the truth.

* * *

CNN had become the largest purveyor of news worldwide, largely because of its incredibly efficient web of intelligence gathering. The KGB could have done no better. Items poured in from places as remote as the South Pole, so it was no surprise when a fax titled 'British Commonwealth, ex colony Zawanda, in battle with UK over aid' passed across the desk of the sub-editor responsible for the African Continent. Nothing of his had been broadcast now for close to two weeks, and he needed to improve his insert rate. With this in mind, he grabbed the fax and headed for the Programme Editor's office on the other side of the bustling newsroom.

His luck was in. News was slow today and the PE snapped at the Zawandan story. He called together the editing team and laid down how the story would be developed. "Run it tonight, just the bare bones," he said. "And Harry," addressing the outside broadcast chief, "you arrange a personal interview with this fellow Zawutu. Where's the nearest camera team?"

Harry referred to a clipboard resting on his lap. "Kenya" he said.

"Right. Get them moving. Jane," to the travel executive, "visas and all the usual paperwork for Zawanda." She nodded.

★ ★ ★

Zawutu leaped at the opportunity. To be invited to advertise his difficulties by way of a CNN network broadcast was manna from heaven. "Give them anything they want," he told Moi eagerly. Stripped of all the usual problems associated with getting into an African state so soon after a coup, the CNN team were in Zawanda within a few days and the interview scheduled for two days later at the Palace.

On the day, lights were assembled and tested, sound equipment laid out and volumes adjusted; transmission dishes aligned and Zawutu's shiny brown face shine patted over with matt powder.

The producer, Ms Carpenter, briefed the President. "Just answer as it comes to you," she said. "There'll be no tricky questions, but I would like something controversial if possible."

Zawutu smiled at that. Why else would they be here?

The presenter, a well-known face to millions across the world, watched the producer count down until only one finger remained exposed, then as that too disappeared he looked directly into the camera with his well-practised expression of serious intent and spoke.

"Tonight we are with President Frederick Zawutu, President of the small African state of Zawanda." He turned to Zawutu. "President Zawutu, may I begin by congratulating you on your Presidency."

Zawutu nodded modestly.

"The thought uppermost in the minds of most people must be the Ushkuu massacre which took place immediately after the coup that brought you to power. Can you elucidate what happened to provoke such a vicious attack on the Ushkuu tribe?"

Zawutu had been expecting this and launched himself into a well-rehearsed reply. "There was no provocation." He smiled convincingly. "The whole affair was most unfortunate. A few over-excited young men from an Eshanti village set about their neighbouring Ushkuu village in a spirit of fun, celebrating the demise of Brigadier M'gabi, an Ushkuu despot who had victimised the Eshanti during his reign of office. It got out of hand and spread rather more rapidly than we could respond. I moved as fast as I could and brought it under control within a couple of days."

"But there are rumours that the army regiment sent to quell the trouble became involved itself and did more damage than the civilians?"

"Rumours are everywhere," Zawutu said, waving his hands all-embracingly, "but they are just rumours."

"Did you not discipline the regiment, though?" the presenter insisted, milking the only hard facts his researchers had managed to uncover.

"Well, yes. But only for overzealousness, and only in a few instances."

"You execute your officers for being overzealous then, do you?" A smug smile into camera.

Zawutu frowned at that. "The exercise of our military code of discipline is a matter for courts martial. In this case a death sentence was obligatory under the law. The officer in question was an accessory to murder; he connived in a death. There was clear evidence of previous antagonism between the two parties and the officer misused his power and authority. For that he was executed, as he would have been in any other state with capital punishment."

"And that is it? That is all there was to it?"

Zawutu leapt at the opening. "No. Not quite. One must analyse the background. Serious unrest is not natural to this country," he said, tongue in cheek. "However, long years of deprivation bordering on famine, blatant denial of basic human rights and genocidal cleansing by previous governments was bound to leave a residue of inter-tribal friction, and that was the situation I inherited. Since then I have been active in healing bodies and minds and bringing my people a better standard of living."

He left off there. He did not want it to seem that he was using the interview as a soap box, yet that was exactly what he had in mind.

"Very laudable, President Zawutu, but there is little progress evident on those fronts. How do you propose to advance your humanitarian policies in the light of the difficulties you have just enunciated?"

"I see you have done your homework, but none too well," Zawutu shot back with a disarming smile. "But you are right. Progress is slow. Unfortunately, without the resources to implement essential reforms it becomes virtually impossible to move on. We do what we can, but we need money and credit. Our copper mines are producing, but slowly, and the price of copper is on the floor. Other than the revenue from mining, we are constrained to the aid generously provided by the United

Kingdom, for which the people of Britain have our most grateful thanks. But it isn't enough, and sources of funding are difficult, if not impossible, to find in today's economic climate."

He paused again, leaving the fly floating temptingly in the current, hoping it would be snapped up eagerly by a presenter with some minutes yet to run.

"But isn't it in everyone's interests to help a country like Zawanda?" the famous interviewer asked. "The alternative, it seems to me, is another Somalia. It must surely be beneficial to invest in a healthy, eventually self-sufficient state situated in the very centre of Africa – a sort of fulcrum." He glanced towards the producer in self-gratification at spotting that one.

Zawutu smiled. He couldn't have written it better himself.

"Of course," he said, also turning to face the camera. "But how do you persuade the wealthy nations? Most are inward looking; most are struggling to paper over the cracks in their own policies, fighting to keep the opposition at bay, manoeuvring to remain in power. They have no mental or physical resources left over from those activities with which to assist countries like Zawanda. Indeed, the whole of Africa is the victim of exactly that kind of limited thinking.

"Let me give you an example. If the same value of aid that is pouring into stricken African countries today had been made available a decade or so ago, the inexorable slide into poverty and decay would have been checked then and you would be seeing an entirely different continent, an Africa self-sufficient, an Africa making its fair and proper contribution in the world, an Africa proud and stable, standing up among the best, not on its knees as we see it honestly displayed on Western television almost every day. Children are starving, there is famine and pestilence, land is eroding away, new deserts are forming and spreading ever outwards. Of course, it's too late now for the worst countries. Short of a miracle, the situation cannot be reversed for them, the damage is already too great. The rest of the world will be supporting them for ever more, pouring in money and material in increasing amounts just to keep them ticking over."

He paused again to allow the terrifying prospect of an Africa well on the way to permanent ruin to be assimilated. He glanced at the presenter ready to anticipate any interruption, and indeed, the great man leaned forward, about to speak.

Zawutu gave him no chance. Turning his eyes back to the camera he continued, remorselessly: "My hope is that the cruel lesson has been learned, that the same slide into oblivion will not be permitted to occur here in Zawanda, and, of course, in the other genuinely struggling African nations who may yet be saved by prompt action. I pray that there are a few students of African history among today's Western politicians who will speak out in favour of early remedies at reasonable cost rather than delay until the situation is beyond redemption. In my view the world can do without more African countries on the permanent dependency list."

He halted to let the agitated presenter speak. He felt sorry for hogging the limelight, but it was essential to his strategy.

"I understand your frustration, Mr President," the interviewer interjected hurriedly, as if his batteries might run out before he could regain the initiative. "But Zawanda is hardly a good risk."

Zawutu cut in sharply. "There you go, always the commercial angle, profit and loss, the balance sheet mentality. You haven't understood a word I've said. But taking your point as valid, even by commercial standards, inward investment in Zawanda today gets the country into self-sufficiency and will eventually show a return for the generous. Fail to invest now, and a few years out much more money will be required just to keep us ticking over like the others. Another endless round of famine aid and no long-term solution. Yet another bankrupt, dependent nation. Now, sir, does that make any sense?"

"I take the point," the presenter said hurriedly, discomfited by Zawutu's waspish response. "But tell me, what if no assistance is coming? What does Africa do then?"

"Revolution, civil war, genocide. The Zawandan tribes are building up to it now. Only my promise of a better future keeps the peace, but how long will they believe me if I don't deliver? Frustration is the root cause of all the terrorism and civil unrest we see in the world today. If no one listens, if no one will compromise, then force is all that's left. People will not sit down for injustice or see their families starve."

"Are you saying that in the interests of your people you would resort to terrorism?" The presenter had ceased playing to the camera now. Totally absorbed by the dreadful prospects being outlined by his guest, his gaze had not wavered from Zawutu's lips.

"I'm saying that terrorism is a possibility. Not instigated by me or my government, but coming spontaneously from dissatisfied and frustrated tribes for whom inter-tribal conflict has been a way of life, off and on, for centuries. Once they overcome their cultural differences and mass together in common cause, anything might happen. I am holding those instincts at bay in Zawanda, but for how long? And it isn't only Zawanda. Revolution could spread across the whole of deprived Africa where billions of poor souls are at risk of extermination from disease, starvation and neglect. Such uprisings would not be the small, internal affairs we are seeing now, but major alliances against the developed countries of Africa, maybe spreading even further. Starving families will kill for food for their children. A spark is all it takes, and Zawanda could well provide the detonator."

The presenter wiped his brow, yet it wasn't hot inside the Palace. "That is a terrible scenario," he said, clearly affected. "Surely it could never happen?"

"Don't you believe it," Zawutu said with another direct look into the camera lens. "It isn't far away."

The producer was waving her hand in a circle above her head to signal wind up. The presenter turned full face to the camera and delivered his epilogue. "There we have it, straight from the President's mouth. Aid or war; assistance or terrorism. Will the whole of Africa become a cauldron? Only politicians in far-off places can, according to President Zawutu, prevent it. Goodnight from CNN, live from the Presidential Palace, Zawanda, in Central Africa."

The red light over the camera went out and the presenter leaned across and thanked Zawutu. "I hope you're wrong about all that," he said with genuine concern.

Zawutu shook his hand and held onto it for a moment. "We can only wait and see," he replied ominously.

★ ★ ★

Henry Beauchamp placed the transcript of the interview on the table at his side and sighed loudly. His wife looked up quizzically from her embroidery.

"Something wrong?" she asked.

"No, not really, my dear. It's just this fellow Zawutu, the new President of Zawanda. He's suffering from large fish in small pond syndrome."

His wife nodded. "He's upset you, Henry. Admit it."

Beauchamp laughed. "I suppose he has in a way, but let's not waste the evening talking about Zawanda. We have few enough evenings together these days as it is."

Mrs Beauchamp agreed, and returned to her sewing.

The following day a question by the Leader of the Opposition gave Beauchamp the opening he sought. He rose to the despatch box, cleared his throat and addressed the House in sonorous tones.

"I have studied the full, unexpurgated transcript of President Zawutu's TV interview and I can tell this House categorically that the cataclysm he forecasts for Africa is not founded on one single identifiable thread of evidence. There is no trans-African unrest, as he would have it. The countries where trouble has occurred, or may do so in the future, are in general under scrutiny by the United Nations or policed by United Nations forces. Improvement is everywhere in Africa. We in Britain have listened. President Zawutu is wrong to say we haven't. In real terms Britain has increased Zawanda's aid package annually by more than UK inflation. And additionally, an ex gratia parcel of aid was to have been provided to assist in reconstruction following the recent coup, although the massacre of the Ushkuu tribe which followed that coup made it impossible for Her Majesty's government to follow through with that assistance. It has never been our policy to reward transgressors."

"Hear hear!" issued from all levels of the back benches.

"What about South Africa, then?" a Labour member shouted. "You lot didn't cut off their aid despite the murderous nature of apartheid."

Beauchamp frowned and Madam Speaker called out: "Order. Order", forcing Beauchamp to sit. "The Foreign Secretary," she said when relative calm had been restored. She nodded at Beauchamp, who rose.

"The honourable gentleman opposite is, as usual, years out of date." A titter rippled through the ranks behind him. "As for Zawanda, threats from that quarter will help no one. President Zawutu is, I am sure, an honourable man, but he would do well to refrain from raising spectres that do not exist. We are too level headed in this House to be taken in by that kind of scaremongering. We deplore such provocative language. Who knows what trouble such wild incitements to violence might stir up for others in the region? My Right Honourable Friend opposite was right to raise the Zawandan issue and I am grateful to him for the opportunity to set matters straight. Her Majesty's Government does not bow to threat from whatever source it comes, whether from Presidents, terrorists or other irresponsible extremists."

He sat down, glowing with pleasure at the resounding cheers that rang in his ears. The PM looked pleased, too.

* * *

Next day a copy of Beauchamp's House of Commons statement reached Zawanda, and Zawutu was furious. Far from persuading Britain to ante up more aid, he had obviously alienated HM Government further. Not that he automatically believed Beauchamp's words. It was Question Time in Parliament, after all. He smiled.

"Damn and blast them all the same!" he expostulated. "Why won't those pompous asses listen?" Frustration burned painfully in the pit of his stomach.

Then he cooled down. Politics is a hypocritical art, he reminded himself. What was said inside Parliament was not necessarily what was meant. Words were for soothing anxious breasts and could always be twisted in the interests of expediency. And it would be expedient, surely, for Great Britain to heed his cry for help. Even the arrogant British must recognise the imminence of real trouble in Africa. To claim that all was well was playing the ostrich.

He smiled to himself. Of course Beauchamp would come back with an improved offer, if only to reduce the impact of the CNN broadcast. Countries other than Britain had heard it too, countries with more at stake in the region, poor countries which would look to Britain to head off disaster.

Meantime, he must make sure that Zawanda could defend

her integrity, protect her borders and successfully resist internal opposition. The Ushkuu were no walkover.

He dug out an old address book from the depths of a drawer and opened it at G for Granby, Richard. He had no idea whether the number was still the same, but he dialled anyway.

"Arms Incorporated," an affected female voice in London intoned.

"Can I speak to Mr Granby?"

"Who's calling please?"

"Just tell him it's Freddie Zawutu."

The plummy voice asked him to hold, then another, deeper one burst upon his ears, one he recognised instantly from way back.

"Freddie, you old fart, how are you? Or should I genuflect first and call you Your Highness?"

Zawutu laughed. Richard Granby had never been one for showing much respect; his Wellington and Cambridge education had done nothing to improve him in that regard.

"Richard" Zawutu said with almost forgotten affection. "No need for ceremony on the phone. How's the weapons business?"

"So, so, old chap. Trouble is, the big boys, your actual governments, have the largest slice of the market. Not that I could supply main battle tanks or fighter bombers. No, to be honest my market is small countries looking for a few rifles and a box or two of hand grenades. Is that what you're calling about? Need some new weaponry, do you?" Granby sounded keen to supply.

"Possibly," Zawutu said carefully. "I am in the market. Depends what's available and at what price. Look, can you come out to Zawanda? At my expense of course."

"Will there be something in it for me?" Granby asked his tone a little desperate.

"I guarantee it," Zawutu said cheerfully.

"Then you're on, old chum. Oh, will I need a visa?" He seemed to find the question amusing.

Zawutu smiled to himself. "As a matter of fact, yes. But that will be arranged through our honorary consul in Battersea. You should receive it through the post in about seven days. No exceptions I'm afraid, just because you're invited by the President." Try that for size, you old bastard, he said to himself, enjoying the nostalgic cut and thrust.

After a few minutes more of chat, Zawutu hung up. He stared at the phone. Yes, Granby would do nicely. Always a wild card, even at college. He recalled what he knew about his old college chum. He remembered he had moved into arms sales at a time when wars were ten a penny and money could be made relatively easily with the right contacts. But the peace dividend had obviously hit him hard and alternative work for a scraped pass degree, Cambridge notwithstanding, could not be all that easy to find. Yes, Granby was his man all right. Poor chap couldn't afford to be choosy, nor for that matter, pricey. Cheap weapons, probably Czechoslovakian, but that didn't matter as long as they worked and the ammunition came with them. The expenditure could be handled – just - but it would hit Treasury reserves pretty badly. Still, better to be almost broke than out of office.

He told his secretary to find Major Moi. A little while later a boisterous hammering on the door heralded Moi's arrival. He stood outside these days, waiting permission to enter.

"Come," Zawutu called after a moment's pause. Moi entered.

"Lucky I was in the Palace," he said. "The girl has gone home. I did what you said."

Zawutu smiled knowingly. Moi would be glad to see the back of the poor creature he had despoiled so brutally; an end to what he had been describing privately as the unnatural coddling of an Ushkuu.

"Uudi stays" he said.

Moi gave a leer. "Yes, of course, Mutti. She stays."

Zawutu ignored the inference, mainly because it was true. "Sit down Josi, I have news." He went on to explain about his call to Richard Granby, then added, "I want you to go to England and escort him safely back here. I know you're very high powered for such a menial task, but for all I know he could have ripped off half the countries hereabouts and I want him in Zawanda in one piece, not gracing one of our neighbours' jails. You are the only man I can trust to get him here safely. It is important, Josi."

Moi frowned. He had no love for the English and had promised himself never to return to that land of pompous, arrogant arseholes. "Is it really necessary, Mutti?"

"Yes, it is. It's vital."

Moi shrugged. "Very well, then, but this Englishman had better move quickly and cause me no trouble."

"That is for you to arrange," Zawutu told him, and he had to smile. The thought of Richard Granby being jostled along by a less than happy Moi had a touch of farce about it.

"That is all for now. You did compensate the girl for her injuries?"

Moi grimaced. "I did, Mutti."

★ ★ ★

Beauchamp sat in the commons dining room at lunch with the junior minister responsible for African affairs.

"A dessert, do you think?" he asked.

"Perhaps not," Jameson replied, lifting his glass of claret ostentatiously to the light and gazing through it. "Good colour, this," he said.

"Sorry to leave you with the Foreign Affairs committee this afternoon," Beauchamp went on, ignoring his junior's posturing. "But as you know, the PM has called a strategy meeting. The budget deficit again. God knows how we shall resolve it without alienating half the country. One thing I can tell you, though, overseas aid is in for a considerable chop, and Zawanda heads the list. But for God's sake don't mention it to the committee."

"I shan't say a word," Jameson assured him, "But I'm sorry for President Zawutu. He really is giving it all he's got. The country is peaceful, for the moment anyway; tribal integration is working, new schools are on the drawing board, medical facilities are improving, the copper mines are on stream. The man is working miracles over there. Reducing his aid will only cause him to thrash about even more violently and create more problems for HM Government."

"I'm not talking about reducing aid to Zawanda, but stopping it altogether," Beauchamp said quietly across the table.

"My God!" Jameson exclaimed sibilantly. "He's been a naughty boy in some respects, but no aid at all will cripple his economy altogether. Give him a few more years and it could be very different, but to cut him off now, immediately, is going too far, Minister."

Beauchamp shrugged. "It's a Cabinet decision. There's nothing I can do, much as I'd like to."

Jameson looked him in the eyes and saw truth in them. Well," he said sorrowfully. "How he'll manage without our aid I shudder to think. You know, I can almost sympathise with his intemperate outburst on CNN. He must be quite desperate already, let alone when this catastrophe strikes."

"You mustn't become too involved, Peter," Beauchamp cautioned. "Zawanda is, after all, only one of the many to lose out, and whilst I agree that Zawutu ploughs every penny into improving the lot of his people, unlike his predecessor who stole most of it, I'm afraid it is our own budget difficulties we must worry about."

"I see that," Jameson said understandingly. "But who will tell Zawutu?" He feared it might fall to him.

"Leave that to me," Beauchamp said, looking at his watch. "I must fly. Let me know how you get on with the committee. I don't believe they have much to gripe about. Billy Tranter will ask why we did nothing to stop the Ushkuu slaughter, but you should be able to field that one easily enough. We knew nothing about it until it was over. Stick to that and you'll be all right. And now I really must fly. Thanks for lunch."

"But I thought…" Jameson spluttered, stretching out a hand in supplication at Beauchamp's retreating form, "you invited me," he ended lamely.

A day or so later a signal came in under protocol rules, informing the Foreign Office of an impending visit by the Zawandan Interior Minister, Major Josi Moi. Beauchamp pondered his copy, then made a note to talk to Jameson about it. An opportunity arose the next afternoon.

"As you know, Peter," he began after amusedly observing Jameson go through his routine of examining the room wall to wall before sitting down, "it is usual for visiting Commonwealth Ministers to pay a courtesy call sometime during their stay in the UK. Of course, a country the size of Zawanda would normally be delegated to a junior FO Minister, you in this case, so I hope you won't mind if I see Minister Moi myself. With you in attendance, naturally."

Jameson blinked, then slowly smiled. "An excellent idea, Minister. You'll pass on the bad news at that meeting I take it?"

"Indeed I will, Peter." Beauchamp said, swelling at his own subtlety. He tapped the chased leather top of his desk with an insistent forefinger. "What do we know about this fellow Moi?"

The first thing Jameson had done when a copy of the cable had landed on his desk was to gather all the information they had on Moi. He hoped the Minister would appreciate the effort, but perhaps not, considering the paucity of facts available. He rested both hands on his crossed knees and spoke regretfully.

"Not a lot, Minister. Luckily I had to swot up on Zawanda for the committee grilling yesterday, which went very well, incidentally, and Moi came up in the process. He's pegged with turning the army onto the Ushkuu, but Zawutu denies ministerial involvement and claims that a few malcontents in the army did the damage. He blamed the CO and has punished several of the officers; he actually executed one. But the waters in that area are exceedingly muddy. What we do know for sure is that Moi himself attended Sandhurst, where the MoD had problems with him. Unlike Zawutu, who was a model student, Moi was trouble from the start. He laced a competitive platoon's water with a native laxative and damn near killed the lot of them, so say some, though that undoubtedly is an exaggeration. It was pretty uncomfortable for a while, but never fatal, the inquiry elicited. The Directing Staff had a good laugh about it in private, apparently.

"I rang Sandhurst this morning in case they could add to our knowledge of the man. Moi is a typical tribesman: tough, ruthless and unscrupulous. But he is an old chum of President Zawutu's from village days. Moi helped him through the loss of his father in '75 and owes his position to that."

"But can we talk with him? Is he literate?"

Jameson took the blatant arrogance in his stride. He was used to such remarks from his Minister and had taken to emulating him in that respect. It was obviously politically correct for the moment, anyway, and he wanted to be recognised as being in the forefront of fashion.

"Oh I expect so, Henry," he said. "He managed Sandhurst and he is, after all, a full blown Minister in his own country."

Beauchamp nodded. "All right Peter. Let me have a full brief on the man as soon as maybe and inform Zawanda that I will be pleased to receive their Minister of the Interior."

★ ★ ★

"No Mutti. Not that, please," Moi pleaded when he heard. "Not the British Foreign Office."

CHAPTER FOUR

Moi complained widely about Zawutu's acceptance of the British FO invitation. He had no experience of international protocol and secretly feared coming face to face with a British Minister of the Crown. He resented the superior attitude of white people and hated it in the British, but at the same time he had to admit to himself that they were very clever in quite extraordinary ways.

"Can't you say I'll be too busy?" he suggested over a drink with the President on the study balcony one evening.

"Come on, Josi. All you have to do is shake hands and pass on my best regards," Zawutu counselled. "Listen to what the minister has to say and tell him how we rely upon British aid to fund the many improvements we have in progress and planned. If there's a function to attend, a dinner, a reception, or anything like that, we'll know in advance, but if nothing has been advised already I wouldn't worry about that. Then just shake hands again, say goodbye, invite him to visit Zawanda and leave. Grab Granby and get on the first plane out of there. Oh, and if the Minister has anything to say about my TV interview, tell him it was for local consumption only... no, don't say that. If you have to say anything, say we're sorry we were misunderstood."

Moi kept nodding throughout, but was clearly nervous. "Can you write it for me, exactly what I have to say?" he pleaded. "I can learn it very well. Better, though, if you say no."

Zawutu smiled kindly. "You know I can't do that. The invitation has the force of a command. But I'll write it for you. Send my secretary in as you leave."

After dictating the crib, Zawutu told the secretary to give the finished work to Major Moi, then sat back to reflect upon why Henry Beauchamp would want to meet Josi personally. He half wished now that he had not ordered Josi to the UK, for apart from his lack of experience and rough manners, he simply would not be able to handle the unexpected.

He wondered about alternatives, but Granby had to be brought safely in, and Moi was the man for that. If only this Foreign Office thing hadn't come up. Even armed with all the likely scenarios, and rehearsed, Josi could well be flattened by the first item to fall outside his visit remit.

Cancel the visit altogether; arrange another time with Dickie? There was no time. The tribal issue would not wait. Perhaps if Josi stuck rigidly to his script with the addition of a last resort, fail-safe phrase like "I am not empowered to reply to that, I will refer it to my President" he might manage. Drilled remorselessly between now and the meeting, he could just survive the confrontation. Maybe. If Josi was good at anything it was performing exactly as instructed and precisely as trained – when it had nothing to do with the Ushkuu. The risks were there. Were they acceptable?

★ ★ ★

Moi prepared for his trip with meticulous attention to the detail of his dreaded meeting with the British Foreign Secretary. He had rehearsed his lines to exhaustion under the tutelage of

Zawutu personally, and although he felt a little better equipped to handle the confrontation his imagination continued to trouble him. Zawutu had been patient, but Moi felt that underneath Mutti regretted that he had ever allowed it to go this far. Too late now, and anyway, getting Granby safely to Zawanda must take priority. Mutti had insisted.

Zawutu himself took Moi to the airstrip, schooling him to the very last second. Poor Moi, who hated flying, climbed from the Presidential Mercedes and stood at the foot of the three steps up to the aircraft cabin. "This is something I do not want to do Mutti," he pleaded, clinging to hopes of a last minute reprieve. Zawutu smiled broadly and took Moi's hand in a reassuring valedictory shake. "You'll be fine, Josi. Just remember what you have been taught. Have a safe trip and call me every day. Now, off you go."

He took hold of Moi's elbow and guided him up the first step. The squat figure, round as a barrel, looked quite forlorn in an off-the-peg suit, tailored to fit but still fitting only where it touched and hanging like a corrugated sack on his disproportionate frame.

Zawutu shook his head in despair as his Interior Minister paused at the cabin door to wave. "Only Allah knows what they'll think of him in England!" he mumbled to himself as he climbed back into the car. "If only he could have travelled in uniform. That at least fits him."

He watched through the car window as the small ten-seater took off and felt a cold shiver as the familiar umbilical to his Minister was severed. Moi was now on his own, a prospect enough to depress anyone. But with no alternative the risks would have to be borne.

★ ★ ★

Moi didn't like aeroplanes, particularly these small ones that hopped and skipped through the sky as if bouncing from one air pocket to the next. He sat white-knuckled, holding tightly to the arms of his narrow seat and staring directly ahead. If he looked through the window he knew he would be sick.

"Coffee, sir?" the stewardess enquired, a pretty Nigerian girl who under normal circumstances would have evoked a bawdy response from Moi. But not today. He glanced quickly at her and shook his head, then resumed staring at the bulkhead in front of him.

"Tea? a cold drink? We shall be serving a snack in about an hour, perhaps you would rather wait?"

"Nothing," Moi spat angrily, his stomach already reacting adversely to her culinary suggestions. He belched loudly. The girl made a face and walked away.

The flight lasted two and three quarter hours, including one stop for fuel and the embarkation of three more passengers on a bush-like airstrip in the middle of nowhere. During all that time Moi had sat rigid, fighting nausea, determined not to show weakness of that kind in public.

In Lagos he picked up British Airways flight 074 to London Gatwick. His VIP status had been notified ahead and the first-class cabin crew, familiar with the sight and peculiarities of Third World government ministers, gave him every attention, much to his personal satisfaction. The sheer size and comfort of the Boing 747 reduced his feelings of anxiety, and because it was a night flight he could at least sleep through the worst of it.

Settled in his first-class seat and about to nod off, he suddenly felt a deep rumble in his gut, followed by another undisguised belch. He was hungry. He found and glanced through the previously discarded dinner menu and liked what he saw. Perhaps he would eat after all, and take a good stiff drink to start.

"Excuse me," he called to a passing stewardess, who halted, leaned over and replied: "Yes, sir?"

"I will eat, but first bring me a whisky," he said.

Two whiskies, a full first-class BA meal with wine and a vintage port to follow, made him forget he was flying. The smooth passage of the 747 and the darkness outside removed all sense of being suspended in the air by a couple of slender wings and four massive engines. Moi unfolded his blanket and tried to get comfortable, until he saw his neighbour across the aisle stretched out full length, seat back reclined and leg rest extended.

He rang for the stewardess. "Like that," he said, pointing sideways. He sat upright while the girl activated buttons and pressed knobs and when everything was in place he stretched his legs on the expanded leg rest, snuggled under his blanket, head and all, and moments later began snoring gently. He did not even notice the cabin lights dim for the night. Each time he turned over he woke, but soon drifted off again, and by 0400 hours next morning, when the cabin crew woke everyone for breakfast, he felt quite refreshed.

He took his turn in one of the toilets, where he shaved, using a travelling electric razor contributed by Zawutu, splashed water on his face, dried it on his handkerchief and thought brightly that this could be any normal morning on the ground. The flight had been smooth and quick and he felt rested and ready for breakfast.

The aircraft touched down a few minutes late, at 0535, and taxied neatly to its landing ramp. Moi was first off, handed over to a hospitality steward for the walk to the VIP lounge where the Honorary Zawandan Consul, in company with a junior from the British Foreign Office, awaited his arrival.

"Minister," Abu Simbli said, extending his hand and drawing Moi into the room. "This is Mr Goodly from the FO – er, Foreign Office."

Moi shook hands with Goodly. "Thank you for meeting me," he said formally.

Simbli, a middle-aged Zawandan immigrant with a business of his own in Battersea, had acted as Honorary Zawandan Consul to Great Britain through three coups and had welcomed Ministers from each of those administrations in just this way. He had abandoned hope of ever seeing the same face twice. But as long as the cheques kept arriving each month he would continue to do the job for his old country. It required very little of his time, to be honest.

He glanced at this new man, raising an eyebrow at his crumpled appearance. He put it down to the overnight flight; but why, he wondered, was he travelling alone? Zawandan ministers usually moved with an entourage larger than that of the British Prime Minister.

"Welcome to the United Kingdom," Goodly of the FO was saying loudly to Moi, as if the better to be understood. "The Secretary of State extends his welcome too, and looks forward to your visiting him the day after tomorrow. I have given all the details to Consul Simbli. Now, if you will excuse me, I will leave you to your own people. Good morning Minister, and enjoy your stay."

As soon as the door closed behind the Briton, Simbli waved Moi to a seat. "If I could have a minute, please, Minister?"

Moi sat and began fidgeting with his hands.

"Here are the briefs for your meeting with the SOS, sir," said Simbli. "The Foreign Office is nothing if not meticulous in providing us with every minutia." He handed Moi a large brown envelope and observed a worried frown form on his minister's face. He hastened to rephrase himself. "They give us names, times and places and clear instructions how to get there, they say who will meet you, for how long the meeting is to last, and usually they provide advanced notice of any subjects that may have arisen since their formal communication with your office in Zawanda." He felt relieved that Moi seemed to be relaxing. "You have a suite reserved at the Inn on the Park. I will take care of the account after you leave. And if there is anything I can do to make your stay more comfortable, please do not hesitate to ask, sir."

Moi took the OHMS envelope and slipped it into his brief case.

"Maidens. What about maidens?" he then asked ingenuously. Simbli stared at him. His dark brown features flashed with disgust, but he controlled his tongue. Pimp he was not and never could be. The matter had never come up before, not for him anyway. He had always assumed that one of the visitors' accompanying aids attended to intimacies of that kind, but Moi was on his own, of course.

Simbli spluttered for a moment. "I'll have a word with someone at the hotel," he said eventually, trying not to grimace. "Perhaps they can suggest something."

Moi nodded. "OK, can we go now?"

Fortunately, at that moment a BA hospitality girl poked her head round the door. "The Minister's baggage is cleared and loaded into the car," she said politely, with an engaging smile.

"Thank you," Simbli said, glad to be on the move. He motioned for Moi to follow the girl.

★ ★ ★

Just over one and a half hours later, Simbli said goodbye to his charge in the hotel lobby. "You have my number. Ring if you need anything," he said.

"Maidens," Moi replied in his normal speaking voice, drawing strange looks from a gentleman seated in one of the easy chairs clustered to the right of the entrance.

Simbli had hoped he'd forget. "Erm, yes, of course," he said, dreading having to raise such a salacious subject with the concierge. "I will ask someone to call you in your room," he ended, and departed hurriedly for the concierge counter on the other side of the lobby.

Pleased that he had arrived without any of the things occurring that he had dreaded, Moi finally entered his hotel suite and began to unpack. As soon as he had finished he looked at his watch. The time was almost eleven o'clock. He should ring Granby. The call to Zawanda could wait. It was lunchtime there and the President would be eating.

He looked up the number for Arms Incorporated on the list Zawutu had given him and dialled. Nothing happened. He tried again, then dialled the operator. "This phone doesn't work," he complained angrily. "I dial and get noises."

"I'm sorry sir. Are you dialling nine for an outside line?" the female operator asked patiently. Foreigners!

Moi felt the heat reach his cheeks. "Of course I am, but I told you it doesn't work," he said aggressively, to cover his ignorance.

"What number do you require, then sir?" the young lady asked calmly.

He told her and was immediately connected. Granby himself answered the phone.

Moi wasted no time on niceties. "Major Moi here. I'm to take you to Zawanda. Meet me here, the Inn on the Park, at six this evening, in the bar."

An educated voice came briskly back: "I'm not sure I can."

Moi smiled his twisted smile. Another arrogant Englishman, but Mutti had said this one had nothing to be arrogant about. It had been a joke, but Moi did not understand college humour. "Be here," he said abruptly and rang off.

After going through the FO file he had been given, he

dozed fitfully until about 3 pm, when he glanced at his watch and swore. Swinging his legs off the bed he grabbed the phone and dialled the operator.

It was a new girl, on the second shift. "Yes, sir. Can I help?" she asked at once.

Not wishing to make another mistake with these stupid British telephones, he gave her the number of the President's office in Zawanda and asked to be put through.

"You can dial direct from your room, sir," the girl said helpfully.

"No I can't," he shouted angrily. "I've told you already, the bloody phone doesn't work with the outside, so just get me the number, girl."

The young operator began to explain that she had only just come on duty, but Moi's irritated response persuaded her not to pursue the issue. Instead she asked him civilly to hold for a moment, and she would certainly have words with her predecessor, who should have left a note on the special instructions pad. It was an unfamiliar code which would take a moment to run down.

"I'll call you back," she said eventually, not wishing to be shouted at again for the delay.

Moi fretted, then the phone rang. "You're through," the girl said quickly and threw the switch with a relieved sigh, raising her eyebrows to her companion. "Foreigners!" she said without expansion.

Zawutu's voice came on loud and clear. "Josi, how was the trip?"

"Easy," Moi boasted. "I was met by Simbli and a man from the British government and now I'm in my hotel."

"Have you contacted Granby?"

Moi snorted. "Yes. He tried to be difficult, but I told him I want him here at six. He'll come."

"OK," Zawutu said. "But take it easy. I want him here willing to cooperate, remember. What about your visit to the Foreign Office?"

"I've got all the information. There's only one problem and that's what I want to talk to you about. They have added a subject."

Zawutu stiffened. "What subject?"

Moi picked up the relevant page from those scattered on the writing table and quoted, "British policy towards ex-colonies, their degree of dependency and future self-funding," he enunciated carefully, reading it word for word.

Zawutu felt it like a sword thrust. "Self-funding!" he repeated.

"What do you want me to do?" Moi asked plaintively. "This isn't on my list. Do I tell them to talk to you?"

Zawutu thought for a moment. "Don't say anything. Ask Simbli to deal with it, to get the details in writing so that I can deal with it later." Even though it could be nothing, he had learned the wisdom of stretching things out to allow time for proper study. "And don't forget, you're there for Granby, do you understand. Get him here safely."

"Yes, Mutti. I will," Moi said as if swearing an oath.

"Is there anything else?" Zawutu enquired out of habit, impatient to hang up and reflect upon what Beauchamp might be up to.

"Well, there is something," Moi said in a serious tone "Did you know that in London it is very difficult to find maidens? Simbli spoke with a man at the hotel here who asked many questions. How old, what colour, man or woman, and how much money? Whoever heard of paying money for a maiden?"

Zawutu, despite the other, potentially serious, news, could only laugh. Trust Josi to reduce everything to basics! "I'm sorry to hear that," he said, trying to sound genuinely concerned.

"Perhaps you should pay too then, if it's the culture over there."

Moi snorted at that. "Pay? Well, maybe, if I can't find a maiden for myself."

"Now look, Josi, no getting into trouble," Zawutu cautioned anxiously. The last thing he needed was a scandal involving a Zawandan minister. "Promise me."

Moi promised and rang off with an Eshanti farewell, astounded that Mutti should agree to paying for what is after all a man's natural entitlement. He shook his head disbelievingly.

At six he was in the first floor bar nursing a whisky and waiting for Granby to arrive. The two restaurants were hardly open, though an enterprising waiter did come across and offer Moi a menu.

"Will you be dining, sir?" he asked.

Moi took the leather-bound menu and laid it on the table. "Probably." he said, and the waiter left.

No identification signal or token had been agreed upon for the meeting, but Moi felt importantly that he could hardly be overlooked. He sipped contentedly at his drink, ignoring the surreptitious stares his unkempt appearance was attracting.

After a few minutes, a tall, well-made man, with fair, naturally wavy hair and a grey streak just visible at the peak, walked in, glanced around and made a beeline for where Moi was sitting.

"Zawanda?" he enquired hesitantly and offered a tentative hand.

"Moi. Major Moi, yes."

"Good." Granby replied, letting his hand drop when the ugly little man did not take it. "Can I get you a drink?" he then asked, noticing Moi's almost empty glass.

"No. Sit down and we'll talk," Moi said rudely.

Granby paused, eyed this upstart from a third-rate ex colony and heartily disliking what he saw. "I'll get myself a drink, then," he said defiantly.

Moi raised a hand and a waiter came scurrying across. "Tell him what you want," Moi said and looked away.

"G and T," Granby ordered and chose a chair opposite Moi at the small, round, glass-topped table. He eyed the crumpled suit and stubbled chin and wondered what the hell Freddie had landed him with. A bloody native, he said to himself. Chum Freddie sends me an ignorant bloody native!

Into the silence the waiter returned and completed the ritual of a bowl of nuts, a paper coaster, the gin and a questioning glance as he poised the tonic bottle above the rim of the glass.

"To the top," Granby informed him, and once it had been done turned his attention back to Moi.

"So what's the plan?" he asked imperiously in an effort to assert control. Moi downed the residue of his whisky in one and ignored, or misunderstood, Granby's tone. "We leave for Zawanda as soon as I'm finished at the Foreign Office."

"And when will that be?" Granby insisted, unimpressed by Moi's name-dropping and wondering why the Foreign Office would bother with such an insignificant little creature as this.

"If I knew that I'd tell you," Moi answered curtly. "Our Consul will make all the arrangements. You've got your visa, so be ready to move any time from Thursday."

Granby nodded. "OK," he said, but there were matters to be made clear and he set about it undaunted. "As long as it's understood that I'm dealing directly with your President. When I spoke with him he just said he was sending someone to assist my travel. I didn't expect a diplomat, but it makes no difference to me either way. Freddie said you'd assist in getting me to Zawanda and that's OK with me."

Moi stiffened at the description 'diplomat', the insult making him deaf to Granby's rebellious tone.

"Diplomat?" he bellowed, then reduced his decibels in the face of inquisitive glances from all around the bar. "I am the Minister of the Interior."

"Sorry," Granby said. Surprised, he struggled to conceal a contemptuous grin. "I wouldn't have guessed you were so important."

Moi actually preened the sarcasm of Granby's remark lost on him.

"Your trip just happens to coincide with my visit to your Foreign Office," he lied glibly. "And the President asked if I would accompany you back, that's all. So bear that in mind, and bear in mind who I am."

Granby bowed his head mockingly. "Yes, Minister."

Moi stared hard, seeking the insult, but with his experience of the British limited mainly to bellowing RSMs and patronising officer class instructors he chose to let it pass. And anyway, tribal custom decreed that when all has been said you depart, so he stood and walked out, leaving Granby to foot the bill for both drinks.

"You little shit!" Granby hissed at the retreating figure. He had expected an invitation to dinner and keen anticipation of a decent meal for a change had mobilised his appetite. He felt ravenous, but a glance at the menu prices put eating in either of the restaurants here way beyond his present financial circumstances. He sighed, paid three times what he would pay anywhere else for the two drinks and left to find a pub.

Moi took a room service meal, intending then to go out and find himself a maiden, but unconsciousness overtook him and he fell asleep stretched out on the bed minus only his jacket.

★ ★ ★

Maidens were truly hard to find in London. Next evening, two discos, three bars and a night club had brought Moi nothing. A few maidens, black and white, had condescended to talk to him and been more than eager to accept his hospitality, but none had shown any inclination to submit themselves to the hands, or other appurtenances, of this ugly, almost dwarf-like creature. By 2 am he was utterly bewildered. In Zawanda, maidens appeared to fall over themselves to be bedded by him; Moi did not know that they were in fact herded there by de Lancy and never forgot the terrifying experience that followed. Astonishingly, he believed himself to be attractive, and as the morning wore on he became increasingly more frustrated.

The dam burst in the Park Tower Casino. He misunderstood the well-dressed young woman at the roulette table who smiled at him and accepted a drink. She claimed later not to have agreed to accompany him back to his hotel suite, but Moi, stimulated by her low-cut dress and tantalising uplift, thought she had. "Come," he said, grasping her by the arm and hauling her towards the door. She resisted, and when Moi refused to release her she cried out in fear. The rumpus quickly attracted two very large men dressed in loose dinner jackets who appeared from nowhere. They took Moi firmly by the elbows, lifted his feet just clear of the ground and assisted him speedily from the premises. No one knew who he was, so the incident was soon forgotten. Just another punter who knew no better.

Raging at the perceived injustice, Moi flagged down a taxi and instructed the driver laconically: "To the Inn on the Park."

The following morning, the day of his meeting with Beauchamp, he was still angry. The insults of the previous night still smouldered in his mind and he took it out on the breakfast waiter, snapping at the poor man, who was in fact a Spaniard and not one of the hated British. Nevertheless, the Park Tower incident had cranked Moi's loathing of the British up another notch, exacerbated by his anxiety about the forthcoming meeting, and any target would do.

Simbli rang at nine to confirm arrangements. He would meet Moi at the hotel and they would travel to the Foreign

Office together. Moi was a great deal less than courteous in his response. He didn't want this meeting and actually thought about not going, but Mutti would have his balls for breakfast if he didn't go. He sighed deeply. Why was life outside the village so complicated?

* * *

Jameson, admitted by Beauchamp's private secretary, briskly covered the long walk from door to desk. "Good morning, Henry," he said, eyeing with envy on the way, for the hundredth time, the panelled room, the antique furniture and original old oil paintings ranked on the walls in a seemingly random fashion, yet somehow perfectly arranged. He reached the leather-topped oak desk with its finely carved curlicues at the corners and thought ambitiously - One day perhaps?

"Peter. Do sit. Tea?" Beauchamp asked, indicating the requirement to his secretary, who hovered in the doorway. To Jameson he added, "I'll be with you in a minute," and gave his attention once again to the papers in front of him.

Jameson had been the member for Ormskirk for ten years, and before that for a constituency which had been lost in one of the strategic boundary changes. He felt himself to be in the mainstream of politics and looked forward with well-placed confidence to assuming higher office in a year or two. His eyes, behind their lenses, were not kind eyes. Ruthless by nature, he used his physical bulk to intimidate and conquer, yet he could be charming, with an attractive smile and smooth words. Today he wore a plain grey suit, pressed to perfection and cut to hide an incipient waistline bulge.

Tea came on a tray. The best china, sterling silver, and a plate of assorted biscuits.

"Now," Beauchamp said, papers put aside and tea in hand.

"Minister Moi will be with us soon." He glanced at his watch. "Leave me to handle the aid business, though I can't say I'm looking forward to it. Young Goodly amplified your brief on the man after meeting him at Gatwick Not very reassuring, I'm afraid. But that's what we're here for, eh?" he added pompously.

Jameson agreed. "I'll leave it to you then."

Several desultory topics later the intercom buzzed.

"Yes?" Beauchamp enquired.

"Minister Moi has arrived, sir,"

Beauchamp eyed Jameson and seemed to stiffen his shoulders.

"Very well. Show him in."

As the door opened Beauchamp rose to his feet, walked round the desk and advanced upon the two men who had entered. He knew Simbli, of course, and had studied a photograph of Moi, but even that had not prepared him for the reality of this untidy, almost deformed figure, dressed in a shockingly ill-fitting suit. Even his shoes were dirty. Beauchamp controlled his surprise and stretched out a hand.

"Minister," he said warmly, as the proffered hand was taken. It felt as though he had taken hold of a well-fed slug, and he found it a struggle not to remove the spotted handkerchief from his breast pocket and wipe his palm. Later, he did manage a surreptitious cleansing rub on his trouser leg.

Moi mumbled a reply, then gathered himself. His progress through the corridors of British power had not done his already twanging nerves much good, but he did manage to blurt out: "And President Zawutu sends his best regards to you and the British people." He felt pleased that he had got his first lines out correctly.

"Thank you, and please give President Zawutu our warmest congratulations when you return to Zawanda." Beauchamp then turned to Simbli. "Consul."

In contrast, Simbli's hand felt surprisingly cool and dry. Beauchamp almost sighed with relief. "Tea, gentlemen? And please be seated."

Jameson was then introduced. During the tea ritual he asked specific questions about Zawanda in order to fill the gaps in his political and economic profile of that country. Then, with nothing more to discuss, Beauchamp judged it time to present the poisoned chalice. He coughed to clear his throat.

Moi sat comfortably in his chair, thoroughly relaxed. He had followed his brief, and with growing confidence had concluded that these British politicians were really no more than pussy cats. Nothing unexpected had arisen, and in boasting of his place and pride in Zawanda he had completely forgotten about the 'added subject'.

"Aid," Beauchamp began, a stern expression now riveted onto his face.

Moi blinked. "Aid?" he repeated, sitting up. Now what had Mutti said about aid?

"Yes," Beauchamp confirmed. "Aid." He looked to Simbli for understanding, on the basis that the subject was difficult enough without the Zawandan Minister becoming confused. Simbli reiterated the word 'aid' in the Eshanti tongue for Moi's benefit and then nodded.

Beauchamp took a deep breath. "It is my proud duty," he went on. "To inform you that Her Majesty's Government finds it no longer essential for the United Kingdom to continue to provide financial assistance to Zawanda." He paused there and smiled, as if to soften the blow, but Moi did not understand the kindness and so, after a moment for assimilation, he spat out an extremely crude Eshanti expletive.

"I beg your pardon?" Beauchamp asked, looking to Simbli for an explanation.

"A Zawandan expression of surprise, sir," Simbli offered,

placing a cautionary hand on Moi's arm. Jameson frowned, regretting now that he had not arranged for an interpreter.

"As I was saying," Beauchamp went on patiently. "Zawanda is now in sound, capable hands. Her economy is improving, the tribes are peaceful and you can look forward to a truly independent existence from now on. The Commonwealth applauds what you have achieved."

He hesitated over the rest of his prepared speech, concerned lest Moi should emit another of his native expressions of surprise, but it had to be said. He decided to ad lib.

"I was about to extend HM Government's displeasure at your President's handling of the Ushkuu matter, but that is water under the bridge now."

Moi turned to Simbli and spoke in their own language. "Water? I thought they were talking about aid?"

"They are," Simbli said. "Water under the bridge is a Western expression meaning the event is past and can be forgotten."

Beauchamp waited and Jameson cursed again his neglect over the provision of an interpreter.

"I'm sorry, Minister," Simbli said, refocusing on Beauchamp. "Minister Moi asked for clarification, that's all."

At least he's listening, Beauchamp thought, but to what? During the exchange between the two Zawandans he had observed Moi's expression change from mystification to downright derision. He wondered why.

"Thank you," he said anyway. "To continue. We also had some difficulty understanding why President Zawutu should seek to criticise the United Kingdom on television." Then he smiled again to withdraw the sting and went on more easily, "But the important thing is that Zawanda is improving in every direction and we are pleased to assist in that process by removing the crutches and letting you walk for yourselves."

"Crutches?" Moi enquired.

"Another expression," Simbli added hastily with an apologetic glance towards Beauchamp. It was clear to him, if not to Moi, that the cut in aid had nothing to do with Zawanda's so called magnificent progress, nor her misdemeanours. Cold, ruthless economics was what it was all about; budget pressures, no doubt. Of course, none of this showed on his face as he secretly admired the British sleight of hand. He glanced at Moi and gripped the man's arm more firmly in case of a sudden reaction, but Moi shook it off.

Beauchamp, unaware of the byplay, continued. "Therefore, all aid will cease from next year. Mr Jameson will provide the details before you leave."

Moi had listened, but he had recognised only the key phrases which told him that all aid was about to cease. He raked his memory for instructions covering this event and found only blank spaces. He panicked.

"You cannot do that to us!" he shouted, falling back on his own inadequate resources and simultaneously waving a bunched fist at Beauchamp. "I said how much we rely on your aid and you nodded. Now you say no more!"

Moi moved to stand, but Simbli pressed him back into his seat.

"This is bad news," the Consul said directly to Moi, pre-empting another outburst by struggling to hold him down without showing the strain. "But let us at least be diplomatic about it."

"Diplomatic?" Moi exploded, still boiling from Granby's misdescription of the first evening. "Balls to that!" And he at once withdrew into his native language for the rest, the words spitting out like machine-gun bullets with such vehemence and ferocity of gesticulation that Beauchamp physically recoiled.

Simbli glanced anxiously at Jameson, not sure how much the Englishman understood of the language, but on seeing only blank concern he turned his attention back to calming Moi. Then the Secretary of State took hold and came up from his seat in some alarm.

"Is he all right?" he enquired solicitously. "A brandy, perhaps?"

"He's a Muslim, Henry," Jameson reminded his boss automatically. "Another tea might be more appropriate."

"No. Brandy," Moi gasped, his eyes bulging, his face beaded with sweat.

"Get him one, will you, Peter," Beauchamp ordered as he leaned anxiously across the desk. "A doctor? Does he need a doctor?"

Simbli shook his head. "No. He's fine. It was the shock, you understand. He'll be all right soon."

Beauchamp shook his head in dismay. Never before had he experienced such an untrammelled demonstration of naked emotion here in the Foreign Office, let alone in the presence of the Foreign Secretary.

Jameson came back with a good measure of brandy, which Moi took in one gulp and then held out the glass for more. Jameson glanced at Beauchamp, who shrugged and nodded his head.

"Can I get you one, too?" Jameson asked Simbli politely.

Simbli shook his head. "I am a practising Muslim," he explained unaffectedly. "But a cup of tea, perhaps?"

"Of course," Jameson said. He understood the embarrassment Simbli must be feeling and wondered whether to exploit it or not. He decided not and instead gave Simbli a sympathetic glance as he passed on his way to the drinks cupboard.

Moi got his brandy and Simbli his tea as Beauchamp looked on, flabbergasted by it all. Then Simbli stood, abruptly, and brought Moi with him. "Thank you, Minister," he said and nudged Moi in the ribs.

"Ah. Yes. Thank you," Moi repeated, the two very large brandies having calmed him somewhat. He offered his hand instinctively. Beauchamp hesitated before reluctantly taking it.

Jameson led the pair to the door, where Moi hesitated and half turned to speak, prevented by a strong consular hand on his elbow. "Not now," Simbli said forcefully in Eshanti.

In the car, Moi sat back, exhausted and silent, much to Simbli's relief. The last thing he wanted was a heated discussion with this awful little man. It was true that the news from the Foreign Office was devastating, but that did not excuse Moi's bad manners. He also feared that Moi's temper had corrupted what little he had understood of the proceedings. What tale would he tell President Zawutu, he wondered?

 **CHAPTER FIVE**

It was Thursday morning before Moi made his call to Zawanda. Back in his room the previous evening, having rid himself of the long-suffering Simbli and gobbled a bag of nuts and a packet of crisps, he had rung down to the concierge and ordered a maiden as he would a meal from room service, desperation finally unzipping his pocket.

"A what sir?" the concierge enquired.

Further exchanges achieved nothing; the employee was not the one Simbli had approached and this one did not see pimping as part of his contract of employment. ""Try Soho or Half Moon Street," he suggested brusquely.

Moi cursed, rang off and went to put his shoes back on. Then he suddenly realised that he had no idea where Soho or Half Moon Street were and in sheer frustration he emptied his mini bar of everything alcoholic by the simple process of consuming it all. So on Thursday morning he had a throbbing head.

"Zawanda," he shouted at the operator, and immediately regretted it. Just the creaking of his bedsprings sounded like peals of bells.

Zawutu came on the line a few minutes later. "Josi, where

have you been? I rang the hotel last night and they told me you were not accepting calls. What's going on?"

Moi swallowed as he strove to get his brain into gear. "I am unwell, Mutti."

"Unwell?" Zawutu said. "Whenever were you unwell? Pissed maybe, a hangover certainly, but unwell, never. So stop messing about and tell me what happened at the Foreign Office yesterday?"

There followed a long silence which Zawutu abruptly ended by shouting down the phone: "Josi, for Allah's sake pull yourself together. What happened at the meeting?"

Moi cleared his throat, his brain throbbing still from the painful effects of last night's excesses. "Don't shout at me, Mutti. My head."

"The meeting, Josi. Never mind your head."

"They're pissed off with us for the Ushkuu job and your TV appearance. And there's to be no aid," Moi emitted in one painful burst.

Zawutu frowned. Josi must have got it wrong, have misunderstood.

"Tell me again," he demanded.

"No aid. None at all," Moi confirmed, shaking his head as if to reinforce what he was saying, and then he suddenly stopped as everything inside felt as if it had broken loose. He winced.

"Are you absolutely sure they said no aid at all?" Zawutu insisted.

"Yes," Moi replied, holding his head still to save it from bursting.

Zawutu felt the hot hand of disaster clutch his vitals and suddenly felt sick. "My god!" he said quietly, the terrible news sapping the energy to be angry. "I expected a reduction, but to be cut off completely..."

He searched through his mental inventory of what this

would mean to Zawanda. It only made the agony worse. He feared most what it would do to the tribes, the Ushkuu in particular, already so resentful that they were dangerous.

"Did you appeal?" he asked Moi in desperation, quickly realising how futile the question was.

"Oh yes, Mutti. Very strongly," said Moi, rescuing what he could from the situation. "It wasn't my fault, Mutti," he ended fearfully.

"Of course not," Zawutu told him "What did they say when you objected?"

"I'm not sure," Moi confessed. "They told us there would be no aid, I complained and then we left."

Zawutu realised that whatever the reality, it had been beyond Moi's ability to comprehend fully or deal with adequately. A slow, burning anger rose in his breast as he recognised how the British had taken perfidious advantage of Moi in this.

"All right, Josi," he said gently. "You concentrate on getting Granby here as quickly as possible. Forget everything else."

"I will do better this time, Mutti," Moi said the need for self-preservation uppermost.

Zawutu told him not to worry, hung up and placed a call to Abu Simbli. He at least should know what really happened.

"I have been expecting you, sir," Simbli said as soon as he recognised the caller.

Zawutu repeated what Moi had told him. "Is it true?" he wanted to know.

"Yes sir, it is," Simbli confirmed.

"Was there nothing you could do?"

"No sir. To be honest with you, it was all I could do to restrain Major Moi from hitting the Foreign Secretary. As it was he launched a scathing attack on the British establishment in the crudest of Eshanti, which, thank Allah, no one understood. I would not tell you this except that it makes my relations with the FO people so much more difficult. But to answer your query, there was nothing I could do at that time. So, it remains that no further aid will be forthcoming after the end of this year, and in my view that ruling is cast in stone."

"Thank you, Abu, for assisting Major Moi," Zawutu said, making no apology for what had obviously been an extremely difficult task. Nor did he bemoan the depth and sliminess of the shit the British had landed him in. Instead he spoke calmly.

"I hope we shall see you soon in Zawanda, and in the meantime I hope you can mend a few fences over there."

Simbli sighed and said he hoped so too, then rang off. Zawutu thought for a while, then placed a call to Whitehall to speak with Jameson.

★ ★ ★

Abu Simbli delivered Granby's flight tickets to Moi's hotel room just before ten on the morning of Friday for the following day's flight, leaving Gatwick at 1330. Moi had worried himself sick since his conversation with Zawutu. To be told not to worry meant nothing at this distance; what mattered was what happened once he was back inside Zawanda. The strain and his vivid imagination had left him on edge and snappy. He snatched the tickets from Simbli's hand, glanced at the detail, asked about transport to the airport and dismissed the Zawandan Consul with as much ceremony as he would the room-maid.

Next, he rang Granby. "Be at this hotel at nine tomorrow morning," he instructed him tersely, and rang off.

A moment later the phone rang. Moi picked it up urgently, thinking it might be the President.

"Granby here," an irate voice announced. "Look Mr Moi, if you have made travel arrangements then I'm ready to discuss them with you, but I won't be ordered around by you or anyone else."

Moi frowned angrily. "You'll do as I say," he said with some force. "We leave for Gatwick at nine fifteen, so be here by nine as I say."

"And if I'm not?"

"I shall come and get you," Moi threatened in a voice rimmed with ice.

"Now just a minute there…" Granby began.

"No. You wait a minute. My President wants you in Zawanda as soon as possible. You have a contract."

"There is no contract," Granby shot back. "So you tell your President to get stuffed. I'm not interested." He swore at the phone and slammed it down onto its rest "Bugger Freddie, sending a moron like that" he fumed to himself. "Money or no money, I'll not be pushed around by that cretin."

Petulantly, he placed a call to Zawutu. "Freddie," he began in a controlled voice. "How are you?"

The call caught Zawutu unawares. He looked at his watch. Almost lunchtime. He had hoped it might be Jameson with news that Beauchamp had relented over the aid issue. Richard Granby's voice surprised him.

"Dickie? I was hoping you would be well on your way by now," he said, masking his disappointment.

"Well, it's your man, Moi. He's being rather unpleasant, Freddie. Ordering me about as if I were a squaddie, and you know I'm not the type to submit to that. I was hoping you might have a word. Frankly, old boy, I'm not at all keen the way things are."

Zawutu took a breath. He had more need of Granby now than ever. Without aid to smooth the way, keeping the peace could well be a bloody business and Granby's weapons would be vital.

"Sorry about that, Dickie," he said emolliently. "Josi has had a very taxing time in London and that may have shortened his fuse a little. I tell you what, why don't I give him a ring, smooth things out a bit? How would that suit you?"

Granby let the offer hang in the air for a minute, then responded ungraciously: "Well all right. But I won't put up with his boorishness a moment longer. Honestly, Freddie, it's beyond a joke."

"Of course," Zawutu oozed. "I understand. Leave it to me."

After replacing the handset Zawutu clicked his tongue impatiently and rang Moi.

"Josi," he opened, allowing no room for Moi to interrupt. "Now listen carefully. I need Granby ready and willing to cooperate when he gets here. You know the old saying, 'a ruffled hawk flies slowly and achieves nothing.' I have important matters to arrange with him. Do you understand?"

Moi nodded at the phone, then he spoke. "He has said words then. But I can't back down, Mutti, you know that."

"Of course you can't," Zawutu said. "Not immediately. Get Simbli to deliver the flight ticket to Richard and smooth things over. But after that I expect you to keep him sweet and deliver him to Zawanda happy and ready to work for us."

"Good," Moi said. "That is clever Mutti, but this man is arrogant like all Britishers, and I don't know how long I can keep myself from acting badly."

"Just try, Josi. Just try," Zawutu said despairingly. "Remember how important he is to us."

Moi pondered over that. There were many arms dealers in the world, so why all this fuss over Granby? Mutti was up to something, he thought as he rang off.

Simbli achieved the desired result; Granby appeared at the hotel at 9 am as required. He forebore to offer a hand, having had it ignored last time. Instead he smiled rather stiffly and said good morning. Moi nodded and spoke in his own language to Simbli, who had arrived a few minutes before.

"No need for you to come after all. Granby and I can manage."

Simbli shrugged his shoulders, shook hands all round and walked out to the hire car with them.

Moi slept all the way to Gatwick, and once in the airport lounge partook himself of a large whisky to quell the beginnings of flight anxiety. He had remained silent, partly to avoid saying the wrong thing and partly because of his fear of aeroplanes, but mostly because Mutti had been most insistent about not upsetting Granby.

Granby, at first nervous and overstrung, soon relaxed when it was clear that Moi intended to keep his own counsel. He ordered a coffee and drank it in silence, and still nothing was said between the two men, a situation which carried over onto the aircraft itself.

In broad daylight, flying took on an entirely different aspect for Moi. Although not as seriously uncomfortable as he would be later in the smaller aircraft, he nevertheless suffered and struggled against air sickness for most of the leg to Lagos, sitting hunched up in his seat and staring straight ahead.

Granby, for his part, could not resist taking a wicked pleasure in Moi's discomfort. He ate his meal with much relish and ceremony, accompanied by murmurs of appreciation and an occasional glance at his companion, whose growing distress was very obvious by this time.

What Granby considered to be largely innocent, light-hearted fun, with a certain devilment mixed in, gradually and wittingly pushed Moi's temper to its fracture threshold, until the truce between them suddenly shattered.

"Fuck you," Moi hissed. "Once we're in Zawanda..." The threat suddenly tailed off as the 747 dropped a few feet into an air pocket. Moi belched noisily. Granby didn't wait for him to continue. He swung round to his adversary and declared: "I'm not going to Zawanda." He'd had enough. "I'll be taking the first flight out of Lagos."

"And good riddance," Moi said dismissively, temporarily shielded from fear of Mutti's reaction if Granby failed to arrive on schedule by his anger at the Englishman and the misery of the constant nausea. Silence came to seats J3 and 4 and lasted all the way to Lagos.

Later, seated in the lounge at Murtala Muhammed Airport, both men calmed themselves, each concluding quite independently that with only the leg from Lagos to New London remaining surely they could manage it in one piece: Moi because he genuinely feared Mutti's anger, and Granby because the lure of hard cash had grown more imperative with each passing mile.

It was eight thirty in the evening and the last of the two daily flights to Zawanda had taken off two hours ago. "What time is the next one?" Granby enquired.

"Six-thirty tomorrow morning," Moi said. "We shall stay in the airport until then."

"Not on your life, old sport!" Granby exclaimed. "I'm for finding a bed for the night."

Moi too would have liked that, but he could not leave the airport without a visa and visas, for reasons inexplicable to Moi, were denied to Zawandans under rules laid down by Nigeria's military chiefs. He could hardly explain that to Granby, though, for reasons of pride. On the other hand, Granby, as a British subject, could obtain a one-month visa without question, simply by walking out through immigration.

"No. We wait here," Moi insisted stubbornly.

"You might," Granby said with an undisguised flicker of contempt, "but not me. I'll take my passport now if you don't mind."

Moi tapped his pocket for reassurance and ran his fingers

over the bulge representing their two passports. "No," he said with finality. "We stay here."

"Now look here," Granby fumed as the spark reached the detonator. "You hand over my passport or I'll call the police."

Moi smiled superciliously. "Fuck off," he said. "It won't hurt you to wait here until morning. And if you call the police it will be you in trouble. You, honky, are white in a black man's country."

"Bugger you!" Granby replied, furious at not making Moi cough up. He had hoped to terrify the little Zawandan into submission by threatening him with the police, but Moi knew the form as well he did. No one in their right mind would approach the police voluntarily in Nigeria. And something Moi did not know; in certain government quarters here the name Granby was anathema, so with a deep sigh he accepted defeat and flopped down into a plastic seat two away from his tormentor, from which he gazed angrily at the floor and cursed himself for permitting this obnoxious dwarf to get the better of him.

★ ★ ★

Jameson mentioned Zawutu's repeated telephone calls as soon as Beauchamp returned to his office after two official days in Scotland. Zawanda was hot just now and Jameson intended to make the most of his period of glory, ephemeral though it might turn out to be. It gave him immediate access to the SoS and provided an unparalleled opportunity to shine and be remembered.

"I'll speak with him myself," Beauchamp told him. "Wait, will you? I think I can clear this up once Zawutu hears it from me."

The connection made, Beauchamp opened. "I understand you have a problem with our overseas aid decision, Mr President?"

Zawutu, tense from waiting and relieved to hear Beauchamp, was nevertheless staggered by the degree of understatement. "I think you might say that, Foreign Minister."

"Well, let's see what we can do to allay your concerns," Beauchamp went on smoothly. "I assume Minister Moi gave you the gist of our conversation, and in addition he has in his possession our written paper on the subject, which you won't have received yet of course. The position is perfectly simple. Her Majesty's Government feels it right and timely to cut you that extra yard or so of cloth to see how you get on. It is in your country's best interests, believe me."

"So now you decide what is in Zawanda's best interests, do you?" Zawutu said sharply.

Beauchamp tutted. "No, not entirely. I have to take the larger view of the Commonwealth as a whole. Wherever a country can manage to fly solo we believe it should be allowed to do so. Aid always has strings attached, which can be inhibiting to the way a Prime Minister, or in your case, President, wishes to govern. So, as soon as we calculate the time is right to strip away those constraints, we do so. In the case of Zawanda, that time is now. Simple, you see."

"But that is a massive miscalculation," Zawutu pleaded. "I have bills for materials and manpower pouring in. Without British aid I shall be unable to service the existing debt, let alone repay the capital. And then there are the medium-term loans inherited from my predecessor. Those creditors are already snarling at my heels. If you cut off my aid Zawanda will be bankrupt, and I can't believe that is what you desire, nor would it be a good example to the rest of the Commonwealth."

"Oh I think the Commonwealth will understand," Beauchamp responded confidently. "After all, we have done the same for many Commonwealth nations who now thank us for it."

While loyally pressing the argument, Beauchamp's conscience still felt strangely troubled over the way Zawutu was being pitched into the crucible. Still, there was no going back on his agreement in Cabinet to cut overseas aid by the two billions insisted upon by the Treasury. Throwing countries like Zawanda to the dogs was just one of the uncomfortable penalties of narrowing the national deficit. Beauchamp sincerely regretted having to do it.

"I'm truly sorry, Freddie," he said, lapsing into the familiar. "There's nothing I can do. The answer must be no."

Zawutu thought quickly and pulled his last trump from the pack.

"What about the Ushkuu?"

Beauchamp responded as expected: "The Ushkuu, what about them?"

"Well, the tribe is very unhappy, and please don't make the obvious remark. The elders are already plotting to overthrow this government by force, and another bloodletting would not look good, particularly once it was known that you could have helped prevent it. You see, if I'm stalled in improving Ushkuu standards of living it will be used against me by the tribe. Without aid I shall be extremely vulnerable. You understand?"

Beauchamp understood only too well. If what Zawutu said was true, another coup so soon after the last one could prove a major embarrassment. Nevertheless, there was no way he could reinstate the aid package. Maybe there were other routes round the obstacle.

"I hear what you are telling me," he said. "But there will be no monetary aid no matter what the situation." He made a mental note to explore all the alternatives and was about to tell Zawutu so when, unable to prevent himself, Zawutu said angrily: "Britain will regret this, Beauchamp," and slammed down the phone.

In a red rage, his tribal genes in control of his brain, Zawutu's thoughts turned to violence. What was it Josi had said? Yes. Threaten the buggers with a local war. Well, why not? He'd tried everything else. His mind churned with venom and hatred as it reached out beyond the orthodox - and discovered an ingenious solution so radical that it raised the hairs on the back of his neck and caused a small muscle at the corner of his mouth to twitch uncontrollably for a second or two.

"Granby, my old chum, I have a new task for you." he told himself grimly. He stood, faced behind him and turned the Queen's portrait to the wall.

★ ★ ★

Beauchamp had meant what he had said. He had asked around, even dropping a hint to the PM after a Cabinet that Zawanda could explode into violence unless some means were found to prevent it. Masters had nodded, and with only that slender acquiescence to guide him Beauchamp had worked on his fellow ministers, hoping against hope that the PM had not just dipped his head out of habit.

"Clive seems agreeable to a low cost solution," he told Graham Henright, Minister of Defence, over a drink in the Members bar.

"I see," Henright replied with interest. "Well, it so happens that I'm under pressure from the Generals to find more realistic training for the elite regiments, or at least their officers, and a spell assisting the Zawandan army would count in that respect I suppose. A spot of military stiffening might make the Ushkuu think twice, don't you think? Act as a deterrent? Won't do much for the country's economy though."

"Quite," Beauchamp agreed. If he could offer Freddie Zawutu something along those lines it would certainly ease his own conscience, if nothing else.

"Can your staff chaps work something up just in case?" he enquired.

"Of course," Henright said, only too pleased at the opportunity to pre-load an obligation on Henry and at the same time get the Generals off his back. The cost would initially come out of the training budget, of course, but he would charge the FO through the nose for it in the end.

* * *

The light aircraft leg to Zawanda went without a hitch. Granby was so pleased to get aboard the ten-seater after a night spent in a plastic airport link chair that he was almost cheerful. Moi, on the contrary, felt too sick to care. For Granby the prospect of imminent arrival in Zawanda provided a sense of renewal which kept his mind occupied, but he could not resist casting a skewed glance of hatred at the man sitting next to him. The notion of revenge would, he knew, burn on undiminished. He was like that.

The plane called at the same remote airstrip to refuel, then an hour later began its descent into New London airport, a single concrete strip lined on one side by a small cluster of buildings. A radar antenna rotated above one of them, but the range and accuracy of the instrument did not nearly satisfy the requirements for International status. It managed the instrument landing system which kept the airport operating in all weathers well enough, though.

A Mercedes 450 saloon awaited the two men, the only passengers to alight from the aircraft. A gaudily-uniformed driver came over, collected and loaded the baggage, helped Granby aboard, then drove out through a secondary entrance gate which gave access directly onto the main road to New London and the Palace.

"So much for the almighty bloody visa!" Granby said sardonically. Moi ignored him and thanked Allah that this obnoxious Englishman would soon be Mutti's responsibility.

Granby settled back in the leather seat and gazed out at the passing bush, an arid plain dotted here and there with stunted trees and wizened shrubs. In the distance he could see a dark line which he took for trees.

"Is that a forest over there?" he asked Moi, trying to show an interest.

Moi grunted, but glanced in the direction indicated. "Yes," he said grudgingly. "Thick forest. It reaches almost to the outer city limits and the border. There is much forest in Zawanda," he added, unable to prevent national pride.

"And animals, too?"

Moi nodded, his grumpiness melting in the warmth of Granby's enquiries. "Many," he said eagerly. "All kinds. Hunting is good."

Granby screwed up his face at that. "You still kill them?" he asked disbelievingly.

"It is tradition," Moi said, his tone freezing over.

"Sometimes it is better to throw off tradition and grow up," Granby said. "Too many exotic species are disappearing for good."

"Mind your own business," Moi said rudely and turned away to stare out of his side window.

"You little shit!" Granby muttered to himself. "Your time will come."

Moi's head swivelled round as if he'd heard, although he had not. He frowned and turned his back once again. Maybe it had been the wind.

 # CHAPTER SIX

The Mercedes swept through the palace gates into a walled courtyard and pulled up before twin stone and balustraded staircases which rose in connecting arcs to a patio area before the grand entrance. A lavishly-uniformed soldier rushed to open the rear door and Granby stepped out just as Freddie Zawutu appeared through the doorway at the head of the steps and waved.

"Dickie!" the President said warmly as Granby reached the patio and extended a hand. Zawutu took it in both of his and with a nod at Moi, who had come on behind, placed an arm around Granby's shoulders and walked him into the building.

Mumbi stood in the entrance hall dressed in his usual tight pants and jacket; Zawutu hadn't found the heart to correct him. Mumbi had been there an hour already, nervously awaiting the arrival of this so important visitor. His task was to show Mr Granby to the room he had so diligently prepared yesterday. His excitement was understandable, for Mr Granby would be the first official guest since the coup and Mumbi was dedicated to making everything perfect for him.

"We'll talk later," Zawutu said to his guest after an exchange of routine pleasantries. "This is Mumbi. He will look after you while you're here. He has a little English if you speak slowly to him. Anything you want, just ask him, or if it's anything beyond his means, Major Moi or Captain de Lancy, my head of security, you'll meet him later, will handle it for you."

Granby nodded towards the wrinkled, grey-haired old man and smiled.

"Mumbi - that's an easy name to remember."

Mumbi smiled a gap-toothed, juice-stained smile and reached for the bags. Granby thanked his host, and then followed the old man to the right hand staircase and up the first few steps before relieving him of the heavier case in the belief that the elderly servant would never make it to the top otherwise. He glanced around as he went and found himself amused at the tasteless pretentiousness of the decaying Victorian splendour that surrounded him. Gold leaf, tarnished and peeling in places, embellished various ornamental flourishes; elaborate plaster nymphs and winged angels clung somehow to the towering walls of the atrium, their cherubic faces cracked and grubby, missing an ear here and a nose there. Yet in a strange sort of way the overall decay seemed to possess an indefinable charm of its own. A sort of warmth emanated from those neglected artefacts and he began to feel comfortable.

From the head of the stairs, he followed Mumbi along a wide corridor and turned left into a room which at first acquaintance appeared huge, made more so by a solid, heavily-braided four-poster at its centre and oaken chests of drawers and wardrobes on every side. A single window space seemed to occupy most of the outside wall and through it he could discern a balcony railed with what looked like intricately worked wrought iron. An equally intricate metal grille guarded the space.

Mumbi placed his load on the ground and walked over to the window, where he demonstrated how the grille opened and gave access to the balcony. "See," he invited, stepping out.

Granby followed and his surprised expression brought a happy smile from Mumbi. "Good, yes?"

Granby hadn't realised that the Palace faced out on to the bush. He could see the trees Moi had mentioned no more than a few hundred yards from the perimeter, and an intervening area that had at some time been professionally laid out as garden, with lawns now burnt brown and borders containing withered plants, now unidentifiable. It had been beautiful once, he imagined, and he could understand Mumbi's pride even in what remained.

"Yes, very nice," he assured the old man.

Mumbi turned and pointed out the wooden shutters, taking the edge of one and showing how it closed. "For night," he said, pressing together the thumb and forefinger of his right hand and making swooping motions.

"Bzzzzzz," he hummed.

"Insects," Granby said, nodding his head and smiling at Mumbi's mosquito simulation. "I will be sure to close the shutters," he promised.

Led back into the room, Granby swept it once more with a fascinated eye. How incongruous the bulky wooden furniture seemed in such a humidly hot country. But the room had a comfortable feel about it which pleased him. It was remarkably cool for one thing, and certainly spacious. There was even an en suite bathroom, grossly nineteenth century in its ornateness and scrubbed and polished until it gleamed.

"This for you alone," Mumbi said in awe as he proudly threw out both arms to encompass the masterpiece. To his mind, that a bathroom of such magnificence existed at all was miracle enough, but to be reserved for the use of just one person - well, that defied belief. He gazed at Granby expecting superlatives in appreciation. "Thank you, Mumbi," Granby said with a smile. "It's very nice."

The innocence of the old man appealed to him and he

reflected in passing that despite the odd feeling he had about this visit, Mumbi at least seemed uncomplicated.

The old tribesman bobbed his head in pleasure. 'Very nice' was obviously equivalent to 'terrific' in Eshanti and he was happy with that.

"Mutti, er, the President, asks – erm - food. Do you want food? Down," he said, pointing to the floor. "When you want," he ended, relieved to have got it said.

Granby smiled at him again and was for a moment tempted to reach out and pat the old man on the head as one would a pet dog. He felt his face burn at the near miss and covered his embarrassment by saying: "I am fine now. Please tell the President I'll join him when I've unpacked."

"Aaah!" Mumbi cried out, hanging his head in self-mortification. "Me unpack. Me. I unpack. Mutti said so."

This time Granby did extend a hand, but only to lay it on Mumbi's arm. "No. That isn't necessary, Mumbi," he said. "Please, you have done enough for now. Just tell the President I will be down soon."

"Soon." Mumbi nodded and shuffled out of the room, gently closing the door behind him.

Alone, Granby walked over to the window. "Wonderful!" he exclaimed as he gazed out once more across a foreground of neglected cultivation that could easily be rectified and beyond to the forest, which gradually rose to become a range of wooded hills not far distant. It reminded him of his stint in Kenya as a National Service 2nd Lieutenant in the Royal Engineers during the Mau Mau affair. He had wanted to sign on as a regular, but in the stiff competition of those days his poor degree had let him down. Still, he had stayed close to the military with his weapons business. Not the British military, of course; mainly with third world armies and their rebel counterparts. Supplying both sides at once had always seemed the fairest way, but one had to be fast off the mark in case one or both combatants learned about his even-handedness and tried to do something about it.

He shrugged off the nostalgic moment and turned to unpack his suitcases. He emptied them quickly, transferring the contents to drawers and wardrobes, then rinsed the dust from his hands and face and made his way to the staircase. At the bottom he heard movement coming from a room off to one side and made for it.

"Ah Dickie," Zawutu gushed as Granby entered the study.

"You haven't altered much since the Raj was here," Granby commented, as he took in the pictures and furnishings. He noted the picture behind the ornate desk which had been turned to face the wall and nodded at it. "Cleaners?" he suggested.

Zawutu smiled. "Probably," he said, turning it the right way round. Granby saw it was the Queen. Had it been done accidentally, or did Zawutu have other motives for hiding HM's face, he wondered?

He glanced quizzically at his old college chum and was about to make a frivolous remark about it when Zawutu interrupted.

"What about a sandwich or something. Something substantial perhaps?"

Granby got the message. "Nothing for me, thank you," he said cooperatively, but he saw the opportunity to relieve his pent-up feelings regarding Major Moi.

"That fellow Moi is a bloody menace, you know, Freddie. He may be your Interior Minister but his general behaviour leaves much to be desired. He actually threatened me with violence and at one time he was about to hand me over to the Nigerian police." A nice twist that, Granby thought.

Zawutu frowned. "I am sorry, Dickie," he said contritely. "Minister Moi had a very difficult meeting with people from the British government, the Foreign Secretary as a matter of fact, which did nothing to calm his nerves. Josi, that's Moi's tribal name by the way, came away feeling a little bruised and unfortunately you caught the hot edge of his temper. As I say, I'm sorry."

Granby shrugged. "Well, I hope he'll be better mannered in future."

But from within came that undeniable desire for revenge which shocked him. He bore grudges, yes, but this was more than that, and it frightened him.

"Of course he will," Zawutu said determinedly. That Moi didn't like Dickie was plain, but Josi knew the score. Dickie was to be kept sweet and ready to play ball, and if Josi thought he could have his own way over Granby then he had another think coming. A frightener was obviously called for. Tomorrow, perhaps.

"Now, I've arranged a trip into the heartland for you. A spot of acclimatisation before we get down to the serious stuff. There's an interesting range of wildlife out there including lion, zebra and giraffe, as well as plenty of other minor species. As a matter of fact, one of the initiatives I have in mind is to develop a small National Park along the lines of the Serengeti – Zawanda's contribution to preserving the species. Not that we have much poaching here, you understand, but a protected area will attract tourists, and their money." He laughed. "Perhaps you'll give me the benefit of your wisdom when you return?"

"Of course," Granby said, mystified by all this. He had expected to be in and out with a shopping list within a few days and wondered why the diversion. But looking gift horses in the mouth had never been a practice of his, and he had nothing urgent on in the UK anyway.

"I'd love to" he said honestly. "When does this delightful excursion begin?"

"You start out early tomorrow morning if that's OK. Now, what about a drink?"

"Tomorrow's fine with me and I'll have a whisky if you please, old chap." His throat felt parched despite the humidity, or because of it, and a good swig was exactly what the doctor ordered. "You'll need some first-class hotels if you're going to bring in the tourists," he said, reverting to that part of Freddie's conversation relating to a National Park. "Something out in the bush like Tree Tops, a true jungle-type ambience."

Zawutu handed him the drink. "Quite," he said. "I have it all planned in my mind." And you, Dickie, are going to make it possible, he thought to himself. This safari had been a last-minute idea devised to reap a double benefit; pleasure for his guest, and more vitally, breathing space for himself, time to reflect upon the outrageously dangerous money-making scheme which he could hardly believe he was still countenancing.

Granby took a big slug of whisky and coughed heavily. "Sorry, old chap. This is a good malt, too good to slurp down like that."

"Another?" Zawutu enquired, taking Granby's glass.

Granby hadn't seen his old college chum since they had met by arrangement in Camberley on just one occasion during Zawutu's final year at Sandhurst. In those days, Freddie had been intensely serious about his military training and had confessed to wanting to graduate high up the list. Then as if to prove he wasn't altogether a totally dedicated, ambitious cadet, he had taken Granby on a tour of the local public houses, where they drank copiously, chatted up the girls and generally had a wild time. Recalling it now, Granby smiled and gazed again at his friend with affection, for friend is how he chose to describe it, even after so long.

Zawutu certainly had more about him than he remembered. For one thing his English was now almost perfect. Not as heavily accented as he remembered, but not as plummy either as the two Indian tea planters he had once negotiated with who outclassed even the most affected Englishman. And he seemed to know what he was about, too. There had been no hesitation so far in anything he'd said or done. Indeed, now he came to think of it, the safari suggestion had been smoothly peremptory.

He watched Zawutu turn from the cabinet and took the proffered glass.

"Thanks, he said. "When do we get down to business?"

"Soon, Dickie. Soon."

★ ★ ★

The euphemistically entitled 'Special Warfare Course' was due to end at midday. The Hereford directing staff couldn't wait. This third and last of three very secret training courses had been the most difficult. Attended by only a few hand-picked officers selected to match a man specification that read like a profile of Genghis Khan and the Saint rolled into in one, the SAS directing staff had expected a bumpy ride. But this last group had been totally stratospheric.

"Thank God it has only one more hour to run," the Chief Instructor whispered to his deputy, who sat alongside him at the long table on the stage at one end of the hall.

"Amen to that," the Major replied.

The instructor in charge of this final session was speaking into the microphone attached to the front of his lectern. The cloth model which occupied most of the floor space in front of him indicated the damage the exercise had inflicted upon an imaginary Middle East enemy and he was now about to wind up.

"And having achieved the objective at a cost of four of your team, how would you set about the debriefing? Hawthorn?"

"Give those that are left a pat on the back and pay for their drinks," Major Alistair Hawthorn replied seriously.

"See what I mean?" the Chief Instructor whispered with a weary smile. "He actually means it." Then he perked up. "Still, I think we've done an excellent job with this lot, rough though it's been. There's not a conventional thinker left among them, at least I sincerely hope not," he ended with pride.

His deputy whispered back, "I understand from the grapevine that there's a special job already lined up for Hawthorn, somewhere in Africa."

"The further from here the better," the CI confided as he rose to deliver the valedictory address.

"Rather extreme coming from a man whose own background contains some very dark and dubious episodes," the 2ic remarked quietly.

The CI didn't hear.

★ ★ ★

On the morning of his safari, Granby took an early breakfast and bounded down the steps to where a Land Rover waited, heavily laden with jerry cans and canvas. Zawutu couldn't be there himself, so he was met by Moi.

"Good morning, Dickie," Moi said with deliberate presumption. "This is your guide," and he indicated an ebony-skinned, middle-aged man, thin as a stick and bandy legged, who was busy tightening cords around the external load. He wore a bush shirt and ragged shorts, and moved about confidently on gnarled bare feet.

Granby sighed with relief. He had thought for a moment that Moi might be accompanying them.

Moi went on, "Call him Sam." Granby bade the guide good morning and received a nod in return. "In you get then," Moi said as he opened the vehicle door. "And be careful out there. The bush is very dangerous." He smiled crookedly. "Watch out for the lions, they like white flesh."

Granby ignored him, he had been in jungle before, but in those days he had been a stone or more lighter and much, much fitter. He caught a glimpse of himself in the rear view mirror as he climbed aboard, at the thinning fair hair, the faint grey streak, at the creases round the eyes and signs of sagging flesh around the jaw line, and sighed; anno domini has a lot to answer for, he thought miserably as he settled himself into the seat and adjusted his safety belt. But the self-critical phase soon passed and he felt his mood lighten. He was, he told himself, rather looking forward to sleeping under canvas again and roughing it with the native driver and Sam.

Sam jumped into the rear, where the seats had been stripped out to accommodate tentage and a miscellany of other kit, and settled himself on a bedding roll. "OK," he said and the driver suddenly let out the clutch, spinning the rear wheels and throwing Granby back into his seat. Sam had been expecting it and swung by his wrist from the leather strap attached for that very purpose to part of the skeleton framework.

Moi watched them disappear in a cloud of dust and laughed. Granby was in for a rough time. The bush was no place for a spineless honky like Granby. "He'll soon be back with his tail between his legs," he told himself.

He watched a moment longer then turned, and with his crooked smile still in place ascended the broad flight of stone steps and strode in through the Palace entrance. At the President's door, outside which an armed officer of the Palace guard now sat, Moi paused and knocked.

"Come," Zawutu called.

Moi sauntered in. "They're gone," he said. Zawutu raised his eyebrows. "But Granby'll soon be back"

"Maybe, maybe not," Zawutu replied with a knowing smile, "But sit down. I have something to say to you."

Moi sat. "I hear you," he said in the Eshanti style.

Zawutu stood, walked round the desk and took the chair alongside his Minister. "I'm moving you from the Interior Ministry and appointing Balindi to the post." he said baldly.

"But he's an Ushkuu!" Moi was shocked into shouting the words out.

"Yes, he is," Zawutu said calmly. "Which is exactly why. With the Ushkuu plotting, and I know they are, Balindi is the best man. He is more acceptable and should be able to handle his own people without creating any more unrest." He was accusing Moi of nothing, but the inference was there.

Moi remained silent. He had never understood Mutti's obsession with fair play for the Ushkuu, and still smarted over the girl.

"Well?" Zawutu asked, breaking into Moi's bitter reflections.

"I… I don't know, Mutti," Moi said. "I have kept the tribes busy, as you asked."

"I know, Josi. Too busy perhaps, but times have changed. We have important things to do for Zawanda, you and I, and I want to free you up for that. I want you as my Minister without portfolio." He stood and began pacing.

Moi sat up, uncomfortable now. Without portfolio? What did that mean? To be without something sounded bad. He crossed his legs, then uncrossed them in a nervous reflex, his brain working overtime. Mutti's moods were unpredictable these days, and this sudden change of job to one without something called a 'portfolio' disconcerted him.

He had observed a marked change in Mutti recently, a sort of hardening. He spoke more and more in the harsh, biting way of the Tribes and seemed to dwell within himself, all of which was very unsettling. Neither one thing nor the other. He waited.

"Here's what we do," Zawutu said, coming to a halt at the ornamental fireplace and turning to face Moi. A small overhead light cluster threw faint shadows over Zawutu's face, making it difficult for Moi to read his expression. He squinted, the better to observe the facial changes. Important. Vitally so, with Mutti's strange new mood swings.

The anxiety he was feeling brought to mind an old Eshanti proverb: "The tongue and eyes of a man are like the two ends of the T'rmor bird; one draws you in with a sweet song, then the other shits on you. It is wise to watch both ends at the same time.' He strove to catch a sight of Mutti's face.

"We buy ourselves a bomb." Zawutu announced. Then with more vigour, "A bomb, Josi."

Moi stared at him as if he were mad, then after recovering his voice he spluttered: "But we have plenty of bombs, Mutti. Not big bombs, but big enough. Why should we need more? I don't remember you saying we needed bombs from Granby?"

Zawutu laughed grimly. "I didn't. This is a new requirement, Josi. This would not be any ordinary bomb. This would be a very big bomb. An atomic bomb."

"What?" Moi gasped. "What are you saying? Where would we buy such a bomb, and what for?" He stood up, unable to remain still at these startling revelations. "An atomic bomb? But they're extremely dangerous things."

"Exactly," Zawutu said, walking swiftly over to Moi and gathering him up so to speak and striding away with him.

"Oh yes," he said as they paced together. "Of course they're dangerous. Incredibly dangerous. Certainly dangerous enough to make other countries sit up and take notice, particularly the big ones who want to keep nuclear weapons for themselves. Britain for instance." He halted in his stride and faced Moi, his face alight with passion. "Beauchamp may think he has marginalised Zawanda, but I intend to dissuade him from that view."

There was a pause while Moi digested another new word – 'marginalise'. Then his face cracked into its twisted grin. "Yes, of course. With such a bomb we would be very powerful." Then he frowned. "But how will that get us money?" The subtlety of the scheme was beyond his reach.

Zawutu thumped him on the back. "Think, Josi, think. The rest of the world will pay us not to use it."

Moi's frowned. "Ahh!" he said, still struggling to see the fuller implication. In his philosophy weapons achieved their purpose by being used. To succeed by not using them was an entirely new concept, and hard to grasp.

"How much will they pay?" he asked at last, clearing his mind of the turmoil of confusion.

Zawutu waved the question aside. "Leave that to me. The first thing is to locate our bomb and arrange its purchase, which is why Granby is here. Now, it's very late

★ ★ ★

Zawutu found peace in Uudi's embrace, a haven away from all the anger and frustration he had been experiencing lately. Such heavenly release with such a willing partner. In their mutual passion neither quite understood what was happening to them.

★ ★ ★

It had been a dusty, bumpy, uncomfortable journey so far through plain, bush and forest, and neither the driver nor Sam had broken silence since lunch, if you could call a gritty sandwich and a mug of tea from a leaky flask lunch. Clinging for life to a flying Land Rover which thunderously ignores protruding rocks and earthy humps as it careers along at constant speed is not the best environment in which to hold a conversation anyway.

Granby sighed with relief when Sam called a halt just before dusk. The area was lush with tall grasses, a stand of gum trees lined the bank of a slow-moving river and a smattering of verdant, spiky bushes dotted the landscape. Granby dismounted, took one look at the invitingly cool clear water and made for it. He removed his clothes and threw himself in. If there were crocodiles he hadn't seen any, and Sam didn't seem concerned.

He waded into deeper water and swam strongly against the current until a mistimed breath made him choke, then, coughing heartily, he clambered ashore and gathered up his dusty clothing. One tent had been erected, and a glance revealed his carpet bag standing by the door flap.

"That mine?" he enquired superfluously. Sam nodded. "What about yours?" asked Granby. Sam pointed at two blankets spread under a tree.

A fire was on the go and the savoury smell of meat cooking wafted across on the gentle breeze. Granby's nostrils twitched and his salivary glands burst into copious production. God, but he was hungry.

"How long?" he asked, miming the act of putting food into his mouth.

"Soon," Sam told him.

"OK," replied Granby as he walked over to his tent and carried his bag inside. He emerged fifteen minutes later wearing a clean safari jacket and a pair of slacks and joined the other two round the crackling fire.

"No more store meat," Sam announced, handing a sizzling chicken thigh to Granby. His own, gnawed to the bone, he cast far into the darkness for the scavengers who would visit during the night. "We kill our own from now," he ended. Granby nodded, his mouth too full of succulent chicken to speak. He had no experience of hunting large animals. He had shot game birds, of course, and being an arms dealer had an easy familiarity with all manner of small arms, but nothing more than that.

He swallowed. "I wouldn't mind a bit of stalking and the feel of a high-powered rifle in my shoulder," he said eagerly. "Telescopic sights?" he asked, miming taking aim. He threw his bone away as Sam had done, and took another from the metal grille over the fire.

Sam repeated Granby's movement, bending his head and closing one eye to squint along an imaginary sight. He looked at the driver, Onjojo, and the two broke into the giggles.

"No, seriously, what calibre are we talking about?" Granby asked, a little uncertain now.

Sam rose, still chuckling, and walked over to the Land Rover from where, after some shuffling of cargo, he returned carrying a small bow and a handful of steel tipped arrows. "This is my gun," he said, stringing on an arrow and flexing the bow. "No sights at all." He kicked Onjojo gently in the ribs and the two broke down again.

Relaxing the bowstring tension, Sam laid both the weapon and its missile on the ground beside him, and then sat down again cross legged, enjoying the game.

"You can kill a large animal with that?" Granby asked, fascinated.

Sam nodded happily, sharing the moment with Onjojo. "No bang. No frighten herd." he said instructively. "Tomorrow I show."

Granby marvelled and helped himself to another mug of steaming hot coffee from the large brass jug suspended over the edge of the fire. Around them an extraordinary cacophony of nocturnal sounds filled the night. Toads croaked, insects chirruped and clicked, and occasionally the deep-throated grunt of a larger animal reached them. He felt no fear, which would disappoint Moi. In fact he had not felt as comfortable and at one with his surroundings since - well, since Kenya. The sky tonight was like black velvet studded with diamonds, the air moved gently against his cheek and the sound of the river burbling disinterestedly along its winding course to the distant sea came to him as music. Granby was intoxicated by it all.

"Beautiful," he said, taking a deep breath as if to bottle the ambience for keeps. He yawned. "I'm for bed. It's been a long day." Sam stood again and walked over to the Land Rover. He replaced the bow and lethal missiles inside their wrappings and dug out a Tilley lamp. "You know about these?" he enquired.

Granby said he did. He took the lamp and a box of matches and called goodnight to Onjojo. He thanked Sam for the meal, slipped into his tent and zipped up the fly. In the dark, lying on top of his sleeping bag, he chuckled once more to himself about his telescopic sight faux pas and drifted gently into an untroubled sleep.

★ ★ ★

During the next three days, over terrain the like of which he had never before experienced, he saw lion, cheetah, elephant and all types of what he called antelopes, which Sam called by their Eshanti names. The scavengers were there too – vultures, hyenas, wild dogs – and he had taken a shot at a wildebeest with Sam's bow from fifteen paces and missed by a mile. Sam and Onjojo had clung to one another in merriment, Sam spluttering something in Eshanti which reduced both of them to even more uncontrollable laughter.

Granby laughed with them. "What did you say?" he asked, wiping the tears from his cheeks with the back of his hand.

"You couldn't hit a bull elephant at five paces," Sam said, which produced another paroxysm of laughter.

"You're right. And I wouldn't want to either. They're too big to mess with," Granby managed in bursts.

The safari continued on through the next day and the one

after that and Granby slowly became more proficient with the Eshanti bow. But that was not all. As he trekked, hunted and endured with Sam and Onjojo, he could not help but learn from them about the forest and the animals that inhabited it. He came to recognise those which preferred to do their hunting on the plains and those that preyed among the trees. But most of all he learned about the fragile relationship between man and beast, the spirit of which had been passed on from man to boy over the centuries in this part of the world.

These three fellow travellers, from such diverse social and geographical backgrounds, had discovered a natural confluence of spirit as they worked together with only themselves and the animals for company. So close had they become that when Sam said it was time to set off for home Granby felt sick at the thought of trading all this natural wonder for so-called civilisation.

Their route had been a circular one and New London was not so very far away. They made it back to the Palace by five o'clock on the evening of the fourth day, Granby disconsolate at the ending of what, for him, had been an idyllic period.

Sam too looked downhearted and Onjojo hid his sadness by mumbling complainingly about having to clean the Land Rover. The parting was going to be painful.

It hit Granby harder than he had anticipated. He clambered from the vehicle and looked around as a feeling of *déjà vu* overwhelmed him; it was like going back to boarding school after a super holiday. He occupied himself patting clouds of dust from his khaki shorts and running his fingers through his hair in an attempt to shed what trail sand he could. Sam came up and the two stood, uncertain, then Granby took Sam's gnarled hand in his and squeezed.

"Thank you, Sam," he said with genuine affection. "I have enjoyed myself more on this trip than I have for a very long time."

"Maybe again?" Sam said in reply.

Granby smiled. "Maybe. Goodbye Onjojo," he said as the driver walked round from the driver's side. "And thank you for getting us round safely."

"Much laughter," Onjojo said, his chubby face breaking into a glistening smile.

Then the connection was broken as Moi came ponderously down the steps calling out sarcastically: "Not eaten by a lion, then?" He looked Granby up and down as if searching for bite marks, seriously disappointed that this arrogant Englishman had lasted the course.

Sam interjected with a stream of Eshanti and Moi waved the bush guide away with an imperious flick of a hand before turning back to Granby, a twist of scorn around his lips. "Great white hunter, then, showing off with the Eshanti bow."

"I'm better with the bow than you are with your mouth," Granby riposted angrily and stormed up the stone staircase, waving a final farewell to his newfound friends as he went.

Half way up he heard Moi laying into the two tribesmen and paused. Should he go back and sort the bastard out once and for all? But that would probably only make things worse for Sam and Onjojo, he reasoned, and continued on his way.

He ran into Zawutu in the hall and paused as they came together.

"How did it go?" Zawutu enquired.

"Wonderful, Freddie, truly wonderful," he said exuberantly. "Thank you for everything. I could have stayed out there forever. Look, I want to leave something for Sam and Onjojo before I go. Will you see that they get it?"

Zawutu laughed. "Of course. But don't go round saying how much you enjoyed yourself out there. A white man back from the outland claiming he actually liked it might be an embarrassment. My people don't linger in the bush for fun, I

123

can assure you of that. In fact Josi has a bet with me that you'd be back before this. I'm glad he's lost, not for the money, but because I believed in you. He doesn't know you like I do. Why don't you get cleaned up and join me on the study balcony? Time for a drink, I think."

"Just what the doctor ordered," Granby said and hurried away to his bath.

★ ★ ★

It was almost seven by the time he joined Freddie, drink in hand, served by Mumbi as he had passed through the study. He nodded at Zawutu and stood looking out over the scene available from Zawutu's balcony, reflecting on the magic of a camp fire and the companionship of good native men.

He turned to Zawutu.

"Beautiful," he said. "You are a lucky man ruling this land and these people. Of course, I exclude Major Moi from that last remark. He must be one of the most unpleasant men I have ever met."

He looked across at Zawutu, immediately ashamed of the outspoken criticism. "Look, I'm sorry, I shouldn't talk about your friend that way. It's just that he gets up my nose something awful."

"I have noticed," Zawutu said with a wry grin. "Another drink?"

★ ★ ★

He was putting it off. Faced with the moment the whole plan seemed so bloody puerile, so unlikely. Dickie would laugh the idea out of court, and so he should, he told himself. To give himself more time he got the drinks himself. As he poured, observed critically by Mumbi, he thought of Zawanda and gritted his teeth. Whether Dickie laughed or not, it had to be done.

He grasped the two refills as if they were hand grenades with the pins removed and returned to the balcony. Once there, he stood facing his old college friend. "Richard," he began determinedly. "I invited you here to discuss the purchase of weapons, so we might as well get down to it."

Granby smiled and wondered why Freddie seemed so intense. "Of course, old boy. Just let me have your list."

Zawutu hesitated nervously, wondering how to broach such a crazy scheme without appearing utterly insane. He took a deep breath and then came straight out with it: "Well, there has been a change of priorities. The most important purchase is to be a bomb." He was trying to sound casual, and failing.

"'One bomb? I don't understand. Not my line of business anyway."

"One will be sufficient, Richard, and I want you to make it your business. Look, I don't know how to say this except just to say it. I want you to source and purchase me a nuclear bomb."

He swallowed his whisky in one gulp, then went on hurriedly: "I realise how bizarre that must sound, but I'm deadly serious. What do you think?"

Granby choked on his drink and took a handkerchief to mop up the spill. Finally he looked up and in a voice that sounded as if he were gargling, expostulated: "A nuclear bomb? You must be mad! And just how do you propose to deliver this bomb if by some miracle you had one?. You have no aeroplanes."

"I was thinking more of a missile system than an aircraft type bomb," Zawutu said, pleased by Richard's question. If Dickie was interested enough to ask questions then maybe he could be tempted further.

"It's a joke, isn't it?" Granby said, uncertainly. A smile hovered about his lips, ready to respond to the truth.

Zawutu remained silent.

"And the cost! God, man, you're looking at a small fortune. Tens of millions of dollars, if not hundreds of millions. Now where will you find that kind of cash? You can't do an offset trade deal over a commodity like that, you know. It would have to be hard cash. But what am I saying?" He pressed the cold glass to his overheated brow. "Never mind the money. The whole idea's mad and impossible from the start. I wouldn't know where to look. You just don't put an advertisement in *The Times,* 'Wanted, one atomic bomb size ten'." He frowned. "And it's illegal to trade in nuclear material without all sorts of permits and licences."

He stopped abruptly. Why wasn't he just saying no? Definitely no? Absolutely no?

"This is insane," he said desperately.

"I can guess how difficult it might be, Dickie, but I just thought you might be interested in a million pounds cash up front. A million whether you succeed or not as long as you genuinely try." He watched Dickie rejoin and the greed flare in those deep blue eyes. "A million, cash in hand, Dickie. And four more when the weapon is delivered."

CHAPTER SEVEN

Moi paced the outer office in a frenzy of frustration. What in Allah's name was going on inside? Had Mutti said anything to Granby about the bomb? The two had been closeted in the President's study for over an hour now and no sound of raised voices had emerged.

"You cannot go in," the President's aide warned as Moi made for the door. Moi cursed and let his hand fall from the handle. He had hardly stepped back when the door suddenly flew open and Granby strode out, flushed and unseeing. He shouldered Moi aside and headed for the front entrance without so much as a glance. Moi felt a surge of anger at the insult, but was held back from pursuing his arch-enemy by a burning suspicion that he had been sidelined over the bomb issue. He knocked furiously on Zawutu's door.

"Come."

"Ah, Josi," Zawutu began as soon as Moi entered, without looking up. "Dickie has gone away to think about our offer."

Moi sat down without invitation, the anger on his face as readable as an open book.

"You've spoken to Granby of it?" he burst out. "Already? Without me?"

Zawutu picked up the tension in Moi's words and raised his eyes.

"Yes," he said sharply, then softened his tone. "It's done. Your presence might have caused Granby a problem so it was better done this way." He hoped Moi would take the point, that his overt antagonism towards Granby had been the reason for his exclusion. "And now I want Granby left alone. No provoking him. Sweetness and light until he agrees. OK?"

"But you promised!"

Zawutu cut him short. "It's over I say. You will accept it."

Moi half rose, but sat back when Zawutu motioned for him to stay. "What we are doing for Zawanda is more important than your petty squabbles," he said sternly.

Moi nodded. "I would not have provoked him," he said.

"Perhaps not, but I decided not to take the risk. And anyway, what does it matter how it was done as long the result is what we want? You are a warrior, Josi, and you must obey."

"I obey, oh M'butu," he said, raising his head and using the old warrior form of address to a chieftain.

Zawutu smiled. "Steady on, Josi. Let's not go overboard." Then his voice hardened. "And while we're at it, time to leave the Ushkuu alone. Things have changed. They're reacting badly and I don't want it to get any worse. They must be persuaded that I won't tolerate inter-tribal raiding." He raised a hand in warning and Moi closed his mouth. "I appreciate the way you've diverted their minds from the worsening economic position, but a deep resentment is developing which will only lead to trouble if I don't do something about it. Minister Balindi is responsible for tribal matters now, so you keep out of it."

First the girl, then Granby and now this. Moi lowered his face and muttered something obscene.

"What did you say?" Zawutu asked sharply.

"I will do as you command, Mutti," replied Moi hastily, afraid to repeat the obscenity.

"So be it then," Zawutu said with a forgiving smile, unseen by Moi, who stared angrily at the desktop before him. A silence settled on both men, Moi raging at the accumulation of insults, Zawutu dwelling on the inexplicable but relentless natural law which said that a leader would always arise when things get tough. History was peppered with such people, he told himself; Hitler, Napoleon, Mao Tse Tung, Lenin. Would one such arise to lead the Ushkuu? He shivered at the thought.

"I hope it doesn't come to that," he muttered aloud.

"What?" Moi asked.

"Nothing. Forget it," Zawutu said. "You may leave now."

Moi closed the door without glancing back or bidding farewell, but Zawutu didn't notice. He was too busy cataloguing his own troubles. Since his accession inflation had soared uncontrollably, creating shortages everywhere, and with its rise so had come its running mate, crime.

The army was restless. Its officers, he knew, were watching silently as their President repeatedly failed to deliver on his promises of a better overall standard of living and quality of life. They would stand only so much of that, and then someone, probably an Ushkuu officer, would attempt a coup. He shivered again as his imagination ran riot. Discontented troops, short of rations, down on pay and looking shabbier by the week could easily mutiny, incited by some disgruntled Ushkuu barrack-room lawyer. And Allah forbid, the Officer Corps might even go along with it.

So much to worry about and only Richard Granby with the potential to ease the burden. He made a note to tighten up on army discipline and make good its quartermaster shortages, even at the expense of something less likely to threaten his presidency.

★ ★ ★

The air was muggy, and in the fading light of evening Granby ceased his perambulations outside the Palace gates and turned for home. He walked slowly, deep in thought, aware now of the perspiration that had formed dark areas on his shirt and trickled ceaselessly down his face and arms.

Five million smackers, by God! It was worth doing almost anything for that kind of money. But it was no use pretending he could deliver a nuclear weapon system for it. The up-front million, that was a different matter. Freddie had promised that, even if no weapon were forthcoming, as long as the effort was put in. He could see no problem there. But what on earth did Freddie want the damn thing for in the first place?

His mind reached out, extrapolating for a moment. Say by some miracle he did produce something. There was no way Richard Granby, honest arms dealer as he was, would deliver such powerful merchandise without knowing its end use. This was serious stuff and his conscience troubled him. He wandered back indoors in no hurry, his mind churning with speculation. Too soon he reached Zawutu's study, knocked, paused a moment, then entered.

Zawutu was seated at his desk. He stared questioningly at his guest. Nothing was said until the silence became too much for Granby.

"I must know what your intentions are with regard to the order you want to place," he said finally, speaking in veiled speech as befitted, in his view, the nature of the product under negotiation.

"You will accept the commission, then?" Zawutu replied, leaning forward eagerly and resting both arms on the desk.

Granby shook his head violently enough to cause his hair, now grown longer than he liked, to break loose and fall over his face. He threw back his head to clear his vision. "I'm thinking about it," he said, brushing back the hair with a nervous movement of his right hand. "But I won't even try unless I know more about what you want it for."

Zawutu pursed his lips. "What can I say? There must be some secrets, even between friends. My purpose is political, not military. I have no intention of firing the thing. For one thing Zawanda has no enemies worth wasting that kind of money on, and for another, once it's launched it's gone forever, so what would be the point? No, rest assured Dickie, it will not even be unpacked."

He tried to read Granby's expression and saw only dissatisfaction.

"If it helps, I promise you on the grave of my father, not military. Not a weapon to be used, just a chess piece."

Granby considered the reply. For the life of him he could envisage no purely political scenario that would require a bloody great bomb. Freddie must be balmy, gone over the top; and that raised the spectre of delivering the kiloton power of a modern battlefield nuclear device into the hands of an unstable African. Hardly a responsible act.

He eyed Zawutu carefully. It had been a long time since Cambridge, and Freddie had certainly changed over the years. But was he mad? Granby shook his head. His friend was as sane as he was which wasn't saying much considering the conversation.

"I can understand how you might want to keep the purpose secret, national interest and all that, but look at it from my point of view" he said. "The merchandise can hardly remain secret once I begin putting the word about. There are people who won't like the idea, and I'm too young to spend the rest of my life in jail."

Zawutu guffawed loudly. "Perish the thought. And anyway, as an arms dealer you must have sailed mighty close to the wind now and then. A doubtful certificate overlooked for cash, a bit of smuggling maybe?"

Granby laughed ironically. "Maybe, but this is a different kettle of fish entirely."

"I realise that, and I'm sorry I can't say more to ease your mind. There's a lot of trust required both ways here, which I know you understand as well as I do. I promise you, Dickie, no harm will come to you, nor to anyone else, as a result of my ownership. I can't speak for the risks you might have to run buying the thing, but once it's here you can rest assured your part in it is finished. As I say, you are being paid extraordinarily well for risks which in the event might never arise."

"I'll think more on it," Granby promised, not entirely satisfied. "See you at dinner."

Back in his room, he went out onto the balcony to gaze out at the night sky and listen to the night chorus which he had learned to love. Slowly stripping off his sweaty kit, he reflected upon the conversation he'd just had with the president of a free state. Bizarre beyond belief. He shook his head disbelievingly and questioned why he had listened to any of it, let alone discussed and half accepted Freddie's startling one-item shopping list. It was sheer madness. A thousand rifles, a few hundred boxes of grenades – they would be simple. But a nuclear missile system? He wouldn't even know where to start looking. Still a million smackers and no strings, he could surely go through the motions for that kind of money. Even exert himself a little

Suddenly excited at the prospect, he climbed into the shower and turned on the water.

★ ★ ★

In the hour following Granby's visit, President Zawutu received his Ministers in turn to listen to their bleak weekly reports. He had abandoned the Cabinet system as soon as meetings had begun to deteriorate into free-for-alls. The worsening news they disseminated today saddened him still further. All were in despair and about ready to chuck in the towel. He commiserated with each in turn and provided what little comfort he could, but although he desperately wanted to lighten their individual loads it was too soon yet to let them in on his grand plan.

After the last official had left, he ordered himself a black coffee and ran over again in his mind the sequence of events that would, he had no doubt, be the salvation of Zawanda. The incredible simplicity of the plan delighted him now that he had got the worst part of it over, convincing Granby, or nearly so anyway. He smiled broadly when he considered Richard's role in all of this. So ironic. Poor Dickie, struggling with the moral and personal dilemmas of a situation that would in the resolution contain neither.

Of course Dickie could not source a nuclear missile system, they both knew that. But he could certainly make it appear to the outside world that he was trying. For a cool million up front his friend would deliver that much heat at least, make a few waves, rattle a few cages in the underworld of arms procurement and finally admit failure. With a cool million stashed securely in a Swiss bank account he could walk away rich and conscience free; no harm done. The secret was in the trying, and try he must – and keep at it until he was told to stop. The longer he thrashed about, Zawutu told himself happily, the more waves he would make and the more likely it was that Britain and others would take alarm and realise that Frederick Zawutu, President of Zawanda, had them by the balls. When the shit eventually hit the fan, the outfall would splash far and wide.

"Magnificent!" he said to the picture of HMS *Andromeda* opposite. Which country, he wondered, would be first to offer to buy him off? Cash, credits, assistance, aid, however they chose to cloak it, would pour in from anxious neighbours, the big boys and the non-proliferation Johnnies. What a pity Granby couldn't be told. He'd appreciate the elegance of it. No missile, just the threat of one. What a laugh!

He glanced at the clock on his desk and tidied the top preparatory to taking his shower before dinner. A faint tension in his loins reminded him of Uudi. And why not? Feeling pleased with himself, and more confident than he had for a while, he decided to bring her out of the closet that very night, sit her at table to dine and reveal, to tonight's guests at least, his interest in her. She had become more than a mere plaything. She was bright and profoundly interested in his loose-tongued, post-coital chatter, contributing wisdoms of her own which sometimes amazed him. He had grown extremely fond of her.

There was plenty of time before dinner to take her into the shower and hoist her onto his erection in the way she so enjoyed. Under the beating needles of the shower water her orgasms were more intense somehow, as if memories of her first experience drew her up and up into climaxes that left Zawutu's shoulders bruised and sore from clutching fingers and sharp nails.

As he walked from the study he had a gentle smile on his face. A nascent erection strained at his shorts and he increased his pace. Along the corridor he paused and spoke through de Lancy's open office door.

"Fetch Uudi," he told him. "Tell Major Moi and Mr Granby to dress formally for dinner, then invite Minister Balindi and Minister Agobo and their wives. Get the staff to lay the table for eight."

★ ★ ★

Glowing happily from her pre-dinner lovemaking, Uudi, now in her own quarters, sorted through a wardrobe bursting with clothes gifted for every occasion. Soon, a stack of discarded dresses lay on the bed. Freddie had suggested something light and fashionable, and now she felt sure she had found it. She held the flimsy confection against her naked form and twirled round in front of the full length mirror.

She herself remained sublimely unaware of her radiance, of her exquisitely-formed features, even by European standards, and of her young, sensual body; enough to turn any young man's head. She knew Mutti liked her and she had endured passing remarks and whistles from some of the more intrepid men on the Palace staff, but never had she imagined herself to be anything out of the ordinary. She was wrong in this.

She had not worn this dress before, there having been no occasion for it, but that didn't matter to her. She wore her wardrobe for Freddie alone, until tonight, that is. And as she dressed she trembled with excitement like a child before the Christmas tree. Tonight she would sit at table, not only with Freddie, but with his friends and guests; acknowledged.

★ ★ ★

Granby was disappointed. he had hoped to dine privately with Freddie so as to advance his interrogation over the need for the bomb. Now it would have to wait. De Lancy had told him that the President was to have his mistress to dinner; de Lancy had actually said 'girlfriend' and disappointing though the dining arrangements were, a young native girl at table might be some consolation. Her presence in the Palace was well known, but Granby had never seen her. It might, he thought, be quite entertaining to witness this child striving to hold her end up among mature adults.

He smiled to himself lasciviously. She was probably very good in bed or Freddie wouldn't keep her. But at the dinner table?

Moi just swore. An ignorant Ushkuu maiden at the same

table as the President and his guests was sheer folly. Mutti would regret this.

As planned, Uudi did not appear for pre-dinner drinks. The two ministers, and particularly their ladies, kept a watch for her, intrigued by the sudden dinner invitation and word that Uudi was to join them. Then just as dinner was announced, Zawutu excused himself from his guests and slipped away to return a few minutes later with a raving beauty on his arm. She walked in with head held high, proud and regal in her carriage. Nothing had been stinted. Her make-up was softly and professionally applied, her hair plaited and bound in Ushkuu native style but somehow more gentle. Her evening gown clung to stunningly feminine curves.

Granby drew in his breath. He had had no idea. For a girl so young she gave the appearance of being surprisingly sophisticated, and by God, she was beautiful! To call this vision a mere mistress was as incongruous as naming Zawanda a superpower.

Dinner proceeded without a hitch. It had been laid in a side room rather than in the large banqueting hall, but still the environment was elegant, if faded a little, with chipped gold-painted cornices, slightly worn statues standing in arched recesses let into the long walls and a few paintings mixed with good-quality prints filling the gaps. The ceiling had a scene of some kind laid into it which was unrecognisable apart from a couple of nymphs - or angels perhaps - in two of the corners?

The servants were doing a passable job of clearing and serving under the keen eye of an elderly Itulu retainer who had worked there as a boy before the British left. And Muslim or not, there was wine on the table for those who wanted it.

Zawutu had come to the table confident in Uudi, but even he was amazed and proud at her smooth, eloquent performance. She charmed the ladies and had every man but Moi eating out of her hand with a naturalness that made Granby wonder. As he observed her skilful handling of Freddie's guests he told himself that this was no ordinary village girl, and speculated on where Freddie might have discovered her.

Only Moi sulked and refused to be charmed. He could not bring himself to acknowledge an Ushkuu village girl, no matter how good looking, except in the time honoured way of achieving an erection fit to demonstrate Eshanti superiority. He wriggled and handled his groin in an attempt to reduce the discomfort she was causing him. His rejection of her as an equal deepened, while his appreciation of her carnal qualities improved in proportion. His mind raced with thoughts of fucking the girl, but that could never be. It would cost him his head, and no conquest on earth was worth that. He sat and suffered, blaming Mutti for his frustration.

★ ★ ★

Later, in bed, Zawutu complimented Uudi on the evening. "You made it one to remember," he told her truthfully. "From here on you will be my official hostess, not just at dinner parties but in the general hospitality required of a ruler."

She smiled her thanks, and as if to demonstrate her appreciation, slid her hand under the sheet, walked her fingers over his thigh and wrapped them gently round his ready penis. She was beginning to love this man.

★ ★ ★

Granby left for the UK two days later, mildly frustrated at not having furthered his knowledge of Freddie's true purpose, yet subtly persuaded that he might succeed in satisfying the requirement without risk or danger to himself. He left with two indelible memories; his safari with Sam and Onjojo, and that incredible dinner with the remarkable young Ushkuu child, Uudi. Even the tricky task he was about to venture upon could not entirely erase the afterglow of those two intense pleasures.

Arriving at his home in Battersea, a two-bedroom flat of modest size, he swore softly as the front door jammed against an accumulation of mail. He forced it open, placed his cases inside and stooped to gather the mess of battered, torn envelopes and packages, mostly junk. Letters of importance like arms enquiries were notably few these days.

He sighed, walked across to the drinks cabinet and poured himself a stiff Scotch. This was home. A bleak, modern box of a place without a spark of character or warmth, far removed from the seductive atmosphere of that decaying Victorian monstrosity in Zawanda. He smiled as he recalled his verbal tussles with Mumbi, his attempts to understand the Eshanti's broken English and trying to speak so that Mumbi would understand. Somehow, between them, they had managed.

He drank down the whisky in one, poured himself another and punched the playback button on his answering machine. The messages were mostly from his ex-wife, bitching about arrears of maintenance and threatening court action if he didn't pay up, and the rest wasn't worth listening to either. His glass was empty again, and it seemed sensible to postpone sitting down until he had refreshed it. That done, he seated himself on the sagging settee which, along with the rest of the room, did not seem so bad now he'd had a couple of drinks.

The night flight out of Lagos had been noisy because of a travelling football team, Manchester something or other, he seemed to remember, celebrating a victory. No one had slept very much and they'd drunk a lot, so now he felt like death. He should take a shower and get on with whatever it was he had come home to do, but suddenly it didn't seem so important. He leaned back, closed his eyes and slept, the half-empty glass slipping from his fingers and rolling away on the carpet.

It was mid-afternoon when he groaned and opened his eyes. His mouth felt as if a Black and Decker sander had been at work in there and he felt the simmering throb of an incipient headache.

"Christ!" he mumbled as he struggled to his feet and headed for the nearest means to assuage a dry throat and gluey mouth, the drinks cabinet. Halfway there, he sensibly veered off towards the bathroom. A gallon of water sucked straight from the tap, followed by a hot shower, soon had him feeling at least half civilised. He towelled briskly, then threw on a clean shirt, socks and underwear, slacks and a sweater. What he had to do this afternoon could be done from home.

His business address book on his lap, he began phoning round acquaintances and business colleagues. Most were unavailable and he left messages on their answering machines asking them to ring back. Those that were in their offices began by passing the time of day, but soon turned quiet when Granby spoke the arms dealers' euphemism for guided missiles.

"You don't happen to know where a chap might get hold of a Smart Ballistic, do you?"

The question invariably brought silence, then the reply: "What sort of price range?"

"Probably a hundred million dollars," Granby replied to each.

More silence, prolonged this time. Then: "A hundred mill for one? That is big."

"As big as they get."

"Sorry, old fellow, but no can do. I'll put out the word for you, though."

"Discreetly. Very discreetly, if you don't mind."

"It goes without saying."

Only Harry said more: "I know they're about, but it's too big and dangerous for the likes of you and me, old boy. Maybe I can point you towards a possible intermediary, but I suggest you introduce him to your customer and get out fast."

"I'd be most grateful, Harry. Most grateful."

"Well, I'll see what I can do." And with that, the only helpful, and scary, reply of the late afternoon, Granby hung up. He switched the phone to answering mode and retired to the bedroom, where he donned a suit, checked shirt and plain tie, swept up his credit cards and cash and slipped them into his hip pockets. With a last look round he left the flat in search of a cheap meal and a pint or two of real ale.

In the days that followed all the unavailables called him back, but none of them had anything to offer. In the end he was left with only Harry's suggestion of an introduction. Faced with that reality, his confidence was slipping badly. He wanted to ring Freddie and tell him no, but the prospect of one million pounds held him back. Bugger Harry, too, for being so bloody helpful.

Confirmation of the availability of his Swiss funds arrived by post one week after his departure from Zawanda, and he immediately transferred ten thousand pounds to his current account in Battersea. This greatly cheered up his bank manager, who called him to inform him of the safe arrival of the funds and offer any help Mr Granby might require; a stark contrast to the usual bad-tempered demands to bring his account into credit.

That very evening, flush with cash, he visited his favourite pub, the Hare and Hounds, where minor arms dealers tended to gather and boast of huge sales to this or that third world country; boasts which no one believed, of course. Granby sauntered in and at once noted that everyone was on beer. A real sale called for champers, and there was no sign of that tonight. Still, it was always a lot of fun listening to the creativity of his fellow dealers. He walked up to the bar and called loudly for a bottle of Moet, which drew an immediate crowd. A complete order could not always be supplied from one source and that meant sub-contracts for those able to make up the deficit, and many such hopefuls gathered round.

"Must have been a big one," one of them said through the noise.

Granby patted the side of his nose. "The biggest," he replied into the hubbub. "A glass for everyone, landlord, and one for yourself." This drew a resounding cheer and a lot of envy.

★ ★ ★

The dismemberment of the USSR had had its casualties. Some of the smaller states, forced into independence against their will, were not yet viable on their own. Russia and Ukraine had withdrawn their troops along with their financial assistance, reducing these peripheral states to various degrees of penury. Times were very hard indeed for some of them. However, one or two did find themselves the custodians of a surprising legacy. The strategically placed had been cold war hosts to elements of the USSR's Nuclear Strike Command and many of the missiles still reposed deep in silos way out in the countryside inside new borders. Promises had been made by Yeltsin's Russia to pull in these fringe missiles and destroy their warheads under one of the SALT treaties, but it had not been done.

"No problem," Yeltsin assured the US President. "We have withdrawn all the skilled operators, firing codes and keys. No one can fire the weapons without skilled men and knowhow."

Firm assurances of future dismantling followed, but the weapons remained where they were, extremely valuable assets, potential market makers within a growing demand segment, overlooked and almost forgotten amid the turbulence of Yeltsin's domestic troubles.

Of course, there could be no overt theft without bringing down massive retaliation from Russia, but time flowed on and there had been no stock-take. This malevolent inventory was assumed to be perfectly secure in the light of lack of expertise within the host states, and no one seemed to be counting. But expertise can be bought in, and not all missiles were locked away in silos. Other, smaller battlefield systems, largely forgotten, lay stored behind double steel doors in hardened underground shelters, neglected and unaudited. Of medium yield, capable of ranging out several hundred miles, they were still serviceable and worth their weight in gold.

One unscrupulous President viewed the mobile launcher systems within his borders as state assets which, as the Western nations had demonstrated most successfully with many of their state possessions, could be privatised. In his case secretly, of course, and by the hand of the old Communist State security apparatus which remained intact in his country.

The first few experimental acquisitions took place in dead of night, after careful reconnaissance and surreptitious springing of locks. Over a period of one month, dark, shadowy figures wearing balaclavas, black tank suits and heavy sidearms removed five medium-range weapons systems complete with command modules and instruction manuals, and transported them via country routes to government warehouses now empty of grain. Doors were locked, guards stationed around the perimeter and ferocious dogs placed to roam an insulated space between electrically-charged wires. The shelves were stacked, so to speak, and sales could commence.

CHAPTER EIGHT

The rain had been persistent all day. Large droplets plummeted down, lashing the pavements and rebounding into the air like fractured hail. The street gutters ran swift, and in places flooded the pavement as drains struggled to cope with an unseasonal rainfall. A cold wind added to the misery.

Granby looked out of his window and thanked the Lord he had no reason to move beyond the warmth of his apartment. It was getting dark, so he closed the curtains before returning to the comfort of his chair and the large whisky he had standing on a small, round side table he had pulled up for the purpose. Then he kicked off his slippers, rested his stockinged feet on the coffee table in front of him and pressed the appropriate remote hand set button to bring up BBC1.

The six o'clock evening news had just started, and Martin Lewis was reporting the Government's latest plans to improve educational standards. Granby sighed. It was all so predictable. The present Government could leave nothing alone; it was continually stirring. He recalled the old maxim, 'If it ain't broke, don't fix it.'

Tonight's monologue of bad news made him wonder why he should stay in England at all now he was rich. With taxes rising inexorably and services declining, the gap between income and the cost of living stretched inordinately wide, making life extremely difficult when business was thin, as it had been before Freddie Zawutu had stepped in and saved his bacon.

He sighed. "If this is democracy then it sucks," he said aloud. The notion of moving to better climes was becoming more attractive by the minute, but he had things to do first.

He tilted what remained in his glass and shook the last sliver of ice into his mouth, then rose for a refill. He'd lost the thread of the news anyway and would wait for Panorama, another severe downer probably. Then as he fired the siphon into his glass, the phone rang.

"Granby."

"Ah, Richard. Harry Chalmers here."

"Harry, how are you?"

"Look, weren't you interested in an introduction to certain parties?"

Granby frowned. "Yes I was – am."

"OK. Then I suggest we meet in the saloon bar of the H and H in, say, twenty minutes."

"Are you serious, Harry? It's a god awful night."

"To be sure, but it has to be tonight. Are you on or what?"

For a moment Granby was tempted to say no, but his promise to Freddie worried at his conscience, and anyway, he needed to get a hold of himself before his present mood transmogrified into a really serious depression.

"All right. Twenty minutes, and it had better be good."

"Believe me, it will be," Chalmers said and rang off.

Tossing back his drink in one gulp and placing the empty glass on the round table, Granby went to wrap up for the walk to the pub. It promised to be cold and wet, but one of the penalties of being in the arms business was that when a deal came up you had to be there or lose it to the competition. Not in this case, perhaps, but there were equally powerful motives driving him out into this filthy night.

He climbed into a stiff, newish Barbour, slipped on a pair of short-legged wellington boots, added a scarf and a flat cap and let himself out of the flat. The wind immediately lashed him, driving bitterly-cold pellets of almost solid rain straight into his face. He hunched his shoulders against it and by the expedient of bowing his head and adjusting his cap over his forehead he managed to protect his eyes from the worst of it.

The lighted pub sign came as a welcome sight as he turned the corner into Akerman Street. He pushed through the pub door into the sudden warmth of a crowded, smoke-filled bar and barged his way across to the bar counter.

"Brandy, a double," he instructed the barmaid, then turned to the room at large.

"Anyone seen Harry Chalmers?"

A general negative muttering ensued.

"I knew it," Granby said, only mildly annoyed now that he was actually there. He loosened his scarf and unbuttoned the Barbour. "Might as well have a drink or two," he said to his neighbour, a man he knew slightly. "Means I won't have to go out into the raging bloody elements again for a while." He'd sort Harry out when next he saw him.

He joined a crowd of acquaintances further down the bar and got a round in. "Harry coming in tonight?" he asked, thinking perhaps the bugger might just be late.

"No one's seen him for a day or two," Jack Hubertson said, to the accompaniment of nods all round.

"He's having me on," Granby announced with a laugh. "Said he had a supplier lined up. Odd, though, that he hasn't turned up to spring the joke and get his free drink."

The group agreed; it was unlike Harry Chalmers to forego a freebie.

"Well, I'm not altogether surprised," Granby resumed. "If he has any sense at all he'll have realised the error of his ways and stay out of my way for a while. Dragging me out on a night like this is no joke. It might even be construed as provoking homicide." He laughed. "Maybe he's reconsidered."

Everyone in the crowd laughed along with him.

"Telephone for Dick Granby," the landlord called out above the noise.

"Here," Granby shouted.

The landlord moved along the bar until he was opposite. "It's Harry Chalmers on the phone. You can take it over there." He indicated a hooded booth attached to the wall beside the door.

"Mad fool. Never knows when to give up." Granby said over his shoulder as he left the gang for the phone booth.

"Could be he wants to apologise," someone called after him, but Granby had already passed out of sight among the steaming crowd. He reached the phone booth and lifted the handset to his ear.

"Richard Granby," he announced formally. "And don't piss me about Harry, I'm not in the mood."

"Don't use my name," Harry Chalmers came back, as if he believed the landlord had not already broadcast it. In a strained voice he went on: "I don't know why I let myself in for this. You'll owe me a packet for this one. These people are bloody dangerous, too bloody dangerous for me. I shouldn't have said I'd help, but it's too late for that now."

"For God's sake, Harry," Granby interrupted with a chuckle, convinced now that Chalmers was having him on. "Don't lay it on so thick, old chap. Get to the point."

"If anyone's thick around here it's you. Now listen, pal. The party I spoke of is interested, but he has to be careful. He's agreed to talk to you only because I told him you were acting as the agent of a third world government, and even so he insists on the strictest security. He won't give his name or be recognised. I hope this is frightening you as much as it is me, Dickie. Frankly I'm shitting my pants."

"You're pulling my leg, aren't you Harry?" Granby said sceptically. You don't expect me to fall for all this bullshit? Too much to swallow, old chap. You're not nearly a good enough actor to get away with it, but a good try all the same. Why don't you give up before you make a complete fool of yourself and come round to the Horse for a drink? On me, I promise, and no hard feelings."

"Dickie," Chalmers croaked. "I'm deadly serious. You got me into this, so the least you can do is follow it through. I wish I was kidding, really. What I'm telling you is the gospel truth. Look, if you don't believe me, listen to this. His nibs wants a meet. Do you know the old tanning factory on Chelsea Creek?"

Granby said he did, but was still suspicious.

"Well, can you be there in an hour?" Chalmers went on. "I wouldn't take a joke this far, would I?"

"Not if you've any sense you wouldn't, no," Granby conceded. "But hear this. If this does turn out to be a wind up I'll kill you. And not quickly, either."

The silence that followed spoke louder than a megaphone and an involuntary shiver ran down Granby's spine. Christ, it was for real. The realisation produced a frisson of alarm.

"Bloody hell!" he exclaimed loudly, heads turning in response. "Yes. I'll come," he said faintly down the phone.

Faced with the reality he would dearly have loved to call it off, but his own pride, his promise to Freddie, and not forgetting the five million pounds, made him stubbornly determined to see it through.

"I don't believe all this," he said desperately, still hoping that Harry would burst into laughter and call him all kinds of fool for going along with it.

"You will," Chalmers said. "Now listen. When you get to the factory, come in at the main gate, then round to the right to the old factory main entrance. From there we're to follow a white ribbon. Our Eastern European friend is probably laying out the trail as we speak. Oh, and a warning. Don't try to sneak a glimpse of the chap. Just talk. OK? He wants me there as well. I'm a sort of guarantee that you're kosher, so I hope to hell you know what you're doing. I'll meet you when you arrive, and please, no heroics. And don't be late, old chum. Remember, one hour."

"I'll be there, I promise," Granby said, stiffening his shoulders. "And look, Harry, I'm sorry if I've dropped you in it. There'll be something worthwhile out of it for you, no matter what happens."

"That's some compensation, I guess," his friend replied with a derisory snort. "But I still wish I hadn't started this. I thought it would just be a matter of a simple introduction, but I committed the cardinal sin of saying too much. The blighter knows who I am and where I live, and he sounds dangerous enough for me to worry about that."

"I understand. Look, I'll take over and talk to this fellow and you can bow out with my thanks and a handsome commission. How's that?"

"Thanks Dickie. I just want out. The contribution will be appreciated."

Granby hung up and made for the exit, his worried expression causing added concern among those near the door. "What's wrong Dickie?" someone asked, but Granby ignored it as he hastily zipped his Barbour jacket to the top, tightened the scarf around his neck, pulled his cap from a jacket pocket and jammed it onto his head. Without a word to anyone, he pushed his way out.

The wind instantly struck him again and the rain beat down heavier than before, but he noticed neither. His mind had other things to juggle with. As Harry had just implied, meeting a man powerful enough to supply a nuclear missile system was bound to be tricky to say the least. He'd never done business this way before, nor at this level, and wasn't too sure how to proceed. Shady wasn't the word to describe it. Illegal, criminally stupid and most certainly suicidally dangerous seemed most appropriate.

Assisted by a following wind, Granby ran all the way home to collect his car. The journey to Chelsea Creek on a night like this would be bad enough under normal circumstances, but Harry had insisted on punctuality, or the salesman had, and there was no time to waste. He threw open the door of his flat, swept the car keys from the sideboard and rushed out again.

Getting to his car in the rear car park took another few minutes, then he was in the driving seat and starting the engine. He released the handbrake and took off with a degree of wheel spin that made him wince.

Once on the road he turned East, windscreen wipers at their fastest setting and still not handling the downpour. The digital clock on the dash clicked up steadily towards nine o'clock and progress was painfully slow. He accelerated, but soon let the speed bleed off. In this weather he could hardly see through the windscreen at thirty miles an hour, let alone any higher speed, and the traffic lights along the route seemed to be playing a malevolent game of their own tonight, switching to red just as he approached them.

The street lamps suddenly ran out and he had only his headlights to show him the blurred tunnel of road ahead. The tyres hissed under him and the treads shed rainwater and spat it out in clouds of fine spray that engulfed the rear end of the car. Then, forced to slow even further, his temper flared and frustration and impatience pumped adrenalin into his system.

Suddenly he was there. It was two minutes before nine on the clock as he saw the site entrance. The gates were open. He drove straight through and turned to circle the building anti-clockwise in search of the old main factory entrance.

He saw Harry's car first. Harry had sensibly left the lights on for him. Granby pulled up alongside and scrambled from the driving seat in time to meet Harry hurrying across from the gaping black hole that had once housed huge corrugated iron doors, illuminated now by both sets of headlights.

"Thank God!" Chalmers said breathlessly, glancing from side to side. "This is no place to be on your own."

Granby agreed. Beyond the double headlight beams and the reflected light from an expanse of rain-drenched, rusting corrugated iron wall, the darkness had a spectral feel about it. The old, dilapidated building exuded a distinct aura of threat, intangible yet fearful. The rain beat a tattoo upon its corrugated roof, loose sheets rattled and crashed, and from the distance came the soughing of the wind through fence wires. Further on still the river made a strange complaining sound as it flowed hastily round the peninsula as if eager to be released from the place. The air reeked of sewage and dead fish, and the whole cocktail raised sinister images in Granby's mind.

Nervously he took Chalmers' proffered hand. "What manner of place is this?" he asked with an involuntary shudder. He wasn't one of those who took fright in the dark, but this place, at this time, had a rank evil about it. He shivered again.

"Let's get on with it" he said. "The sooner we're away from here the better." Out of habit, he tightened the collar of his Barbour. "What's the form?"

Chalmers glanced anxiously from side to side, then with obvious reluctance led him to the open doorway. "We should find a white ribbon tied to something here. We've got to follow that. That's all I know," he shouted above the screaming wind.

They paused just inside the building, out of the wind. Chalmers switched on a torch "You got one of these?" he enquired.

Granby shook his head.

"Here, I've a spare," Chalmers said as he handed Granby a small, narrow-beamed plastic model. Granby took it and switched it on.

The ribbon was there all right, tied to a rusty old door handle, a single white strand hanging in serried catenaries from various fastenings as it disappeared into the darkness. Inside, the building rattled and shook as the hurricane-force winds assaulted its rotting fabric. Granby swung his torch beam either side of the path and surmised that the place had been abandoned with everything still in it. Old machinery loomed tall, rusty and derelict, casting weird shapes and moving shadows in the light of the advancing torches. Granby's apprehension swelled still further.

The ribbon progressed along an alley between two rows of these towering machines and the two men followed, flicking the beams of their torches into the darker spaces on both sides, not knowing what to expect. They came to a crossroads, where a small hut-like structure stood, probably a long-deserted foreman's office. Here the ribbon terminated abruptly. Granby estimated that they were somewhere close to the geometrical centre of a large machine room.

Chalmers, who had remained silent thus far, leaned over and whispered, "He must be close."

Then out of the darkness of the hut came a sudden voice. "Velcome, gentlemen!"

Granby jumped and grabbed hold of Chalmers' arm. "Hold still, for Christ's sake," Chalmers hissed.

"I apologise for the dramatics," the voice went on. It sounded Eastern European. "But as you will understand, this is a sensitive matter we are about to discuss. Please don't move from where you are. My colleagues are watching in the shadows and any move on your part will be prevented with whatever force is necessary."

Granby's gaze swept the area, but he could see nothing.

"We have no wish to know who you are sir," he replied. "Merely to do our business and leave."

"That's good. Very good," the disembodied voice replied. "Let us begin."

Chalmers interrupted. "Look. I've done my bit. I have no business to transact, so is it all right if I slip away now?"

"Not yet," said the voice abruptly. "I require your friend's bona fides corroborated, if that is the correct language? Perhaps you can assist in that?"

Despite the accent, the man's English was superb, Granby noted. Not that it mattered under these dire circumstances. Just as long as there was understanding.

Chalmers looked wistfully at Granby and spoke to the hut. "OK, but as I told you on the phone, Mr Granby here is acting for a national government, isn't that enough?"

"Words, my friend."

Granby intervened. "It's true. I have a letter from the President of the country involved." He reached slowly into his inside jacket pocket, retrieved and waved an envelope, aware all the time of presences lurking dangerously beyond the reach of his torchlight.

"Walk forward slowly and slip the letter under the door," the voice instructed. "But no tricks. A cough from the darkness on the left adequately reinforced the warning.

Granby did as he was commanded and stepped back. A light flickered inside the hut and was as quickly extinguished. The voice said, "I am satisfied that there is a letter, but as to its authenticity?"

Granby had suddenly had enough of this cloak and dagger stuff.

"Look, whoever you are," he said aggressively, "I can understand your need for caution, but if we were police or security agents you and your chums would be in the van by now on the way for interrogation." Then he took a flyer. "It isn't as if we don't know whom you represent."

A lengthy silence. Then in more conciliatory tone the voice came back: "Very well. I accept your reasoning. Your friend may leave while we get on with the business at hand."

Chalmers shook his head at the hut. "No, I might as well stay now," he said boldly, encouraged by what he saw as Granby's courageous stand. He was amazed at his own courage.

"As you wish," the man replied.

There followed an exchange of information. The Eastern European defined the weapons that were available by range, yield and physical size, launcher type, electronics and so on, and Granby asked about delivery - when, how, where to, and of course the price and how payment was to be made.

Finally the man in the hut called a halt. "I have told you all you need to know" he said. "When can I expect a firm order?" He sounded impatient to leave.

"I must first talk with my principal," Granby told him "So, how do we get in touch?"

"Through your friend there. You should leave now. As you came, and do not linger," the foreigner instructed sternly.

Chalmers, his anxiety renewed, grasped Granby's arm and began pulling him away. Granby shook him off. "Just a minute," he said defiantly. "I could be spending hundreds of millions of dollars with you. I think I'm entitled to a name."

The voice in the hut chuckled. "Of course. That is only fair. Call me Zivago. Now go."

The way out was easier and quicker, and once the two men were outside the raging night laid into them again remorselessly. Granby was for hanging around to see who emerged, but Chalmers' courage was running out.

"Don't piss about, Dickie. You heard the man. His chums might do you some damage, deal or no deal."

Granby nodded, his bravado expired; it had been superficial anyway.

"OK. Let's go. And thanks again, Harry."

"See you." Chalmers said, making his first smile of the evening as they shook hands. Then both men climbed into their cars and left the site in tandem, turning in opposite directions at the gate. Granby pipped his horn in a valedictory gesture and headed with considerable relief for the street lights in the distance.

★ ★ ★

Back in his flat, adrenalin still high, Granby poured himself a stiff brandy and picked up the phone. Then he glanced at his watch. The affair had occupied nigh on three hours and it was now past midnight, making it three am in the morning in Zawanda. Should he wake Freddie? He decided not to. Tomorrow would do just as well. He sank the brandy, turned out the lights and went to bed.

But sleep would not come to a mind boiling with the thrill of having achieved the impossible. And having earned another four million pounds to boot. How could a chap sleep with that on his mind? He got up, went through into the sitting room and mixed himself a whisky and water. Then he had another, and another, and finally fell back and slept where he lay, the glass, as usual, falling from his relaxed fingers, bouncing and rolling away across the carpet.

He was still there next morning, his head muzzy and a mouth like the bottom of a parrot's cage. He groaned as he stood and stretched the ache from his joints. "God, I feel awful," he said aloud to the empty room.

His neck had a crick from sleeping with it twisted on the arm of the settee all night and he rotated his head to ease the pain. He ran his fingers over the stubble on his chin and made for the bathroom. There he shaved, electrically with his spare, for his usual cutthroat would have done a lot of damage in his shaking hands. Then into the shower.

As the pellets of steaming hot water bombarded his skin he reflected that, of course, Freddie could still get cold feet even at this late stage in the game, and in a perverse way he hoped he would. But the payment had been earned. A missile system had been sourced. Freddie owed him.

But as he stepped into a warm bath towel, such ethics as he possessed began to nag at him. His conscience began to whisper that he should inform the British authorities.

"Christ Almighty!" he muttered to himself. "If a tuppenny ha'penny place like Zawanda can get a nuclear missile why not Libya or Iran, for God's sake? Or the IRA even? He shuddered at that.

His awakened conscience continued working on him all through breakfast, and by the time he had poured himself a second cup of black coffee he was all but ready to ring the Ministry of Defence and confess. The ease with which he had acquired a nuclear missile, subject to Freddie providing the funds of course, troubled him deeply. Someone should be informed.

But in the end, avarice, disguised as loyalty to Freddie Zawutu won through. He also recognised the perils of dropping a word in the wrong official ear and landing himself in all kinds of trouble with the security services; a distinct danger in his case and his line of business. That finally settled it for him.

He studied his watch. Freddie would have been up for a couple of hours by now.

Moi answered the phone. "Oh it's you," he said rudely. "I'm not sure Mutti wants any calls this morning."

"Just get him," Granby ordered impatiently, eager to get it

over with before he changed his mind, to make the commitment past all redemption. "He'll want to hear what I have to say."

Moi grumbled and Granby heard the handset clatter as it struck a table top. After a short pause he heard the sound of someone picking up the instrument and Zawutu's voice followed.

"That you Dickie?"

"Yes, it is. I've good news. A success, you might say. I've managed to find the equipment you wanted."

Zawutu had been anticipating an admission of failure and had been getting ready to tell Richard that it didn't really matter and thank him for trying. Then the penny dropped. He tried to speak, but his mouth was dry with shock.

"The deal is more or less tied up," Granby said into the vacuum, puzzled by Freddie's lack of response.

"But you can't have!" Zawutu managed at last.

"No, I have, really," Granby replied. Perhaps Zawutu's odd behaviour was amazement at the speed with which the task had been completed. "It's a bloody miracle, I know, but there it is. I've got all the delivery and payment details and all that, so all that remains is for me to confirm the order with Zivago. That's what the Russian chappie, or whatever he is, calls himself by the way. It's a code, of course," he gabbled on. "I must confess, though, Freddie, I wasn't too happy with how easy it was. Had second thoughts there for a while, but I did promise."

Zawutu, impatient now with Granby and unable to accept that a nuclear device could be acquired that easily, said angrily, "I don't have time for this nonsense, Dickie. Just tell me the truth. I'll understand."

"But it is the truth," Granby asserted calmly. "I can understand your incredulity, but I have actually pulled it off." He paused. "Look, this isn't safe, talking like this over an open line. Phones have a way of attracting eavesdroppers. Better if I come out to Zawanda. We have three weeks to confirm the order, plenty of time to get the cash in place and make arrangements to receive the shipment."

Zawutu began to realise his friend was telling the truth. But how was he going to tell him it was all a deceit – that there was going to be no four million pounds?

"Very well," he said at last, ducking the issue. "You make your own arrangements, and never mind the visa. Just let de Lancy know the date and time and he'll meet you."

He replaced the handset. Better leave it until Dickie got here. He walked away from the phone, stunned, shaking his head disbelievingly. What an imperial cock up! He had arranged to buy a missile system he didn't want, and couldn't pay for even if he did. What in Allah's name was the world coming to?

# CHAPTER NINE

"Just the one?"

Zivago, or Colonel Sergei Grigorovich, as he was better known in his native Byelorussia, nodded. "Just the one so far, but it is a beginning. I was lucky to be in England when news reached me of a potential customer."

"And the price?"

"As you instructed, sir." He tried hard not to cough. Despite the ministerial size of the office the air in the room was thick with cigarette smoke and getting denser by the second as the grossly-overweight Minister pulled heavily on an evil-looking black cigarette. The ceiling, once a pleasant cream colour, now wore a patina of brown tar which ran over onto the walls, showing a tide mark of discolouration. A long, sagging pencil of ash teetered on the end of the cigarette and looked about ready to join its predecessors on an already grey -streaked suit front.

Sergei watched fascinated. He almost sighed audibly when the ash sheared off and descended onto the Minister's lapel, to be brushed away with the habitual flick of a hand.

"Very good, you have done well," Defence Minister Dimitriov Lupin said. "But until money changes hands we can't be sure, can we?"

"Er, no," Sergei admitted, tearing his eyes away from the new column of forming ash. "But from what I gleaned, Zawanda is urgently in need of such a weapon."

"Zawanda? Where the hell is Zawanda?"

"Africa, sir. Almost the geographical centre. An English arms dealer named Granby is brokering the deal for the Zawandan President, name of Zawutu, Lieutenant Colonel Frederick Zawutu."

"Ah! A military regime!"

"I didn't question too much. Just enough to be sure that Granby is authorised to negotiate. As to them paying, it is a government purchase after all."

The Defence Minister managed to nod without disturbing the fragile column of new ash. "Well, let us hope you are right. Now, what about security?"

A fresh ministerial exhalation of smoke, carelessly inhaled, assaulted Sergei's healthy throat membranes with sufficient bite to make him start coughing beyond control. "Excuse me, sir," he said, affectedly replacing his handkerchief into the cuff of his jacket sleeve. "The tail end of a chest cold."

Lupin dismissed the apology with a wave of a hand. "Get on with it," he urged impatiently.

The Colonel cleared his throat once more before resuming. "The man Granby wants his commission, and his colleague, Chalmers, is shit scared," he said hoarsely. "Neither man is going to the authorities, I'm sure of that. Oh, there might be rumours of course, but who will believe them? Nuclear weapons for sale? No. It is too far-fetched. And anyway, we were very, very discreet. No one knows me or where I come from. All negotiations were conducted in secret in a dark, obscure location and without any of our embassy team being seen. It was the first sale, too, which means that no security service can have anticipated the event. Future sales will be more risky, of course, and the longer we keep selling the riskier it will become."

The Minister paused to light another cigarette, then replied harshly: "Do you imagine I am not aware of that? I would have preferred it if you could have found one customer for the lot."

The Colonel stiffened to attention. "Yes sir." Where, he wondered, would he find a customer desperate enough and rich enough to buy the number of battlefield nuclear weapon systems Minister Lupin intended to liberate? He could think of only one such country, and Iran did not have any freedom of manoeuvre, monitored closely as it was by the Americans.

"Leave," the Minister commanded, and Colonel Grigorovich replaced his cap, saluted, turned about and walked briskly to the distant door. Lupin watched him go, his hooded eyes observing the body language; stiff, unhappy. Grigorovich was a good officer, one to be trusted. Ex-KGB, now serving with the Byelorussian security apparat, he would do his best, but would it be enough?

Lupin shook his head doubtfully, his heavy chins wobbling with the effort. He crushed out his butt end in an already overfull ash tray before disposing of the lot into a convenient waste bin and picking up the direct line to the President.

"Lupin here," he announced. "We have one customer for operation Troika. A small African country called Zawanda. The President is a man named Zawutu."

Lupin had in fact already been briefed on Zawanda. His feigned ignorance in front of Grigorovich had been a ploy to test Grigorovich's customer knowledge and attention to security. He had been less than impressed by both.

He continued, "Our information is that Zawutu attended Cambridge University in England, where he took a second in political science. Then to RMA Sandhurst followed by regular Zawandan army. You will remember the coup out there which brought him to power."

President Anatole Gorgio, tall, with bushy grey hair and

jowls to equal Lupin's, interrupted. "Only one, Dimitriov? I thought we had agreed all?"

"I doubt whether that will prove possible in practice, sir," Lupin replied cautiously. "Colonel Grigorovich has been casting his line as liberally as security will allow, but so far only Zawanda has taken the bait. Of course, he is severely inhibited by the urgent need for discretion, and it is early days yet."

"Absolute discretion, yes," President Gorgio said anxiously. "If Russia or America get wind of what we're up to they'll come down on us like a ton of shit. Where is Grigorovich now?"

"Here, in Minsk sir, making arrangements for shipment."

"Very well, but no more oneses and twoses. Get your man out to the Middle East. That's where the business is."

Our friends the Russians are there too, Lupin was going to say, but he held back. As he lit another cigarette he thought carefully about the implications of Colonel Grigorovich attempting to make nuclear sales in the Gulf without inside help. Disaster, surely. Anatole must know that. After all, the Russians had held sway in that part of the world for years, so any indigenous help that might be offered to Grigorovich was bound to be second best. But maybe Anatole knew that full well and was following an agenda of his own on this one?

The thought brought a frown of profound concern to Lupin's brow. For the life of him he could think of no political scenario that called for such recklessness. Let Grigorovich loose and sooner or later Western intelligence would be bound to take an interest, and then presumably go ballistic when they discovered he was hawking nuclear weapons in the Middle East. A scandal of that magnitude could bring no good to Byelorussia, so why was Anatole so gung ho about pursuing sales out there? Could it be that the money side had blinded him to the dangers?

Whatever the truth, he believed the outcome could only accelerate the downfall of his old friend; he could think of no other ending. His smile broadened with satisfaction, for he was next in line.

"Something the matter, Dimitriov?" the President enquired at the silence.

Lupin pulled himself together. "No sir. An urgent message, that is all. I will see to it that Colonel Grigorovich is sent to the Middle East at once and that our embassies are informed." He reached for and lit another cigarette just as the President's phone clicked off.

★ ★ ★

As deep in the bush as it is possible to get in such a small country as Zawanda, a man of medium height, of typical Zawandan build and colouring, a year younger than Zawutu and as well schooled and trained, sat at an Ushkuu tribal gathering surrounded by chieftains. Until recently, Lieutenant Colonel (Retired), Joshua Ingabe had been in command of 1st Ushkuu Regiment based in Qurundi, Zawanda's second largest urbanisation. His resignation had been sudden and dramatic, the result of Major Moi letting 2nd Eshanti Regiment loose on the Ushkuu. Joshua had simply walked out.

His instant departure had created a serious dilemma for Major Moi. He feared anything which might remind Mutti of the Ushkuu affair. Consequently, he had done his best to keep the resignation a secret, threatening dishonour, discharge and much pain to any officer who spoke of it. Of course, he knew Mutti must hear of it one day, but he prayed that by then his unquestionable involvement in the Ushkuu episode would have been mainly forgotten. The army was not currently a close interest of the President's, thank Allah.

Had Zawutu known the truth at the time, he might have stepped in and saved himself a heap of trouble, but as it was

Joshua Ingabe now sat with the chiefs, cross-legged at the ceremonial fire, as was the custom, discussing revenge.

Back then it had been the turn of the Ushkuu to provide a candidate for training at Sandhurst and Ingabe had been selected to follow Zawutu to that hallowed establishment, where he had done well, graduating well up the list on merit, not just because he came from the Commonwealth. His subsequent regular army career had elevated him to the rank of Lieutenant Colonel ahead of his contemporaries, and but for Moi he might have made it to the very top of the army after Zawutu. As it was, this extremely capable soldier now sat scheming against his erstwhile employers.

He had been at it for a while now. A cadre of Ushkuu army deserters formed the backbone of the Zawandan Liberation Army, an unoriginal name but one which Ingabe thought described exactly the purpose of the organisation. Currently these ex-regulars were engaged in giving basic training to the flood of Ushkuu warriors pouring in from the villages, volunteers mostly, though some had been ordered there by their chiefs. In time-warp villages where civilisation had hardly progressed and old crones still crudely circumcised nine-year-old maidens with unsterilised knives, the rebel army thrived. Their weapons and weapon training came courtesy of Unita rebels just across the border in Angola, to be set against future concessions once the Ushkuu were back in power.

"It is a miracle that Zawutu has heard nothing of us yet," Ingabe was saying.

"El Hamdu Lillah," (Allah be praised) one scholarly chief replied. The others nodded their agreement.

"When do you attack?" another asked directly.

Ingabe had been expecting it. "We shall lay siege to Qurundi," he pronounced firmly.

The chiefs murmured among themselves. Siege? Tribal wars

did not require such a wasteful and boring strategy. It was straight in, kill, capture a few maidens and out again. The concept of siege was alien to them. The muttering intensified. Ingabe ignored their carping and continued his presentation.

"Since the coup, 1st Ushkuu regiment has been run down to two under-strength companies and Zawutu has not moved to reinforce it. It's a soft target and I would expect the Ushkuu regulars still serving to come over to our side as soon as they learn who we are."

The chiefs, understanding that part of the plan better, nodded sagely.

Ingabe continued: "The main elements of the regular army are stationed in New London and will therefore require time to organise, ammo up and move to relieve Qurundi. As we all know, they're in pretty poor shape and Zawutu will be unable to rely on his Ushkuu officers and ORs once news of our rebellion breaks. Mixed regiments, remember."

The chiefs remembered and nodded to one another.

"We're not yet strong enough to take and hold the city, so, once the regular army has mobilised and closes I shall pull back into the bush. But we will have been seen, our fist will have been felt and Zawutu will know he has a serious problem."

The chieftains smiled broadly and hammered the floor with their intricately-carved wooden staffs, indicating unanimity. Then, after the usual long-winded courtesies, the meeting broke up with Ingabe in joyful possession of tribal consensus.

* * *

De Lancy sat on a folding chair in an old, deserted attap cow herder's hut beyond the edge of the city, listening to two scruffy, sweaty, Ushkuu informers who were in it for the money. The light was fading, and the gloom inside the hut made him motion the two men closer.

"This meeting was yesterday?" he asked sceptically.

"Yes sir," the elder of the two replied as he shuffled nearer.

"Impossible!" de Lancy said. "An Ushkuu army? I'd have heard something."

"It's true," the younger man said emphatically. "I have seen it with my own eyes, across the border in Angola. Our warriors are training with Unita rebels."

De Lancy's hard blue eyes narrowed. "You will regret it if you are lying to me," he said with such menace that both men prostrated themselves in fear, the younger one clutching hold of de Lancy's boot in a gesture of submission, mortally ashamed that it was to a despised half caste. Then the elder spoke.

"You may have my wives if I lie," he said, looking directly up into de Lancy's eyes; an insult in Ushkuu culture but casually ignored by de Lancy, who wanted only to squeeze the truth out of them.

"Don't flatter yourself," de Lancy said scornfully. "What would I want with your shrivelled women? I fuck only women of the Eshanti. Keep your ugly wives, it's your testicles you should be worried about."

The man instinctively reached down to his groin, breaking eye contact.

"These are as precious to a warrior as his arrows," he pleaded, fingering the threatened portions of his anatomy. "Believe me, your honour, at the risk of my balls, I can prove what I say about Ingabe. Just let me guide you and you will see for yourself." He glanced sideways at his young companion, who lay whimpering, and kicked him into silence in front of this lowly mixed blood.

De Lancy tapped his swagger cane on the man's head. "Stand!" he ordered, revelling in the power he held over these pure-bred tribesmen. "I will send an officer with you, and a few soldiers in case of trouble. Be ready by five this afternoon. Five days, no more, and I want all of you back here by six o'clock in the evening of the fifth day."

"It shall be so," the younger of the two said and received a slap across the face from his elder for interfering.

"Go!" de Lancy commanded, and the two scrambled to their feet and rushed for the door. He watched them until they were eaten up by the night, then climbed aboard his Land Rover and drove himself back to the Presidential Palace. Had he persevered he might have discovered Ingabe's plans for Qurundi, but in his haste to inform the President he had failed to acquire the most vital piece of intelligence.

Once at the Palace he made straight for the President's study where Zawutu had the Ushkuu Interior Minister, Balindi, with him.

"Yes?" Zawutu said curtly when de Lancy burst in unannounced. He was about to reprimand him for an unwarranted intrusion, but held back on seeing the state of him; dusty, heated and clearly agitated about something.

"It is urgent and very important, sir," said de Lancy apologetically.

Zawutu studied him for a moment, then turned courteously to Balindi.

"If you don't mind, Hamad. A security matter. We'll talk again later."

As the Minister walked out De Lancy opened the door for him, but no greetings were exchanged. De Lancy smiled to himself. To be ignored as a half caste by all sides suited him admirably. No single tribe could accuse him of bias, and all feared him. What could be better for the chief of internal security than to be virtually invisible?

"What is so important?" Zawutu asked as soon as the door closed.

"I have very serious news, Mr President. Trouble is brewing."

"I thought we already had all we could handle," Zawutu muttered, a rueful smile lifting one corner of his mouth. "What is it now?"

"Two of my Ushkuu informers tell me that their tribe is arming under Colonel Ingabe. He meets regularly with the Ushkuu Chieftains and they have provided him with their best warriors."

Zawutu jolted upright in his chair. "Rubbish! We would have heard."

De Lancy shook his head. "That's what I thought, but I'm persuaded of the possibility. Apparently Unita rebels are supplying weapons and conducting training in Angola. It has been seen by my men. So, with your permission, sir, I propose we mount a reconnaissance to ascertain the truth of this. I need your authority to detach a small platoon under a reliable officer. My informers will guide them and within a few days we will know for sure."

Zawutu pulled at his lower lip, then rang for his aide. "Fetch Major Moi," he snapped, "and hurry." He turned back to de Lancy. "How many Ushkuu are there already trained and under arms, do you know?"

"My people have not counted, but they think it could be many. The Ushkuu villages are very thin on young men, so they tell me."

"Shit!" Zawutu said with vigour. "That's all I need, a bloody Ushkuu uprising. And how will the army behave?"

De Lancy nodded. He understood the problem. Since the President had integrated the regiments, no single-tribe units remained. Every formation, therefore, had within it the seeds of Ushkuu mutiny.

Zawutu's own thinking went even further. Over and above the threat of mutiny there remained the general demoralisation of the regular army to be considered. He hadn't yet corrected the shortcomings in that area, and he profoundly regretted it now. The million he'd paid Granby had depleted his reserves, an investment on which he had gambled, hoping that it would mature in time to stabilise the country. If the Ushkuu became active before that could be achieved, he could say farewell to his grand plan. If only he had better maintained the regular army as he had promised he would. He cursed himself again for his neglect. Right now the troops were neither materially nor psychologically equipped to take on freshly-trained Ushkuu warriors. Particularly warriors led by Joshua Ingabe, an officer for whom he had the highest regard.

A knock at the door saved him from slipping into irrevocable self-recrimination. "Come," he called.

Moi strolled in nonchalantly, but at once he felt the tension in the room. He looked into Zawutu's eyes, then let his gaze drop. Something was seriously wrong here. He slid into the chair indicated and waited in trepidation to find out whether he had transgressed against yet another of Mutti's newly-invented rules. Childlike, he had always accepted tribal law as immutable, drummed into him from the cradle with as much force as had been applied to the teachings of the Koran, and he simply could not come to terms with Mutti's meddling. Even Presidents were not above God's law, and Mutti would surely pay the price.

Zawutu waited until Josi was settled, then spoke bluntly. "We have a problem. The Ushkuu are organising under Colonel Ingabe. Captain de Lancy's informers have witnessed young men being trained across the border in Angola. They are, it seems, well-armed and well-motivated."

Moi almost sighed with relief, but there was always a personal risk where the Ushkuu were concerned. He brushed the news aside with an exaggerated shake of his head, and, aware of the danger to himself, turned on de Lancy.

"That's nonsense," he said scornfully. "My own spies have

seen nothing. There have been no weapons used by the Ushkuu against the Eshanti. I have watchers in the villages, so I would know. Nothing has got out of hand."

"The Ushkuu are out of hand!" Zawutu snapped back.

"Not through anything I've done," Moi blurted out without thinking and covered up by looking sharply in the direction of de Lancy. De Lancy's lips tightened and he opened his mouth to reply.

"Certainly not by anyone else's doing," Zawutu interjected before de Lancy could respond. "But to be fair, I always knew something like this might happen. It was unavoidable eventually unless things improved, and they haven't. So there's no need for you two to start accusing one another. Recriminations are counter-productive right now, so keep your antagonisms under control." He stared warningly at Moi. "If Captain de Lancy is correct, and I'm ready to accept that premise for now, an Ushkuu uprising is imminent."

He paused to order his thoughts, then looked at Moi. "You will provide Captain de Lancy with a platoon of Eshanti infantry under a reliable subaltern." Then to de Lancy: "You say you have guides who know where Ingabe's training camps are?"

De Lancy nodded.

"Very well. How long before we know?"

"Five days, sir."

"Right. Meanwhile, Josi, liaise with Defence and arrange for the troops to be paid all their back pay. Draw the money from the Zawandan Central Bank. Print some more if you have to. We can sort the mess out later. Then stocktake weapons and ammunition and let me know the result by the day after tomorrow. Oh, and I want to know the percentage of Ushkuu in each regiment, particularly the number of officers. Got it?"

Moi nodded. An open, legal, uncomplicated scrap with the Ushkuu – this he understood and relished.

Zawutu turned to de Lancy. "Get your recce off as soon as you can. I must have the truth of this. Five days, you say, before we know for certain? Well I suppose that will have to do, but take note I want to nip this thing in the bud before it develops into something we may not be able to control." He paused again, then went on as if talking to himself, "Perhaps I should talk personally with Ingabe. We were friends once, before the massacre."

He stared accusingly at Moi, made up his mind and addressed his next set of instructions to him. "Set up a search for Ingabe and invite him to meet me here at the Palace. Give my word that he will be given every courtesy and protection. I'll give you a letter for him. Meanwhile, do everything you can to placate the Ushkuu. No more provocations, and repair the damage wherever your bullies have been active.

"And one final warning. Find Colonel Ingabe peacefully. Whoever you send must understand the prime directive: quietly, gently and without confrontation. Is that understood?"

Moi bowed his head in acceptance and inwardly fumed at the straitjacket unjustly imposed, as he saw it, on his future actions. There had been potential until now.

Addressing de Lancy again, Zawutu said: "Do your best to tell the Ushkuu through your spy network that I, their President, will see that the Eshanti are punished for any trouble they've caused and that reparations will be paid."

He saw an ugly grimace appear on Moi's face and lost his temper.

"Don't be such a fool, Josi!" he blasted at him. "Do you want armed insurrection?"

Moi flashed a glance at de Lancy, angry and embarrassed that Mutti would speak to him like this in front of the half caste. He shook his head miserably.

"No Mutti," he said, when what he really meant was 'yes please, Mutti'.

"Very well, then. Are you both clear about what is needed?"

De Lancy nodded with pleasure. He felt elevated by his part in this. He had been first to discover the plot, his President had upheld him in front of Moi and was now entrusting him with clear, unequivocal responsibility for a key element of the response. Half caste or not, he was a major player. He grinned impishly at Moi and received a threatening frown in return.

Zawutu ignored the interplay. "Right. Let's get on with it then."

Moi and de Lancy stood, saluted and made for the door, where Moi unceremoniously elbowed de Lancy to the rear.

Alone, Zawutu reflected on his choices. Paradoxically he felt Moi to be the best man to calm the Ushkuu. Balindi was no longer trusted by his tribe; a turncoat, a traitor, was the least they called him. No, with Moi out there doing the apologising the chiefs would at least feel they were dealing with the perpetrator of their ills and hopefully be more receptive because of it.

And what of Ingabe? From what he remembered, the Colonel was a damned good soldier who would always seek to avoid bloodshed if it could be achieved with honour. To a soldier of Ingabe's calibre, honour and glory were to be valued above life itself, and he must therefore convince his old colleague that loyalty to the nation held the greater honour, that in time there would be one state, indivisible and homogeneous.

He sighed deeply. Richard Granby was due tomorrow. It could not be at a less auspicious time.

★ ★ ★

The countryside looked quite different to Granby's newly-educated eyes. What had appeared before to be bare, uninteresting scrubland now had the vista of a beautiful plain alive with the very spirit of nature. As the car motored dustily between expanses of familiar bush, he spotted here and there signs of animals passing, and was even able to identify the spoor of some. Nostalgically he recalled the time he had spent in the bush with Sam and Onjojo and the skills he had learned from them.

In the seat alongside, Simbli, the Honorary Zawandan Consul to the Court of St James, kept his silence. He was here on different business altogether. He was, after all, an Ushkuu.

* * *

Slumped in his swivel chair behind an empty desk, Zawutu sat wondering how he could deal with Granby's terrifying success and at the same time prepare to defeat an Ushkuu rebellion? His shoulders sagged, his eyes were dull and staring and his brain seemed unable to grapple with the menacing escalations. Then a knock on the door jerked him out of his misery and accelerated the problem into real time.

"Come," he called, sitting up and rubbing his eyes. Today he had chosen civilian clothes, a dark suit and Cambridge old boy's tie, and now he began fiddling with the trouser creases, easing the knees as he waited.

Granby walked in accompanied by a Presidential aide and Consul Simbli. "Thank you," Zawutu said to the aide, who withdrew.

"Abu, how good of you to come," Zawutu said, standing to extend a hand in welcome. The hand was touched rather than firmly taken, the meaning missed in the ominous significance of Granby's arrival. "But I wonder if I may have a private word with Richard here before we get down to business?"

Simbli nodded and retired from the room.

"Dickie. How very nice to see you again." Zawutu said as soon as the door closed. He walked round from behind the desk and shook his friend's hand vigorously with both of his, overdoing it enough to bring a shy, embarrassed smile to Granby's lips.

"It's truly a pleasure to be here." Granby said genuinely. "And nice to have been missed so much." He gazed at Zawutu, wondering why all the emotion. Too much physical contact worried him, but he knew the Zawandans were prone to it and had given up trying to avoid it. It just seemed strange coming from Freddie.

"Flight OK?" Zawutu asked next, hating himself for dodging the burning issue.

"That stretch from Nigeria to here is a bit of a bore, but it passes over some grand country and the plane flies quite low so that one gets a good view."

"Good. What about some tea – or something stronger?"

★ ★ ★

Tea was also being dispensed across town in New London barracks, where Major Moi was engaged in briefing the new CO of 2nd Eshanti Regiment, Lieutenant Colonel M'Nango. The regiment had retained its Eshanti title despite the revolutionary mixed nature of its establishment. Nowadays, twenty-five percent of the regiment were Ushkuu, and it was exactly that proportion which currently engaged the minds of both men, for quite different reasons.

"Take only those you can trust," Moi was saying.

M'Nango nodded. "All Eshanti then."

"No," Moi said urgently. "The President would not accept that. Just make sure the Ushkuu you do take are loyal and trustworthy. Difficult, I know, but I'd use administrative staff only, you know, cooks, drivers, clerks etcetera. No front liners. I wouldn't involve any Ushkuu in the actual search if I were you. They can't be trusted."

He added this casually in front of M'Nango's adjutant, who was also present, so that if things went wrong, as he sincerely hoped they would, he could say he had specifically warned the CO not to use the Ushkuu other than as support troops. He knew this advice would be ignored.

"And the objective?" M'Nango enquired.

"Find Ingabe and fetch him to the Palace. Give him this letter from the President, and for your own sake do not get into a scrap with his troops." Another smart let-out.

"But if they start it?" M'Nango persisted, remembering the witch-hunt that had followed the last wild excursion of 2nd Regiment. He wanted crystal clear rules of engagement, in writing.

Moi frowned. "Use your initiative," he snarled. "You're a Lieutenant Colonel, for Allah's sake!"

The CO smiled grimly. "Indeed I am, Major," he came back, emphasising Moi's rank. "But tell me, does this mission have the approval of the President?"

"Don't fucking well mess me about, Colonel," Moi bellowed, dangerously angry now. "Haven't I just given you a personal letter from the President to Colonel Ingabe? And you'd do well to remember who I am. A Major, yes, but a Minister also and a personal friend of the President."

Unperturbed, M'Nango fingered the envelope and carefully studied the presidential seal. "I suppose it's all right," he said reluctantly, hesitant still. "Are there no written orders, though?" Moi's briefing had been far too vague, too damned loose by far.

"There isn't time for all that staff duties bullshit," Moi said dismissively. "I've told you what's required, let that be enough and let's get on with it."

M'Nango stared at the ugly little man. Moi clearly had no intention of providing proper orders. He weighed the presidential letter in the flat of his hand and considered his options; he had none, other than to accept or refuse and take the consequences. Finally he curled his fingers round the letter in a gesture of acceptance.

"Very well," he said. "How long do I have?"

"As long as it takes," Moi said, a sardonic grin spreading his features. "But don't loiter. You are dismissed."

The CO and the adjutant stood, saluted and marched out, leaving the CO's office to Moi.

"He's a shit, that man," M'Nango confided to the young captain as they walked across the parade ground together. "And I say that as a father to a son. Keep away from him. He despoils everything he touches."

The adjutant had heard rumours about Moi and the 2nd and would have liked to learn more, but a glance at his CO's grim features warned him off.

★ ★ ★

Back in the office, Moi rubbed his hands. With a bit of luck the 2nd might yet do some serious damage to the Ushkuu during the search; a last opportunity to take a few out before open warfare flared, a conflict he relished and felt sure Zawutu could not prevent. His devious little mind turned at once to thoughts of self-interest and exploitation.

M'Nango walked briskly towards the gymnasium, muttering petulantly to himself, calling himself every kind of fool for accepting Moi's open-ended set of orders. His adjutant ignored him, as was his duty.

Once inside the gym, waving his Company Commanders back into their seats, he became all CO again, positive, commanding and impressive. His orders were specific and precise and followed exactly the Staff College procedure. "Any questions?" he ended as prescribed. There were none. "Very well, gentlemen. Synchronise watches."

That done, his Company Commanders dispersed to issue orders in turn to their Platoon Commanders, who went on to brief Section Corporals until all levels of command and control had been tasked. The 2nd was nothing if not efficient these days. By late evening the regiment was loaded up and ready to move out.

In allocating responsibilities, M'Nango had not taken much cognisance of Moi's advice regarding the 2nd's Ushkuu contingent. Rather than leave them out of the search proper, he considered it most appropriate for the Ushkuu officers and senior NCOs actually to conduct it. That way the risk of Eshanti troops running amok would be much reduced and it might even persuade Ushkuu villagers to be more receptive.

Of course, regular Ushkuu soldiers were these days considered virtual outcasts by their tribal leaders, but nevertheless, M'Nango figured that it was better that his Ushkuu should take any stick rather than risk Eshanti retaliation. The Eshanti would act as escort and back-up in case of trouble.

Remembering again the post-coup slaughter, and determined to prevent a repeat, M'nango had made it brutally clear, on pain of hanging, that the Ushkuu were not to be harmed nor their villages vandalised. "If they fire on you, duck," he told his men humorously as they dispersed to embark for the operation. A safe joke, he reckoned, for if that moron Moi was to be believed most of the headstrong young Ushkuu warriors were across the border in Angola anyway, leaving only the aged and the very young occupying the villages.

★ ★ ★

Beauchamp clicked his tongue as he read the intelligence report. The more he read, the more sceptical he became. Simon Battersbee, the MI6 officer responsible for the Central Africa

Desk sat opposite, legs crossed, studying the upper set of shoe-laces as though they were the wrong colour. His bald pate reflected the sunlight streaming through the window, making the few remaining wisps of blonde hair seem the intruders.

Beauchamp looked up. "What level of confidence would you allocate to this?" he enquired testily, stabbing at the report with a stiff forefinger.

Battersbee lost interest in his shoe and removed his spectacles to eye myopically the sheaf of papers under digital assault.

"I'm not sure sir," he said, commencing vigorously to polish the lenses with a blue and white spotted handkerchief. "We got it from our man in Moscow. He got it at a British Embassy social evening where the Byelorussian Military Attaché, ex Nuclear Forces, whispered it into our military chap's ear. He was a trifle tipsy. Probably just boasting, but we can't ignore it." He fiddled with the earpieces until satisfied, replaced the handkerchief in his pocket and crossed his legs the other way.

Beauchamp waved a hand impatiently for him to go on.

Battersbee coughed. "Er where was I? Oh yes. Colonel Grant, our military resident, mentioned it to the Ambassador, who dispatched a 'Flash, Eyes Only' signal. We've tried corroborating the information, without much success. We know there are nuclear weapons out there unaccounted for, but so far there has been no evidence of them being moved across borders. As I said, I simply don't know what credence to attach to this intelligence." He looked apologetic and shook his head as if bewildered.

Beauchamp studied the man opposite. Was this the best MI6 could produce, he wondered?

"But Zawanda!" he exclaimed, his tone loudly disbelieving. "The bloody country's bankrupt, according to its President. Where on earth would he get the money for a nuclear missile system?"

Battersbee shrugged again. "Zawanda is unstable, Minister.

Who knows what Zawutu might do under that kind of pressure?"

Beauchamp frowned. "I simply don't believe it," he said firmly. "But keep me informed."

Three days later Battersbee was back, not so vague this time and without affectations. "Sir, we now know more," he said authoritatively. "It seems a deal of some sort has recently been negotiated between Zawanda and an Eastern European middleman. A dubious small-time British arms dealer named Granby is alleged to have met the Russki, or whatever nationality he is, here in London. An offer has apparently been made and awaits acceptance."

Beauchamp was still having difficulty with all of this. "I still think its rubbish. Misinformation," he said emphatically. "Zawanda hasn't the resources. And, incidentally, how've you learned so much all of a sudden?"

Battersbee's expression hardly changed under Beauchamp's aggressive scrutiny. He calmly went on: "Special Branch have spoken with a Mr Harold Chalmers, who claims he was present at the said meeting. Chalmers himself is an arms dealer of sorts, apprehended two days ago attempting to move a few rifles across the Irish Sea, to Southern Ireland by the way, no IRA connection. He was caught red-handed and offered the Granby-Russian meeting as a trade-off. SB thought it worth mentioning to us and we were most appreciative. It begins to make sense, you see sir, the Moscow titbit, and now this."

"You think so?" Beauchamp said thoughtfully. "I wonder. It's such an unlikely scenario. This chap, Chalmers, you say, is most probably lying through his teeth to save himself. He's heard a whisper and hopes to capitalise on it. Keep me informed if anything else turns up" he ended abruptly.

Battersbee went to demur, but Beauchamp had already reached for his phone.

"As you wish, sir," the MI6 man said resignedly. What more

proof did this man need, he thought disgustedly as he stood to leave the room. He ran his hand over his scalp as if it were thick with growth, hesitated, then submitted, turned and walked away. The last words he heard before closing the door were: "How's that little matter of a military team for Zawanda coming along?"

Beauchamp glanced up the moment the door clicked shut. Had Battersbee heard something in the overlap? These MI6 people were past masters at manufacturing mountains out of molehills and a military excursion to Zawanda would be most excellent grist for their devious mills. He sighed. Nothing was simple these days.

"Ready when you are, old chap," Henright's voice boomed in his ear, drawing his attention away from the machinations of MI6. "A Major's command, of course, and we've selected a good man. Major Alistair Hawthorn. He's just completed a special staff course which equips him well for the task."

"Good. Can I ask you to put him and his men on some sort of warning to move, say two weeks?" asked Beauchamp.

"Of course, Henry," Henright said without hesitation. "I assume this matter, whatever it is, will be approved by Cabinet eventually?"

"Naturally," Beauchamp replied confidently, for he had absolutely no intention of carrying the can alone for whatever might come of this. And having thus reminded himself of the hidden minefields, including Simon Battersbee's possible time bomb, he next called the PM.

"Are you serious?" Clive Masters asked in surprise. You had better come over at once."

* * *

The PM listened carefully to Beauchamp's account of his meetings with Battersbee and sat silent while his Foreign

Secretary played down the significance of the intelligence he had received.

"I can't say I agree with you, Henry," the PM said finally. "We are obliged to take this matter seriously. Better if it goes to Cabinet."

Beauchamp smiled cynically. "Of course, Prime Minister." He recognised in the PM another dodgy soul unwilling to shoulder the risk.

★ ★ ★

At the emergency Cabinet that evening, after a plethora of uninformed alarm and dark forecasts of disaster, Beauchamp managed to quieten everyone down by persuading them of his own scepticism. It was with obvious relief that the military provision was unanimously approved. "To be exercised at the express determination of the Foreign Secretary," Masters added as a postscript. "That's all for now, gentlemen." He closed the file before him. "Henry will keep everyone informed, won't you Henry," he demanded pointedly, for Beauchamp was renowned for the selectivity of his circulation lists.

"Of course," Beauchamp said, smiling all round.

The PM almost rubbed his hands as he rose. Having been cornered by Beauchamp, he had artfully manipulated a potential personal embarrassment into a collective one. No one could point a finger now, least of all Henry B.

As the meeting broke up, Defence Secretary Henright came alongside Beauchamp. "Well, Henry. Looks as if you got what you wanted. Can't say the PM seemed awfully pleased with the way the Foreign Office is handling things, though, what did you think?"

Beauchamp contained himself as he deflected the barb. "We'll see. I think you'll find I'm right. Zawanda simply can't afford a nuclear weapon and Clive has not yet grasped that fact. By the way," he went on with a completely benign expression, "Would you mind putting MY army chaps at one week's notice?"

CHAPTER TEN

2nd Regiment fanned out into the countryside in the search for Ingabe. Ushkuu villages were surrounded and the inhabitants questioned. Here and there a headman received a roughing up, but all claimed to know nothing. Officers, under severe stricture, were careful not to go too far in extracting information.

On the second day the CO tightened the reins on his sub units; he had to. His Ushkuu complement of officers and senior NCOs had proven inadequate for the size of the task; too few of them and too slow. So, very reluctantly, he carefully chose and briefed a number of Eshanti officers to augment the search force, thereby hoping to improve the chances of finding Ingabe sooner rather than later. He himself travelled constantly from place to place keeping in close touch with events.

At about mid-morning of the third day, his small personal convoy ran into an ambush between two villages and a fire-fight developed. Two Eshanti soldiers were wounded, and if there were any casualties on the other side they were carried off when the raiding party withdrew. M'Nango thought deeply about the incident and concluded that he had been served notice to leave the villages alone. Anything else would have lasted longer and been more bloody.

From then on search parties moved with scouts deployed in the van and on either flank, and tension mounted.

The dry season still had some time to run before the annual rains came and nature renewed itself. Months of searing sun had sucked all the moisture from the land. A quilt of dust lay over everywhere and even the slightest movement created dense clouds of particles which clogged throats, turned sweat into mud and generally made any kind of movement unbearable. Here and there, tempers flared.

On day four the pressure burst and a village was put to the torch. An Eshanti corporal, nervous, suspecting there were armed men somewhere in the vicinity and frustrated at listening to the headman's repeated refusal to divulge Ingabe's whereabouts, lost control of himself. He rushed in, clubbed the headman to the ground and set fire to the council hut. The rest of the dwellings quickly followed. In flagrant disobedience of orders to cease and desist screamed out in panic by the Ushkuu subaltern in charge, the section rampaged through the village with flaming torches.

When the CO heard he immediately had the section and the officer rounded up and sent back to barracks under close arrest, while he himself visited the scene to apologise and make offers of assistance. When he arrived at the village, or what was left of it, it stood deserted. Even the dogs were gone. He stamped angrily over the charred ground, swearing vociferously.

"It was unfortunate, sir," his Adjutant said comfortingly. "In the circumstances we have been very lucky. Only one breakdown of discipline in four days."

The CO grunted. "That's right, Bwandi, but I'd feel better if we could find that elusive bugger Ingabe. Where the hell is he? Much longer out here with no result and we could be facing another outbreak of blood lust like the last one." He stared at the ground in thought and after a short period, said: Look, let's take a break from this awful bloody heat. Get the Company

Commanders to come in and I'll read them the riot act one more time. Any recurrence of this" - he swept his hand round the charcoal-blackened area - "will result in courts martial, not just for the perpetrators, but for their officers as well, all the way up to Company level. President Zawutu will no doubt see to me personally." He grinned wryly.

* * *

The man under discussion sat in a council hut not three miles away in a village which straddled the Angolan border. He was arguing with the assembled chieftains.

"It was not a deliberate act," he declared vehemently. "Only the one village has been harmed and I'm willing to believe it was accidental. Colonel M'Nango has controlled things well so far. If he was intending to do damage we would have felt the full force of it before now. Let us wait."

"No," said Barrabussa, the senior Ushkuu Chieftain firmly. "They must be made to pay. You must attack at once. The Eshanti Colonel took no notice of your warning and now it is time."

Ingabe rose to his feet. "The target is Qurundi," he said unequivocally. "We shouldn't dissipate our energies fighting the one regiment and so reveal our strength before we're ready. I have spies out at this moment attempting to discover why 2nd Regiment is out of barracks. It could be as simple as an exercise gone wrong."

"But they are going from village to village." Barrabussa said, scanning the assembly for support. The chieftains murmured their concurrence and began talking together of retaliation. Ingabe knew he had to stop this or lose his army back to the chiefs.

"Look," he shouted into the babble. "Let me deal with it my

way. Surely it's better to learn what M'Nango is up to before we go blindly off, unprepared, starting something we might not be able to stop. Remember the Ushkuu proverb, 'Once fallen over the cliff it is too late to regret the first step'."

The chiefs looked at one another. "It is good advice," Barrabussa said, rising to his feet. "Perhaps we should find out first." Heads nodded, and before the tide could turn yet again Ingabe wound up the meeting; an Ushkuu chieftain's nod was as good as his word.

Ingabe walked wearily across the compound to the hut set aside for him. This constant squabbling with the chiefs drained him every time, diverted his energies, did nothing to calm the anxieties that gnawed at him. Despite careful planning and a deep-felt confidence in the abilities and courage of his new army, he knew very well how things could go terribly wrong on the battlefield. Rarely did actions conform to plans. Indeed, commanders were trained to expect chaos and do their best to anticipate and reduce its effects.

He lay on the blanket spread on the floor and tried to unwind, but his mind raced like an ungoverned engine. He grunted, rose to his feet and walked across to the council hut. The chiefs would still be there exchanging boasts.

"I regret," he said to those remaining. "But I must return to my headquarters."

The paramount chief nodded his permission. "Go well and arrive," he said, using the customary Ushkuu farewell to a traveller.

Ingabe rounded up his driver and adjutant and was back in his own command post within the hour. The duty officer had nothing to report, making it possible for Ingabe to manage a half decent night's sleep.

Next day, shortly after breakfast, just as Ingabe was about to leave on a visit to a training camp, a patrol leader came hurtling into the headquarters with the news everyone had been waiting for. "They are searching for you, Utari" he said between deep breaths.

Laughter rang through the commandeered attap long house; all looked at Ingabe for his reaction.

"Me? Why me?" Ingabe asked, mystified, flagging down the laughter.

"There is a letter from President Zawutu, so it is said."

"Who said?" Ingabe demanded.

"An Ushkuu soldier, sir, who wants out of the dust and back to his girlfriend in New London. He was at the Simbibi water hole when we found him, said he was going to desert."

"They want you dead. This is a trick," an elderly Major warned.

Ingabe ruminated for a moment on this odd turn of events. "I will see this letter," he said. "Can you find Colonel M'Nango's headquarters?" he asked the young officer who said he thought he could.

Ingabe scribbled a note, signed it and placed it in an envelope. He sealed the flap and handed the buff envelope to the subaltern. "See that the Colonel gets this," he ordered.

A rumble of dissent came from the staff officers present. "Enough!" Ingabe barked. "We will follow this through. Now we wait."

He did not wait long. Within one day an Eshanti subaltern, clad in the fighting skirt of an Eshanti bush warrior, was thrust through the ZLA Headquarters doorway pinioned between two Ushkuu NCOs and followed by a staff officer.

"This Lieutenant says he has a message, sir," the staff officer said.

Ingabe came to his feet. "You are from Colonel M'Nango," he said confidently, recognising the Eshanti skirt.

The subaltern controlled his breathing and stood to

attention as best he could, looking anxiously at the notorious and elusive Colonel Ingabe. "I am, sir."

Ingabe gestured to the escort to release him. "And what has the gallant Colonel to say to me?"

Still breathless, the subaltern spilled out the message he had carried at the run for three miles. "Colonel M'Nango wishes to meet you on a one to one basis, unarmed, on neutral territory. He suggests the Itulu village of Enbiti. He says you know where it is. That you and he spent some time there once."

"When is this meeting to be?" Ingabe asked without hesitation.

"Careful, sir," the staff officer cautioned. "This could be a trap."

"I think not," Ingabe replied. He remembered the village and the night he had spent in Enbiti as M'Nango's prisoner, caught napping while on a recce. President Zawutu had been there too, a major then, umpiring the exercise. The three had shared Zawutu's rum ration that night, a ration augmented by several bottles from the depths of Zawutu's field pack; he had been a wild one in those days.

Ingabe faced the Eshanti subaltern and repeated "When?"

"Colonel M'Nango will be in Enbiti at ten tomorrow morning. He will wait one hour and then, if you do not come, he will continue the search until you agree to meet him. As a sign of good faith he will stand the regiment down for twenty-four hours. sir."

Ingabe thought for a moment. "I understand there's a letter?"

The runner reached into his sweat-stained skirt front and extracted a damp envelope bearing the presidential seal.

"How did you find us?" the staff officer interjected, still extremely suspicious.

"Your lieutenant came barging straight into our HQ, sir.

Only the letter he carried to our Colonel saved him." Then hoping to improve his own potentially parlous situation, the young Eshanti went on hurriedly, "But he is well. Fed and comfortable. He told us the way only after all was explained."

Ingabe intervened. He had finished reading Zawutu's letter.

"Enough" he said. "I will meet with Colonel M'Nango tomorrow." He spoke to the staff officer. "See that this young man is made comfortable. He stays here until all is over."

Briefing his staff, he faced a flood of objections and advice, but bluntly refused any kind of escort and prohibited the placing of snipers around Enbiti.

"If I am to stop the 2nd's incursions into Ushkuu territory I must attend this meeting honourably. The President's letter has promised safe conduct and Zawutu is an honourable man. There will be no danger to me," he said confidently. "My friend M'Nango will see to it."

* * *

Colonel M'Nango arrived first, early in fact, so as to witness the arrival of his erstwhile colleague Ingabe. He chatted desultorily with the village headman until an upsurge of excitement at the eastern approaches to the village signalled Ingabe's presence.

M'Nango kept his eyes firmly on the Ushkuu Colonel as the distance between them shortened. Then as the two men came together, before aught else could be done, the Itulu headman and a delegation of tribal elders performed a traditional Itulu welcoming ritual, as befitted such a serious occasion. That done, M'Nango made the next move by offering his hand.

Ingabe took it willingly. "I do remember" he said with a broad grin. "I must have been the best looked-after prisoner of war ever. I was pissed on rum most of the time, and so were you, and Freddie Zawutu."

M'Nango grinned back. Then his face fell. "It's not like that these days," he said sorrowfully. "The army doesn't enjoy those sorts of jaunts any more. But perhaps I shouldn't be telling you that."

Ingabe shrugged. "I know how it is," he said.

M'Nango smiled wryly. "I'm sure you do." Then he turned to the headman and asked politely: "Where may we talk?" He swept the cluster of residential huts with his left hand.

The headman turned and indicated an attap building specially set aside for the meeting. He then ceremoniously escorted the two officers into it. Inside was food and several pannikins of the local fermentation.

"Please help yourselves and ask for anything you desire," the headman said as he waved forward two nubile young maidens dressed only in the short ceremonial skirt normally reserved for the annual fertility rites or when neighbouring Itulu chiefs visited. To extend the same courtesy to outsiders was a rare event and a great honour, a measure of the importance the Itulu placed on this meeting. They had no desire to be caught between the two sides again.

Ingabe thanked him, truly touched. "We have not much time, my friend, otherwise it would be an honour to lie with your maidens."

The Chief nodded and waved the two girls away, pausing for a moment to permit them time to exhibit the customary degree of disappointment before departing. He watched them throughout with a critical eye, then turned back to his guests. "Call if you need anything," he said from the doorway, shooing away the inevitable flock of children that had gathered at the entrance as if by magic.

Ingabe waited until the coast was clear, then addressed his opposite number. "It's a genuine pleasure to see you again. You know, I miss the regular army," he said.

"You shouldn't have resigned. There was no need," M'Nango reminded him, sniffing the contents of a wooden jug before pouring some of the contents into a ceramic mug. "Have some. It's papala juice" he said, offering the mug to his guest. Ingabe took it, nodded his thanks and shrugged.

"I thought there was a need, and anyway, I wouldn't have lasted five minutes with that idiot Moi high up the arse of Freddie Zawutu."

"True, true!" M'Nango said with a sigh. "We have lost some other good Ushkuu officers for that very same reason, but we're not here to discuss recruiting needs. You've read Freddie's letter, I take it? I have no idea what it said, but I am ordered to deliver you to the Palace. With your permission, of course, and I hope you will accept and allow me the pleasure of your company that far at least."

"Of course, old friend," Ingabe said. "When do we start? But first I must let my people know what is happening."

"Your runner is still with us" M'Nango reminded him. "Give him your message and I will arrange for him to be dropped off somewhere close to your HQ. If it hasn't already moved." He gave a knowing grin.

Ingabe nodded. "That will do nicely."

★ ★ ★

The news that Ingabe had been found reached Zawutu at the Palace later that afternoon, relayed by the second in command of 2nd Regiment. The major had driven cross country to deliver the message and hadn't even paused to dust himself off.

"Thank you very much, Major," Zawutu told him. "Get yourself a drink before you leave, and a shower if you want one." He passed the officer over to his secretary to be looked after.

★ ★ ★

The sun shone on London with a rare brilliance. It had rained on and off for several days before, and this would be the first opportunity the pavements had to dry out, for umbrellas to be furled and left at home.

Clive Masters hardly noticed the weather. Deep in preparations for a visit to France, he had been head down over his desk for most of the day studying the various briefing documents. It was close to four o'clock when he glanced at his watch. Tea time. Time to join the family.

He tidied his desk, religiously locked away all the sensitive material and was about to leave when his PPS knocked on the office door and popped his head round.

"President Clayton on the red line, Prime Minister," he said.

"Damn!" the PM exclaimed. He hadn't taken tea with Jane and the children for… how long? Too long.

"Put it through to my private quarters," he told Parkins, determined not to miss this opportunity to spend time with the family. "I'll be there in just a minute."

Once upstairs he said hullo to the children and kissed Jane on the cheek before excusing himself with a shrug. "President Clayton on the phone, dear." He turned and walked across the sitting room, took up the red instrument from the bureau and seated himself on a convenient chair.

"Clive Masters," he said into it. "What time is it there? It's tea time here," he said, thinking he was speaking to one of the President's staff.

"And I'm late for lunch," Clayton replied sharply, "I presume you know what is going on in Zawanda? My people tell me that that crazy President, Zawutu, has ordered himself a nuclear missile from somewhere in the old USSR. Franklin Doberman, you know, my CIA chief, came to me with it like a possum with its tail on fire. He's very upset that your security service didn't inform him."

Masters switched his brain rapidly to the subject. "We've only recently heard ourselves," he said truthfully, silently cursing that Clayton had got wind so soon. "But I'm sure MI6 will copy you as soon as we have corroboration."

"Corroboration, for Christ's sake?" the President shot back. "It's a concrete fact already. Your lot are too damned complacent, Clive. No sense of danger."

The PM ignored the American's bluster and replied calmly: "Our analysis is that Zawanda can't afford that kind of money. The country is on its beam ends, and no one is going to supply a nuclear weapon without cash on the barrel head."

Masters heard mumbling from the other end and realised at once that the President had a network call set up over there, damn him. All his advisers on tap while he had none to back him up. He butted in sharply.

"Zawutu is flying a kite. As I said, he can no more afford to purchase an advanced weapon system than, well, than he can breathe under water." He glanced shamefacedly at his wife for the lame ending. She smiled comfortingly back at him.

"That's all very well," Clayton came back in determined fashion. "But Zawanda is an ex British colony and a member of the British Commonwealth. This fuck up is your pigeon."

The PM, stung, had opened his mouth to respond in kind when he caught sight of the children through the corner of his eye.

"Look, Orville," he said with considerable effort. "I don't need you telling me…"

At that point the head of the CIA interrupted. "Mr Prime Minister. If I may interject here?

President Clayton cut his man off abruptly. "Hold it right there, Franklin. This conversation is between heads of state."

There came a muttered apology down the line, then the President continued in a more congenial tone. "Clive, it isn't so much that Zawanda is messing around in the nuclear pond. I know you and your people can deal with that adequately enough. What I'm more concerned with is that nuclear weapons are obviously available on the open market, and that is a frightening prospect for peace. We must find out who's marketing them and where they're stored and stop them being moved around. I hope you'll agree to a joint effort; CIA, MI6. Meanwhile, Zawanda must be hauled into line."

The last sentence sounded very much like a direct order to the PM, who had no doubt it was meant as such. The special relationship, he realized, had turned suddenly very chilly indeed.

"Of course, Orville," he said, anxious to appear accommodating. "No one understands that better than the British government."

You'll see to Zawanda, then?" Orville persisted remorselessly.

"Indeed I will," Masters promised rather too easily, for he had no idea how he would deliver on that assurance. He made haste to modify his words and found himself addressing a dialling tone. The President had hung up on him.

"And fuck you too," he said sotto voce into the instrument before slamming it down angrily. Tea with the family had turned out to be a mistake.

★ ★ ★

Richard Granby was seated on a creaky chair on the balcony beyond the President's study, enjoying a sundowner. "You know, Freddie," he said. 'This is what the Garden of Eden must have been like." He swept a hand across the vista which was visible from the first floor balcony.

Zawutu chuckled. "Well, Zawanda must be the only country

in the world not to have laid claim to it. But it is beautiful, isn't it. That's why I'm so determined to bring it on."

Granby nodded. "But are you sure this missile route is the best way?"

"Maybe not. Not the way things have turned out," Zawutu said regretfully.

"I'm not with you? You wanted a missile system, and I've got you one. You should be over the moon."

Zawutu swallowed his whisky in one gulp "Dickie, I've a confession to make."

★ ★ ★

The latest reports on the increasing agony being caused to Iraq by UN sanctions hit Saddam Hussein's desk at about the same time as Colonel Grigorovich disembarked at Saddam Hussein International Airport, Baghdad, from the Iraq Airways flight out of Amman, Jordan, on a so-called liaison visit. It was not an unusual event. After all, Russia had been the main supplier of Iraqi arms for many years and it had been commonplace for Eastern bloc military advisers to be seen coming and going. And even now, after the humiliation of the Kuwait episode, Saddam's old friends had not abandoned him entirely.

Coincidentally, later that morning in Libya, via Algeria, intelligence whispers of Zawanda's excursion into nuclear weaponry crossed borders. Granby, it seemed, had been far too liberal in his enquiries and now a large part of the world watched belatedly as Zawanda's ambitious foray into the dark, ominous arena of mass destruction progressed.

China didn't like it because it wasn't their sale; Russia remained silent because they were somewhat embarrassed by it all; Europe left it to the UK, as did the USA; Argentina wondered why they hadn't thought of it, and Japan planned higher production of cars and electronics while there was still time. The smaller countries, accustomed to dramas of many kinds, merely readied themselves to vote their view when it came up in the UN, as it was bound to do.

Only in central Africa was there silence. No one was saying much there.

In Iraq, Grigorovich was met at the airport by a subordinate of General Hamad Fawazi, the person with whom the visit had been arranged. Grigorovich's brief, intensely studied on the aircraft on the way out, had noted that Fawazi and a Dr Victor Mikaivitch, a Ukrainian expatriate nuclear physicist, between them had run Saddam's nuclear programme until the UN destroyed the factories, or thought they had. Fawazi was the military brain, Mikaivitch a builder of bombs when circumstances permitted.

On arrival at the defence building, Grigorovich was shown into Fawazi's office, where he was offered a chair and an Arabic coffee, a gritty concoction served out of a long spouted brass jug into small cups without handles. Grigorovich swallowed it gamely and found he had two more portions to endure to satisfy Arabic rules of etiquette. He managed not to grimace.

Throughout the unpalatable ceremony he had been secretly reflecting that he was here on a fools' errand. For despite vigorous objections to those pulling his strings, he had been told he must go.

"Iraq is the last place to try and sell nuclear bombs," he had suggested politely to Minister Lupin. "The UN has the country sewn up tighter than a gnat's arsehole."

Lupin had smiled patiently. "The President wishes it."

And that had been the end of the conversation.

* * *

"Is this true? That we have in Iraq a Russian Colonel hawking nuclear missiles?" Saddam asked of Tariq Aziz, his Foreign Minister.

Aziz nodded. "General Fawazi has accommodated him in the Guest Palace. It came as a severe shock to the General, and to Mikaivitch, when Grigorovich, that's his name, explained his purpose for being here. Fawazi thought it best to keep a close eye on this ambitious visitor and considered it best done in official quarters."

Saddam threw his hands in the air. "If only," he said with profound longing.

"I know," Aziz responded. "Oddly enough, Grigorovich shares your sorrow. He as good as told Fawazi that he had come here against his better judgement, on the express orders of the President of Byelorussia. He is not expecting to sell us anything, he says."

"Na'am," Saddam said sadly. "There is no possible way we can deceive the UN Inspectors."

And there the matter rested. Saddam spent the rest of the day reading and signing papers, then he went to bed and dreamed that a nuclear holocaust launched from Iraq had devastated Kuwait. He woke up severely disappointed and hardly touched his breakfast.

Tariq Aziz suffered no such torment, being of a more pragmatic turn of mind. He arrived at his office at his normal time and sorted through his In tray. Among the papers therein he came across a note left by the night duty officer marked: 'Information only.' It referred to a country called Zawanda and described rumours circulating in the Middle East that Zawanda had entered into the murky business of nuclear weaponry.

It did not take long for Azizi to put two and two together. He rang General Fawazi.

"Hamad. This fellow Grigorovich, he's still under your protection is he?"

Fawazi assured Aziz that he was.

"Well, there's an interesting rumour doing the rounds to the effect that a small African country called Zawanda has acquired, or is about to acquire, nuclear missiles. I shouldn't think there are too many nuclear salesmen around, so perhaps our good Russian friend knows something about it. Will you enquire for me?"

Fawazi said he would; he had computed the same odds as Aziz.

Grigorovich did not hesitate to confirm, with pride, that he had indeed sold a weapon to Zawanda.

"One? Delivered?" Fawazi asked.

"Yes, sadly just one. Awaiting delivery instructions from the middle man," Grigorovich explained.

Fawazi nodded slowly. "You have been busy," he said with a touch of irony, then in a more straightforward tone, "Your superiors must be pleased with you."

Grigorovich shrugged. "It won't last. If I sell nothing here, and I won't, the triumph will soon be forgotten."

"I know the feeling," Fawazi said, empathising with his guest. His Corps had been the only one to bloody the Americans' noses in the Iraq desert, yet he had suffered Saddam's wrath equally with those commanders who had buckled under Allied pressure. "We'll have a drink later."

He left his guest's suite and returned to his own office across town.

"You were right," he told Aziz on the phone. "He did sell to Zawanda."

"I thought it couldn't be a coincidence," Aziz said. "Maybe we can exploit this knowledge. Don't lose him, whatever you do."

Fawazi assured him he wouldn't.

Aziz replaced the receiver and sat thinking about the

possibilities. He came to the conclusion that Saddam Hussein must be told before he could complain about being kept in the dark. The only problem was that he was currently chairing a key strategic meeting of the defence chiefs and would not smile upon an intrusion. Nevertheless, Aziz considered it more prudent to interrupt and be kicked out than not say anything at all. Even then he hesitated outside the conference room door before knocking.

Saddam heard the knock and looked round to see his bodyguards moving to intercept the intruder, then saw them hesitate when they recognised who it was.

"Yes?" Saddam said curtly, clearly displeased.

"I wouldn't break in unless it was important," Aziz said by way of explanation.

Saddam waved the guards back and gestured for Aziz to move closer.

"What is it?" he said irritably.

Aziz stepped forward and bent to whisper in Saddam's ear.

"What?" Saddam exclaimed loudly, more from disbelief than from impaired hearing. Aziz repeated the message. Saddam sat bolt upright.

"Is this true?" he asked.

Aziz nodded.

The senior officers around the table looked anxiously at one another. Whisperers had cost the heads of many of their colleagues before now.

"Thank you, gentlemen," Saddam said next. "We'll finish this another time."

There was a collective sigh of relief. Chair legs scraped and papers rustled as the company hastily swept up paperwork and stood to clear the room with as much dispatch as possible. Alone with his Foreign Minister, and, of course, his omnipresent bodyguards, Saddam first asked for confirmation of the whispered message, in case he had misunderstood. Aziz spelled it out *en clair*, ending with the suggestion that perhaps Iraq could also benefit from Zawanda's good fortune.

"But how?" Saddam asked, surprised at the proposal.

Aziz shook his head. "I'm not sure, but it bears thinking about."

Saddam looked askance at his Foreign Minister. "Had it not been for our misunderstood assistance to Kuwait and the subsequent criminal interference by the UN, we would have had a nuclear arsenal of our own by now. How can a minor country like Zawanda achieve this wonderful thing?"

Aziz shrugged, as much in the dark as his President.

"But I like the idea of exploiting Zawanda's good fortune" Saddam said enthusiastically, always alert to the possibility of making the best of propitious circumstances, a trick he had learned the hard way during his ruthless climb to the leadership of the Ba'ath Party. The Party had grabbed the reins of government simply by wiping out the Iraqi monarchy; not a unique route to power in the Middle East. Since then the Party, and Saddam, had held on by sheer brute force. Murder, imprisonment, torture and hostage taking were the norm. Purges regularly cut swathes through the senior ranks of the armed forces and party officials. The merest whiff of subversion or hint of personal dissent, an overheard remark, were enough to initiate a major blood-letting. In the recent past whole villages had been wiped out, mainly Kurdish ones, and on at least one occasion by the ruthless, indiscriminate use of Sarin, one of the more virulent of the nerve gas agents. Saddam Hussein didn't just have a hard streak, the man was granite all through, without heart or conscience, and pathologically paranoid. The world knew it, his cabinet knew it, his people knew it, even his immediate family knew it, and all treated him with extreme caution because of it.

"It seems to me," he said thoughtfully, "That Zawanda could be persuaded to assist a friendly neighbour."

"But Zawanda's in the middle of Africa," Aziz pointed out. "Hardly a neighbour."

"Don't try and teach me geography," Saddam said curtly. "Neighbours are not necessarily neighbours in space. There are other connections. Think of one."

Aziz did. "I looked Zawanda up before I came, and, Allah be praised, they're predominantly Muslim" he said, pleased to have remembered.

"There you are, then," Saddam said with a broad smile. Brothers in Islam."

Aziz nodded, but could not for the life of him see where all this was leading. Discovering a religious commonality in no way suggested a means of exploitation.

A knock at the door interrupted further conversation.

"Come," Hussein called and the door opened to admit a flustered General Fawazi. "Sorry I'm late," he said ingratiatingly, having arrived to join the strategic conference and to his confusion finding only Aziz and the President seated together at the long conference table. He couldn't be that late, surely? One had to be so careful.

"Urgent business," he added, looking to Aziz for assistance.

"Sit," Saddam said distractedly. "You are aware, I suppose, of this miracle purchase by...?" He frowned and turned to Aziz.

"Zawanda," Aziz replied.

Saddam waited for the General's response.

"Indeed I am, sir," Fawazi replied, with some relief that his absence from the strategic meeting had obviously been forgiven, or at least overlooked in the unfolding of this new drama.

"I asked Tariq if we couldn't exploit Zawanda's good fortune," Saddam went on. "Brothers in Islam, you know."

"I think maybe we can," Fawazi said casually.

Saddam sat up sharply, surprised, his question having been mainly rhetorical. "Go on," he said animatedly.

"We buy one off Zawanda." Fawazi responded. The idea had

sprung from something Grigorovich had said about delivery arrangements to Zawanda and the vendor's despondency at selling only one missile. He looked in turn at the two men opposite, seeking their acclaim.

The boldness of the suggestion stunned Saddam for a moment, and Aziz too; the latter was first to recover. "We'd never get it into the country," he said, half questioningly.

"Oh yes we would. We'd fly it in," Fawazi said, the plot gathering flesh even as he spoke. The two looked at him in astonishment.

"Yes. I said fly it in." Fawazi reiterated. "All we have to do is disguise the destination and fudge the manifest. No one can check on direct flights from one willing nation to another. From Zawanda to one of our military airfields, say."

Saddam looked to Aziz for comment.

"I suppose it is possible," Aziz said slowly, his words tinged with residual doubt. But then his manner grew in confidence as his thoughts crystallised. "Yes, I believe Hamad is correct. With Zawanda acting as a screen, taking receipt and concealing the onward movement, it could be done, just. The main difficulty would be avoiding UN inspectors. But as the General says, if we can slip an aircraft, or however many it takes, into one of our northern military airfields while diverting UN attention elsewhere, say to the Kuwait border, we might create sufficient clear time to dispose of the hardware into a secure hiding place."

Saddam reached for General Fawazi's hand across the corner of the table and shook it. "Mabruk" he said. "Many congratulations. I believe you have given us a workable plan. Tell, me," he asked of his Foreign Minister, "do we have diplomatic representation in Zawanda?"

"I think not," Aziz replied, puzzled.

"Well, it's time we did. See to it. Tell their President, er – what's his name?"

"Zawutu," Aziz supplied.

"Zawutu, that we will accept a reciprocal arrangement at our expense. Embassy status, of course. They can have the old British Embassy building. I don't suppose we shall see the British back here for a while."

Aziz, almost as devious as Saddam, grasped the implication at once.

"Of course. Our man on the ground, to help things along. I'll see to it without delay."

"We will meet again when we have more details," Saddam said, rising to his feet. "Meanwhile, you, General, select the airfield, and arrange for Mikaivitch to receive and handle the weapons. I'll instruct my cousin Ali to deploy the Mukhabarat in search of secure locations to secrete the missiles once they get here."

Fawazi butted in, feeling he had the right since it was his plan.

"We don't need complete missiles, sir. Just the warheads. We have missiles of our own, despite the UN inspectors."

Saddam nodded. "That makes it much easier. Without all the launchers, generators and propulsion hardware we stand a much better chance of success. Well done again, Hamad."

The mini meeting broke up with Saddam Hussein exhibiting more bounce than he had since his ill-fated venture into Kuwait. The other two were buoyed up by it too, for it might augur a remission in their leader's pathological behaviour. He did not seem to be able to put the Kuwait débâcle behind him; perhaps this would do it. But Allah help them if something were to go wrong, Aziz thought. Saddam might not be clinically mad, but his disregard for human life was legendary, and never more so than recently.

* * *

Over the following few days, Tariq Aziz initiated his part in the plot. He despatched an emissary to Zawanda, ostensibly to explore the possibility of establishing diplomatic relations, but also to make contact with Major Moi, whose nascent opposition to the ruling regime had become known. The Iraqi's name was Hassan. He travelled via London on a Jordanian passport, purporting to be a Palestinian, and checked into the only decent hotel in the capital, New London, from where he rang Major Moi.

The choice of Moi as initial contact had come from Iraqi Intelligence staff. They knew of his position as Minister without Portfolio and judged it better to approach him rather than the President direct. His opposition views and growing antagonism towards Zawutu's way of doing things were an added reason, as he would be more receptive to the game plan and therefore willing to throw his weight behind it.

"We should meet," Moi said in English, the language Hassan had used.

"Say no more on the phone."

Hassan frowned. "If I am to say no more, how will I know where to meet you?"

Moi was silent, then spoke tersely. "I know where you are, don't I?" he said and rang off, leaving Hassan none the wiser as to time or place. He could not know, of course, how secretive little meetings like this were handled in Zawanda, particularly by Moi, master of the devious.

The first intimation the hotel manager had that a VIP guest dwelt under his roof was when Major Moi stamped into the hotel demanding instant attention.

"At once, sir," the manager mumbled obsequiously, calling for the register and running a finger down that day's entries. "One o four," he said, looking to Moi for further instructions.

"A private meeting room, then, and bring me a whisky and Mr Hassan in that order."

The manager bowed, issued a string of orders to the reception staff and personally escorted Moi to his own office suite. "You may use this sir," he said. "No one will worry you here."

Hassan was quickly found and escorted to where Moi waited, glass in hand. The Iraqi entered, smiled and advanced, hand outstretched. "Major Moi?"

Moi shook it perfunctorily as he eyed the stranger up and down. Typically Arab, he thought, even in a suit. Swarthy and equipped with the almost obligatory Iraqi moustache, medium build and height and sweating badly. He looks worse than I do in civvies, Moi grinned to himself.

"Sit," he said, indicating a leather-covered chair on the other side of the manager's desk. "Now, what can I do for you?"

Hassan took in his surroundings in one sweep. It looked shabby and it smelled of something unpleasant, which meant it really was bad. He brought his gaze back to Moi and took a moment studying the Zawandan. Could this pygmy-like figure possibly be as powerful as the intelligence briefing had suggested? He decided that he must be and answered accordingly.

"President Hussein sends his compliments and wishes you and your family every good health, sir."

"Yes, yes," Moi cut in impatiently. "But why are you here?"

Hassan blinked, unused to such unseemly haste. Arabs, Iraqis in particular, preferred a more circuitous route, opening with the proper courtesies and exchanges of cultured conversation, only then getting down to the core business. He took a moment to collect himself, then replied carefully with what he thought to be the correct degree of servility: "I understand you may be in a position to advise me."

Moi smiled his crooked smile. "That depends," he said enigmatically.

Hassan smiled back and reached into his inside pocket, from which he withdrew a fabulously ornate gold cigarette case. "Do you mind?" he asked politely. "So many people do nowadays. Mind, I mean." He watched Moi's eyes focus greedily on the gold. 'Got you,' he said to himself.

Moi shrugged, eyes denying his feigned insouciance. "Please yourself," he said.

Hassan took his time selecting a cigarette and extracting a gold cigarette lighter, the twin of the heavily gold encrusted case, while he covertly observed Moi's reactions. He wondered why a man so obviously greedy would want to appear belligerent. But there was little to be gained from guessing. Enough that he had gauged the avarice of the man.

"Depends on what?" he asked innocently once he had enjoyed his first inhalation.

"On whether it will cost or benefit me."

Hassan smiled inwardly at the blatant invitation to offer a bribe.

"Oh, I think benefit would be the correct description," he said.

Moi smiled again. "That is as it should be. Perhaps we might now exchange views."

Two whiskies later for Moi, two mineral waters for Hassan, a deal had been struck; Moi had agreed to press the proposal for a diplomatic exchange directly with President Zawutu. "No point going through that Ushkuu bastard, Balindi," he said, referring to the one appointment he wholeheartedly deplored. "I will gladly see to it for you."

"And for the ten thousand British pounds I will pay you," Hassan added, sealing his end of the bargain.

CHAPTER ELEVEN

Joshua Ingabe received a welcome worthy of a prince. Colonel M'Nango delivered him straight from the outland, dusty, travel-grimed and all, into the Palace yard, where a guard of honour had been drawn up. As he stepped down from the open-topped Land Rover the Regimental Band of his old regiment, 1st Ushkuu, brought in specially from Qurundi, struck up the National Anthem and Ingabe came to the salute out of habit.

Zawutu waited for the last strains to die away, then strode forward.

"Colonel Ingabe, I see you. You are doubly welcome." He took Ingabe by the arm and led him to the right of the infantry line, where the Captain of the Guard reported the parade: "Present and ready for inspection. Sir."

Ingabe stiffened his shoulders and as the band began a slow march he quite naturally fell into step with the guard commander and traversed the double ranks as if it were the old days and these were his own troops. He walked smartly round to the front of the guard to take formal leave of its commander and compliment him and his men on a good turnout. He glanced back nostalgically as he accompanied Zawutu up the palace steps and into the building.

Once indoors, Zawutu clapped Ingabe on the back. "Like old times, eh?"

Ingabe smiled broadly. He was not as tall or well-proportioned as Zawutu, but as a professional soldier he had looked after himself.

"I am sorry, my friend, that we meet under such unfortunate circumstances," Zawutu continued. "But let's not become too depressed, eh? As I recall, you have a taste for a good malt?"

Ingabe shook his head. "Later, perhaps."

"As you please," Zawutu replied understandingly. He had no wish to jeopardise this vital meeting by appearing overzealous or devious.

They walked into Zawutu's study and sat opposite one another on the two ancient club chairs. Ingabe glanced round at the pictures hung on the walls.

"Nothing's changed in here," he remarked.

Zawutu smiled. "It's as the British left it. I don't think we could do it better. You know, of course, why I invited you?"

"I have an inkling."

"In which case let's not hunt the impala upwind. We'll do this the army way. Straight up, officer to officer. I want you to call off the Ushkuu."

Ingabe blinked at the directness, averted his gaze then smiled and re-engaged Zawutu's eyes. "What makes you think I have any influence in that direction?" he asked.

Zawutu sighed. "I had hoped we could do this without all the usual fencing and ducking. I know perfectly well what is happening on the border."

Ingabe looked quizzically at Zawutu. "What border?"

Zawutu leaned back in his chair, clasped his hands in his lap and fixed his ex-colleague opposite with a deeply cynical gaze. His tone matched it.

"This is sad, my friend. I remember you differently. I remember you as a patriot who would do anything for Zawanda."

Ingabe's eyes flashed angrily. "You have the nerve to question my patriotism?" He leaned forward in emphasis. "Why else do you think I am here? And speaking of loyalty, why have you not kept your promises to your own people, let alone the Ushkuu? Zawanda deserves better, all the tribes do and I shall achieve it for them." There, he had said it.

"You have set yourself a dangerous task, my friend," Zawutu said, shocked, yet somehow relieved by the admission. He leaned forward to close the gap between them by several more inches. "If you oppose me the army will whip your rebels and we shall both have blood on our hands. I had hoped that as reasonable men we could prevent that happening. We still can, Joshua."

Ingabe hunted for the truth in Zawutu's eyes, deciding how to respond.

"I'm genuinely sorry," he replied. "I appreciate that you don't have the resources for much, but you could have done more. Spending money on weapons and ammunition – and don't deny it, I know about Mr Granby – takes it away from the people. What do you want weapons for if you believe in peace?"

Zawutu sat up in alarm. How could Ingabe know about the missile deal? But of course, he couldn't. He relaxed.

"Defence against outsiders, that's all," he said convincingly. "There is always the danger of one of our larger neighbours pushing his luck immediately after an internal coup, you know that. I have to make good our material losses. You would do exactly the same."

Ingabe nodded. "Maybe, but I would put other things first."

"Of course you would, but you don't have to, do you?" Zawutu said cuttingly. "If you were sitting in my seat it would be a different matter, believe me."

"I must go," Ingabe said abruptly. "This is a waste of time."

Zawutu reached out an open hand in a gesture of appeal.

"Please, Utari. Let us prevent any more bloodshed among our people. Just say what you want from me."

Ingabe hesitated. The offer was clearly genuine, but he already knew he could not dissuade the chiefs; he had seen the red in their eyes. He rose reluctantly.

"This is sad, Freddie. I will try, but you know the chiefs. You will honour your pledge of safe conduct?"

Zawutu stood too. He nodded. "Of course. But do you think the chiefs will listen to me if I talk to them direct?"

Ingabe smiled a brief smile. "I believe you want the best for Zawanda, but it cannot come as long as the old tribal ways persist. You have gone some way towards integration, but that cockatoo Moi is ruining everything for you and you do nothing to stop him. The Ushkuu chiefs have had enough, and even if I wanted to rein them in I doubt I could. They want retribution and without me it would be absolute slaughter. You see my predicament. There's no way they'll talk to you. You know how it is, they would fear your persuasive tongue might alter their vision of an Ushkuu victory." He held out a hand. "But I will try, Freddie. I will."

Zawutu took and held it.

"Of course, keeping the maiden Uudi here doesn't help your case" Ingabe went on, shaking his head. "Rather like shooting yourself in the foot."

Zawutu looked hard at Ingabe. "I don't understand. She's Ushkuu, yes, but that's nothing new."

"You really don't know?" Ingabe asked incredulously. "Princess Uudi is the eldest daughter of the Ushkuu Paramount Chief, Barrabussa."

Zawutu was stunned and looked it. Now some of the exceptional things he had noticed about her began to fall into place. "No, I didn't know and that's the truth," he said. "She's beautiful and clever and I treasure her, but how come she kept me in the dark about her family?"

"She likes you, that's why," Ingabe said. "She pleaded with

her father to be allowed to stay, then told him she would anyway. He's disowned her, but to the tribe she is still their Princess. They are affronted and very, very angry. With you, not her."

Zawutu's heart leapt when he heard that Uudi had chosen to stay with him, but keeping her here now, how could he justify that? "What should I do?" he enquired seriously of Ingabe.

Ingabe shrugged. "Her family won't have her back and the tribe won't forgive you anyway, so you are caught between a thorn and a spiky bush."

"I'll marry the girl," Zawutu said without thinking it through. He loved her, and from what Ingabe had told him she felt the same. "Wife of the President of Zawanda is higher in status than Ushkuu Princess and that should satisfy your tribe. It could even help to bring the tribes together." He smiled broadly, well pleased with himself at having solved several problems by the one simple, eminently desirable act.

Ingabe smiled too. Zawutu was about to make a terrible mistake. The mixing of tribal blood through marriage was a taboo which even presidents could not ignore. Even the Eshanti would baulk at such a marriage. Certainly the Ushkuu would, and what of that evil bastard Moi? He'd go spare.

"What a wonderful idea," he said clapping Zawutu encouragingly on the back. He took hold of Zawutu's hand again and shook it vigorously, but it was an empty gesture. In his mind the die was cast. He had come here wanting only to right a wrong, but in the process he had learned how easy it would be for him to become the next President of Zawanda.

CHAPTER TWELVE

Zawutu sat at his desk reflecting upon the impossible position he had painted himself into. Nothing seemed to be working out. Ingabe had gone back to his rebel command leaving a sense of inevitability behind him; Granby had taken umbrage and refused to switch the missile deal off; Moi was more trouble than he was worth and Britain remained obdurate. He sighed with frustration. Then the phone rang.

"Secretary Beauchamp for you, Mr President" his aide said.

"Put him through," Zawutu said wearily, mopping his brow with a tissue.

Beauchamp's opening tone was silky smooth. "President Zawutu," he began formally. "I hope you are well?" He left no time for a reply. "I wonder if I might raise a small matter that is of some concern to Her Majesty's Government."

Zawutu's pulse quickened. "Small, you say?"

"Well, only in the sense that we cannot believe all we are hearing from our intelligence services."

"Which is?" Zawutu said. He mentally scrolled through a list of matters that might be of interest to British intelligence and came up with only one.

"I know it's ridiculous," said Beauchamp. "But someone has

started a rumour that Zawanda is shopping in Eastern Europe for a rather large weapon system and I thought it only fair to let you know that Her Majesty's Government views such rumours with some dismay. The PM has therefore asked me to ascertain the truth of the situation."

"Of course," Zawutu said accommodatingly. He felt an irresistible urge to give an enormous 'whoopee'. The British knew, and it worried them. At last something good was coming his way. He struggled to calm himself and managed finally to respond reasonably coolly.

"I can't imagine where such a wild story might have originated. It is true that I'm hoping to re-equip the Zawandan army with modern small arms, if I can find the money, but nothing more."

Beauchamp coughed. "How's the tribal situation?" he asked incongruously. "The last time we spoke you were expecting trouble from the Ushkuu?"

The abrupt change of direction flummoxed Zawutu for a moment. Geared to deny and defend, the unexpected shift caught him wrong footed. Had Beauchamp somehow divined a connection between the Ushkuu problem and shopping for missiles, he wondered? Unlikely. It would take an enormously imaginative leap to connect those two things, particularly since no direct link existed outside his own brain. He decided to play it as if the question was an innocent one.

"Thank you for asking. Things have certainly deteriorated since last we spoke, which is why I urgently need to replace the army's conventional weapons. Nothing of the calibre you suggest, though. What use would a single missile be against simple tribesmen?"

"Quite!" Beauchamp replied. "I take your point, but I'm still concerned about your Ushkuu problem."

Zawutu hesitated to answer. He had not prepared himself

for this line of discussion. Indeed, if Beauchamp planned to catch him on the hop he was succeeding. He felt suddenly inferior and gritted his teeth.

"Yes, well, so you should be" he began aggressively. "The Ushkuu are mobilising under an ex-army half colonel named Ingabe, and he's good, which makes the situation all the more dangerous." He paused to let that information sink in, then resumed: "If I had available even the mediocre level of UK aid we used to get I might be able to nip Ingabe's ambitions in the bud, but as it is…" He left the alternative hanging in the air like an executioner's axe about to fall, then added mischievously: "Maybe a big missile is just what I need to frighten him off."

"Don't even think of it," Beauchamp said urgently, his voice adopting an involuntary dictatorial tone.

Zawutu smiled to himself. He'd rattled the smug bastard's cage at last. Could he push the advantage home?

"If you would change your mind about the aid position," he said bluntly. "You must see that I am bound to do my best for Zawanda wherever I find the means."

There followed a prolonged silence, and when Beauchamp did eventually reply he sounded sincere. "I can't rescind a Cabinet agreed position, much as I'd like to," he said. "That you are having difficulties is not in dispute, but that won't restore the aid programme."

"What will restore it?" Zawutu asked sardonically. "Me getting myself an atomic bomb?"

The silence stretched before Beauchamp came back: "I'll ignore that provocative remark," he said in a conciliatory tone. "I understand how you feel, but threats won't solve anything. Look, maybe there is another way. If it's a deterrent against the Ushkuu you're looking for I think I might be able to oblige."

He took a deep breath. He was about to commit the Government to expenditure beyond his authority, and in doing so would cross ministerial boundaries. But the PM wanted this missile crisis settled. By any means, he'd said.

He let go the breath and ventured into proscribed territory.

"Firstly, Britain can supply the new small arms you need, on long-term credit, which probably means free of charge. Secondly I can arrange the loan of a quite substantial British Army Liaison Team, ostensibly to train your chaps on the new weapons, but also to help stiffen your regular army against the Ushkuu. A clear message that Britain is four -square behind you. This fellow Ingabe might think twice about causing trouble when he knows the British Army is on the ground in Zawanda keeping a close eye on him."

Zawutu almost dropped the phone. Not only was the offer astounding, but Beauchamp sounded equally surprised to be making it. The missile threat had worked somehow; never mind that it had got him into all sorts of trouble. The joke was that Zawanda couldn't afford that kind of money anyway, but if Britain had deceived itself into believing otherwise, even to the extent of re-arming his army free of charge, how could he refuse?

The aid issue would not go away, of course. The urgent need for cash would remain, but from little acorns… And with the nuclear card now on the table and the potential to play it up to its full face value, only Allah knew what might yet be achieved.

He didn't much like the inclusion in the deal of a British Army contingent, though. It smacked too much of Big Brother, suggested a degree of mistrust. But given his tacit agreement not to wade any deeper into the nuclear pond, he should, he figured, be able to negotiate that away.

"I accept your offer of weapons," he said. "But a British Army presence in Zawanda would be too reminiscent of colonial days. Not that they were bad, but recalling them militarily might not have the effect you suggest. Indeed, I believe it might go entirely the opposite way and force Ingabe into reacting before your people are on the ground in sufficient strength to make a difference."

"One thing goes with the other," Beauchamp replied with a note of finality. "No Liaison Team, no weapons."

Zawutu began to argue vociferously, but Beauchamp was adamant.

"Oh very well," said Zawutu ungraciously. He had a niggling feeling that he had been manipulated yet again. "When will all this come about?"

"Very soon," Beauchamp replied. "The MoD and our ordnance people will let you know."

The conversation tailed off soon after that, Beauchamp eventually pleading a visitor and hanging up. He turned to face Jameson, who was gently placing the extension on its rest. "Well, what did you make of that?" he asked.

Jameson shrugged and pushed his spectacles further onto the bridge of his nose in an habitual gesture. "He's lying about the missile, of course, but I'm inclined to believe he is in serious trouble with the Ushkuu Tribe."

Beauchamp nodded. "I agree with you, but with our army chaps on Zawandan soil he won't be able to do much without us knowing about it." He chuckled. "You know, maybe the Ushkuu will indeed be deterred by our presence in Zawanda. Walked right into that one didn't he?"

Jameson smiled. "Be honest, sir, you gave the poor sod no choice. I just wonder, though, whether the PM will go along with re-arming the Zawandan army, or, for that matter, agree to the military assistance you just promised."

Beauchamp sniffed and looked down his nose as if he had suddenly detected something rather unpleasant. "That is none of your business, Peter, and I don't see he has any choice in the matter."

★ ★ ★

Granby sat in the second creaky old chair on the study balcony nursing a whisky, waiting for Freddie Zawutu to break the silence. Freddie had been strangely withdrawn all evening, and as the silence extended to the point of embarrassment Granby coughed conspicuously to remind him of his presence.

Zawutu slapped at a mosquito on his neck and missed. "Let's go inside," he said. "They're beginning to bite." His uniform was streaked with sweat from the heat of the day. He found uniform more congenial than civilian clothes, as the open neck, short sleeves and plenty of changes made it easy to stay comfortable. Unlike some other African military rulers he had not promoted himself to Field Marshal, nor had he awarded himself a clutch of spurious medals. Plain Lieutenant Colonel Frederick Zawutu was good enough, and Granby admired him for that.

Once in the study with the shutters closed, Zawutu suggested another drink. A further silence descended while he poured them; Mumbi had been dismissed for the night. Then, drinks refurbished, Zawutu stood back and looked down on Granby sitting in one of the old club chairs.

"Look, I'm sorry, Dickie," he said, his dark brown face reflecting his sorrow. "Things have been happening rather too fast for my liking. It's about the weapon offer. I've thought about what you said and quite frankly I don't want to go ahead with it. To be honest, I never expected you would succeed as you have. Nothing against you, but the odds were not in your favour, be honest. I can't pay for it anyway, and what would I do with it if I could?"

Granby held up the hand with the glass in it, almost in self-defence at the rush of words. "OK. OK, Freddie. No need to go on. I'm disappointed, but I understand." Actually he felt relieved, but there was too much money riding on this to admit it. He had never liked the idea from the beginning, or so it seemed to him now.

"You want me to tell the Russkies no I suppose" he said. "Well, I'm not keen still. They're a nasty bunch to cross. And what about my four mil? I did source your missile after all and it isn't my fault that you don't want it."

Zawutu smiled sadly: "I owe you that, Dickie, and I only wish I could honour it, but funds are a little short just now. I promise I'll pay you the balance as soon as I can. I mean, you've already received the one million deposit and that should last you until I can scrape the rest together."

Granby looked hard at his old college friend, at the new creases in his face and the sagging shoulders. "I had no idea things were so bad. Just hadn't noticed. Of course I'll wait." He meant it too, but he couldn't help feeling disappointed at the postponement; would Freddie ever be able to pay?

"Thank you, Dickie," Zawutu said, pleased that Granby had accepted the bad news without argument. "So will you return to the UK and close down the missile deal?"

Granby lowered his eyes. He recalled that terrible night in the old tanning factory and shuddered. He couldn't go back there. But even to Zawutu he could not admit fear.

"I can't promise anything, but I'll do what I can" he said. He could see how desperate Freddie was to get out of the fix he had placed himself in, but the silly old fool shouldn't have started it in the first place. Perhaps after a few drinks in the H&H he could con Harry Chalmers into passing on the cancellation. But it might not be possible.

"It's just that the vendors might be difficult to contact that's all, so it may take a bit of time," he said weakly.

"The sooner the better, all the same" said Zawutu.

Granby shuddered again, then squared his shoulders. For

another four million, even if he had to wait, it was probably worth the pain. "

I'll leave as soon as your secretary can arrange a flight" he said.

"Another whisky?" Zawutu said, cheerful now. He reached down and took Granby's glass.

* * *

Major Alistair Hawthorn was not impressed with his new posting, independent command or not. He'd never heard of Zawanda; had had to look it up in his World Atlas. And there, after a scrupulous search, he came across this tiniest of blobs in the centre of an otherwise enormous continent.

"It could easily be mistaken for an oversized full stop," he said indignantly to a fellow officer over a drink in the Depot mess. "It has to be a mistake."

"Very likely" his companion said. "Since they cut MoD Stanmore to the bone all sorts of errors have emerged. A friend of mine found himself in Bosnia when his posting order distinctly said Belize."

"Christ!" Hawthorn said. "I didn't know it was as bad as that."

"Believe me it is, old boy."

"Well, I'd better talk to someone about it then," Hawthorn said. "And make mine a double, there's a good chap."

His telephone call to Postings Branch, Stanmore, next day was rather direct and a shade unmilitary, due partly to a lingering hangover.

"Look," he began aggressively at the unfortunate Major at the other end. "I don't know what's going on, but I don't much fancy Zawanda as a posting. A training visit, OK, but a proper term posting? There's obviously been a major balls-up somewhere."

"Wait one moment," the Staff Officer replied as he put down the handset. He grinned at the instrument before stepping across the corridor to the open door of Colonel Simpkin's office.

"It's Hawthorn, Colonel," he said. "Bang on time. He's pissed off about his posting, as was expected. What shall I tell him?"

"I'll take it," the Colonel said, pressing the appropriate button on his phone unit.

"Major Hawthorn? Colonel Simpkins here."

Hawthorn repeated his concerns, adding the occasional 'sir' but still managing to be subtly insubordinate. Simpkins grimaced in amusement down the phone. Hawthorn was well named. He was certainly prickly.

"Major," he said in his most severe voice. "After that little performance I wouldn't change your posting even if I could, which I can't. Your appointment is courtesy of the Foreign Office and I suggest you tackle them about it. I'll give you the number you want." He gave Hawthorn a private direct number. "And the best of luck," he ended, winking at the Staff Major, who had eavesdropped from the doorway.

"These specially-trained officers will be the death of me one day" he confided, shaking his head. "Prima donnas, all of them."

Hawthorn's ensuing conversation with a plummy-voiced senior Foreign Office civil servant did little to modify his inherent dislike of that particular brand of officialdom, but in the end he agreed to hold his fire until the official briefing.

"Wednesday next, old chap, say ten, followed by a spot of lunch," said the civil servant.

On the prescribed Wednesday, in a sparsely-furnished back room of the old War Office Building where an overhead projector had been set up, a small team of men in civilian clothing detailed the reasons for sending a British Army team to Zawanda. Hawthorn listened passively to veiled references to nuclear weapons and promises of an unusual degree of freedom once on the ground. He was given a condensed version of events in Zawanda; the tribal situation, the recent coup, the Ushkuu massacre and a rundown of the leading political and military figures currently in power. A more protracted history of President Frederick Zawutu followed, from which Hawthorn found himself already strangely attracted to the man.

Throughout he had maintained a blank expression, despite the fizz that consumed his innards. Only when the missile issue came up had a transient flicker appeared in his eyes.

"And, of course, you may select your own team," the most senior man at the table said. Hawthorn blinked hard. Never had he been offered such a gem. Zawanda might not be too bad after all, he told himself.

"A cool one, that," was the post-luncheon comment of the MI6 representative, the inscrutable man who had sat in the darkest corner of the room, listening.

* * *

Hawthorn, taking the MoD at its word, gathered together his choices. A small Signals troop to operate the rear link to the UK; an Intelligence section under an Intelligence Corps Sergeant, which somehow gratuitously gathered two oddballs whom he was sure were MI6 agents masquerading as soldiers; a Subaltern painfully levered out of the elite SAS Regiment after an initial blunt and offensive refusal by Hereford had been immediately overruled by the Defence Minister himself; four augmented troops of the same who between them possessed a range of skills of which even Hawthorn was not certain; and finally a full Rifle Company of Light Infantry from his own Regiment, along with the usual complement of cooks and admin types. Then, at the last minute, when it was decided that the first instalment of new weapons would travel with the troops, a team of three REME Armourers was included to service and commission them.

With his new command currently occupying a large aircraft hangar at RAF Lyneham, Hawthorn stood in the midst of his officers and warrant officers rounding off his final briefing.

"We've no time here to learn about one another before we go," he said. "So we'll bed down as a unit once we reach Zawanda. OK?" He then dismissed the group, all but for Lieutenant Jimmy Harwell, the SAS Subaltern.

"All right, Jimmy?" Hawthorn enquired. Fortuitously, they had met in the Officers' mess at Hereford during Hawthorn's course there.

"Fine, sir," Harwell responded. A stocky young man of twenty-three with a ready smile and clear hazel eyes just a little darker than his hair, he had come into the SAS via Sandhurst and Hawthorn's own Light Infantry Regiment, but it had not been until Hereford that the two had met. Hawthorn had spent most of his regimental time elsewhere whilst Harwell had gone Para, then SAS.

"Has your kit arrived yet?" Hawthorn asked, referring to a package of high security equipment shipped from Hereford.

"Already loaded, sir," Harwell informed him blandly.

Hawthorn nodded. He had taken to this lad, but not just because they were from the same Regiment. In fact he could not put his finger on exactly why. Perhaps he could discern reflections of his own rebellious nature and desire for the unorthodox in the youngster. He smiled at that.

There was in fact only seven years between them, and looking at them together one would think even less. Much the same build, and a straight way of looking at you.

"Better see to your Troopers, then," said Hawthorn. He returned the Subaltern's salute and watched him walk away, reflecting that a secondment to the SAS was no mean feat for a young officer. It placed him among the very best in the rough, tough world of special forces and Hawthorn recognised how lucky he was to have him on board.

On the apron, the four C130s dedicated to the transit were lined up ready to receive their cargoes of men and weapons. It was 3 am and the mission had a Restricted classification only. A military training team on loan to a Commonwealth country was nothing out of the ordinary, after all.

★ ★ ★

Granby had been in the UK only twenty-four hours when he received an unexpected phone call. "Am I speaking to Mr Richard Granby?" a heavily-accented voice enquired.

"Probably," Granby replied, recognising a Middle Eastern inflexion in the caller's voice and playing it canny on that account. He had once suffered a very bad experience in that part of the World. "Who is asking?"

"My name is Ahmed. Could we meet somewhere? You choose."

Granby frowned. Since the Russian business, still to be resolved, he had come to hate mysterious invitations; 'blind dates', he called them.

"About what?" he asked.

"You are an arms dealer, are you not? So, I want to talk about arms."

Not the usual approach, but business is business, Granby reasoned.

"OK, let's meet at the Horse and Hounds public house in Akerman Street. Do you know it?"

"I will find it," the man said.

"Seven o'clock tomorrow night then." At least in there he would be among his peers, and relatively safe.

The mention of arms drew his thoughts back to the Russian problem. He hadn't been able to trace Harry Chalmers. Someone said he'd gone abroad, and it looked as if he would have personally to close down the Russian deal after all.

He searched among the loose papers in his desk drawer until he found the number Harry had given him. He stared at it for a long time, then reached for the phone, paused and withdrew his hand. Best leave it for a day or two, he told himself, resenting the fear that invaded his senses at the thought of contacting that sinister invisible Russian, or whatever he was.

He brushed his hair back from his forehead and grabbed his coat from the peg in the hall. A jar in the pub would cheer him up, he figured. As he left the flat he failed to notice two men in a car parked across the street.

Next evening, after too much of the day spent pacing his claustrophobic sitting room and debating whether to call the Eastern European, he repeated his walk to the Horse and Hounds, feeling thoroughly downcast. He had never known such angst. Sweat had actually run down his face while he had dithered about calling the owner of that sinister voice, and it wasn't hot by any means. He'd been in stickier situations, but there was something about this one that terrified him.

Once more into the jaws of uncertainty, he thought dramatically as he paced his way to Akerman Street. Once again he failed to notice the two watchers, who were parked further down the street this time.

He arrived at the pub shortly before seven to be greeted exuberantly by the old crowd, expecting more largess, but when he didn't offer, one of them, hoping it would be noticed, bought him a glass of beer instead.

"Cheers," Granby said, glancing around for a Mediterranean type. He spied him seated alone at a table in the darkest corner of the bar.

"Excuse me a minute, chaps," he said, placing his glass on the bar. "Spot of business. shan't be long. Get the next round on me." He placed a twenty-pound note on the counter and walked away.

"Ahmed?" he enquired tentatively as he approached.

"Mr Granby," the man said in reply, coming to his feet and indicating a chair across the table.

Granby surveyed him in some detail; swarthy, black pomaded hair, moustached and perfumed and wearing an oversized suit, a flowered shirt and a gaudy tie. He sat down.

"I get you a drink?" the Arab asked.

"Thank you, but I have one waiting," Granby replied, nodding towards the bar counter so as to indicate that he must get back to it soon.

"I understand," Ahmed said. "So down to business, eh! Isn't that what you English say?" He smiled broadly.

Granby nodded.

"I represent Iraq," the Arab went on, the smile fading now and his voice dropping as he leaned across the table.

Granby sat up at that. Iraq? Now what did Iraq want with a second-rate arms dealer? An alarm bell sounded deep inside his head.

"We have learned that you have sourced a nuclear missile for our Muslim brothers in Zawanda. No. Please do not deny it," he said forcefully, placing a finger across his lips in emphasis as Granby, shocked into rebuttal, opened his mouth to speak. "We know it to be true and wish only to assist our Zawandan Brothers."

Granby wished now that he'd accepted that drink. "Assist Zawanda?" he repeated vacuously.

"Yes. Of course." The Arab was exuding sincerity. "It is our desire that Zawanda purchase two systems. One for them and one for us. And as a gesture of goodwill we will pay for both." He paused to allow for full assimilation.

Granby glanced around surreptitiously. Discussing openly the purchase of two nuclear weapons across a table in a public bar seemed to him, to say the least of it, incongruous. He stared at the man opposite.

"You can't be serious," he said hopefully. "Iraq is sanctioned and monitored by the UN. How could you possibly get a nuclear device into your country?"

The man hardly hesitated. "That is our problem" he said tersely, then relented. "No, I'm sorry. Of course you are entitled to know. We need your cooperation and must be honest with you. You're right; we could not bring such a thing into Iraq directly. But a few flights in and out of Zawanda would probably go unnoticed, particularly if we are shipping, say, vaccines. We are permitted to import medicines for our children. It can be arranged, believe me, and we will see to it that Zawanda is not involved in anything that can be construed as illegal. Firstly, though, there is the matter of the principle and an agreement. President Hussein hopes that President Zawutu will not refuse Iraq's generosity and thereby risk our country's displeasure."

Granby looked up sharply at the implication, only to see his table companion nodding slowly in reinforcement. He stared back boldly despite the acid multiplying and sloshing around in his poor abused stomach. This bloody nuclear nonsense was getting far too convoluted for his liking. He could actually feel the stress building like a tourniquet around his chest. It had been bad enough at the beginning when Freddie had first mooted the scheme, but now, with Iraq demanding to be involved, the Russki waiting for news and himself the only negotiator, things were suddenly becoming very dangerous indeed. Why the hell had he listened to Freddie in the first place?

He shuddered and glanced back over his shoulder to where his chums were gathered at the bar. The contrast between the cheerful ordinariness just a few feet from where he sat and the almost tangible tension now apparent at the table was hard to believe. His friends wouldn't believe it, that was for sure.

"I'll convey your wishes to President Zawutu," he said, turning back to face the Iraqi, panic momentarily contained.

"Meet me here tomorrow at the same time," the Iraqi said. "You can contact President Zawutu in the meantime and bring me an answer?" He smiled broadly again. "Are you sure I can't get you a drink?"

Granby shook his head. "Better get back," he said, glancing meaningfully over his shoulder at the bar.

"Until tomorrow then."

Granby watched him leave, then left himself. "Your change, Dickie," someone called after him, but he was too immersed in the developing drama to notice.

Back at the flat he threw off his coat, poured a large whisky and sat pondering the complications that were now scuttling out of the woodwork in their hundreds.

★ ★ ★

The man in the car down the street made a note in his notebook: "Subject returned 2100".

"He can't have been thirsty," his companion quipped as he slid into the passenger seat. "Didn't touch a drop. Talked to an Arab gent then left, pale as a ghost. Something frightened him, I'd say."

"Hmm" the driver said. "He ought to be shitting himself. Fancy a burger? There's a place round the corner."

★ ★ ★

Granby took up the phone and held it for a moment before dialling. "Hullo Freddie," he said when Zawutu finally picked up the direct line. "I've some very bad news for you." There was no point beating about the bush.

"Not more," Zawutu said with a huge sigh. He had just come from a shower with Uudi with all its excitement and protracted sexual engagement, and he was physically tired.

"Afraid so," Granby pressed on. "I'm not sure I should talk about this over the phone, but we only have until this time tomorrow. Does your Consul have secure communications?"

"An old scrambler, that's all. No cypher or code machines."

"Well, that's better than nothing. What's his number and address?"

"He's here in Zawanda, Dickie. Don't you remember?"

"Granby clicked his tongue. "Of course. But surely there's someone at his home who can let me use the kit?"

"Look, I'll get Simbli to ring his wife and tell her to expect you," Zawutu offered. "Here's the address." He read it out from a slip handed to him by his aide. "You're frightening the life out of me," he went on.

"That makes two of us," Granby said. "Talk to you soon." He swept up his coat again, found the car keys and went out into the night.

The car started and he reversed out of the parking space and onto the street. There he pulled into the kerb whilst he consulted the London A to Z, then set off for Battersea. The surveillance car fell in behind.

At Simbli's house he was received with some sense of urgency by the eldest son, who led him to his father's study and pointed to a bulky red phone unit on the desk. "Scrambler," he said succinctly and departed.

Granby picked it up, dialled, got through and asked what he should do next.

"Press the bloody S button," Zawutu replied sharply. "Thought you were an engineer!"

Granby, too preoccupied to take umbrage, did as he was bid. There was a crackling sound, then the line cleared.

"Can you hear me?" he asked.

"Clear as a bell," Zawutu assured him. "Now, what's all this about?"

Granby held back for a moment. What he had to say was too bizarre for words, but it was real enough.

"Your damned missile is what it's about," he began accusingly. "The whole bloody melting pot has escalated right out of control."

Zawutu frowned. "Don't tell me the suppliers won't accept our withdrawal?"

"Your withdrawal, if you don't mind," Granby reminded him. "No. It's much worse. I've been approached by a diplomat, or at least I think that's what he was. Represented Iraq, he said. He insisted you buy at least two Big Boys and give one to Iraq. They'll pay for both. Generous of them, eh?"

"Insisted? Insisted?" Zawutu barked down the phone. Then he quietened as the full import penetrated. "You're kidding me, Dickie. Christ, I never wanted one of the damned things, let alone two. This just won't do."

Granby hardly noticed the Christian expletive. "I wish I was kidding," he said. "And before you tell me to tell them to get stuffed, let me caution you that the offer comes with threats. Threats that to my mind make it virtually impossible for you to refuse. Get Iraq a nuke or else, that's pretty well how it was put to me."

"What in Allah's name did you say?" Zawutu asked, reverting to Islam and trying to sound reasonable at the same time despite the thunder in his head.

"That I'd consult with you, of course."

"I see. Well, perhaps you'd better do that then out here. Maybe together we can conjure up a way out of this." He ran his hand across his brow and was surprised at how damp it felt. "It never rains but it pours," he told Granby, recalling the proverb from his Cambridge days.

"God, what a mess!"

"Ah well, about my coming out, there's another problem. As I said when I first rang you, you only have until tomorrow evening to decide."

There followed a long silence. Then Zawutu spoke bravely. "What happens, I wonder, if I say no?"

Granby snorted down the phone. "I wouldn't even contemplate it," he said. "Iraq can cause you enormous grief. Saddam Hussein has terrorists all over the place, and what if he supports Ingabe?"

Zawutu thought about that for a moment. "Yes, you're right," he said. "But I need time to weigh this up and sort a few things out."

Granby frowned. Sort what out, he wondered? The play was already set and well into the second act.

"There is no time," he said impatiently. "The sorting's already been done in Iraq. It's my neck on the block, remember, so I reckon I should have a say."

"Of course, Dickie," Zawutu replied in a more conciliatory tone. "What have you in mind?"

"I reckon we should agree in principle and then claim that the Russian contact is unavailable, that I won't be able to place the order until he shows up. If you go along with that I'll tell the Iraqi tomorrow."

Zawutu frowned. He realized that Dickie was in the firing line, but this was Zawanda they were discussing. Nevertheless, there appeared to be no alternative.

"OK" he said reluctantly. "You go ahead with that. Meanwhile, we'll try to fathom a way out of it here."

Granby had been thinking and a glimmer of a solution had formed in his brain. "Freddie, I've an idea. You never actually wanted the weapon, did you? So you'll have no use for the one Iraq is offering to pay for. Why don't we offload both the weapons to the Iraqis and claim the cash equivalent of one of them for your trouble and generosity. How's that sound?"

Zawutu hesitated, then exclaimed: "Brilliant, Dickie! But can you actually negotiate it?" His own inclination had been to stonewall the Iraqis until he found a way round the dilemma, but Dickie's idea was better.

"We can but try, but there's no avoiding the main problem. You're going to have to accept a few dicey flights in and out of Zawanda, I'm afraid."

Zawutu hardly paused. "I expect we can manage a few surreptitious flights through New London Airport, unnoticed, or at least disguised," he said cautiously.

Granby coughed. "Of course, if it comes off you'll have more than enough to pay me the balance of what you owe me."

"Do this for me and it's yours out of the proceeds," Zawutu replied without hesitation.

* * *

At 0030 the pilot of the leading C130 began his descent into New London Airport. Hawthorn sat looking forward at nothing. A pattern of lights could be seen well to the left – New London, he assumed – but in front, a black space.

During the flight he had moved among his command, familiarising himself with key personnel. He knew a bit about Jimmy Harwell's background and concentrated first on his 2ic, Captain Butler, and the three Platoon Commanders.

Butler had come up through the ranks, been RSM of Hawthorn's Regiment until his commissioning two years ago. Hawthorn had chosen him, against fierce opposition by the regimental CO, because of his active service experience; Falklands and The Gulf. In his estimation one couldn't have a better man at your side than a good ranker who'd been under fire.

The Subalterns were much of a muchness. Three good lads, eager and excited at the prospect of serving overseas in the relative smallness of a Company Group. Hawthorn's reputation had preceded him and there had been competition for the three junior appointments. Lieutenants Harkness and Williams and Second Lieutenant Phil Storey had been chosen and now considered themselves extremely lucky to be where they were. Hawthorn had spent a little time with each of them on the way out and was satisfied with what he found. They seemed to have a grip on their platoons and knew their stuff.

The black expanse out front seemed to stretch forever.

"Where's the bloody airfield?" Hawthorn called to Squadron Leader Hughes, piloting the aircraft.

"Blacked out," the co-pilot shouted back. "We're on instruments, if you can call it that. Their radar isn't the best in the world. Landing lights at two hundred feet if we're lucky."

"Sod this cloak and dagger stuff," Hawthorn remarked to Butler sitting alongside.

At two hundred feet the runway suddenly appeared between two strips of flickering lights and Hawthorn could swear he heard loud sighs of relief from the flight deck.

On the ground, Moi stood outside the departure building watching the first of the RAF C130s touch down. Three more followed in quick succession, the last one triggering the shutdown of the main runway lights. Only faint blue taxi lights remained for the crews to follow. Then a 'Follow Me' truck came out and took up a position in front of Hawthorn's plane, leading it to a parking spot near a pair of massive steel-wired gates which gave access to the main road.

Brakes squealed, the airframe sighed forward and settled back, then the ramp opened. A lone figure appeared, paused to look around, then continued down to the hard standing. Behind him the three other aircraft were taxiing in.

Moi stepped forward and saluted. "Major Hawthorn?" he enquired civilly.

Hawthorn returned the salute, nodded, and took a moment to compare the man before him with the photographs he'd been shown. The pictures had been immensely flattering, he decided, but perhaps the diffuse lighting here on the airfield only made it seem so.

"We have transport ready for you, your men and the weapons," Moi informed him in only slightly broken English. "You will be billeted with our Second Eshanti Regiment in New London Barracks and the President will see you personally the day after tomorrow."

Hawthorn smiled to himself at the brusqueness. He'd been warned about this little fellow and responded accordingly. Maintaining a strictly professional visage he said a curt "Thank you, Major," and turned to his second in command, loitering on the ramp.

"OK. Everybody off. Unload the kit and vehicles, but leave Jimmy's stuff for his chaps to deal with. What about your weapons?" he asked Moi.

"I have men ready to unload them," Moi said, waving forward a group of Zawandan soldiers.

"They're in the last aircraft," Hawthorn explained to the young Zawandan officer in charge.

Suddenly all the airfield lights went out, plunging the whole area into total darkness, lit only by the sidelights of the vehicle convoy waiting to take on its load, and the few British Land Rovers and three-tonners already on the tarmac.

Concealed in the secondary growth on edge of the Ulu, a lone Ushkuu observer had witnessed the landings through a less-than-effective night sight and mentally recorded the disembarkation of troops and a number of cases which, he mistook for their equipment. The bulk of the new weapons were in the rear aircraft just commencing unloading, and in his haste the Ushkuu spy did not wait to count those.

Moi knew someone from Ingabe's lot would be out there, but Zawutu had ordered him not to interfere. "Let them see the British arrive," Mutti had said. "Give them something to think about."

As soon as the four Hercules were clear of soldiers and payload and had laboriously refuelled from 44-gallon drums using hand pumps, they taxied in line to the end of the runway, led again by the 'Follow Me' truck, which continued to the end of the strip and parked there in order to indicate with its roof light that most critical point, the outer threshold. There would be no other lights to assist the take-off.

Squadron Leader Hughes spooled up his engines and released the brakes. He had taken off in almost total darkness many times before. Much easier than landing, he always said. One was, after all, already on the ground. He lifted off in plenty of time to clear the truck and the fence beyond and set a heading straight for Lyneham. By full dawn New London airport had been restored to its sleepy old self, the Ushkuu observer, Hawthorn and Moi's vehicle convoy long gone.

The journey to New London Barracks took just over an hour. Moi peeled off early into the city, leaving one officer from the 2nd to guide Hawthorn in. Inside the gates a Regimental policeman waved the convoy to a hard standing area in front of which was what looked like a row of garages. Hawthorn climbed down.

"Major Hawthorn?" a round-faced, tubby Eshanti officer enquired, saluting punctiliously. "Major Abulu. Second in Command of 2nd Eshanti Regiment. Welcome to Zawanda."

Hawthorn thanked him and asked about the men's billets. Abulu waved forward a sergeant, who took no time at all in allocating waiting guides to each element of Hawthorn's force and supervising their dispersal to a line of basha huts across the other side of the parade ground.

"I think they'll find them comfortable" Abulu said as the last column departed. "And your quarters are this way," he added with a smile that sparkled in the camp street lights.

The two set off in a different direction from the men, towards the officers' quarters, and on the way Abulu chattered incessantly, leaving little room for more than a yes or no in reply; mostly he asked about the UK and specifically about Aldershot, where he had once attended a course.

"Here we are," he said finally, throwing open the door to a corner room along an open veranda.

Hawthorn blinked when he saw it. It was more like a hotel suite than anything he had ever been used to at home.

"This is mine?" he asked, flabbergasted.

"All of it."

Abulu led him round inside. There was a bedroom, a sitting room and an en suite bathroom with separate shower. "Colonel's accommodation," Abulu explained. President Zawutu ordered it for you."

Private Jimmy Smith, Hawthorn's batman, had trailed along behind.

"Shall I unpack, sir?" he enquired, his eyes everywhere.

"Ah, yes," Abulu added. "Your batman's room is right next door." He pointed. "And your officers are all along the veranda."

Hawthorn nodded. He told Smith, "See to yourself first. Then you can put my kit away." He turned to Abulu. "Can we see the men's accommodation now?"

It all looked very satisfactory once he got there, unexpectedly so in fact. Typically tropical. It comprised attap bashas with plenty of ventilation and quite sanitary looking ablutions; four men to a partitioned area, and Hawthorn found them all laughing and stowing their kit. He spoke to the

Corporals, warning them of the fire risk in such conditions. "Like living in a haystack that has never seen rain," he reminded them.

The Platoon officers were very properly moving about, seeing to their men, and Butler, the 2ic, moved tirelessly between them, accompanied by the CSM. A Zawandan NCO also tagged along; his job was to show the British senior NCOs their quarters in the Sergeants' Mess when they had finished. Hawthorn was pleased, and said so.

"See you in the mess, then," Major Abulu said, saluting smartly. "Breakfast is at six." He then set off for his own bed, already composing the hyperbole he would pass on to his inquisitive colleagues about the new arrivals. The 2nd's new CO, Lieutenant Colonel M'Nango, was elsewhere tonight.

Hawthorn did another round of the OR's accommodation, chatting to the men as they settled in, and finally made tracks for his own lavishly-appointed rooms, embarrassingly lavish in fact, but he could live with that. On the way round he had told the officers and the CSM to gather in his suite as soon as they were free, which occurred some fifteen minutes later.

"Gentlemen," he began as soon as the last officer arrived. "We start work at once. Reveille here is five thirty, that's an hour and a half away roughly. No one gets to bed, so I hope you and the men managed forty winks on the aircraft."

The Platoon Commanders mumbled noises that sounded like "Yes, sir."

"Very well. By 0600 I want the weapons trucks unloaded, the cases checked and a random selection of the contents inspected by the REME armourers. You see to that," he instructed Butler. "Meanwhile I'll find out where the magazine is. Any questions?"

Butler spoke. "The cookhouse, sir, and our HQ? When will we be given the locations?"

"Before you need them," Hawthorn said. "We'll need late breakfasts for everyone, assuming our cooks are permitted into the dining hall and there are rations for us. You can check on that as well," he told Butler.

"Anything else?" There was nothing. "Thank you gentlemen. Let's get on with it then."

The meeting broke up, leaving Hawthorn alone to take a shower and check that his batman was comfortable in the adjacent servants' quarters before heading off to find the 2nd's duty officer to ask him the whereabouts of the camp magazine and whether it could store the number of weapons transhipped?

★ ★ ★

Granby found Ahmed seated at the same table in the hostelry. "You have news for me?" the Arab asked without ceremony.

Granby sat down opposite as before. "The deal is on," he said, equally brusquely. "With conditions. Iraq pays Zawanda the equivalent of one missile in cash. You take everything and President Zawutu agrees to tranship the purchase, whatever its size, but tranship only. There can be no question of storage inside Zawanda, or delay for any reason. Straight in and out again."

"Agreed," Ahmed said without demur. "I leave the details to you. Zawanda's money will be placed in a bank in whatever country and under whichever name President Zawutu requires. This will happen as soon as the systems, however many there are, leave Zawandan airspace."

"No," Granby said boldly, the arms negotiator in him automatically taking over. "I believe a deposit of at least one third would be appropriate, and another third on arrival of the weapons in Zawanda with the balance once the cargo leaves Zawandan airspace, as you suggest. The suppliers also want something up front as a gesture of good faith, you see."

Ahmed smiled. "You should have been an Arab, Mr Granby."

Granby hardly viewed that as a compliment, coming from an Iraqi.

"Yes, maybe, but what do you say?"

"One quarter up front and one eighth on arrival. The remainder on clearing your airspace."

Granby gazed hard at the man opposite. It was clear that he would obtain no further concessions.

"Very well," he said. "But if no period payments are received Zawanda reserves the right to dispose of the hardware as it sees fit."

Ahmed reached out a hand. "The British way, then. Let's shake on it. We can hardly put it in writing." He chuckled. "A drink on it too. I'll have a Scotch. Oh by the way, would you know whether President Zawutu has agreed to our offer of a diplomatic exchange?"

Granby shrugged. "I know nothing about that" he said, and made a note to ask.

* * *

"I told you he was lying about the missile," Jameson said as he handed Beauchamp the latest Int Rep. Beauchamp ran his eye over the page devoted to Zawanda and frowned.

"The bloody fool. What does he think he's playing at?"

"More to the point, who's paying the piper? Jameson added significantly. "Zawutu can't be doing this on his own."

"We'd better find out, then," Beauchamp said. "Have a word with Simon Battersbee at MI6, and I'll brief the PM."

Jameson nodded and for the millionth time ran his eyes round the Minister's office; at the gallery oils and prints displayed on the walls, the exquisite furnishings, the elegance of the whole. One day, he promised himself.

"Where can I reach you?" he enquired from the door.

"I'll call you," Beauchamp told him.

The PM frowned deeply when shown the Int Rep. He had been closeted with his Private Secretary going through his replies for today's PM's questions session when Beauchamp had arrived at Number 10 demanding to see him. No one had advised him of the earlier phone call asking for this meeting. His staff were afraid to disturb him, so, unbriefed as he was, the visit and its purpose came as a bit of a shock.

"I hope it isn't already out of hand, Henry," he said, looking up into Beauchamp's face. "I'll have President Clayton on my tail as soon as his people get a sight of this, so let's get our fingers out and find some answers before that happens."

But he was too late. The red phone rang stridently just as Beauchamp was about to close the door.

"That's the Americans now, I guess!" Masters threw at him peevishly. I'll get back to you."

He lifted the handset. "Prime Minister," he said, buzzing for his Private Secretary at the same time.

"Hold for the President, please Prime Minister," a detached female voice intoned. There was a second or two of silence, then the stentorian tones of Orville Clayton came booming down the phone.

"Prime Minister?"

The PM said it was he, and wondered impatiently why the Yanks were so fastidious with protocol at first and then deteriorated into the most awful slang. At least that had always been his experience of their dialogue.

The PPS popped his head round the door at that instant and Masters waved him urgently in. "President Clayton," he mouthed silently, pointing at the phone, then indicated the nearest chair.

"Well, hell, Clive," the President articulated. "We thought you had this Zawanda business under control, and now we find Zawutu has actually made a deal. What in God's name is going on?"

"I wish I knew," Masters conceded. "We got the same intelligence ourselves only a few hours ago and haven't had time to evaluate it yet."

He grabbed a printed sheet offered by his PPS.

"Just come in from the Foreign Office," the secretary hissed.

"Orville, I've just received a preliminary report." He quickly ran his eyes down the document. "Zawutu appears to have done it, against the odds. We've had the arms dealer fellow, Granby, under surveillance, physical and electronically I'm told, ever since he returned from Zawanda. Apart from a couple of meetings with the spurious Iraqi Business Attaché working out of the Saudi Arabian Embassy he hasn't been anywhere, made any suspicious calls or even sneezed without us knowing about it. We do not like the Iraq connection, however."

"Well if you don't know, and my people say they don't either, Zawutu must be cleverer than either of us give him credit for," replied Clayton. "I hope you've taken that on board over there and adjusted your approach accordingly. And by the way, Iraq? I don't like the sound of that. How the hell did Iraq become implicated?"

"I don't know that they are," Masters said frankly. "All we know is that Granby has met this Iraqi a couple of times. Maybe he's pitching for a weapons order for when UN sanctions are lifted."

"And maybe not. An Iraqi meeting with a man who has undoubtedly been involved in negotiating the purchase of at least one nuclear weapon is kinda scary. Hope to God there's no connection Clive, for all our sakes."

"I shouldn't think so Orville," Masters replied emolliently. "Saddam can hardly draw breath without the UN monitors knowing about it."

"Maybe, but Zawutu must be stopped anyway and this nightmare prevented from spreading. It's a Commonwealth matter, Clive, which we left to you, but it's gone ape as far as we can see. I cannot allow a nuclear weapon of any type to reach Zawanda, so please be effective. I don't want to be seen to be interfering, but as I say, at all costs those weapons must not reach Zawanda, and let's see if by working together our security services can't get a fix on this Iraq business."

The PPS scribbled a note and slid it across the PM's desk. It read "See if Clayton can lay some weight on Byelorussia. MI6 say that's the source."

Masters nodded. "I don't think you need to worry about Iraq, Orville, but I wonder if you could perhaps do something to assist me with the main business, Zawanda? Could you lean on Byelorussia? My intelligence people tell me the weapons are coming from there."

"The CIA is of the same opinion," Clayton concurred. "We've been expecting something like this for a while now, but Zawanda, for God's sake! Who'd have believed it? Anyway, I'll see what we can do, but a direct approach isn't on so don't expect too much in that direction. Russia is the best conduit for what we want to achieve, but the Bear is not on the best of terms with some of her old Soviet Union states. She's ripped off too many of them. And, of course, Byelorussia is naturally at the top of the discontented list. On the plus side, Byelorussia has no economy to speak of and is still receiving a small aid package from its old Russian masters. Perhaps Yeltsin can do something with that. But you know all this. Just keep us informed from your side. The situation must be resolved and I expect – cancel that, I hope – to hear something positive very soon."

Masters bristled. "There is nothing for America to be concerned about," he said huffily. "As you say this is a Commonwealth matter. I'll be in touch." Then, unwilling to listen to any further carping from across the Atlantic, he abruptly put down the phone and addressed his PPS.

"Get the Chief of the Defence Staff over here, and Henry Beauchamp too. I'll not be lectured to by the Americans. I want this nonsense stopped once and for all, and with absolute guarantees. Let's find out what the military and diplomatic services have to offer, shall we?"

CHAPTER THIRTEEN

Ushkuu commanders at every level kept vigil on their synchronised wrist watches and at precisely 0630 the assault on Qurundi began. 1st Ushkuu regiment, in garrison, had not felt the need to put out sentries or outposts, there being, after all, nothing to fear, or so the senior Eshanti officer in residence had believed. Those Ushkuu officers who had secretly been privy to Ingabe's plans - most of them, as it happened - immediately mutinied and took the entire Ushkuu complement along with them. They didn't try to control the wild men who at once began executing the few Eshanti officers serving with the regiment, pleading afterwards that nothing could have prevented it.

Eshanti Other Ranks fared better. They were rounded up, given a ritualistic beating and locked in police and military barracks under guard. Ingabe had ordered it so. The civilian population, meanwhile, being mostly Ushkuu, debouched en masse to welcome Ingabe's troops into the city, and so Qurundi fell with hardly a shot being fired.

Ingabe could not believe his luck at just how easy it had been. Just a few short hours to capture a whole city! So overcome was he with his success that in a fit of euphoric megalomania he changed his plans on the hoof and decided to advance on New London without delay. His staff counselled against it, although the chiefs applauded it. He went ahead with it anyway, conveniently abandoning his own recent tribal meeting arguments against precipitate major action.

Zawutu could do nothing. The New London regiments were under strength and had no experience yet with their new weapons. The army's Ushkuu contingent had become restless and unreliable, though outside Qurundi not yet overtly mutinous, which was worse. They remained under discipline, but like a fuse of unknown length they smouldered away unpredictably.

Hawthorn carried on as normal, ignoring the tension and polarization taking place around him. His only concession to the situation was to order the carrying of loaded weapons at all times and instructions to shoot if shot at.

After a great deal of effort Zawutu eventually managed to assemble one understrength battalion made up entirely of Eshantis hastily thrown together from New London garrison regiments. He gave command of this hotchpotch to the 2nd's CO, Lieutenant Colonel M'Nango, with orders to march on Qurundi with what he had, well short of a full fighting regiment.

Just short of Qurundi M'Nango encountered the van, then the main force, of Ingabe's rebels advancing rapidly towards New London. A ragged engagement ensued in which the Eshantis found themselves outgunned and outmanoeuvred. M'Nango had no alternative but to withdraw, but he did it slowly, forcing the Ushkuu to fight bitterly for every inch of territory and take many casualties on the way.

Ingabe beat his breast when he heard. "Zawutu knew what he was doing when he gave command to Kwaka M'Nango," he spat out angrily. "He's good, he'll do his best to slow us down so that we do not get to New London ahead of the British."

This notion that the British were bound to come to reinforce Hawthorn's Company had been fermenting in the back of his mind for some time now, encouraged by snippets of intelligence supplied by Zawanda's Honorary Consul to Great Britain, Abu Simbli, who was of Ushkuu blood. But this was the first time he'd spoken of it openly. His solitary thoughts, accentuated by the heat and frustration of the current action, had made the prospect of British intervention appear more certain than ever. His dream of power was fading in proportion to the rise of these anxieties. Now he panicked and called forward his reserves from obscure villages where they were still under regimental training, and green.

His Chief of Staff, a Sandhurst-trained Major, advised against it. "It is too soon, they're not ready and we'll have nothing left," he cautioned wisely, but in his dark mood Ingabe chose to ignore him.

The startling order was received by the rear echelon commander and disseminated to the various host villages. Soon two columns of Ushkuu reinforcements formed up and started out along the only two hard routes to New London; the aim was to be up with the main force by nightfall the next day.

About two miles into their march they were suddenly halted by trees felled across the roads and driven into cover by ferocious small arms fire. The untested recruits panicked and ran. The officers, unable to stop them by shouting, drew their weapons and fired indiscriminately, killing and maiming until discipline was restored and a defence organised.

A radio report of the incident reached Ingabe one hour later.

"How the hell did M'Nango get behind us in that strength?" the stunned Ushkuu leader yelled furiously, his already black mood degenerating rapidly. No one dared answer. "Send patrols back," he bellowed. "I want to know numbers and the extent of M'Nango's intervention back there."

Nothing was said about the killing of Ushkuu reserves by their own officers. Such a thing was only to be expected when troops deserted under fire. Obliged now to protect his rear and flanks, Ingabe could do little else but relax his unrelenting forward pressure on M'Nango. This in turn presented the Eshanti Commander with time to dig in and prepare a serious, static defence. Uncertainty reigned in both camps; neither commander understood exactly what was going on.

"Sir," Ingabe's adjutant said hesitantly, approaching him some hours later; Ingabe had been as dangerous as a wounded lion since the first radio message. "We have a prisoner, but he's near to death."

Ingabe banged his fist on the table. "At last, some action!" he said as he rose to follow the young Captain outside to where an Eshanti tribesman lay on the ground, untended and bleeding profusely from a stomach wound. The injured man groaned, but the shock had not yet fully worn off and the real agony begun.

"What has he said?" Ingabe asked the sergeant standing over him.

"Nothing, sir," the sergeant replied.

"Help him speak" Ingabe ordered, and the sergeant stamped down with a heavy boot on the man's wound, at which the captive screamed and fainted.

"Wake him," Ingabe said.

A bucket of water roused some semblance of consciousness and Ingabe knelt beside the poor fellow. "There's medical aid for you if you answer my questions," he said kindly.

The man groaned.

"How many Eshanti behind us?" The sergeant raised his foot menacingly. "Two hundred!" the man screamed.

Ingabe looked up sharply at the officers now gathered round. "Impossible!" he said. "The man's lying. M'Nango can't have many more than that overall."

"Not M'Nango," the prisoner groaned hastily as the sergeant's boot descended menacingly to within an inch of the bloody hole in his stomach. "Major Moi."

"Moi? What's Moi got to do with it?" Ingabe repeated, frowning with disbelief. He leaned closer to catch the man's fading words.

"Eshanti warriors from the villages. Major Moi brings them to fight."

"Nonsense," Ingabe said, nodding to the sergeant, who ground his boot heel on the man's stomach.

"It's true, master!" the man screamed. "Not M'Nango, Moi."

Ingabe studied the man's face. "It is true then," he muttered to himself, the unfairness of it welling up in him. The man heard and nodded with all his remaining strength.

"Put him out of his misery," Ingabe then ordered as he rose to his feet and walked away. A single shot resounded behind him in the still evening air.

Back in the command post he sat down heavily on his canvas chair. His Chief of Staff stood hesitantly at the entrance.

"For Allah's sake come in," Ingabe said impatiently.

Encouraged, the Chief of Staff entered. "What do we do about Moi?" he asked cautiously. He had no intention of raising the question of the ignored advice that had got them into this fix.

"In the first place I don't believe he has two hundred men," Ingabe said, thinking more calmly now. "If we squeeze him between the reserves and a unit from our main force he'll quit or ooze out of the way like pressed toothpaste. He can't possibly have the strength or firepower to resist an organised attack in strength."

But he was mistaken again. Moi was, if nothing else, a bush warrior with a Sandhurst-trained knowledge of guerrilla tactics. Craftily, he had exploited the President's wedding announcement to persuade Eshanti tribal chiefs to support his flag. Taboo, he'd cried. Eshanti cannot marry Ushkuu. The chiefs had agreed and given up their best warriors to him. He now had command of some two hundred and fifty Eshanti warriors, some of whom preferred to fight close in with spears and bows to great effect, but the majority of whom were properly armed with modern weapons acquired from Unita.

Moi had not shied from doing a deal with the Angolan rebels on the promise of safe havens on the Zawandan side of the border once he was in power. The fact that an identical arrangement had already been made with the Ushkuu only demonstrated that Unita had very sensibly backed both horses. Masters of the bush, Moi's irregulars did not conform with Ingabe's plan. They did not fade away when squeezed from both sides, nor did they capitulate. Instead they harassed and struck by night preventing the reserves from moving forward to join the main body and at the same time successfully drawing to the rear a substantial part of the Ushkuu main army facing M'Nango.

When the Eshanti Colonel learned of Ingabe's problems, he believed implicitly in the suggested cause. Something significant had certainly halted the Ushkuu push towards the capital, and Moi's reputed intervention fitted the case like a glove. He radioed the astonishing news back to Zawutu. "He's got a small army back there," he said excitedly.

Zawutu turned to Major Hawthorn. "You heard that," he said. "Josi Moi, he met you at the airport. He was my Minister without Portfolio until he dropped out of sight a while ago. And all this time he's been recruiting round the villages. Probably to challenge me for the Presidency."

He saw Hawthorn's raised eyebrows and smiled. "It's expected here in Zawanda, a challenge. But never before by a member of one's own tribe. That is new, if it comes about."

"Thank you Kwaka," said Zawutu into the radio. "Make the most of the reprieve. Hold Joshua Ingabe for as long as you can. We'll get reinforcements to you soon. Out."

Hawthorn waited until Zawutu had laid down the microphone. "But in that case, why would Moi fight on your side?" he asked.

"Because he hates the Ushkuu more than he does me," Zawutu said cynically.

Hawthorn nodded. "Makes sense I suppose. Do you think he will agree to a unified command until the Ushkuu affair is settled?"

"Probably not," Zawutu said, shaking his head. "I'm afraid I've alienated him beyond redemption. He thinks I'm too soft on the Ushkuu and shouldn't be marrying an Ushkuu maiden."

Hawthorn nodded casually again. The President's wedding plans were of no interest to him.

"Still, he's doing you a favour by taking on the Ushkuu and forcing Ingabe to look over his shoulder. Gives you a little more time to organise and train your own people. If Colonel M'Nango can hold Ingabe's main thrust and Major Moi can be persuaded to accept some measure of coordination, you should be in good shape to crush this uprising. Pity Moi is so stubborn."

"With your help I might not need him," Zawutu said. "Which is why I sent for you. I'm sorry our original meeting became waylaid by this Ushkuu business, but now you are here, apart from welcoming you to Zawanda, which may not be the best place to be as things are, I wanted to discuss the future. If matters get any worse I shall assume personal command, which includes you and your British troops. The Ushkuu will think twice before challenging your people."

Hawthorn hesitated for a moment; the prospect of joining in sounded very attractive, but he had his orders.

"I regret, sir," he said formally, "but that's not possible, I'm afraid. I received specific orders from London only this morning forbidding me from becoming actively involved. I should never have asked the MoD in the first place, but orders are orders. Once you've asked and been told no that's an end to it."

Zawutu looked crestfallen. "But you'd like to help?" he pressed, having noted a hint of disappointment in Hawthorn's voice.

Hawthorn smiled. "But as I say, orders."

"Then I don't understand your orders. Your Foreign Secretary assured me that you would act to stiffen my army. His words exactly."

"I don't think the Foreign Office has any say in that respect," Hawthorn explained. "It's the Secretary of Defence who lays down the rules of engagement. The FO is only the sponsor, so to speak."

"But you're here, you can't stay neutral," Zawutu insisted, raising his eyebrows quizzically.

"True," Hawthorn went on. "My orders are to assist the legal head of state, which is you, but only with training and advice. I serve only you, so in that respect I'm on your side, but not under direct command, sir," he reiterated firmly.

Zawutu frowned. "Maybe I'll talk to your seniors in London. Clarify this, or get them to change their minds."

"If only you could," Hawthorn said sincerely, knowing how remote such an outcome was. It made him remember the other 'eyes-only' signal he'd received that morning. His small intelligence group had almost frothed at the mouth when they had seen it. "Could you drop something into the conversation when you're with the President?" one of the now admitted MI6 chaps had asked. He had shaken his head, but now he reconsidered. Zawutu seemed receptive enough.

"What about this fellow Granby?" he opened casually. "Isn't he an adviser of some sort? A weapons man, I believe. Where's he when he's needed?"

Zawutu looked up sharply at the impertinence. "How do you know about him?" he asked briskly.

"Part of my briefing," Hawthorn admitted. "Richard Granby, arms dealer and adviser to Zawanda, is how it was put to me."

Zawutu scowled, then his face cleared. "Yes, well, he's doing a little job for me in the UK. He'll be here soon."

Hawthorn kept a straight face as he recalled the exact context of the relevant signal: "Granby has dropped out of sight in the UK. Is he in Zawanda?"

"Are you sure he's in the UK?" he asked, rather too quickly.

"Sure? Of course I'm sure," Zawutu replied, his suspicions alerted. "Why do you ask? It's no business of yours."

Hawthorn realized his mistake and shrugged his indifference. "I just thought he might be more useful to you here right now, that's all."

"Well, he isn't here and that's that," Zawutu said curtly, firmly ending that line of conversation. Hawthorn backed off at once.

"Is there anything else, sir?" he enquired.

"Not for the moment, Major. However, I shall be requesting the UK to place you under my command."

Hawthorn saluted and left the room, hoping like hell that Zawutu would succeed, but knowing there was little chance.

★ ★ ★

"Don't be ridiculous. I couldn't ask him outright about nuclear bombs now, could I?" Hawthorn complained later to the MI6 man. "I did learn, however, that Granby is still in the UK. Your people must have misplaced him. Careless, I'd say."

★ ★ ★

Back in the bush, south of New London, Moi continued to delay Ingabe's reserves, hitting hard, disappearing like a puff of smoke on the wind, then attacking again, relentlessly. He had received several presidential messages asking if he would agree to the regular army staff coordinating his group of irregulars, but he was not in this to help the Eshanti traitor. Killing Ushkuu was fun, and the more he killed the less power to Ingabe, even if it did help Zawutu temporarily. But he could not accept the leadership of the man he would eventually usurp, perhaps kill. Even to Moi's twisted mind that seemed dishonest.

In Ingabe's camp the tactical planning meeting had been in progress for an hour now. "As long as he straddles our lines of communication we can't move forward, and each day more regular troops reach M'Nango" Ingabe's Chief of Staff reiterated for the third time, determined to get the message through. And for the third time Ingabe replied: "And each day risks the arrival of more British." He glanced again at the map. "I know the situation, so don't go on about it. I agree Moi must be dislodged soon and I have thought about how. I believe the most effective way is to fight fire with fire."

The CoS shook his head. "A full assault is the only way to defeat him," he said, looking round for support and finding none.

"No," Ingabe told him, aware of the general feeling in the tent. "Order the regiments to select their best hunter warriors, those who know the bush and have hunted it. Give them plenty of firepower and turn them loose on Moi's men. They are not to stand and fight, but to search out, butcher and bolt. They must do this over and over until Moi is so busy defending himself he has no time for anything else."

"It shall be done," the CoS said keenly, eager now to save face.

Ingabe didn't usually embarrass his senior officers in this way and regretted having done so. He felt worse when the CoS felt it necessary to explain himself.

"I just thought it might be quicker to hit him with an orthodox attack" he said. "But your scheme will give that bloody Eshanti pig a taste of his own medicine."

Ingabe smiled. "Quicker, yes, but not as effective. Both plans have equal merit, but I think we can sacrifice speed for certainty in this case."

* * *

Granby flew in from Frankfurt, a place he had reached courtesy of a colleague who had ferried him across the Channel in a small boat usually used to smuggle arms to North Africa, and another friend who had supplied him with a false passport; not unusual tactics in the arms trade.

"Good trip?" Zawutu asked when Granby joined him in what was now called the War Room, a cellar under the Palace.

"Had to be a bit careful," Granby replied. "A few days ago I noticed a tail. Special Branch probably. As soon as you told me that the Right Hon Beauchamp had questioned you about you know what, I figured I'd be in the frame as well. Two men in a car. Too arrogant for their own good, seen too much TV I reckon. I was able to slip them easily when the time came."

"And the deal?"

"Four aircraft, five at most. They'll fly in two complete weapon systems, crated as machinery. The Iraqis only want the warheads, but the vendors won't go for that. It's all or nothing, they say. I don't know what Saddam's going to do about that, but it's going to be complete systems in those planes. Anyway, no one will have access to the contents of the cases until they arrive in Iraq. The flight plan is from Minsk to Namibia with a refuelling stop here, allowing enough time to transfer the weapon crates to Iraqi planes and reload the Russian aircraft with genuine boxes of machinery from the incoming Iraqi aircraft."

" So, four or five planes in and out and the job's done."

"That's about the strength of it, yes," Granby said. "But you'll have to keep that British Major out of the way whilst all this is going on. How are you two getting on anyway?"

Zawutu dismissed the question with a wave of the hand. "It's irrelevant. I didn't want him here, but now he is I'm warming to him. Actually, I wanted him under my command for the duration of the emergency, but the British won't countenance it. Training and advice only, they insist." He smiled wryly. "Mind you, Hawthorn is keen to do more. Could be a useful conduit to the UK actually, and only time will tell how his presence here might be manipulated."

"Not unexpected, though, that the British are reluctant to let him become actively involved" Granby offered, his mind on his own problems. "What about the Ushkuu? Are they likely to make a push for the airport? Be bloody embarrassing if they took it before the Russkies passed through. Ingabe couldn't have chosen a more inauspicious time for his little adventure."

Zawutu frowned. "Well, the strip is vulnerable. It wouldn't take much for Ingabe to reach it with a small force anyway. It's not in his direct line of advance, though, and on the face of it it holds no strategic value for either side as it happens, so perhaps he'll leave it alone. And anyway, Josi Moi is in among the Ushkuu LoC with a small army of guerrillas. He's causing Ingabe more problems than the whole of the regulars put together. With Josi operating where he is, the airport should be safe for now."

Granby accepted the drink Mumbi handed him. "Who's in overall command?" he asked. "Whoever it is will have to ensure the airport is secured until this Iraq deal is concluded."

Zawutu took his own glass and swallowed a large measure. "Field command of the regular army is with Colonel Kwaka M'Nango at the moment" he replied. "Josi Moi is a loose cannon unfortunately, doing his own thing. He won't accept joint command. And anyway, the way things are I expect to take overall command myself before too long. Maybe my awkward friend Josi will conform then. Who was the last English king to lead his troops into battle?"

Granby shrugged. "History was never my subject. But what about Moi? Why is he being so difficult? As if that's anything new."

Zawutu smiled. "He's ignored all my communications and is obviously following an agenda of his own. He wants things his own way, but to achieve that he'll have to come on board sooner or later, you'll see."

Granby nodded. "With your permission, then, I'll start preparing for these flights before Ingabe or Major Hawthorn gets wind of anything. You'll be too busy to handle it yourself, so if you'll give me a letter of authority I'll get started. I have four mil riding on a satisfactory outcome, remember!"

Zawutu laughed. "I won't forget. And I appreciate your offer of help. You know this deal inside out, so you're obviously the best man for the job. I'll issue instructions to those you'll have to deal with, but for God's sake keep it simple and straightforward. A routine refuelling with the cargoes switched after the airport is closed for the night. I'll provide troops for that."

"I'll get some sleep then," Granby said, finishing his drink and rising to his feet. "I'm whacked. I'll start organising things tomorrow."

"One more thing before you go," Zawutu said, rising from his chair in one athletic movement. "Iraq has been pressing for a diplomatic exchange, tried to get it done through Josi Moi, but the Ushkuu put a stop to that. As far as I know, the Iraqi Consul, or whatever he calls himself, is still with Josi. I want it made clear to your Iraqi contact that Zawanda will honour its contract without assistance or policing. There will be no exchange of diplomatic credentials. Beauchamp would immediately smell a rat."

Granby threw out his hands. "That slimy Iraqi bastard said nothing to me about this. I'll enjoy telling him to get lost. Leave it to me."

"Goodnight then, Dickie," Zawutu said, confident in Granby's abilities.

★ ★ ★

Hawthorn was getting tired of the number of signals pouring into his HQ.

"Sitrep on N weapons?"

"Sitrep on Granby?"

"Threat analysis?"

"Do not, repeat not, become embroiled in the civil war."

"We have rejected President Zawutu's request for your direct assistance."

And so it went ad infinitum. Things were difficult enough without the chairbound johnnies in Whitehall bombarding him with stupid questions. Disappointing, though, their refusal to allow him to participate. He should never have asked, of course. But there were more ways of skinning a cat, he thought, smiling to himself. He sat at his desk turning ideas over in his mind, whilst outside his men continued with the crash courses he'd laid on to get more trained Eshantis into the field.

★ ★ ★

NATO radar had been monitoring Byelorussian airspace for years; diligently throughout the Cold War, but rather casually since the wall had come down. Suddenly there came an order for all stations with arcs covering air lanes out of that country to search the skies with maximum vigilance, twenty-four hours a day. The operators of a British station in Northern Germany read and signed the instruction and wondered what it was all about.

Only one of their number missed the briefing. He was on leave. Returned now, he took over his shift at 0200 hours, scanned the log and signed it without questioning the Red Alert status. No one had bothered to explain it to him.

By 0300 he was beginning to get worried about the amount of overlap information pouring into his printer from adjacent stations: 'nothing seen', 'routine internal traffic', 'nothing seen'. Then came the one that really alarmed him: 'bogey in the crease'. The word bogey had not been used since Byelorussia had run exercises along this border, testing NATO's air response by pushing heavy bombers right up to the line. 'In the crease' meant a bogey trying to slip between two radar scans.

He felt his pulse race as he focused his attention on the overlap. There it was. An aircraft. Heavy too. No transponder code. He listened out on the civil wave band for North German Air Traffic Control to interrogate the intruder. On demand, the aircraft squirted its code, apologised and was accepted.

The British operator, curious now, called up the flight plan on his screen: Machinery for Namibia, refuelling in Zawanda. He sighed with relief. Routine.

The printer crackled. He glanced at the message and frowned. Bogey reported as suspicious, the emerging paper roll said.

"For God's sake, what's going on?" he said aloud, scared now. Had war been declared without him knowing? He pressed the buzzer for the Duty Officer.

"What is it, Simpkins?" Captain Rollason said as he rushed into the darkened room, fastening his shirt front as he came.

Simpkins glanced round, apologised for disturbing him, and on being told it was OK ran through the events of the last few minutes.

"Dead right," Rollason said of the neighbouring radar security report. "Did no one tell you we're at red alert over something or other?"

Simpkins shook his head.

"Well we are, and all suspicious aircraft are to be reported."

"But ATC accepted him, sir," Simpkins demurred.

Rollason shook his head admonishingly. "No legitimate flight tries to avoid military radar by flying down the crease, my lad, transponder off and well adrift from established air lanes. You know that." Simpkins nodded glumly. "Never mind, we've got him now," Rollason said, rubbing his hands together and mentally composing a signal for transmission to HQ BAOR.

★ ★ ★

"What now?" Masters complained when Beauchamp interrupted his morning dictation.

"A report from BAOR, Prime Minister. A cargo aircraft has departed Byelorussian air space on course for Africa. North German air traffic control confirm the ultimate destination as Namibia with a refuelling stop in, of all places, Zawanda. Our radar chaps say the pilot tried to avoid military surveillance until he was pegged by German Air Traffic Control and had to show himself."

Masters frowned and waved his secretary from the room. He waited until the door closed, then spoke.

"Is this positive, Henry? Couldn't be a simple pilot error, could it?"

"Our people don't seem to think so" Beauchamp said,

staring firmly down his nose at the PM. "I had thought that Zawutu wouldn't or couldn't do this, but I'm persuaded now."

"The bloody idiot," the PM sighed. "Do the Americans know?"

"I expect so. The report came from NATO," said Beauchamp.

"Better get a signal off to our diplomatic and military people in Zawanda warning them to be on the alert. Meanwhile, I'll call Orville Clayton before he rings me. Can you let me have everything you have on the flight, including our own people's technical assessment?"

Beauchamp nodded. "I have it with me," he said condescendingly. He placed a 'TOP SECRET' file on the PM's desk.

"I'll call you," Masters said brusquely, cutting Beauchamp off from overhearing the exchange with America.

Beauchamp snorted. "Very well, Prime Minister. I hope the President won't be too rough."

Masters opened the file and studied the contents before placing the transatlantic call. The connection was made almost instantaneously, but the President took his time answering it.

"Just been told," he replied to Masters' anxious query. "You beat me to the phone by a millisecond. My people think we should intercept that goddamn plane and force it to land inside NATO territory."

"I think not," Masters said urgently. "It might be exactly what it purports to be, a genuine flight carrying machinery to Namibia. Then what?"

"And I might be the Pope," Clayton said impatiently. "I told you before, America won't allow the export of nuclear weapons from any source."

"But didn't you talk to the Russians about preventing this?" Master's went on, politely shifting the blame. "If you truly believe this delivery to be the one we both fear, then Yeltsin has let us down. I suggest you speak to him again and I'll add my weight if you think it will help. In any event, my people estimate that one aircraft won't be enough. They say there'll have to be at least one or two more. Perhaps we can try to stop those."

Clayton coughed to clear his throat. He did not take kindly to being lectured at by a British Prime Minister and a Conservative one to boot. Nor did he like being criticised for failing to persuade the commies to act.

"The Russians are cold on the idea of interfering in Byelorussia," he said gruffly. "They have enough on their plate with Georgia and Chechnya, they say. Yeltsin suggests I talk directly to Anatole Gorgio, but he doesn't hold out much hope short of threatening military force, which the American people would not tolerate for what is only a suspicion at this stage. Yeltsin is not against us doing something in our own airspace, however, which is why I want to stop that aircraft before it crosses the Mediterranean."

Masters' face tightened. "That would be air piracy," he said firmly. "And not something the UK could condone. We have no proof of delinquency, Orville, and if you recall, there are already British troops in Zawanda and contingency plans to fly in significant reinforcements." He bit his lip at the lie. "Zawutu is up to his neck fighting a tribal war and hasn't the resources to handle the covert importation of rogue missile systems as well." He glanced down at a list of options hastily provided by the MoD and chose the top one. "Our people out there will occupy the airport and intercept the aircraft. That will prevent any future flights landing and leave only the first load on the ground under our control. If it's genuine, we let it go. If not, we confiscate the contents, then let it go."

There was a silence broken only by the American President's breathing. Then: "Very well. It's your pigeon I suppose, but please keep the Pentagon informed. I agree to your plan without prejudice to any action the USA might be forced to take if things go wrong." And with that threat hanging in the air, he rang off.

Masters rang for Jameson. "Get Defence on the phone. Graham Enright himself," he commanded.

★ ★ ★

Within a few hours, an Infantry Brigade of the Rapid Reaction Force had been placed on standby for Zawanda and Hawthorn was reading a signal; the tenth of the day:

Sec Class TOP Secret, EYES ONLY. Priority FLASH.
Time 14.20Z
MILAS Zawanda
Info. Cabinet Office
MS 2
MI 6
MI 10
AG 14
MET 5
USA G1.

One aircraft believed to be carrying BIG BOY en route Namibia. Int expect landing in Zawanda, refuelling and unloading. You are to occupy New London Airport and inspect incoming cargo. Aircraft liveried in Byelorussian colours. Cargo, if suspect, to be confiscated and held for further investigation. Aircraft to be released thereafter.
President Zawutu NOT to be informed and NOT to be consulted.
3 Air portable brigade on standby for Zawanda. If despatched you are to brief the Brigadier and come under command.

Secstate.

Hawthorn read the signal again. The Sigscentre was deserted, standard procedure for the receipt of Eyes Only communications, so he had no need to disguise his feelings. He glanced again at the time signature and cursed. "Why are they always too late?" he complained bitterly.

Zawutu had called only a few minutes before to say that Moi had beaten off an Ushkuu attack on the airfield and now occupied it himself. Could Hawthorn help? He had answered no, for even though he now had orders to occupy the airfield, his subsequent request to take it using necessary force had been denied. To 'occupy' and to 'take' had quite different connotations in military parlance. He should of course signal back, explain the current situation at the airfield and request new orders, pointing out that with Moi occupying the facility the Air Portable Brigade could be faced with an opposed landing.

He called for the Signals Sergeant. "Code this," he said, then dictated a simple sitrep explaining the airport situation and ending with "I say again, request permission to take airfield by force in order to intercept suspect aircraft and clear and hold strip for arrival AP Brigade".

The reply winged back by return. "No change to previous orders. Definitely no aggressive action. Consider Major Moi's occupation sufficient to deter further flights and prevent unloading of nuclear cargo by Zawutu. On despatch of AP Brigade we shall revisit the question of airport security. Has suspect aircraft actually landed Zawanda?"

"How the hell should I know?" Hawthorn exclaimed to himself, staring angrily at the time signature and suspecting the worst.

★ ★ ★

In fact it had landed, over two hours before, observed by Ushkuu scouts who didn't know one aircraft type from another. They reported it as a British arrival.

"Just one plane?" Ingabe had queried, and upon confirmation assumed it to be a late British weapons delivery. He was aware of the small arms deal with Britain. Abu Simbli, Zawandan Consul to Great Britain and now Ushkuu spy, had told him of it.

"We cannot allow Zawutu to get his hands on those new weapons," the CoS said.

"Exactly," Ingabe agreed. "Do we have troops near enough to occupy the airfield and take the weapons for ourselves?"

"Yes," the CoS said, and was ordered to deploy them immediately. A patrol from Moi's guerrilla army observed the movement of Ushkuu troops towards the airport and informed Moi.

"No chance," Moi said determinedly, and set off himself with a sizeable party to intercept. A brisk skirmish ensued which drove the Ushkuu from the scene, but not before the Russian aircraft had been damaged and the crew had fled to the safety of the trees. Moi had them rounded up and persuaded them that he represented the new Zawandan government and would look after them. They were given food and escorted back to his HQ that night.

At about the same time, heavyweight agricultural tractors equipped with long steel ropes rumbled onto the strip and by morning the plane had disappeared. Moi then left a few men in conspicuous positions around the perimeter and withdrew his main force.

★ ★ ★

"What the hell happened?" Zawutu demanded of Granby. "Why was that bloody aircraft left on the tarmac?"

"I didn't want to draw attention to it," Granby explained petulantly. "It was agreed that it would remain there until dark, when your chaps would unload it. I told you that was the plan."

Zawutu ignored this, knowing it was the truth. "And now Moi's got control of it? It hasn't taken off, for instance?"

Granby shook his head. "No, not as far as we know. Have any of your people been down there to take a look?"

"We can't get near it. Moi's on the airfield and the Ushkuu are in the near vicinity. I had hoped that Hawthorn might help, but he's still adamant he's only here to advise. And anyway, it would be stupid to let him anywhere near that plane. So, as I don't have the men to do it myself..."

"...there's nothing to be done," Granby ended for him. "If you can regain control of the airfield I might be able to reschedule the remaining flights, but it means doing it from here. I daren't set foot in Blighty. They'd have me in irons in the twinkling of an eye. And then there's the problem of the first delivery. If that goes missing it means at least one incomplete missile system and the whole damned plot probably compromised. All it needs is one half-intelligent fellow to take a look inside one of those crates and recognise bits of rocket and we're all in trouble. I'd better let the Iraqi know what's happened and try to ring the Russki."

Zawutu acquiesced willingly, glad in a way to be shot of the problem for now. There was nothing he could do anyway.

★ ★ ★

Two more signals came in pestering Hawthorn about the Russian aircraft and finally, in exasperation, he instructed the Signals Sergeant to pull the plug. "Technical fault, OK? And no answering the phones, either. We've radio contact with the President's War Room, yes?"

"Yes sir."

Hawthorn smiled to himself; free at last. He could now exercise the massive authority intrinsic in his orders: "In the event of communication failure you are to act as you see fit in furtherance of your overall objectives".

CHAPTER FOURTEEN

The patrol despatched by de Lancy to recce the presence of an Ushkuu army on the Angolan border never returned. Weeks overdue, de Lancy reluctantly accepted that they were irretrievably lost, overtaken by events. He reported them missing, believed dead, or deserted more like, and turned his attention to other matters, one of which was to take a look at New London airfield. The President had ordered it. "Is there an aeroplane on the tarmac?" he wanted to know.

De Lancy had been surprised to have been tasked with this unusual recce, but accepted it without question. He did, however, wonder to himself where else one would one find an aircraft if not at an airport. Nevertheless, if the President wanted to know, he would find out.

He set about the task with his usual vigour and had lost five men deserted to Moi's irregulars before calling it off and explaining to the President why. "There is little point in losing individual men like this," he said carefully. "The only way is to go in in strength. And why is Major Moi stealing our Eshanti warriors?" he added, genuinely confused by this turn of events.

Zawutu had removed his shirt in the midday heat and his dark skin shone with a fine patina of perspiration. "Moi!" he bellowed, squeezing his hands together as if they were round Moi's neck. "Moi is a fool."

Then he calmed and relaxed his bulging biceps. "I can't spare men for the airfield," he said more reasonably. "Every man is needed at the front. Your paramilitary squads can keep a watch on the approaches to the airport and if Moi's men move away or a gap develops, slip in and get me the information."

De Lancy promised he would and retired feeling much relieved that President Zawutu had understood. For a moment he had feared Zawutu's strength, but now he smiled. Moi was in serious trouble. Unsure of how one stayed hidden and at the same time close enough to exploit a weakness, he made his way to the barracks to discuss the problem with Major Hawthorn; English officers had knowledge and much experience.

On reaching Hawthorn's small HQ, he was shown into the Major's office.

"Hullo," Hawthorn said, offering the only spare chair. "What can we do for the head of security?"

De Lancy hesitated a moment. The contrast between this starched officer and Zawutu's half nakedness had the effect of seeming to reverse the importance of the two men. Hawthorn's clean, stiff uniform and hard, penetrating stare seemed to shrink de Lancy. He had heard the President speak freely with the Britisher and act on his advice, even seek it, before committing himself. That was power. But, of course, the President would be here long after Hawthorn had gone.

De Lancy pulled his chair closer to Hawthorn's desk, the aura of the British presence fading somewhat. He began by describing the President's order to ascertain the status of the airfield and went on to explain how it had been impossible to get near enough to the runway to see anything. He spoke in a middle-class English accent acquired from his father, a skill he had always been proud of.

"Lost several good warriors in the attempt" he said. "Not killed, of course, they simply went over to Major Moi." He was still mystified by that. "To be honest, I don't understand why the President wants to know about one particular aeroplane, but he gave me this photograph of a machine like it." He waved a glossy print.

"Russian?" Hawthorn enquired casually, without looking.

"Why, yes," de Lancy exclaimed. "Well, Byelorussian, but how did you know that?"

"It's a long story and not one for general consumption. Do I take it though that President Zawutu thought you might find one like that on the airfield?"

"It looks like it," de Lancy said with a tilt of his head. "Why else would he ask?"

"Perhaps he's anxious the Ushkuu don't get their hands on it. I assume that if it is there Major Moi has it now?"

De Lancy shrugged. "That's a reasonable guess. I hate being beaten by that moron." He stopped there, unready to admit such open dislike for Moi, who was still a friend of the President, as far as he knew, and an enigma at the moment.

Hawthorn registered the antipathy. De Lancy wondered anxiously if he had said too much already and abruptly brought the conversation back to its original context.

"I wonder if you can help. I need to get past Moi's screen and obtain the information for my President. Can you advise me, sir?"

Hawthorn smiled at the transparency. "I should think you've done all you can in that respect," he said gently so as not to embarrass the Captain further. "If bush-experienced warriors can't get through, then no one can. The only way now is to take Moi on in strength. That way you'll keep control and prevent desertions to Moi's guerrillas."

De Lancy smiled happily. "That's what I told the President,

but he hasn't the men. I think he also does not want to pit Eshanti against Eshanti. Anyway, I am to observe and slip through if an opportunity presents itself."

"I suppose that's all you can do for now," Hawthorn confirmed, smiling at the pedantic English usage. He thought for a fleeting moment of his SAS contingent and quickly dismissed the idea. It would be nice to know whether or not that Russian plane had in fact landed, but he could not disobey a direct order. Still, with his communications down and no one to say no, he might take time to reconsider a scheme he'd had burning inside his head for two days now. He knew he wouldn't get permission if he asked, so best just get on with it, he told himself happily.

Staring blankly at the opposite wall of his office, he ran the idea through his mind again. Of course, it would not do just to discover the whereabouts of the Russian aircraft. If he was going to visit the airport it must achieve more than that; it must prevent the follow-on aircraft from landing, and that meant cratering the runway. What a beautifully wild idea!

"Thank you anyway," de Lancy was saying.

Hawthorn pulled himself back from the pleasure of planning a spot of action to respond generously. He stood to see de Lancy off and watched his guest's departure, wondering why the man was so disliked. He could not know, of course, of the tribal dimension, so he had put what he'd heard down to jealousy. There was no doubt de Lancy was close to the President and enjoyed his full confidence. A powerful position in a land where power was sought so assiduously.

Alone again, Hawthorn sat quietly, his mind playing out the airport plan like a computer game. Then he sent for his SAS subaltern, Jimmy Harwell.

* * *

Zawutu took command of the army at 0800 hours the following morning and informed Hawthorn of it. "Come and see me," he ordered in cavalier fashion, then softened it to: "I'd like your advice, if you can spare some time this morning." Hawthorn said he would come immediately.

In the War Room beneath the Palace kitchens, Zawutu was busy at the map display when Hawthorn entered, escorted by a young Eshanti officer. The large scale maps occupied one whole wall and a glance at the layout told the visitor all he needed to know about the urgency of the situation. The Ushkuu were beating on the City gates, that much was clear, and the arrows indicating Moi's activities were markedly few and far between.

Zawutu turned to greet him. "Thank you for coming," he said formally, then grinned ruefully. "You can see the mess we're in." He pointed at the spread-out map. "Ingabe is in the suburbs and making ground, and Moi has turned very quiet for some reason. I need your expertise here and I'm not afraid to admit it."

"Are you sure you should be doing this? Taking command yourself?" Hawthorn replied instead. "Shouldn't you and your government take yourselves off to a safe place until the armies have sorted this mess out?"

"Please!" Zawutu said, throwing his hands out towards the depressing map layouts. "I can't leave Zawanda now. If I left it would be seen as a defeat. I've sent the government to Zaire, and Uudi is with a relative in Kenya, so there's only me to worry about. I stay."

Hawthorn shrugged. "So be it."

Zawutu had risen a whole tower block in his estimation. Most African heads of state in his position would have scarpered by now, to their boltholes, to wherever they'd stashed their aid pension funds. He glanced at the map.

"You can't hold the city," he said definitively, protocol forgotten in deference to tactics. "It's too sprawled-out and you don't have the troops to defend it. You could lose a lot of men if you tried. Ingabe has the advantage, he can outflank you at every street corner and mop you up piecemeal."

"So?" Zawutu asked, cognisant of Hawthorn's superior experience and only too ready to learn from it.

"Withdraw and establish a new line, out in the open where you can see the enemy." He moved to the map. "Here, in the hills behind the city. Occupy the heights, secure your flanks, and you can hold Ingabe till the cows come home. With the Impolo valley behind you he has nowhere to go. And if he's mad enough to try to dislodge you by frontal assault up those hills, he won't last long. He is Sandhurst trained, I assume."

"A year behind me," Zawutu confirmed.

"There you are then. We've all read the same text books. Get yourself established on the heights with plenty of provisions and the best he can do is lay siege. After that it's a matter of who can hold out the longest. And I must tell you that I don't think the British Government will want to see you defeated."

"You mean British troops?"

Hawthorn held his tongue. Another idea was germinating.

"Look, I should be getting back," he said as an excuse for avoiding the question. It had struck him during the conversation that to immobilise the airfield he would have to act soon, before Zawutu pulled out of the city. After that, distances would be too great and the country too open. Then, given a fair wind, and if he accidentally placed his command into the thick of things, or was ordered by Zawutu to occupy a seemingly safe position which later turned out to be not so safe, he might coerce the MoD into committing the stand-by Brigade. They wouldn't want to lose a British Company to native troops. What would history say about that?

Zawutu, meanwhile, grasping the straw of Hawthorn's words, glowed at the thought of British reinforcements, for that was how he saw any further British involvement, as reinforcing Hawthorn. It occurred to him that Hawthorn might not then be in command, but once a second British Company was on Zawandan soil, he, President Zawutu, would give Hawthorn overall command; he saw the need for only one more Infantry Company. Ingabe wouldn't stand a cat in hell's chance against the Zawandan Army led by half a British infantry regiment under Hawthorn.

"I'm most grateful," Zawutu said as Hawthorn turned to leave.

* * *

Moi had felt the sting of Ingabe's counter-guerrilla tactics. He had lost too many men to the Ushkuu rebels to continue his current hit-and-run methods and had therefore decided to cut his losses and pull back into deeper bush country to the west. The Ushkuu reinforcements, taking advantage of the lull, broke through and joined up with the main Ushkuu army just as its advance guard was feeling its way into the perimeter of New London.

For part of this time Moi, despondent and furious at the poor turn of events, had sat in a shallow cave worn into the side of a large rock face, reflecting upon his new circumstances. His two hundred or so men (he hadn't counted lately) occupied the dense scrub all around to a radius of about half a mile, with sentries out even further than that. Even so, Ingabe's men continued to harass these outposts, but they gradually melted away as they were recalled to take part in the fight for the City.

Moi fretted and fumed, balancing his desire to kill Ushkuu with his obsession to be President. Finally he concluded that the only way to defeat the Ushkuu was to appear to accede to Zawutu's request for a single command and, once the enemy was beaten, work from within to unseat Zawutu. He could, he figured, carry on killing Ushkuu and at the same time weaken Zawutu's hold on the Presidency. He complimented himself on such a masterly plot, then called together his lieutenants who, to a man, agreed the plan.

"We march tonight," Moi said, and the meeting broke up.

* * *

Back in his own small HQ, Hawthorn sent for Lieutenant Harwell, the adrenalin buzzing.

"We'll have to do the airfield tonight, Jimmy," he said. "Zawutu's pulling out of the city and we'll have to conform, so tonight or tomorrow night are our last chances."

Harwell nodded. "I'll get things organised, then. Will you be coming with us, sir?"

Hawthorn smiled. "Wouldn't miss it for the world."

Harwell saluted and left. He had never served under an officer like Hawthorn before. No SAS officer would dream of pulling the plug on communications with the War Office; none would dare. And then, to head for the airport with intention of blowing up the runway. Magnificent!

Hawthorn called for his batman. "Get my battle kit assembled. Lightweight order, and see if Lieutenant Harwell can spare me one of those natty machine pistols his chaps carry."

"Sir" Private Smith responded, recognising what was happening. "Will I be coming too, sir?"

"Do you want to, Smith?"

"I should be with you, sir."

"Very well then," Hawthorn said with a grin and wondered how many more requests he'd be receiving before the day was out. Training others was, for a fully-trained soldier, an extremely boring pastime. After long hours driving elementary weapons drill into Eshanti skulls it was no wonder his men wanted a break, and what better than one with a bit of excitement thrown in.

He watched Smith leave; a good infantryman, he reflected as he reluctantly addressed himself to the pile of paperwork on his desk.

The door rattled to a heavy knock. "Come," Hawthorn said, glad of a reason to leave the official work until later.

"Granby," the tall, fair-haired figure said as he entered. "We haven't met." He extended his right hand.

"Well, and good morning to you," Hawthorn said, standing and taking it. "Major Hawthorn, OC British Assistance Mission, BAM for short."

Granby smiled. "How apposite. I hear you've been looking for me?"

"Well, only in a perfunctory sort of way," Hawthorn confessed. "My masters in the MoD seem concerned to know your whereabouts, that's all. Why don't you sit down?"

Granby accepted the offer. "I didn't know I was so much in demand," he said with a cheeky smile.

"Well, you'll be pleased to know I can't snitch on you at the moment, my communications are down."

"Really?" Granby said. "In today's high-tech world I should have thought the army would use satellite dishes and computers and things of that ilk."

"So we do, but even they break down occasionally. What can I do for you?"

Granby pulled the chair a little closer, as if preparing to impart deep, dark secrets, then said blandly: "As you know, President Zawutu has taken personal command of the army, and I'm only getting in his way. My job's more or less at a standstill for the time being, so he suggested I should attach myself to you. Something about being with my own kind."

Hawthorn looked hard at his visitor. "That might not be so

easy," he said. "We'll be moving soon to conform with the President's movements. And before that I have a little task to perform which will leave us very little time to look after you."

"Don't you worry about me," Granby said, affronted. "I can look after myself. I'm not altogether ignorant of military matters, you know. I did a short service stint in the Sappers."

"Explosives?" Hawthorn asked, suddenly interested.

"Of course," Granby replied.

"Welcome aboard," Hawthorn said delightedly. "I don't suppose you'd care to join up again, for the duration that is?"

Granby raised his eyebrows. "Join up? At my age?"

"Well, only in a manner of speaking. I can't enlist you, of course, but I'd appreciate you becoming a temporary soldier rather than a civilian, then you won't be in the way and I can use your explosives expertise."

"It's been a while," Granby said. "I'm probably years out of date."

"Plastic, cortex, guncotton, primers, safety fuse, detonators, ignitors – nothing's all that new."

Granby felt a buzz. "Are you serious?" he said, leaning forward and gripping the edge of Hawthorn's desk.

"Indeed I am," Hawthorn assured him. "In fact we're off out tonight to crater the runway at New London Airport, if you'd care to join us."

"You've got Beehives, I suppose?" Granby enquired, referring to a special directional explosive device designed especially for blowing holes in roads.

"I'm not sure," Hawthorn confessed. "Jimmy Harwell, the SAS sub, he'll know more about that. Why don't you have a word with him? Oh, and one more thing. If you come on this one tonight you're under Harwell's command, that's if he agrees to take you."

"Understood," Granby said, the mixture of excitement and

anxiety gripping his stomach like a vice. Never in his wildest dreams would he have believed he'd be on active service again after so long. "OK. Jimmy's probably briefing whichever Troop he's using, which means you'll find him in the basha next door but one from here. Go have a chat and get kitted out."

Granby came to his feet and almost saluted, halting his arm at waist height. "No hat," he said, grinning like a child just given a present.

"Take care," Hawthorn said, and with a deep sigh returned reluctantly to his paperwork.

★ ★ ★

Moi moved his guerrillas through deep bush in a wide sweep around the Ushkuu. By 3 am he was the other side of New London Airport, where he paused to collect the men he'd left on guard there, including a bonus of regular army deserters, then swung right towards the capital.

Just as Moi changed direction, three darkened, specially-adapted Land Rovers left the city, motoring rapidly and on a course convergent with Moi's guerrillas, though they had no way of knowing this.

Unknown to either column, an Ushkuu patrol, on a bearing destined to intercept the two in a shallow valley ahead, moved on at a good pace. The NCO in charge heard the SAS Land Rovers approaching and immediately laid an ambush where the track passed between the steep sides of a rain gulley in the bottom of the valley. He thought the vehicles were Eshanti.

As the SAS vehicles zigzagged through the dried-up rain gulley they came under intense downward fire from the Ushkuu on both sides.

"Keep going," Harwell yelled to his driver in the lead vehicle. "Fast as you can."

The heavy, .5 calibre machine guns mounted on three hundred and sixty degree swivels in the back of each Land Rover engaged the tops of the embankments and at the same time Harwell fired the smoke dischargers attached to his front and rear bumpers. Accelerating hard, the Land Rovers cleared the next bend and ran slap bang into another, much larger group of enemy stretched at right angles across their path. It was Moi, though they didn't know it, and he thought they were Ushkuu.

"Turn when you can. We'll go back through!" Harwell screamed into his driver's ear. "The smoke screen had developed nicely behind them and he estimated it would provide adequate cover for their escape.

The lead vehicle swung round and climbed part way up the bank at an astonishing angle before roaring back the way it had come. The other two followed into the smoke and suffered a hail of unaimed fire from above which kicked up stones and chips of rock from the track ahead and twice pierced the bonnet of Harwell's Land Rover without causing catastrophic damage. A scream from behind, followed by a drop in the rate of machine gun fire, which, swiftly taken up again by the number two on the gun, indicated their first casualty; a ricochet strike in the left thigh, painful but not life-threatening. A field dressing was quickly applied, and a syringe of morphine unceremoniously jabbed into his thigh soon made Trooper Jones as comfortable as a careering Land Rover would permit.

Hawthorn had remained a silent passenger in the second vehicle. This was Lieutenant Harwell's show. He ducked as the air above his head parted with a crack to the passage of high-velocity rounds, then glanced round to check on number three. So far all the Land Rovers were still mobile. They cleared the smoke, rounded the bend which had led them into this mess and at full throttle made their way back to New London.

Safely in barracks, with Trooper Jones sedated and the

crumpled bullet removed from the fleshy part of his thigh - no permanent damage had been done - Hawthorn re-enacted his Hereford training course style of debriefing. "Well done, chaps," he said. "The drinks are on me when everything's tidy." He nodded to Harwell and Granby to follow him into his office.

Once behind closed doors, Lieutenant Harwell began. "Who the hell was that second lot? They were too thick on the ground for a routine patrol, surely, and did you notice how the firing continued long after we were clear?"

From the passenger seat in the third vehicle things had happened too quickly for Granby to see much, and he'd had his eyes screwed tightly closed throughout the most violent manoeuvres anyway, but his hearing had not been impaired. "Yes. Odd that," he said, looking to Hawthorn for an explanation.

"Damned if I know," Hawthorn said. "One thing's for sure, they caught us napping tonight. So, we go again tomorrow, this time in heavier numbers, moving tactically, Phil Story's platoon leading. It'll take longer, but it'll be safer."

Jimmy Harwell shook his head. "If I may, sir?"

Hawthorn nodded.

"Better if we go in fewer numbers, actually sir. I think you'll agree, this is a purpose-designed SAS operation and I suggest you let me run it as such. With one LR and a demolition team, cross country, I promise you I'll complete the job tonight." He looked straight into Hawthorn's eyes as he spoke.

Hawthorn held the subaltern's gaze with his own while he thought about it, then he said: "It'll be our last chance. Are you sure?"

"Positive, sir," Harwell said boldly.

"So be it, then."

"And amen to that," Granby said, having watched the modern army at work. In his day a subaltern would never have dared contradict a Major, but then this was his first experience of the SAS. Perhaps they were permitted such luxuries because of their privileged position. Harwell was certainly a strange bird, but a demon in action if tonight was anything to go by, and a likeable lad too.

"Get some rest," Hawthorn counselled. "We'll deal with tomorrow's stuff tomorrow. And Jimmy, wake Captain Butler, give him my compliments and ask him to call on me now."

Harwell saluted and left, followed by Granby, for whom the night's excursions had been draining. He hadn't done this sort of thing since his Kenya days and was feeling the effects of a sedentary lifestyle.

Butler, Hawthorn's 2i/c, a straightforward ranker with a remarkable knowledge of Queen's Regulations and the Manual of Military Law, had been specifically chosen because of his fighting experience and because he always gave meticulous attention to the minutest administrative detail. Every action-minded OC needed a Butler.

"Sir," Butler said as he entered, clad in a lightweight dressing gown his wife had bought him specially for Zawanda.

"Ah, Gordon! Sorry to wake you, but our dash for the airfield did not go too well last night, so we're having another bash at it tonight. I need to know what President Zawutu has been doing while I've been away."

Butler stifled a yawn. "Sorry sir. Well, I kept in touch with the War Room as you instructed and it seems we are expected to be in prepared positions by dawn the day after tomorrow." He looked at his watch. "No, cancel that, it's tomorrow now. I've warned Lieutenant Harkness to be ready to carry out a recce at dawn." He studied his watch again. "In one hour from now. We've been allocated a steep-sided three-crowned hill at the entrance to the Impolo Valley where the President thinks we'll be well out of the way. It lies about two miles behind the main

Eshanti positions. Here," he said, indicating the location on the wall map. "Harkness has orders to lay the position out and get everything ready to receive the main group."

"Digging in?"

"No sir. I hadn't envisaged there being any need. We're non-combatants as far as I know."

"Hmm. Look, it's almost time for Reggie Harkness to leave. Ask him to wait. I have a few orders to dish out here, and I must see how Jones is doing, then I'll be with him."

Butler nodded and turned to leave. "Oh, Gordon," Hawthorn said, causing his second in command to pause, "I don't suppose we can get Jones medevaced the way things are, so let's keep him with us. No Zawandan hospital, OK? And by the way, you may have to see the unit into position. I might not be here to help."

Butler nodded again. He had half expected it anyway and had already made provision for Jones.

★ ★ ★

Moi sent a minor chieftain into New London to contact the President and explain that two hundred-odd Eshanti irregulars under Major Josi Moi were camped on the plain between the city and the hill country, ready to receive orders. Zawutu beamed when he heard.

"At last. Let Major Hawthorn know," he ordered his signals officer.

CHAPTER FIFTEEN

Having removed Uudi and the majority of his Cabinet to Kenya and Zaire respectively, Zawutu felt free to prosecute the war with renewed vigour. He at once set about organising the withdrawal from New London. Hawthorn had implied that Britain would not want to see the present regime fail, and with Moi and his two hundred men waiting in the wings, the future looked decidedly rosy for a change.

"Ingabe has come to the end of his reach," he said to his ADC as the pair left the Palace. "We'll be back, don't worry."

In the distance he could hear the sounds of battle, an energetic rear guard doing what it could. The main elements had begun withdrawing just as the last glimmer of sunlight disappeared below the horizon.

"Break clean," Hawthorn had advised. "Get as much space between you and Ingabe as you can, right from the start."

The Army's logistics staff had been busy moving transport vehicles and supplies to a number of suitable locations deep in the range of hills behind the city, where they were now well concealed in ravines under heavy camouflage. The operations staff, as well as managing the withdrawal sequence, were engaged in maintaining a deceptively stout defence put up by a relatively small but effective rear guard, under cover of which the main force was gradually slipping away into the deepening darkness.

On the verdant plain which lay between the city and the mountains, Moi had parted his command like the waters of the Red Sea to allow safe passage for the main army, and there he waited. By dawn the evacuation was more or less complete, with Zawutu's men digging in on the forward slopes of the heights above the town, and below, on the Serentipo Plain, Moi poised to cut into Ingabe's flanks as soon as the Ushkuu army debouched from the City suburbs into open country.

Zawutu reached his command position at two forty-five in the morning to find Colonel M'Nango already in occupation. The hastily-prepared bunker was rather small, too small to accommodate the two officers and the radio men, M'Nango complained.

"It'll do," Zawutu told him, refusing to let anything deflate his new-found buoyancy. "How's the withdrawal going?"

M'Nango referred to the map already spread across one of the earth walls.

"Everyone's moving to time so far," he said.

Then suddenly, before he could enlarge further on the tactical situation, a series of massive explosions ripped through the night, bringing a shower of loose soil down from the roof. A sudden splash of bright light lit up the bunker entrance, and was gone.

"What the hell was that?" Zawutu gasped as he dived for the door.

Following close behind, M'Nango glanced anxiously at the roof before calling forward to Zawutu, "Ingabe? Blowing the main road perhaps?"

Zawutu turned as M'Nango came alongside, flicking soil debris from his hair. "What for? He has no need."

M'Nango shrugged. He listened to the echoes dying slowly

in the hills and could think of no answer. Nothing else stirred but the occasional crackle of small arms fire from the edge of the city. After a moment's listening the two men returned to the shelter of the dugout.

Zawutu spent no more than a second wondering about the detonations; whatever they might have been, he could do nothing about it. Ever the pragmatist, he brushed aside the mysterious bangs to concentrate on current events, of which the most important just now was the state of defensive preparedness.

He listened to the sitreps as they came in over the radio and watched M'Nango feed the data onto the map. As the night wore on the concentration of Chinagraph circles containing regimental titles began to look impressive. Then just before dawn the rear guard joined, and deployment was complete.

"Moi's turn now," M'Nango remarked as he carefully placed the Chinagraph pencil in his breast pocket; Chinagraphs were like gold.

The first glimmer of dawn was beginning to spread from the Eastern horizon. A faint daylight crept into the bunker and alerted Zawutu to the new day. He made his way above ground, followed by M'Nango, and marvelled at the nascent sunlight, its rays dancing among the water crystals suspended in the morning mist and making the air sparkle like a mass of tiny suspended mirrors. He listened for signs of fighting, but the air seemed relaxed and quiet.

"Ingabe will know we're gone by now" said M'Nango. "The question is, will he come on in a rush or be more cautious?"

"He'll be impatient enough to push on regardless if I know him," Zawutu replied. "He wants this over and done with as quickly as possible, remember."

The heat from the sun was at last burning off the mist and visibility was slowly improving, but not enough to permit a clear view of the whole plateau area where Moi waited.

Then suddenly it became academic. A terrible cacophony of deadly small arms fire rose like a wave from the plain below.

"That'll have stopped the Ushkuu in their tracks," M'Nango remarked as the President snatched up a pair of high-powered binoculars and made a rush for a forward observation post. He panned across the area below, but still the morning mist denied him a clear view. Muzzle flashes appeared like sparklers where deep shadows still held back the feeble light of day, but men and their movement remained invisible. There was only the noise of battle, punctuated by screams where a bullet found a victim.

It went on for over half an hour, then petered out. The mist was lifting fast now, and into a widening area of clarity Zawutu aimed his binoculars. If Ingabe had triumphed over Moi, he should expect to see Ushkuu advancing. There were none.

"Looks good," he said to M'Nango. "Let's get a sitrep from Moi."

"The Ushkuu had been caught like a gazelle with the wind in its ears," Moi said. "They have pulled back to lick their wounds. With mortar and heavy machine gun support from you I can hold them for the rest of the day."

"Let it be so," Zawutu said. "And thank you, Josi."

Eventually of course, Josi would be driven off, but the time gained would be invaluable. For the British to come perhaps, or to weary Ingabe and the Ushkuu chiefs. Certainly time enough to prepare the definitive counter-attack as advocated, again by Hawthorn, who, it seemed to Zawutu, was quite incapable of recommending anything but attack and victory.

★ ★ ★

Harwell led his team out of the bush to the foot of the British mission's new hilltop location. It was five o'clock in the morning and later than planned. Twice on the way from the airport they had been forced to turn back and search for a different route through trackless bush laced with steep, dry watercourses. Two vehicles had left barracks just before midnight the previous night with Hawthorn and Granby in the second, the former determined not be left out and Granby coming along for the ride. When Hawthorn had advised the SAS Subaltern of the change of plan from one Land Rover to two, Harwell had merely saluted and replied: "Of course, sir." He figured he knew Hawthorn well enough by now to expect the unexpected from this so-called ordinary infantry officer whose behaviour was anything but ordinary.

This second attempt at the airfield had gone well, or as well as could be expected for an operation taking place across unknown and unrecced bush country. Moi's guerrillas had moved on earlier and Ingabe was fully occupied in the city, which left the route clear and the trip unchallenged. Laying charges and setting timers on the blackest of nights had been achieved without interruption and Granby had performed his part well.

Once final checks had been completed the two-vehicle convoy had set off on a heading for the new location at the entrance to the Impolo Valley, but an early compass error, not realised until the lead Land Rover almost crashed head first into a deep wadi, had led them well off course. A study of the inadequate local map and a comparison with the ground in the dim light of a narrow-beamed torch had shown that they were almost back at the airport.

"We've gone wrong," Harwell had said with a shrug. "If we follow the wadi we should come out here." He showed Hawthorn on the map.

At that moment the charges at the airport detonated, lighting the sky and creating a sudden rush of air and dust.

"Too bloody close for my liking," Granby had exclaimed to

Hawthorn from the ground behind the second Land Rover. "We should have been further on than this by now."

"Give Jimmy a chance. The maps are none too good and this is new country, remember."

Granby grimaced. "Even so…" he began, then he shut up.

Once they were again on the move, the new directions had proved not to be correct either, leading to further delays until the young SAS officer had finally pinpointed their correct location. After that it became a clear run for home.

With the Land Rovers refuelled and recamouflaged in patches of bush at the foot of the hill, the demolition team climbed up the steep slope, to be met at the top by Captain Butler.

"This way, sir," he said to Hawthorn, leading him towards the command tent. "You are over there, Jimmy," he said pointing to the left as he went. "And you, Dickie, are with Lieutenant Harkness, in that direction."

"Show me the layout first, Gordon," Hawthorn said. "And I'll drop in on Jones."

The feature they occupied was actually two hills with a high valley between, over which ran a zigzag track; a saddle, in Ordnance Survey terms. Hawthorn viewed the track with a professional eye. It could just about handle a small car, but nothing bigger; obviously the Impolo valley did not attract too many visitors. And from the map it was clear that the long, deep river valley went nowhere except to an escarpment wall which delineated the Zaire border. He ran his eye up both slopes of the saddle and concluded that nothing could pass along that track as long as he sat on both hilltops.

"We occupy both peaks?" he asked Butler.

"No. sir. Only this one."

Hawthorn made a mental note. "I'd like to walk over to the other one."

From that peak he looked down to where the Impolo

emerged from the valley and turned left towards the north. The gorge here was almost vertical and the one river bank looked virtually impassable except on foot and in single file. He nodded to himself, satisfied, though why he had gone to the trouble when his command had no combat role, he could not have explained. Perhaps he could not help being a soldier and seeing things from a soldier's perspective.

He smiled. "Just keeping in practice," he said to Butler, as if he would understand.

About an hour later he and his officers sat together in the mess tent partaking of a good old English breakfast. Congratulations flowed copiously, the whole command sharing in the night's success. "Jimmy's show," Hawthorn told them, directing all the praise to the young SAS Subaltern. Then he asked of Butler: "No news from President Zawutu, I suppose?"

"None sir."

"Well let's see if we can raise him after breakfast. Oh, and get the Sigs Sergeant to rig the antenna. Better let London know what we've done and how we're fixed."

★ ★ ★

Ingabe paced up and down the map room in his command post on the edge of the city with a fury that frightened the officers present. "Who let Moi through?" he demanded. "It is Moi out there holding us up, isn't it?"

The bravest of them spoke up. "Yes sir, but you wanted us to drive Major Moi off the main roads so that the reserves could come up, and that's what we did. Your brilliant idea of putting out counter guerrilla teams dispersed the Eshanti guerrillas as you said it would, but there was no way we could contain them after that, not without taking men from the main assault on New London."

Ingabe frowned and dashed rivulets of sweat from below his

chin with the back of his hand. "Not good enough," he said unreasonably. "Now we'll have to do it all again. He has to be removed from the Serantipo Plain or we'll never get close enough to Zawutu's main army to defeat him, and time's running out."

He resumed his perambulations and asked himself why on earth the British reinforcements he considered inevitable had not left the UK yet; Balindi reported them still in barracks. If he could shift that bastard Moi there might still be time before the British arrived. President Ingabe enthroned, fait accompli.

"Why don't we go round?" another officer remarked sotto voce to his neighbour.

"What was that?" Ingabe demanded, halting half way across the floor and swinging round to find the speaker. The young officer who had made the remark half raised a hand and let it fall again when Ingabe's eyes focused on him.

"Well?" Ingabe bellowed

"Or we go round, sir," the embarrassed officer mumbled to the floor.

Ingabe liked it. Had he not been so angry he would have thought of it himself. "Well done, young man," he said kindly. The officer looked up and smiled. "It'll take longer, but longer than what? Who knows how long it might take to shift Moi? Even the lion knows it is better to go slowly than to fail." He moved to the map board.

"If Zawutu is dug in in these hills, he must be tanking water from the Impolo river," his logistics officer contributed. "That's what I'd do anyway."

"Of course! And if we can get round behind and cut off his water supply, he's done for. Thank you Captain S'Umbar."

S'Umbar threw out his chest and glanced proudly at his fellows. Two satisfied officers.

Ingabe wasted no time. "Major Malib, your Battalion will

lead. We'll swing left in a wide sweep through the area where the bush is thickest, and we leave at dusk. No noise, bush discipline all the way or we'll alert Moi to what we're doing. Understood?"

Heads nodded and a ripple of "Yes sirs" ran through the assembly.

"Thank you gentlemen. We'll win this war, never fear."

To dignify this tribal squabble with the title 'war' was the same as calling Zawanda a world power, for no more than two or three thousand warriors were engaged on either side. But for Zawanda, where tribal skirmishes occupied tens of warriors, and never as many as a hundred, the numbers in this conflict were significant and the fighting bitter; and replacements were drying up. During the early honeymoon period, volunteers had signed up in significant numbers on both sides, but as the struggle had become unusually protracted so recruiting had dwindled to single figures and now there had been none at all, Eshanti or Ushkuu, for over three days. Instead, wherever a village had fallen under the control of the opposite tribe, the young and old were moving out to create a new problem. Long crocodiles of Eshanti refugees weaved their way out of Ushkuu-occupied territory towards the Angolan border, while similar streams of Ushkuu departed Eshanti-held territory for Zaire. The United Nations refugee organisation rushed its representatives in from Rwanda. The hardships associated with trekking for miles carrying household bundles and babes in arms, the harassment, starvation and deprivation along all the routes out of the country, was familiar ground to these aid workers, but without adequate resources they were powerless. Zaire and Angola, accustomed in their turn to refugees flooding across their borders, had already called for international assistance to house, feed and care for the multitudes.

Neither side in the armed conflict responded to UN appeals

for clemency and assistance in persuading refugees to return to their homes. Indeed, neither side was honestly aware of the genocide being perpetrated by loose bands of lawless youths in the villages and towns, and neither side could spare men to act as policemen. The outcome was that the final stages of this confrontation would be fought with unit strengths as they now stood - roughly equal - and damn the refugees.

With Major Malib in the van, Ingabe's forces set off just as dusk began creeping over the plain.

★ ★ ★

Hawthorn's first signal to London was short and pithy: "Eshanti vacated New London yesterday to new positions in hills to West of city. New London Airport runway cratered by this unit."

The signals room in the Old War Office building came alive.

"Hawthorn's transmitting again, sir," the duty signals officer shouted to his superior, who at once rang the Foreign Office. A telephone link created for just this situation switched in, allowing direct communication between the FO in London and Hawthorn in Zawanda.

"Is the subject aircraft at the airport?" was all the FO wanted to know.

Hawthorn tutted and replied "No".

"Where is it then?" the FO man asked.

"How the hell should I know?" he drafted, then screwed the signal sheet up and threw it on the floor. Instead he sent: "Either one never landed, or if it did it has disappeared.

"Disappeared? How? Where to?"

He sighed deeply. "If I knew that it wouldn't be missing, would it?" he muttered to himself. But he suppressed his impatience with those at home and sent: "You were aware of Major Moi's occupation of the airfield at the relevant time."

"Go to voice," the next incoming signal ordered and the

Signals Sergeant obeyed, after glancing at Hawthorn, who nodded. "If that's what they want."

Everyone knew that voice was much less secure than cypher; scramblers were much easier to break than encoded signals, but whoever was in charge over there today seemed prepared to accept the risks.

"Hullo, Sunray speaking," Hawthorn opened.

"Sunray Major here," a voice he didn't recognise came back. "That aircraft must be found. We're certain one landed in Zawanda and did not take off again."

"I am unable to leave this location," Hawthorn explained drily. "As I told you, President Zawutu is dug in on the hills outside New London with Ingabe and the Ushkuu pushing across the Serentipo Plain. Any movement by me will attract attention from one side or the other and both are very trigger happy. And anyway, I understood you didn't want me involved?" He grinned mischievously at Captain Butler as he said it.

There followed a pause, presumably while consultations took place. Then the London Sunray came back: "Confirm that it is absolutely impossible for you to move from your present location to institute a search."

"Absolutely," Hawthorn replied.

"Very well. There is no point in you remaining where you are. You are to evacuate your command to Zaire until such time as the conflict is resolved. Arrangements will be made at the border."

Hawthorn spluttered in disbelief. "But I've just told you in simple language that I can't move from here, neither to search for aircraft nor to evacuate to Zaire. Movement of any kind would be fatal as things are. And anyway, what about reinforcements? I understood the Rapid Reaction Brigade was on standby for Zawanda? There's no guarantee Zawutu will win here, you know, and another change of government would be disastrous for the country. I suggest you think about that. The Brigade could put a stop to this ridiculous fighting, and at the same time find your aeroplane for you." He held up crossed fingers to Butler. "Oh, and remember, the runway is out of action."

"We have redesignated 6th Airborne Brigade," the London voice came back. "Meanwhile, remove your command to Zaire as ordered."

"How many times must I repeat myself?" said Hawthorn, knowing he was being insubordinate but fed up with London's lack of understanding. In fact he was more afraid that they suspected what he was up to, but he was equally bent on staying where he was.

He tried again. "It's not possible, I tell you. I am the officer on the ground and I reiterate, we're surrounded by hostile tribes.

"Withdraw under a flag of truce," the FO insisted.

Hawthorn held back. To reply was to accept.

"Pull the bloody plug," he said to the Signals Sergeant in a defiant tone of voice. "Cable fault." To Butler he said, "and raise the Union Flag. That's as neutral as I intend to get. 'O' Group in twenty minutes."

Twenty minutes later the officers were assembled, seated in a semicircle at the foot of the tree against which Hawthorn leant. He briefed them on his conversation with the Foreign office, paraphrasing the insubordinate bits and adding his own interpretations. Then he ended by saying, "Unfortunately the question of our withdrawal to Zaire remained unresolved when the black box on the signals kit packed in again."

Butler looked up sharply at the fib, but hastily looked away before the others noticed.

"So, I have decided to hang on here until we can fix the rear link radio."

Murmurs followed that announcement. Few, least of all

Lieutenant Harwell, believed that what they had just been told was the whole truth and nothing but the truth. Harwell studied his OC, searching for the gleam in his eye, a characteristic he had picked up in Hawthorn whenever he was about to do something not quite in step with his orders. And there it was, like a beacon, a dead giveaway, apparently beyond Hawthorn's control. They would not pull out of here while there was still a fight to be had.

Hawthorn continued: "With matters so fluid and Colonel Ingabe determined to unseat the President, the situation could become very nasty indeed. My rules of engagement extend me plenty of latitude should communications fail, and absolute freedom should we be fired upon." He grinned evilly at that. "So I figure we should prepare ourselves to be fired upon."

A louder murmur accompanied this statement, but no one's eyes left Hawthorn's face.

"I'm not with you, sir" Butler threw in. "Who can fire on us back here?"

"Who knows?" Hawthorn replied enigmatically. "I want the whole unit dug in tactically on both peaks." He glanced meaningfully at Butler. "One and Two Platoons left and right respectively and Three Platoon here with me. You, Jimmy, out in front, over there on that hill." He gestured to an unoccupied mound across the small plain to the front. "Admin to bring the vehicles closer in and stay with them. Everyone to be on full operational routine from now on."

The suddenness of the announcement seemed to still even the sounds of breathing.

"Any questions?" Hawthorn asked, as was customary. There was a silence as if all present were turned to stone.

Then Harwell spoke up: "When fired on we fire back then, yes sir?"

Hawthorn noticed the 'when' as opposed to 'if' and smiled at the subaltern. Jimmy had the makings. He understood.

"No. Not you, Jimmy," he said smoothly. "As I said, you're over there and out of sight. The rest of you may engage anyone foolish enough to take you on. I say again, this unit is on a war footing as from now."

"Will the Air Portable Brigade come in, sir?" Lieutenant Williams asked anxiously.

"I don't see how they can stay away," Hawthorn said with another boyish grin. "But it will be the Paras now we've ruined the airport runway. With our comms down and stuck out here you can be sure they'll give it some thought. Then of course, there's another small matter that should stir them into acting soon."

"Another matter, sir?" Butler enquired from under raised eyebrows.

"It's hush hush," Hawthorn said, placing a forefinger over his lips. "Something to do with an aeroplane, which needn't concern anyone here."

"Understood, sir. When do we open comms again?"

"When we've something to say, and not until. Jimmy, will you hang on please? I've got separate orders for you."

★ ★ ★

The mini Cabinet had been gathering for only a few minutes when the Prime Minister walked in, bang on time, which was unusual. "Sit, gentlemen," he said and took his place at the oval table. He had a sour look about him which prompted the others to seat themselves quickly instead of indulging in the usual pre-Cabinet chatter.

"Zawanda," Masters opened, panning the assembly with an icy glare. "President Clayton is giving me stick over that damned Russian aircraft. Fortunately there have been no further take-offs from Byelorussia, so we appear to have stemmed that aspect, for the present anyway. Which leaves that one single aircraft in Zawanda. Intelligence is positive it's there, but no one has actually seen it." He raised his eyebrows at Henry Beauchamp.

"That's true," Beauchamp confirmed. "No one has actually set eyes on it, or at least no one who is talking to us."

"I may be able to shed some light on that situation," Graham Henright, SoS for Defence, offered. "Just a few hours ago, too recent to disseminate, we were in communication with Major Alistair Hawthorn, officer commanding the British Assistance Mission in Zawanda. He has been to the airport and his people have cratered the runway to prevent any more landings. He reports that there was no aircraft there then. In his opinion, Major Moi, you know, Henry, the uncouth fellow who made such a scene in your office, his guerrillas occupied the airport during the key period and may have taken and hidden the bloody thing."

"Hidden a full sized cargo aeroplane?" Masters exclaimed incredulously. "Where's this Moi now?"

"With Zawutu, apparently."

"Well, get Major Hawthorn to quiz him then."

Henright coughed in embarrassment. "Well, Clive, that's not as easy as it sounds. Either Hawthorn is really having trouble with his radios or he's deliberately avoiding us. We ordered him to Zaire, but he may not have heard us. At this moment in time we are out of touch I'm afraid. He's in the field with Zawutu and there are no phones. The international lines into Zawanda are inoperable anyway."

Masters stifled a grin which would have cracked his severe expression, and he felt much better for some inexplicable reason. He had seen Hawthorn's 'P' File when vetting him for the Zawandan job and what Henright had just said about the man did not surprise him.

"If you have an unorthodox task to perform, you give it to

an unorthodox performer," he said. "I thought you trained Hawthorn specially to be that kind of maverick, Graham?"

Henright grinned sheepishly. "Indeed we did. So I suppose it's rather churlish of us to expect normal reactions from a chap like that. Anyway, he's stuck on a hill to the rear of Zawutu's main army and the theory is that he's simply not going to do as he's told. What he's really up to no one knows, and the Generals are smiling. As you know, they objected strongly to political control of Hawthorn's command."

"No point in pursuing a vacuum then, is there," Masters replied. "If he comes on line again ask him about this what's his name, Moi. Presumably President Zawutu isn't going to admit anything."

"Unlikely," Beauchamp said. "He ordered the missiles in the first place, we know that now."

"OK, so what do we do next? I want Clayton off my back."

Beauchamp glanced at Henright and received a nod in exchange.

"There's the Para Brigade, Prime Minister. Graham has it under notice for Zawanda, if you remember?"

"Seven days' notice, actually," Henright interpolated.

"Yes, seven," Beauchamp repeated with a smile at his colleague. "But we need a good reason to commit it. We can't just drop in. The civil war in Zawanda is an internal affair by all international standards, and we dare not interfere without drawing down the ire of the Commonwealth upon us, and probably a large proportion of the rest of the world as well. We simply can't afford to be seen to be interfering in one of our ex-colonies. What would the others make of it?"

Masters sighed. "I take your point, Henry. Now, am I right in assuming that the Russian aircraft is definitely still in Zawanda? Iraq was mentioned at one time."

Beauchamp nodded. "It's a reasonable assumption it's there,

yes. I can't speak for the Iraq connection, of course, but there's been nothing about them from the Int people so we must assume that any arrangement they did have has been cancelled."

"OK, so the aircraft, if it's there, can't get far if Major Hawthorn has blown up the airstrip. As far as we know everyone involved with the pesky thing is otherwise engaged at the moment – Zawutu, Moi and Granby. Where is Granby, by the way?"

"We're not sure," Beauchamp said. "I guess he's in Zawanda, but in what capacity is uncertain."

"Right. But to go back to what I was saying, it's very unlikely there will be any change to the current position as long as fighting continues, and I think I can persuade President Clayton of that. I can also tell him that we'll drop the Paras in at the first legal opportunity, with orders to find and confiscate the cargo and tidy things up out there."

"Graham," he said, addressing the Defence Secretary. "Put the Paras on twenty-four hours' notice and develop a scenario which places Hawthorn's command in serious danger, serious enough to warrant us mounting a rescue mission. Which means no more talk of withdrawal to Zaire, you understand?"

Henright and Beauchamp both nodded.

"And you, Henry, you talk to Zawutu's neighbours and sound them out about us going in to get our lads out."

Beauchamp nodded again.

"That's all for now," Masters said, rising to his feet. "Keep me closely informed." The meeting broke up with the Prime Minister more sanguine than when he had arrived.

★ ★ ★

Moi found he had no Ushkuu left to fight. They had all disappeared, but to where? He put out patrols, and the longer-ranging ones soon caught sight of Ingabe's rear guard moving swiftly through the bush in a movement clearly designed to encircle the main Eshanti army. The patrol reported back and Moi at once informed the President.

"Can't you cut them off?" Zawutu enquired anxiously.

"No. I'm not equipped to take on the whole of the Ushkuu army. And anyway, they are too far ahead."

Zawutu nodded. It made sense. "Very well then. You had better come in and join us here." Two hundred more men on the ground would be much appreciated.

Moi hesitated. He had no wish to be absorbed into Zawutu's order of battle. By operating independently he could keep his men together, whereas if he joined up with Zawutu, many of his warriors would desert. They felt no loyalty to a President who had openly declared he would marry an Ushkuu maiden, and if Moi was to succeed on his journey to the Presidency he would need all his men.

"We'll pursue Ingabe and try to force him to turn and face us," he said, proposing the only alternative Zawutu might accept.

"It might work," Zawutu conceded, but he was too bright not to see that Moi had other reasons for not wanting to come under direct physical command. He could read Josi like a book.

"Good luck," he said at length. "And let me know how you get on."

He looked grimly at M'Nango. "Ingabe's bypassing us to get to the rear. Josi's pursuing him and hopes to turn him, but I don't hold out much hope. I'm afraid we're in another bad situation," he ended with a sad smile. "Where is Hawthorn now? I could do with him."

M'Nango shrugged. He did not approve of always falling back on the British when things went wrong. He had to admit, Hawthorn had been right every time so far. But that was not to say that he or the President would not have come up with the same solutions had Freddie had not been so eager to consult.

"Didn't we allocate him a hill near the Impolo Valley?" It was a statement rather than a question.

Zawutu nodded and referred to the map. "Here," he said, pointing to the spot.

In the corner of the dugout the radio operator had been panning the operational frequencies which would normally have been carried on separate radio sets. But with radios in short supply because of failures which could not be repaired in the field, Zawutu had only the one to handle all his traffic. The radio link allocated to the British Liaison Team had been crackling with electronic noise ever since it had come on net following the move from the city. But now, suddenly, as the operator paused on the frequency, a carrier wave swept aside the atmospherics and an English voice burst forth.

"Charlie one, this is Charlie one. How do you read me, over?"

"Charlie one, we are receiving you strength nine, over."

"Charlie one, fetch Sunray, over."

"It's the British, sir," the operator said excitedly, interrupting Zawutu's conversation with M'Nango and pointing at the set. "Asking for you, sir. They're using strict RT procedure and their call sign is Charlie One."

Zawutu smiled at M'Nango. "Allah is on our side after all." He took up the microphone and pressed the switch. "Charlie one, Sunray on set, over."

"Charlie one, Sunray minor speaking" said Hawthorn. "We are in a new location. We visited the airport and blew the runway but found no aircraft. Presume Major Moi knows where it is. Suggest you enquire. London very keen to know its whereabouts."

Zawutu frowned at Hawthorn's mention of aircraft. He'd obviously been briefed by London. His frown increased when

Hawthorn spoke of Moi's connection. What did Josi want with an aeroplane and part of an atomic bomb? He shook his head in confusion. But for all of that, Hawthorn had done him a great service by blowing up the runway. Both the Russians and the Iraqis would understand the implications of that and bear no grudge, he hoped. He pressed the mic switch.

"Charlie One, Major Moi is acting independent of main army. Currently he is in pursuit of Ushkuu and out of contact. I know nothing of any aircraft, but will interrogate Major Moi when communications are re-established. Pleased to hear you are in position. Are you tactical? Over."

"Charlie One, regret, no official change to rules of engagement, but we're here nevertheless, over."

Zawutu turned to M'Nango. "Now what does he mean by that?"

M'Nango shook his head. "Strange warrior, that Hawthorn."

Zawutu shook his head in agreement and turned back to the radio set.

"Charlie One, here is latest sitrep. Ingabe is attempting to encircle me, pursued by Moi. If the circle is closed my quartermaster staff tell me we can survive only three days without water." He waved the message sheet he had just been presented with and mouthed "Is that right?" and received a yes in return. "Charlie One, I say again three days, over."

"Charlie One, but you were supposed to be self-sufficient, what happened to the stockpile?"

"Insufficient containers. We are tanking water in from the River Impolo. Only course now is to withdraw before we're cut off. Do you concur? Over."

Hawthorn looked at Butler and Granby, both of whom were present, and grimaced. "Charlie One, agree your appreciation. Only safe course is to pass through me into the valley behind. Suggest you move quickly with minimum baggage and establish a rear guard stop line on the plain below and in front of this position, over."

"Charlie One, will comply," Zawutu said as if replying to a senior. "Watch out for us. At least Ingabe's on the move and way out to a flank. He'll never get here in time to interfere with the withdrawal. Out."

Hawthorn handed the microphone back to the operator and walked out into the open, followed by Butler and Granby.

"Our President is definitely accident prone," he said regretfully. "He's got himself into one hell of a mess again. Ingabe could win this, you know."

Butler looked confused. "What about the mess we're in?" he protested. "I heard you say that President Zawutu should pass through us into the Impolo valley. By my reckoning that leaves us between the Ushkuu and the Eshanti. In the front line."

Hawthorn smiled. "Yes, I suppose it does. But we're neutral, are we not?" He glanced up at the Union Jack rippling out in the stiff breeze from the top of a trimmed tree trunk. "British. Ingabe can't remove us from here without using force, which I shall very naturally resist, as per my orders."

A slow smile spread on Granby's face. "And of course, we're dug in here like a steel cork in the neck of the valley and no one gets in without our consent, yes?"

"I suppose so. How very perspicacious of you, Richard."

"But we can't fire on Zawandans, sir," Butler complained.

"We can if they fire on us first, Gordon," Granby said, nudging the 2i/c in the ribs and looking to Hawthorn for confirmation.

CHAPTER SIXTEEN

The appellation 'Hawthorn's Hill' had already been taken into common use by the squaddies, and no one knew where it had originated. Nicknames, often scurrilous ones, were the currency of troops in the field. They tended to name everything in sight, creating familiarity wherever they went as if that made them feel more comfortable in dangerous surroundings. Wherever they found themselves was home to them, if only for a short time.

The searing sun beat down on open trenches roofed with ponchos to absorb the direct rays. Dust and mist swirled on the updraughts from the plain below, reducing visibility, but by early afternoon it had usually dispersed, leaving a clear view of the range of hills opposite, beyond which Zawutu was encamped.

The main Eshanti army had been on the move since 0200 hours, their logistical units having climbed and passed through the British positions at approximately 0230. They were followed by 3rd Eshanti Regiment, which had filtered through quickly in disciplined Company groups. The New London Regiment was next, two Companies of which had already entered the valley with a third currently on its way. 2nd Eshanti and a makeshift battalion made up from the remnants of two Ushkuu Regiments would be last through, hopefully before dawn.

Hawthorn had been awake on and off all night waiting for Zawutu's HQ to appear. With, at a guess, only one or two more battalions to come – he was not privy to Zawutu's actual order of battle - he was getting worried. He called up Harwell, concealed on the crest of the opposite hill.

"Sunray here. Any sign of Sunray Major?" he enquired.

Harwell scanned the further peaks and hollows through light - enhancing binoculars. "Nothing so far," he replied. "But Eshanti formations have been moving through the valleys below all night and I wouldn't know one unit from another from up here. A mist is beginning to roll in, too."

Hawthorn clicked his tongue impatiently. Tactically speaking, Zawutu should have been among the early movers, so where was he?

"OK." he said into the microphone. "Once the Eshanti are through and clear let me know. Then warn me of your first sighting of the Ushkuu. I trust you are appropriately concealed, over?"

"Wilco. And if the Ushkuu come over this hill they'll walk right over the top of us without knowing we're here."

"Very well. Out."

★ ★ ★

With Moi in hot pursuit of the encircling Ushkuu, the Serentipo plain lay empty and open to Ingabe's reserves, which were just now leaving the city and spreading out to prevent Zawutu from marching back into it. The city lay quietly sinister in the pre-dawn light, its suburban shanty towns deserted and the affluent, white-stuccoed part of town equally devoid of occupants. Those who had stayed, the shopkeepers and others with assets to protect, had very wisely locked themselves behind stout doors until the matter of who was to rule was settled. The streets smelled of sewage, rotting flesh and all kinds of malodorous waste; vegetable and human. Packs of dogs fought between themselves for the best pickings, pausing only to see off swarms of ravenous rats, which were becoming bolder by the minute. The city had a tired, abandoned look, and it had only been a few days. The Ushkuu reserves were glad to be leaving it behind.

Recce patrols came first, probing the bushland and bare plain, pushing forward into the foothills, surprised that no one was shooting at them. Pressing on, the leading patrol topped the crest of the central peak only to find empty slit trenches and discarded items of equipment.

"They've gone," the astonished patrol leader articulated redundantly.

At that point, a junior officer and a radio operator, sent forward by the CO who suspected that the delay meant something was up, came hurrying over the crown of the hill. "They're gone, sir," the patrol leader reiterated.

The Lieutenant looked around, concurred and grabbed the radio microphone. "The Eshanti appear to have withdrawn," he said politely.

"Bugger," the Major commanding the reserve said to his 2i/c in the equivalent Ushkuu. "Tell Colonel Ingabe what's happened."

"He's more slippery than an eel," Ingabe said petulantly when informed. "Let's get after him."

From then on the Ushkuu reserve moved at bush pace, a steady jog-like trot which ate up the miles, uphill and down without pause for rest, an inexorable momentum which by mid-morning brought them within seeing distance of Zawutu's rear elements; the Eshanti withdrawal was already way behind time. But by then the Ushkuu were wilting from the punishing pace and ready to drop. Nevertheless, the sudden knowledge that the Ushkuu were close behind, and because there was no properly organised rear guard – Zawutu had anticipated a clean break - M'Nango had to improvise as best he could. He turned the tail enders, mainly the rear companies of the make shift battalion, to face the enemy, with orders to shoot and scoot.

★ ★ ★

"Ingabe's caught me by surprise," Zawutu confessed to Hawthorn as they met on the hill in the early hours. "He's managed to get right up behind me somehow."

Hawthorn, pleased that Zawutu had finally shown up, nevertheless swore silently. Bloody man's a walking disaster area, he thought.

"Show me on the map," he said calmly.

Zawutu shone a torch and traced the route his troops were taking, pinpointing the place where the Ushkuu had suddenly appeared behind them.

Hawthorn took it in at a glance. "Look, sir," he said, "there's not much you can do to save those poor sods at the tail end, but you have to stop Colonel Ingabe somewhere or he'll roll you up like a carpet. Your best plan is to establish a stop line on the plain below my hill here to give you time to slip cleanly into the valley. If you don't slow Ingabe here, you're finished."

Zawutu nodded and turned to M'Nango, who had caught up with him.

"What do you think, Zwaka?"

"It's all we can do," M'Nango replied, his breathing laboured from the climb.

"I agree," Zawutu said, with more spirit than the circumstances warranted. "Tell Moi to establish a stop line across the plain down there." He pointed.

At that, Hawthorn butted in. "Moi? He's already in the valley. Came through here about two hours ago and paused to say he'd taken a short cut across the plain and was moving into the Impolo valley on your orders."

The two Eshanti officers exchanged glances. "I gave no such orders," Zawutu said.

"Nor me," M'Nango confirmed.

"Well, he's gone through, so there's no help there," Hawthorn said, stating the obvious.

Zawutu snapped back. "I know, I know. I know what he's up to. He's after saving his strength for when this is all over. He wants my job."

At last it was out.

M'Nango grunted non-committally. In his view this was no time to be playing politics. By the light of his own torch he glanced at his mill board sized map, estimated key distances by eye, looked up and proposed that 2nd Eshanti should form the stop line.

"They're on their way. They should be here soon, almost the last through. And they owe it to you."

"But not you personally, my friend." Zawutu said, nodding his thanks. "I need you with me."

He had perceived the gleam in M'Nango's eyes. The 2nd was M'Nango's regiment, commanded currently, it was true, by the second in command, but nonetheless, M'Nango must be bursting to be back with his own men for this key task. Recognising the powerful draw, Zawutu reinforced what he had just said. "I need you with me," he repeatedly firmly.

M'Nango bowed his head and raised one hand in the Eshanti sign of obedience. "I'll inform the 2nd," he said, and taking Zawutu's radio operator by the arm, he led him a short distance away.

Zawutu went to place an arm round Hawthorn's shoulders, then desisted.

He remembered just in time that such familiarities did not go down well with the British.

"The 2nd will do an excellent job," he confided from a respectable distance instead. "And now I must be off. You'll keep an eye on Kwaka's old Regiment, won't you? It was once mine, you know. Anyway, see that they have a clear run through here when the time comes."

Hawthorn said he would. If there's anyone left to run, he added to himself.

★ ★ ★

The two summits of Hawthorn's Hill were separated by a shallow saddle. The two together blocked the entrance to the Impolo valley "like a steel cork" as Granby had described it. The only exception was a narrow gulley which wound round the base on the northern side where the River Impolo emerged from the valley and curved away towards the hinterland. In Hawthorn's estimation no one could get through there opposed, so he had ignored it in his planning.

Captain Butler clambered up the gentle slope of the right-hand saddle to where Hawthorn sat on the lip of his excavated command post. No one had bothered to camouflage their slits from the air – why bother when there were no aircraft on either side? The spoil had been left where it had fallen during excavation, or in some of the more energetic cases, mounded to provide additional frontal protection. Not having to build overhead cover and conceal the results had been a bonus for the Light Infantrymen and had made it easier for them to settle into their battle positions.

Exercises to test the layout for access, movement and communications had been going on throughout the night, indeed the 2ic had just completed a round of visits to observe an ammunition resupply and casualty evacuation exercise ordered by Hawthorn.

"It went well, sir," he reported. "Did I see Granby down on the forward slopes with some of the SAS chaps? Is that safe considering the Ushkuu can't be far away?"

"Doing a bit of mine laying," Hawthorn said casually.

"But we have no mines!" Butler said, surprised.

"Not your real mines, no. But Jimmy's lads have a few special skills with ordinary plastic explosive, and they're doing whatever they do with it. They'd better be quick about it, too. I want those SAS Troopers back in their hides over there before the Ushkuu get a sight of them. Give them a nudge, will you?"

Butler nodded. "Of course, but you're not thinking of blowing up Ushkuu are you, sir?"

Hawthorn waved a hand over the slope. "Not as long as they stay down there on the plain, no," he said. "But if they attempt to come up here then I'll stop them as best I can."

Butler sighed. "But sir, what you're telling me is that you intend to contest Ingabe's right to move into the valley."

"Not entirely," Hawthorn said seriously. "Only his right to move over this hill, which I have declared British territory for the duration. Now, what about a cup of tea? After you've had a word with Richard, that is."

Inside his CP Hawthorn told his batman to brew up, and then sat reflecting upon the Moi-Zawutu situation. He recalled the moment Moi had appeared outside this very dugout in the middle of the night surrounded by at least four minders bellowing for the 'Britisher'. The 'Britisher' had just got his head down after a tour of Platoon positions and was not due to be disturbed for another half hour. But disturbed he had been, and as he had staggered out into the open he could be heard muttering dire threats to whoever had spoiled his rest, threats which he had repeated in earnest when he discovered it was Moi out there.

Naturally, the meeting had not got off to a good start. Indeed, it had soon deteriorated into confrontation, he recalled, with Moi demanding ammunition and Hawthorn refusing to supply it. The situation had then degenerated into a shouting match which had brought Butler rushing from the forward OP, where he had been keeping watch for Zawutu's HQ group. One of the minders had stepped forward aggressively at that point, to be restrained by Moi placing a firm hand on his arm. Hawthorn remembered Moi's words clearly: "These are English, I'll be fine".

"I see you're dug in for war," Moi had observed calmly, sweeping the nearest positions with an outstretched arm.

"Just a precaution," Hawthorn had assured him.

Moi had smiled his twisted smile "I must be getting on."

Hawthorn smiled too as he recaptured the ensuing scene; himself stepping in front of the rebellious Major and remarking: "My bosses in London are rather anxious to learn the whereabouts of a certain Russian aeroplane, and you're rumoured to know where it is."

Moi had faked a massive show of injured innocence. "Me? Why should I know anything about an aeroplane?"

"Because you pilfered it from New London airport," Hawthorn had said bluntly.

"Not me," Moi insisted. "Try Ingabe. Now I really must be off. Excuse me."

Moi had ignored Hawthorn's outstretched hand, gathered his staff about him and set off at a jog to catch up with the rest of his guerrilla army.

Hawthorn sighed as Smith came in with a steaming mug of tea.

"And one for Captain Butler" he said, taking the cup by the handle. "Didn't I mention that?"

Smith muttered something unintelligible and went out into a breaking dawn. Perhaps Ingabe did have the bloody thing after all, Hawthorn told himself, thinking of the trouble a single aeroplane was causing an awful lot of people.

As dawn illuminated the hills and valleys, Hawthorn's men found themselves looking down through the thin, early morning mist onto the familiar sight of occupied two-man slit trenches. But these were Eshanti trenches, not sited for all-round defence; they were all facing the same way, towards the approaching Ushkuu.

2nd Lieutenant Phil Storey had the forward platoon position and could see the full extent of the 2nd's deployment. He knew what it augured and looked forward to observing the battle from his front row seat.

"Never thought it would be this exciting," he remarked to his Platoon Sergeant, Sergeant Hiscock.

Hiscock looked at his officer. "With Dynamite in charge, what did you expect?" he said, using the Sergeant's Mess nickname for their CO.

* * *

Ingabe felt cheated. His forced march through difficult terrain had achieved nothing. Zawutu was gone, the encirclement a dismal failure. The only small recompense came from the rapid response of the Major commanding the reserve, who had caught up with the rear of the Eshanti army and was continuing to harass it. With any luck Zawutu would be prevented from making a stand and the Zaire border lay just beyond the Impolo valley. Push him across that and Zawanda would be his, and he its President.

He studied the map. "If we move in a straight line from here, cross country, we'll catch up with Major Boboli and reinforce his drive into Zawutu's rear" he muttered. "I wonder why the British haven't come yet?"

The dark prospect had lain heavy on his mind from the beginning and had grown more so with every passing day. But the British had not come, and in their absence the conflict looked set for an Ushkuu victory within the next day or so.

"I believe we'll be in power before anyone can interfere," he said, feeling a sudden upsurge of confidence.

"Yes, sir, but the men are very tired. They were pushed very hard to get here," a young Captain said, to be shushed by a senior Major.

"It is true. The men are tired, but ready to go on if you wish it, sir," the sycophantic Major said, without a thought for the soldiers.

Ingabe looked at him kindly. He favoured yes men. "Let them eat," he said. "It is only a few miles further."

In the event it was next day before Ingabe got his army on the move. His quartermaster department, outstripped by the rapid advance, were way behind with rations, water and ammunition and had struggled throughout the night to resupply. Ingabe fretted and paced and swore and threatened dire consequences if his supply train did not sharpen themselves up. But despite his impatience, his people were happily spared the dark mood which usually accompanied such delays and disappointments. The reason, the tardiness of the British to react. His deepening sense of disaster had thus been lifted, and he found himself empathising a little with the difficulties his quartermasters were experiencing, though not enough to forgive their sluggishness entirely.

By the time the main Ushkuu force did recommence its advance, the bulk of the Eshanti were well on their way to making a clean break of it. Ingabe travelled fast and joined up with his advanced units early on the afternoon of the third day. He conferred with the CO, Major Boboli, who explained that the range of hills to the front was occupied by Zawutu's rear guard and that he had not been able to move against it because his ammunition had all but run out.

Ingabe nodded. "Well, I'm here now and your ammo is just coming up. We'll push on over this range as soon as it's been distributed."

★ ★ ★

Harwell heard Corporal Sanderson whistle softly. The camouflaged lid of the command post was propped up on four stones and would be lowered as soon as the Ushkuu were in sight, but for now there was enough room for the binoculars. Harwell aimed them at a spur that snaked away from him towards the city. Along the spur a ragtag of Eshanti had been holding out against the Ushkuu reserves. Other Eshanti were holding similar positions on the hills on both sides. But now they were moving, rearwards.

"Here they come," he commented to his Sergeant, meaning the Ushkuu. He reached to dislodge the stones holding up his roof just as an Eshanti soldier tripped over it, almost destroying all the meticulous work that had gone into harmonising it with its surroundings.

"Hey, watch where you're going!" Harwell bellowed as he shoved the offended article aside and stuck out his head. The next Eshanti, moving fast, an NCO experienced in fieldcraft, threw himself to the ground and aimed his rifle at Harwell.

"Hey!" Harwell said, raising his hands in the air. "British. Has no one told you we're here?"

The Eshanti NCO hesitated, but when the ground around him began to move and other bodies appeared bearing weapons, he clambered to his feet. In good English he apologised politely and unhurriedly, as if he had simply spilled someone's drink.

Harwell took the opportunity. "The Ushkuu. Where are they?"

"In the valley, sir. They've stopped their advance for some reason and our officers told us to get out while the going was good."

"They're not on your tail then?" Harwell pressed him as other Eshanti streamed past at the jog, avoiding these holes in the ground that looked like animal warrens and were full of strange soldiers with even stranger guns.

"No sir," the NCO replied, eager to be away all the same.

Harwell nodded. "Very well. You'd better get going." As the Eshanti saluted and moved off, Harwell signalled for his troopers to conceal themselves once more. He waited until the last pair had adjusted their camouflage, swept the area to make sure none of the hides was obvious, then stuck up the aerial of his Platoon radio and called Hawthorn.

"The Eshanti have retired," he began, speaking softly over the short range. "The Ushkuu are held up for some reason, but it's certain they'll be stomping over me pretty soon now. I'm going to ground. Over."

Hawthorn responded: "Message received. Out," and handed the handset to the signaller guarding Company channels.

* * *

Ingabe conferred again with Boboli; this young chieftain was no fool, and Ingabe had come to respect his judgement. Having risked Ingabe's wrath by halting the advance and stoutly defending his decision, Boboli had unknowingly risen several notches in the estimation of his Commander in Chief. Ingabe listened, and agreed that the reserve units were too exhausted to take part in the forthcoming assault on the heights before them.

"The main army will attack as soon as the assault units have received their orders" he said. "You keep the Eshanti occupied for now, and when the attack is launched it will be through you. Your people are due a rest."

"Yes sir," Boboli said. No heroics, only satisfaction that

Ingabe had understood. Ingabe studied the young man and liked what he saw. There would be a place for him once this war was over.

The assault went in two hours before dusk so as to allow time for the lead units to fight their way up and over the crests and bounce the next range just as the light was fading. Next stop the valley itself.

Once there, light didn't matter. It was only half a mile wide and a damn great river ran through the middle of it, so no one could get lost. And, thought Ingabe, no one could escape, short of withdrawing over the border. What he didn't yet know was that Hawthorn sat astride the ultimate hill, the one that blocked the valley entrance. He soon would.

CHAPTER SEVENTEEN

"Are your reinforcements in Zawanda yet?" President Clayton demanded, his voice echoing softly in the Cabinet room, where Masters, emulating the American President, had put the call on muted speakers. Beauchamp and Henright were present, along with General Herbert 'Buster' Hilliard, the Combined Chief of Staff.

"No," Masters replied succinctly.

"Hell, Clive, the CIA and the Pentagon are at my throat every damned day over this, and they're right to be. They want to send a task force in to get that goddam nuke, and I'm having a hell of a job keeping the lid on."

"I'm truly sorry, Wilbur," Masters replied coolly. "But even the US could not enter Zawanda legitimately. There is still no absolute proof of a nuclear missile; no evidence, no witnesses. This isn't Grenada, you know. A different situation altogether. And as I told you before, the officer commanding the small British force already in Zawanda was under instructions to find and take custody of any aircraft fitting the description we gave him. Well, he has visited the airport and reported back that there are no aircraft there, of any kind. A civil war is in progress over there, which is occupying all the major players. If that aircraft is still there, nothing is happening to it. Either we wait until the war is over, or invent an excuse to go in."

"But we figured you'd have created a situation, in inverted commas, by now," Clayton complained bitterly.

"Not so easy," said Masters. "Our contingent is surrounded by the warring factions and its communications are on the blink. In the meantime we've been in touch with Zawanda's neighbours and other African Commonwealth members and there would be no objection to British intervention, providing it's legal. And there's the rub. But we'll think of something, don't you worry."

"You have troops ready to go in?" Clayton enquired, a formality for the benefit of those listening in on his side.

"Of course. The Parachute Brigade is on standby."

General Hilliard nodded vigorously.

"That's good," Clayton bellowed, then at lesser volume, more intimately, he went on: "Look, Clive, I really do want to leave this to you, but I'm under enormous pressure at this end. The policy of deterrence must be seen to be effective so that any future prospective purchaser understands the sort of trouble he'll run into if he tries it on. The Iraq dimension, too, is extremely dangerous, but I suppose we can't entirely blame Zawutu for that. Nonetheless, our young President mustn't be allowed to be get away with it scot free."

"We concur," Masters said in a conciliatory tone. "Be assured, we shall not let the grass grow under our feet on this one."

Unable to resist having the last word, Clayton came back with, "I sincerely hope not, 'cos the USA wields a mighty big lawn mower." He immediately regretted it. "A joke, Clive, just a joke. As I said, we'll leave it to you." Even then could not prevent himself from adding, "For the time being, anyway."

"Well, you heard that," Masters said to the assembly as he

replaced the handset. "The Americans are not renowned for their patience, nor for honouring international protocols when it suits them – Grenada for instance. If we want to keep this to ourselves we have to find a solid, acceptable reason to send in more troops. General?"

Hilliard coughed. He was a consummate military politician, but he held little brief for the civilian equivalent. Too slippery. They confused him with their expediencies and double dealings. He was a frontal assault man himself.

"Well, gentlemen," he commenced cautiously. "I understand we have lost contact with our unit in Zawanda, and as you are aware, Hawthorn is operating under political control, albeit Ministry of Defence, but outside the army's chain of command." He paused to glance round as if to indicate it would never have happened had he been in charge. "I advised against the unorthodoxy of it at the time, and…"

"Yes, yes," Henright butted in. "But what about the Prime Minister's question?"

Hilliard coughed again. "As I was saying, gentlemen, it is most unorthodox." he glared at Henright. "And that unorthodoxy is responsible, in my professional opinion, for this present communications blackout. You cannot contact Hawthorn and he, so he wants you to believe, cannot contact you." He smiled knowingly. "The MoD people running Hawthorn have had the goodness to keep me informed, so I am aware of his present awkward placement, but it isn't enough to warrant a full-scale rescue operation. His command is in no danger, as far as we know, so until you can communicate with him again I'm afraid you'll just have to keep your fingers crossed. The risk is that if he is genuinely without serviceable radios and is overrun by one or other of the warring parties, we could lose him altogether and not know about it until it's too late. I can only reiterate, this operation is most improper in the military sense and contains many unnecessary risks." He glared again at Henright.

Masters was shocked at the forthrightness of Hilliard's reply. Someone hadn't briefed him properly. He looked sharply at his Defence Secretary before addressing the CoS.

"I want you to accept, General, that it was absolutely essential to take political control of this situation. A straightforward military presence under army command was satisfactory to begin with, but once we got wind of the nuclear component, things changed dramatically."

"We could have handled it, sir," Hilliard said flatly.

"Perhaps," Masters conceded. "But we are where we are and no amount of hindsight is going to improve matters. I ask you again, what next?"

"Isn't that a question for those running the operation?" Hilliard said.

Masters sighed. These bloody generals were so damned touchy!

"General, I seek your expertise on this. I can understand your feelings about how we had to handle things, but I ask you to put that aside and give me your best answer."

Hilliard almost smiled. He felt he had won a small victory.

"If I know officers like Hawthorn," he said, more cooperative now, "he'll talk to you when he's ready. I don't believe his radios are faulty, he probably got fed up with the sort of traffic he's been receiving." Another rapier glance at Henright, as if to say "and I don't blame him". "And when he does surface I suggest you listen. If circumstances are as critical for him as my military intelligence people suspect, then he'll be very busy. My best advice, sir, is to let the army handle it from here on. Hawthorn is engaged in a purely military operation now, which requires military responses and military advice."

Masters shook his head to conceal a nascent smile. This general was no blimp.

"I can see the sense in that, but the reason we took political control in the first place remains extant; we do not have that nuclear missile. I'm afraid that's the way it is, General, I'm sorry."

Hilliard shrugged. "If that's the way you want it, Prime Minister, who am I to argue? Just remember, though, that it's British soldiers lives you're playing political games with."

Masters scowled. "That borders on insubordination, General," he said. "Military use is always for political reasons."

Hilliard bowed his head in acknowledgement. "I'm sorry Prime Minister, please forgive me. I'm very concerned about Hawthorn and his command."

"I understand, and be assured we won't do anything to place them in more danger than is absolutely necessary." He smiled. "And anyway, it looks as if Hawthorn is doing very well in that direction without any help from us."

Hilliard's turn to smile. "I can't deny that, sir."

"Very well then," Masters said finally. "We await Major Hawthorn; a daunting responsibility for such a junior officer. Thank God the army selects and trains them so well," he added as a genuine gesture of reconciliation to the General.

★ ★ ★

The last few remnants of the Eshanti came scurrying down the reverse slopes of the hill before Hawthorn's without even noticing the SAS men burrowed into the crest. They passed through the 2nd's prepared positions on the plain and continued up and over Hawthorn's hill. Then everyone waited. In the unnatural stillness, the next anyone heard was the sound of running feet and the jingle of equipment buckles, and then a moment later a human tide of Ushkuu came hurtling over the brow in full cry, caution thrown to the wind. Eager and bunched together as they never should have been, they rushed down the slope, each man eager to be first. Consequently they presented a mass target to the 2nd's riflemen, who waited.

Hawthorn held his breath, but he still flinched when the 2nd opened up a withering concentration of fire. Most of the first few reckless ranks of Ushkuu fell, killed and wounded, and the momentum slowed. More were brought down as those still on their feet tried to stop and go to ground, but they were either driven forward by those behind or trampled to death.

Gradually the horror of the situation filtered back through the oncoming ranks and the ambushed army finally split, to wheel away from the deadly swathe of bullets. The two human streams curved away, finding refuge in the gulleys. Those not yet committed held back and were redirected down the rear slopes to join up with the stricken remnants of the first waves trickling back over the difficult terrain between the hillsides. There the Ushkuu paused, licking their wounds while Ingabe fumed and ranted.

"I'll execute those fatherless officers!" he screamed. "Where's their training, for Allah's sake? The advance should have been controlled, the men spread out in the proper way."

But he had not himself experienced or witnessed the full weight of the 2nd's revenge. Had he done so he would have known that nothing could have made it past them, given the mood they were in.

He gathered his officers and heard from those who had experienced the horror of the Eshanti trap just how devastating their stopping power had been. All were now certain that the only way forward was to patrol the area cautiously and ascertain the strength of the opposition.

"I never expected them to make a stand on the plain," one officer said. "In the hills, yes, but on the plain?"

Ingabe nodded. "I wouldn't be surprised if it wasn't that Englishman, Hawthorn, who put Zawutu up to it" he said, half admiringly. "But let's not be downhearted. If Zawutu wants to fight on level ground, that suits me. At least we don't have to fight up these bloody hills any more." His officers mumbled their agreement. "Mount a series of patrols to test the depth of their positions. We can't go round this time. The only way forward is over that last line of hills, so we must defeat him on the plain before he can withdraw any further." Ingabe smiled at the men around him. "Zawutu might like Hawthorn's advice, but this time he's been given a dumb steer. There's no escape for him now."

All this time the 2nd had been pulling back into the Impolo valley. In his eagerness to organise the next, and to his mind, final, phase of the war, Ingabe had omitted to establish observation over his enemy.

When the patrols he'd ordered were debriefed just before dawn next day, they reported no resistance. Indeed, they had swept the plain thoroughly, the leaders said, and found no one in residence.

"They've gone again?" Ingabe screamed at the messenger. "In such a short time? How in Allah's name can the whole of the Eshanti army have disappeared so quickly?"

He sat and thought about it. Of course - the only logical explanation was that the main Eshanti army must already have moved into the Impolo Valley by the time the pursuit had foolishly cascaded downhill onto the plain. What his troops had encountered was a stop line; classic military thinking, and Hawthorn's again, he reckoned. His smile turned to a frown as he reflected that this war was not going the way he wanted. This kind of civil conflict was seldom fought according to British Staff College doctrine. Even rarer was it fought face to face, as this one had been so far. More commonly, a rebel force moved against specific targets such as towns and communications centres. Never did it take on a regular army as he had finished up doing. And once the capital had fallen, so, as a rule, had the government; though not in this instance. With Zawutu still in charge of a substantial loyal army he had to be beaten in the field before the British woke up.

Simbli had reported that the British were, for some reason not to do with the civil war apparently, very twitchy about Zawanda and were definitely making plans. Too late to change any of that now, Ingabe told himself. The finale would take place in a few days in the Impolo Valley, head to head. "May the best man win," he muttered to himself, and immediately regretted it.

Thank the Lord none of his officers was there to hear him. He shook his head to clear it of the insidious germ of doubt.

Then he called together his commanders. "OK," he told them, "So the way is clear into the valley. Let's seize it and use it as an advantage instead of weeping into our beards. Get ready to move at first light tomorrow. You'll need all that time to drill junior officers and NCOs in fieldcraft all over again. There must be no repetition of yesterday's fiasco."

Major Boboli ventured, "I think they've learned that lesson the hard way, sir."

"Maybe, but use the time to reinforce the message."

★ ★ ★

The advance kicked off on time. An early morning mist swirled off the Impolo, creating a dense carpet of vapour that rose to above head height, a natural smoke screen into which the van moved cautiously forward, scouts well out in front. The remainder of the Ushkuu were coming on behind in a wedge formation, one sub unit up and two back all the way up to Brigade level.

The first Ushkuu to set foot on Hawthorn's hill was a warrior from Ingabe's own village, a private soldier with a reputation as a spirit man, one reputed to have the ability to move invisibly through the bush. He was also thought to bring good luck.

The sun was not yet strong enough to burn the mist off and visibility was only a few yards. Private Askari, the spirit man, had his eyes on the ground and could not have seen Hawthorn's Union flag through the mist anyway. He took his first step onto the narrow track that led upwards in zigzag fashion, and was about to take a second when an amplified voice came down to him as if from Heaven. "Stay where you are!"

Askari did not understand a word of it, but Allah didn't have to speak Ushkuu. He screamed, then turned and ran. The rest of the scouts, nervous from their isolation in the mist, heard him, and they also turned and ran until stopped by their Platoon Commander, who had started forward to see what the noise was about.

Ingabe beat his head with his hands. "What does he mean, Allah spoke to him? Is the man mad? And why has the advance stopped?"

A junior officer sent to explain what had happened stood before Ingabe, moving his weight from foot to foot and staring anxiously at the floor. In Zawanda, 'shooting the messenger' was not necessarily a figure of speech.

"Word has passed that Allah does not want us on the mountain" he mumbled.

"Rubbish!" Ingabe spat back. "We'll see about that. Fetch my aid and tell him to get me a walkie talkie." The subaltern saluted and scampered away, relieved to have been let off so lightly.

Ingabe considered the problem. He knew it was no use simply rebutting the scout's account; a gesture had to be made. He waited for his aid to arrive, then shouted loudly so that all in the vicinity would hear and pass it on: "I will go myself and ask Allah to let us pass".

He came forward in a Land Rover driven by his aid and dismounted about a hundred yards from the base of the hill. Frightened men held in place by threats from their officer moved aside to let him through as he strode out manfully, emulating a warrior stalking his first lion. Soon he reached the base of the hill and stared dramatically upwards into the opaque, refracted light. He raised both arms to heaven and called out: "Allah el Akbar!"

He almost shat himself when an answering voice boomed out from above: "Do not advance any further. The slopes are mined."

The infra-red scope in Butler's hands had given plenty of warning of approaching body heat. Ingabe's call to Allah merely corroborated a human presence.

It took a full minute before Ingabe recognised the language. "Who is that?" he called up, terribly afraid that the British had indeed arrived and were established across his path in some strength.

"We are the British Assistance Mission. Who are you?"

He heaved a silent sigh of relief. Not the British then, only Hawthorn.

"I am Colonel Ingabe, commanding the Ushkuu Liberation Army, and you are in my way," he said threateningly. "I demand you let me pass."

Hawthorn himself had scrambled forward and joined Butler in the forward observation trench. He took the portable megaphone from his 2ic and raised it to his lips. "This is Major Hawthorn, sir. I wish I could help you. Unfortunately, for as long as I occupy this hill it is British Sovereign territory and I am expressly commanded not to become involved with either side in this dispute."

Ingabe gasped at the effrontery. "You are impertinent, Major. No part of Zawanda is British. You gave it all up when you left us to fend for ourselves. Now, I repeat, you will let my forces pass or else."

"Or else what?" came the obvious reply.

"Or I shall force my way through."

Much as Hawthorn welcomed a scrap, to take on the whole Ushkuu rebel army would be folly indeed. He temporised. "I think we should talk about this," he said.

Ingabe paused to consider. The Eshanti were well into the valley by now anyway and he needed a full day to march the whole of his army into that narrow defile of uncharted river bed and bush. He could not risk splitting his force half in and half out, and he had no real intention of taking on Hawthorn's group, small though it was; the British would come down on him like a ton of elephant's dung if he did. Compromise was the only way.

"I agree. Let's do it now."

"Sorry again," Hawthorn replied. "But I have to contact London about this. Dawn tomorrow is the earliest." This would give Zawutu more time to prepare.

"Sounds like an invitation to a duel," Butler remarked whimsically.

Hawthorn chuckled. "Well, let's hope it's not. My skill with the native spear is somewhat rusty."

At the foot of the hill Ingabe swore sibilantly. "Oh very well," he conceded. He could do no other. Afraid of what Hawthorn might tell his superiors in England, he felt it better to appear cooperative for now.

"Did you get the gist?" Hawthorn asked Granby, who had sauntered up.

Granby nodded "You're not actually going to get on the radio to London, are you?"

"Not unless I want a whole set of instructions that make no sense, no."

"So, you'll meet old grumbly guts down there face to face in the morning, is that it?"

"What else is there?" Hawthorn replied. "God, I'm hungry. Let's see if breakfast's ready."

Butler walked behind, shaking his head. In his long career he had never served in conditions like this before, under such a cool customer as Hawthorn, who by his very presence kept everyone sharp as needles and loyal to a man, without effort it seemed, and risked his own future so casually. And he hoped he never would again. It was infectious.

On the plain below, the Ushkuu army rested, the fear of Allah's intervention was dissipated by an issue of native beer augmented by the knowledge that it was the British up there, not God.

★ ★ ★

By dawn next day Zawutu had made good progress. He had rested his troops overnight rather than hazard them along the rock-strewn valley floor. Then, as daylight chased away the shadows, his men started forward again, visibility through the river mist just adequate for the men to avoid the natural obstacles along the route. He hoped to reach and secure the escarpment at the head of the valley before Ingabe made contact.

And there was no sign of Moi.

★ ★ ★

Hawthorn rejected suggestions that he should at least take one other officer with him, nor would he agree to snipers watching over him. "It's only a chat," he insisted brightly. "Nothing will happen to me."

Granby and Butler saw him off, Granby descending as far as the forward observation post. "I'll wait here for you," he said.

Higinbottom, the Corporal on observation duty, shrugged cheerfully as Granby jumped down into the trench. He had never been in such demand, and by the top brass as well. The OC and 2ic last night and Mr Granby now. Something to write home about, he thought, suitably embellished, of course. He moved his kit to make room.

The scene below resembled Granby's recollections of a Territorial Army annual camp; men lying about on the ground cleaning weapons, assembling kit after a night's sleep and cooking on hundreds of individual camp fires. There seemed to be no sense of urgency, yet he had the impression there was considerable energy down there just waiting to be released; the very air seemed to buzz with tension.

A cluster of men stood close to the foot of the hill and as Hawthorn reached the bottom, one of them stepped forward; Ingabe.

"Major Hawthorn?" he said. "I've heard much about you."

"And I you," Hawthorn replied.

"Yes. And now we meet as men of arms. I see you." Ingabe saluted, and Hawthorn returned the gesture. Ingabe indicated two rugs laid out on the ground a few paces away.

"We Ushkuu sit when we have serious talk."

Hawthorn nodded. "Makes sense," he said and fell in behind. Ingabe adopted the cross-legged seating style of his race, which Hawthorn found extraordinarily painful. He settled for a sort of sideways, half-lying posture.

"Can I offer refreshment?" Ingabe enquired once they were still.

"Just had breakfast, but thank you."

Ingabe lowered his head in acceptance, then said: "Major Hawthorn, you said last night that your government does not wish you to become involved in our troubles, is that correct?"

Hawthorn nodded.

"Very well then. By refusing passage into the Impolo valley, you are clearly not honouring that wish. In preventing my advance you are ipso facto assisting the traitor President Zawutu."

"Who is the legitimate leader of Zawanda," Hawthorn interrupted, taken a little aback by the Latin tag, but not showing it.

"An unpopular leader," Ingabe argued. "Whom the people want to see replaced. Unfortunately, unlike Britain, we no longer hold elections here, so the only recourse the people have to remove a despot is rebellion, as you may have noticed. The majority favour me in this current affair and that gives me the right under our bizarre, empirical constitution to challenge for the Presidency in the only way we have."

Hawthorn found himself drawn to this man. He argued a strong case, always assuming that the interpretation of Zawandan culture and methodology he was expressing was correct, of course. Nevertheless, Britain wanted Zawutu to remain, and Hawthorn was obliged to pursue that policy by every means. He looked steadily at Ingabe.

"All that you say may well be true, but I'm not here to judge the rights and wrongs. My orders are to sit tight and not provide aid to either side, other than within the remit under which I and my men came here. For your information, that was to provide training and advice."

"So it is you! You are suggesting all these clever little ruses to Zawutu. I wouldn't call that even-handed and certainly not within the spirit of your orders."

"Who said anything about being fair? If I'm asked for advice, I'm obliged to provide it."

"Will you get off that hill?" Ingabe now demanded, frustrated by the way the conversation was going in circles.

"No" Hawthorn replied. "I've explained why not."

"Very well," Ingabe said angrily. "You force me to adopt extreme measures." He rose to his feet and called over two officers waiting on the fringe. "Arrest this officer," he demanded, and they stepped forward simultaneously and took a firm grip on Hawthorn's arms as if expecting the order.

"This is unlawful detention," Hawthorn said calmly, offering no resistance. "I hope you know what you're doing."

Ingabe merely shrugged.

Hawthorn was led to a waiting Land Rover, bundled inside and driven off towards the city. The whole episode was observed by Granby from Higinbottom's trench and by Harwell from his hidey-hole on the hill opposite.

"What'll happen to Major Hawthorn now?" Higinbottom asked anxiously.

"He'll be fine, lad, but it was good of you to ask," Granby said. He climbed from the trench and started uphill as fast as his ageing legs would allow.

Butler and Phil Story met him at the top. "Shall we go after him?" Story asked enthusiastically, more brave than practical.

"I don't think he'd want that," Butler said, surprised that he knew Hawthorn so well.

"Did he leave any orders?" Granby asked.

Butler shook his head. "Not with me, but I know he gave Jimmy Harwell something in writing before sending him over yon." He pointed.

Granby gazed at the trail of dust which marked Hawthorn's progress towards New London. "All we can do now then is follow his last order," he said, facing the two officers. "Which as I recall was something like – 'no one goes over this hill'."

Both nodded their agreement. "I'd better get back to my platoon then," Story said. "Should I go round the others and let them know the score?"

"If you would, please," Butler said, realising with a shudder that command of this madhouse now fell upon him. "Maximum alert. No one to leave their trenches. Richard, would you be so kind as to let the admin blokes know we're going to battle stations? Ammunition is the priority." God, but it was infectious!

Granby did a double take. This once docile, withdrawn, unremarkable officer was suddenly revealing a serious set of fangs. But then command did that to people; the outright, absolute responsibility for the lives of others subjugated all other considerations, and Butler was a fully experienced infantryman after all.

The sun had hardly breasted the rising ground on the left when the leading element of Ingabe's army pushed onto the lower slopes of Hawthorn's Hill. Butler, who had taken up a position in Higinbottom's trench, took a grip on the handle of the megaphone. They'll never believe this at home, Higinbottom thought.

"This is Sovereign territory," Butler bellowed into the amplifier. "The property of Her Britannic Majesty Queen Elizabeth the Second of Great Britain and Northern Ireland." Might as well give them the full title, he thought. "You are advised not to attempt to scale this hill."

Granby, at the flagpole, hoisted the Union Flag to reinforce the message.

A single figure stepped from the mass. It was Ingabe. "Rubbish!" he shouted through cupped hands. "It is you who are trespassing on Zawandan soil. Either you let me through or Major Hawthorn will suffer."

Butler stared down. He hadn't expected that and found himself lost for words.

In his hole in the ground on the hill opposite, Harwell knew exactly what to do. He pressed the ring button on the field telephone and waited for the Royal Signals sergeant to reply.

"OK. Now," he said to the sergeant.

Behind the crest, from his burrow beneath a loose pile of rocks, the sergeant, assisted by his two SAS minders, rigged a portable folding satellite antenna and aimed it in accordance with the set of tables he carried in his manual, using a hand-held prismatic compass to lay the bearing. He then switched on the radio, checked the battery charge and completed a routine self-check. A minor adjustment to the aerial, and all was set.

"Ready sir," he reported over the field telephone.

Harwell pulled Hawthorn's written orders from his breast pocket and studied the procedure. "Hullo Signals Four," he opened into his remote microphone.

In London, the operator on duty, who with his colleagues had spent days and nights listening to nothing but the crackle of electronic noise, almost fell off his chair when Harwell's voice reverberated in his ears.

"Signals Four, wait out" he said, and crossed his fingers that he wouldn't lose the signal. He rang the duty officer. "Hawthorn's back on line, sir."

"For God's sake don't let him get away!" the rotund, well-tailored, pin-stripe-suited officer screamed at him. "I'm coming."

The door swung open, bounced off the wall and slammed shut again behind Pin Stripe, who in his haste to get to the set hardly noticed.

"Give him to me," he shouted, almost ripping the headset from the poor operator's head.

"Hullo. Signals Four," he said, then held his breath. Hawthorn had revealed an annoying habit of switching off in the middle of a transmission.

"Signals four," he heard to his utter relief. "This is SAS Sunray. Regret transmission must be in clear. Matter is urgent and I have no codes. Sunray major taken captive by Ingabe and removed, presumably to New London. Ushkuu army threatening our position which is Map 34, grid reference 224

839. Captain Butler in command. We also have Mr Richard Granby with us. Situation is that President Zawutu is in Impolo valley in company with Major Moi's guerrillas. Hawthorn's Hill, the feature we occupy, lies between Ingabe and the neck of the valley with no other access. Possible that Ingabe will force the hill. I am in separate, secure location in touch with the main force by radio. Instructions, over."

"Wait out" Pin Stripe said. This required bigger fish than himself.

"Signals Four. Have only a few serviceable batteries and cannot recharge. Suggest we arrange a specific time for next comm."

Pin Stripe looked at his watch. "Call me again in two hours, and please don't forget!"

"Wilco, out."

★ ★ ★

Henright yelped with joy. Not only had contact been established but the British team was in serious trouble, their Officer Commanding actually in the hands of the rebels.

Masters took a slightly different view, concerned for the British soldiers and for Hawthorn, who, though they hadn't met, he had come to admire.

"Let's not run any risks with Hawthorn's life," he told Henright. "And I want our lads out of there safe and entire."

"Of course," Henright said compliantly. "Do we launch the Paras?"

"Yes," Masters said without hesitation.

CHAPTER EIGHTEEN

Granby sat in the command dugout staring at the Ushkuu officer opposite. The man had been dumped on him by Gordon Butler, who had materialised from the forward observation post a couple of minutes before with two of them in tow. He had left this one with him and departed in a hurry with the other. "What the hell's going on?" he had called after him, but either Gordon hadn't heard or he had chosen not to.

"Do you know?" he demanded of the Ushkuu.

The officer shrugged. "No good English," he said, but Granby doubted that. He had to wait until Butler returned before being apprised of the situation.

"Ingabe threatened to do injury to Alistair if we didn't comply," Butler explained dourly. He glanced sideways at the Ushkuu. "English?" he whispered.

Granby shook his head. "I'm not sure," he confessed. "But what the hell."

Butler took another sly look and shrugged. "OK. Ingabe wants no more interference from us, and I had to agree. I had no alternative. These fellows, and three more to come, are here to see that we don't do anything silly. I figured that there was no point in calling Ingabe's bluff with Alistair's wellbeing on the line."

Granby nodded and glanced surreptitiously at the Ushkuu minder sitting across the dugout. How much did he really understand?

"Can we go outside?" Granby enquired of him, speaking slowly and gesturing towards the exit.

The Ushkuu nodded, his English apparently good enough to understand that. "I come too," he added, smiling in a friendly way.

As they emerged into daylight Granby spoke in an aside to Butler. "As I said, I'm not sure how much this gook understands, so let's be careful about sensitive matters, eh? How long is this going on for?"

"Who knows?" Butler replied, trying hard not to stare at their escort. "Until Ingabe has achieved whatever it is he wants to achieve, I suppose."

The three walked aimlessly, threading their way between trenches occupied by confused light infantrymen who wouldn't know an Ushkuu from any other native soldier. All they did know was to keep their heads down and carry on as normal, eating, sleeping and shitting, as the Sergeant Major had elegantly put it.

"They've still got their weapons?" Granby said, surprised. He gazed about him as they passed through the rear left Platoon's positions. "And there's plenty of ammunition stacked in the trenches as well."

"I threatened Ingabe with unspecified retaliation if he tried to disarm British troops in the field," Butler explained with a chuckle. "Said the people at home wouldn't stand for it. That's why he insisted on sending these officers, to make sure we behaved ourselves. And he's got Alistair as guarantee"

Granby smiled. "Well done. All we have to do now is find time to ourselves so we can plot a little," he said sotto voce, making eye contact and nodding once.

Butler nodded back, imperceptibly, and addressed their Ushkuu escort.

"English. Who speaks English?"

The officer smiled. "English no good," he said, meaning, Butler hoped, his ability to speak the language.

"Yes, but who is good?" Butler insisted.

The Ushkuu pointed to another Ushkuu officer who was talking to Lieutenant Williams. "He good," he said, calling out and waving an urgent hand in a 'come here' gesture.

"Lieutenant Beriwelli" the second Ushkuu officer said with a salute as he arrived a moment later.

Butler had images of a pair of disembodied wellington boots walking across the plains of Zawanda, and suppressed a smile. Naughty, he told himself. Here the name was probably highly respected.

"I wonder if we might have a word?" he said after returning the salute. "We have a ceremony of changing the flag every midday from the Union flag to the Regimental flag. I hope you will permit us to continue this ancient custom?"

The two Ushkuu officers exchanged glances, Beriwelli interpreting for the other. They swapped a few words in their own language, then Beriwelli turned to Butler.

"What harm can be done by it? Yes, of course you may. We understand the importance of these regimental customs."

"It is important it is done with proper ceremony," Butler continued pompously. "With only regimental personnel in attendance."

"We understand," Beriwelli said. "We will observe from a respectable distance if that suits you."

Butler hid a smile. "Most kind," he said. "So, with your permission." He nodded to Granby, who fell in alongside.

"Brilliant," said Granby. "That was quick thinking, but where's the Regimental flag?" He changed step with a huge skip to fall in with his companion.

"There is one," Butler said. "I just don't know where it is." He giggled at the mess he was in.

Corporal Prithy in the nearest trench had overheard the whole conversation and recognised the dilemma. With great presence of mind he ferreted around in his kit and produced a Serbian flag he had plundered when the unit was in Bosnia and forgotten about. "The Regimental flag, sir," he said with a wink, handing the folded cotton square to his Captain.

Butler took it with a straight face and shook it out. "Thank you Corporal."

He took his time over the proceedings, making each movement slow and exaggerated, all the time praying that the Ushkuu would continue to respect the solemnity of the occasion and keep their distance. He also prayed that the ceremony today would set an enduring precedent and enable Richard and himself to talk together at least once a day without being overheard; they might not always be accompanied by their present 'English no good' jailer, he reminded himself.

Granby held the halliard while Butler removed the Union flag. "Is Ingabe coming over the hill, then?"

Butler shook the Serbian colour out and toggled it onto the halliard. "Apparently not. I think he's nervous of British reaction. Not at all sure about our official status, stupid bugger. We're in the middle of Zawanda, for God's sake."

Granby almost laughed out loud. "So what's he going to do?"

"Go round." Butler took hold of the halliard and slowly raised the colour.

"There is no way round" Granby pointed out.

"There is. The Impolo River turns sharp left just below us and runs through a steep gorge. There's sufficient river bank to allow two or three abreast to get through. I recce'd it when we first arrived to estimate the risk it presented. It would have been suicide, of course, for Ingabe to attempt it if the Eshanti had been there, but Zawutu is long gone."

Granby stood to attention while Butler stepped back one pace and saluted the raised flag. "Strange how Ingabe seems scared of what the British Government might think or do," Granby said, glancing from the corner of his eye to where the two Ushkuu officers also stood at the salute, staring up at the Serbian flag.

"Look Gordon, I've been thinking. You remember young Story offered to go after Alistair and you said no? Well, you were quite right, of course, but what about Jimmy Harwell's lot? They're specially trained for that kind of thing aren't they? And they're over there, untended by the Ushkuu. Do you think we can contact Jimmy without the Ushkuu knowing?"

Butler glanced quickly at the hill opposite. "I hadn't thought of that, but you're absolutely right. I think I know how it might be done. Leave it with me."

Granby winked and relaxed from his position of attention.

"Very moving," the English-speaking Ushkuu commented on their return.

★ ★ ★

The rains were coming. In the distance a rim of black cloud had assembled and started its slow, inexorable migration towards Zawanda. It would take another week or so, running before seasonally lethargic, low-level winds, before it reached the Impolo valley, where Zawutu stood observing the lowering mass and praying it would all be over by then. Once the deluge came life outdoors would become virtually impossible.

Villagers readied themselves by hoarding grain and dried meat. They turned the animals free and found things to occupy the children for the two weeks of the monsoon. But the two armies, out in the open, would literally be swamped. The river would flood its banks and fill the valley from side to side and every track and gulley on every hill would become a raging torrent.

In a perverse way, Zawutu actually welcomed the prospect. He had lost his transport and had only as much ammunition and supplies as his men could carry, which would not last more than a week at best; even less if he had to fight more than one battle. That grim thought made him realise that he had no idea of Ingabe's whereabouts.

"Get me Major Hawthorn" he told his signaller.

The operator got through almost at once and passed the headset to Zawutu. Zawutu gave the call sign and asked his question: "Sunray speaking. Where is Ingabe now, over?"

"Sunray Major captured by Ushkuu," Harwell replied; another example of Hawthorn's foresight, giving the SAS the liaison radio as well as the rear link. "Sunray Minor on set."

Zawutu felt the shock in his chest. "Captured? How was he captured?"

"Taken hostage when pow-wowing with Ingabe," Harwell replied.

"Where are the Ushkuu now?" Zawutu repeated, his mind racing.

"Entered the Impolo valley this morning. They went round Hawthorn's Hill, taking the river route. It took a long time."

"Ah!" Zawutu breathed. "Of course. I regret what has happened to Major Hawthorn and pray that you all come out of this in one piece. Now I must prepare."

★ ★ ★

Hawthorn had been incarcerated in Granby's old room in the Presidential Palace, the door locked and guards placed on duty outside. He ached from the unceremonious way he had been handled coming here. An overzealous Sergeant, out of sight of his officer, had thumped him once or twice, raising a darkening bruise round one eye and leaving him with painful ribs. The Sergeant's Officer ignored it when he saw it and Hawthorn didn't complain.

Putting that aside, he had done the rounds of his quarters, meticulously seeking vulnerable areas where the judicious removal of a wall panel or the uncovering of a ceiling trap would have allowed him some means of escape, but to no avail. The single, large window was shuttered and the walls were three feet thick and solid. On the positive side, however, he had been here two hours already and no one had visited him. He had the time to escape, if only he could find the means.

Suddenly, as if his thoughts had been read, the door lock clicked and a wizened native dressed in overall trousers and a donkey jacket, bare breasted and on bare feet, walked in carrying a tray.

"I am Mumbi," he said, with a smile which revealed a juice-stained mouth in which there were as many gaps as there were teeth. "I bring food." He placed the tray on an ornamental table at the foot of the bed and straightened, and as he did so he was holding one forefinger across his lips. He glanced at the door and waved Hawthorn further away from it.

"I friend of Dickie Granby," he whispered. "I help."

"Can we get out of here?" Hawthorn asked, accepting Mumbi for what he claimed to be. No time to waste.

"Tonight. I fetch food, then we go."

★ ★ ★

Trooper Haldeman, an SAS signals expert left behind by Harwell to operate the SAS – Hawthorn link and now redundant, slipped unseen down the slope, slithering in the dark night from bush to boulder to stunted tree more effectively than any Ushkuu spirit man. From the base of the hill he moved equally carefully across the plain and up Lieutenant Harwell's hill.

"Haldeman, what the hell are you doing here?" Jimmy Harwell blurted out as the trooper fell head-first into the dugout.

"Message from Captain Butler, sir," Haldeman panted, picking himself up and handing Harwell a folded paper. "Couldn't use the radio. The Ushkuu have taken the batteries."

Harwell grunted at the cheek and waved Haldeman to a seat cut out of the earth. He took a moment reading the note in the light from a pencil beamed torch, then read it again, smiling broadly.

"What a bloody good idea," he said to the SAS sergeant sharing the hole with him. "Captain Butler thinks we should go and find the boss."

"I'll alert Two troop," said Sergeant Jackson, matching Harwell's smile.

Harwell waved him still. "Hold on. We don't know where they've put him. Could be the barracks, the jail or somewhere else, or he might not be in the city at all. We'll need more than one troop. Leave one operator to handle all the radio nets and a couple of troopers to guard things here. The remainder come with us."

"What about transport sir? We can't go wandering around on foot. The bloody war'd be over by the time we got anywhere useful."

Harwell pursed his lips and screwed up his eyes in concentration. "Well, we can't get to our own Land Rovers without alerting the Ushkuu over there." He paused. "But there are two other possibilities. The Eshanti dumped their transport a mile or two back, and the Ushkuu must have left theirs somewhere close; they certainly couldn't get it into the valley. So one or other of those vehicle parks should provide what we need. Get a team moving. They're to pinch enough light vehicles to carry everyone. Customary track signs for us to follow, and let's move fast on this one. We'll try the city first as being the most likely. Any questions? No? Well, let's get on with it."

"Can I come too sir?" Haldeman asked eagerly.

"No, Haldeman. Sorry. I want you to get a message back to Captain Butler."

Haldeman made his disappointment obvious, but every job in the SAS is important and he recognised that Captain Butler had to be kept informed. "OK sir."

"Very well. Hang on a minute while I write it down."

★ ★ ★

The very nature of the Impolo valley lent itself to ambush, so Ingabe moved slowly and with extra caution. He had no need to hurry. The valley ended in an escarpment, then came the border. There was no way out for Zawutu. He literally had his back to the wall.

Gingerly and with exaggerated precautions, the Ushkuu worked their way along the valley floor, taking all of that day to cover half of the distance. Ingabe called a halt as dusk overtook them.

"We'll finish this off tomorrow," he said to his aide confidently. "Zawutu is as good as dead, and the British can't complain that I interfered with their soldiers, except to provide guards for their safety. The UK hasn't responded yet with reinforcements and even if they come now they'll be too late. They will find Colonel Ingabe President. Fait accompli."

★ ★ ★

Butler read Jimmy's note, slipped to him by Haldeman, who on his return had taken up residence in the trench nearest the flagpole. The contrived flag ceremony had turned out to be a godsend for passing and receiving information, from and to platoon commanders for instance, and now from the SAS over the way. And since it worked so well, Granby had taken it one step further by conning the senior Ushkuu into believing that the Geneva Convention allowed for a degree of privacy for prisoners of war and had insisted that he and Butler should be allowed to spend part of their evenings unchaperoned.

"In the trench," the officer had said, indicating the command dugout. "No walking."

So, alone in the dugout that evening, Butler paraphrased the note's contents to Granby in a subdued tone.

"Jimmy's been in touch with London," he said almost directly into Granby's ear. "The Paras are coming. Jimmy says Ingabe annoyed the MoD by abducting the Major, surprise, surprise! One battalion will drop near the airport the day after tomorrow and the rest the day after that. A Brigadier Humphries is in command."

"D'you know him?" Granby asked.

"Only by reputation. Known familiarly as Hotpants Humphries because he likes to do everything at the double."

"He and Alistair should get on well then."

Butler smiled. "It's ironic, but I expect Alistair's too much of a one-man band for Humphries' liking. Anyway, Jimmy's off after the OC and I hope to God he finds him before the Paras arrive, or with nothing left to lose Ingabe might just turn vengeful."

★ ★ ★

Mumbi came on time, carrying the dinner tray, which he placed on the same table as before. "Eat," he said. "Long, no food."

Hawthorn nodded and tucked into the food. It was a stew of sorts, though it contained more fat than meat and tasted abominable. Finished, he wiped his mouth on his handkerchief and stood up. "OK," he said. "I'm ready."

Mumbi grinned. "Eat good," he said, then began to disrobe. Hawthorn watched in fascination as the monkey jacket came off, then the overalls, to reveal a sort of loin cloth caught tight at the hips; the Eshanti skirt. Mumbi at once looked ten years younger. He gestured and moved towards the window.

Hawthorn had tried that and found the shutters closed and locked from the outside, but Mumbi inserted a length of tree root, carefully pared to size, into the thumb hole used normally for opening the shutters, gave it a sudden twist, and with a faint creaking sound the shutters swung slowly open.

Mumbi turned and grinned with well-deserved self-praise, then, repeating the 'follow me' gesture, he slipped cautiously out onto the balcony.

Hawthorn moved just as carefully and came up alongside his rescuer, where he squatted down in the darkest corner of the balcony. He searched for movement on the ground and on the other balconies and saw none. The only incongruity seemed to be the branch of a tree overhanging the balcony, which seemed somehow wrong; it was too long in comparison with the other branches and it was resting too conveniently on the balcony rail.

"We go down" Mumbi said, hopping over the balustrade like a teenager and slithering down the suspect bough into the dense foliage of the tree proper.

Hawthorn checked his surroundings once more, then copied everything Mumbi had done.

"We wait," Mumbi hissed, grabbing Hawthorn by the shirt to prevent him slipping down any lower. "Ushkuu listen."

Hawthorn instantly knew what he meant. He remained

absolutely still so as not to rustle the leaves. The Ushkuu might indeed have noticed something and be listening. He took the opportunity to investigate the odd-looking branch and confirmed his first impression; it did not grow naturally from the tree. Mumbi must have wedged it there somehow during the night. He glanced at the old man with respect.

Mumbi moved. Then he pointed to the ground and simply let go. The two hit the ground within a second of one another, Mumbi up and running before Hawthorn could draw breath. Gathering himself, Hawthorn set out in pursuit.

They finished up in a narrow passageway which emerged onto a street outside the Palace walls. From there Mumbi led them into an unlit, malodorous side alley, where again they waited.

Mumbi nudged him and parodied unbuttoning a shirt and pulling it partially out of the trouser waist band. He followed this by reaching down, taking a handful of dirt, spitting on it then mimicked rubbing it on his face. "No look British," he said, grinning unashamedly.

Hawthorn took the whole procedure seriously, as behove a newly-enrolled student of bush artistry, and when he had finished he looked to Mumbi for an opinion. The little man bounced up and down and pointed merrily. "Now Ushkuu," he said and squeezed his nose to show what he thought of that tribe.

From the alleyway Mumbi took them into another, then another and still another, until Hawthorn became totally disoriented. On his own he'd have been on course only as far as the first crossroads. After that he would probably have travelled in ever-increasing circles and finally been recaptured. As it was, Mumbi was reading the streets like an RAC map, pausing here and there to glance round a corner, at each intersection pushing Hawthorn into the shadows. The miracle to Hawthorn was that in all these manoeuvres they had so far met not a single soul.

Then his luck ran out. Mumbi turned into a broader avenue and immediately bumped headlong into an Ushkuu street patrol.

CHAPTER NINETEEN

Few rebels wore uniform, and although this ragtag bunch looked like bandits to Hawthorn, Mumbi knew better. He shoved Alistair unceremoniously into the shadows and hissed: "Ushkuu." He stepped forward, stooping markedly and generally adopting the stance of a sick old man, an itinerant street bum.

"Your honours," he said obsequiously in his own tongue. "I am taking my idiot son to hospital." He gestured behind him to where Hawthorn waited. "He has been beaten by Eshanti pigs."

The leader of the patrol glanced up and peered at the British officer, who, taking a leaf from Mumbi's book, leaned against the mud wall and groaned.

"You lie," the patrol leader said bluntly. He reached out for Hawthorn. "Let's take a look at this idiot son of yours."

Mumbi staggered as if weak and in so doing deflected the extending arm.

"You clumsy fool!" the patrol leader said angrily, swiping Mumbi across the face with the back of his hand and sending the little old man crashing to the ground.

Hawthorn weighed up the odds. The two junior members of the patrol had not brought their rifles to a state of readiness; they still carried them slung over their shoulders and were therefore vital seconds away from being able to use them. The leader had unslung his weapon, but in order to reach out for the 'son' he had transferred it to his left hand. Striking out at Mumbi had further unbalanced him and made it even more awkward for him to aim the weapon. Hawthorn took a second or two to appreciate these facts, then he acted.

"I think that will be enough," he said in English, coming up off the wall and snatching the patrol leader's weapon in one fluid movement. He had no idea whether the rifle was loaded, cocked or whatever, but he had become familiarised with the Russian-built AK during his Hereford course and knew where to find the various levers and bolts to operate it.

He flicked off the safety and prayed as he pulled the trigger. The first two rounds killed the leader and the subsequent two bursts took out the other two. He sighed with relief that the weapon had functioned.

He reached down to assist Mumbi to his feet. "Are you all right, old man?" he asked slowly.

Mumbi stood erect and nodded. "Eshanti," he said fingering his warrior's skirt to explain why the patrol had disbelieved his hospital story.

Hawthorn nodded. "I expect that was it," he said as he dragged one of the bodies into the shadows, then, with Mumbi's help, the other two.

"Better if they're not found too soon," he explained. "The noise will have alerted others"

Mumbi grinned. "Dead," he said. "Ushkuu pigs." He seemed quite unconcerned that he had just witnessed the despatch of the three men. "No talk now," he added, drawing his hand across his throat. He kicked one of the bodies in a valedictory gesture, then took Hawthorn by the arm and resumed the pace of escape.

Gradually, the built-up areas they were travelling through began to thin out. There were no more scares; Mumbi made sure of that by treating each road junction with consummate care. It slowed progress, but Hawthorn was happy to subordinate himself to Mumbi's superior knowledge and skills, full of admiration for the little man's indefatigability and courage. Impatience would achieve nothing anyway, only potential failure; Hawthorn had learned that early on in his military career when as a platoon commander he had lost the chance of taking a prisoner by acting too precipitously.

As they left the last mud hut behind and entered open country, Mumbi pulled Hawthorn down into the deep brush that extended as far as the tree line where the Ulu began, a dark line of trees in the distance. Hawthorn judged them to be at least a quarter of a mile away, a long journey to make in the open under the intermittent illumination of a hazy moon that had been popping in and out of slowly passing rain clouds like a stroboscope. Faint though the light was, it would make the trip that much more hazardous.

Mumbi placed a finger over his lips and pointed to the dense outline, then back at the city and finally to the sky. Hawthorn nodded. A quick glance at his watch told him they didn't have a lot of time before dawn, and he indicated as much to Mumbi.

"Come," Mumbi said by way of reply, setting off at a tangent that seemed totally wrong. But again, Hawthorn was not about to question an expert native tracker. As they made ground, Hawthorn noticed that they were following an old animal trail where the brush had been trampled down and there was less chance of brittle twigs or pieces of dried wood cracking underfoot. He shook his head in admiration. This way they were able to travel at a good speed.

They entered the tree line undetected; at least, no one had challenged them. Mumbi paused just under cover to listen. He shook his head. "No come," he said, indicating the path they had recently followed.

No pursuit, then, Hawthorn told himself, understanding better now Mumbi's mixture of words and gestures. "OK," he said "Good, eh?"

Mumbi nodded, pointed into the forest and started off at a blistering pace. He glanced back now and then to check that Hawthorn was still with him and slowed each time the Englishman fell behind. In this way they made good progress, until Mumbi suddenly held up a hand and knelt on one knee.

"Road," he said in a whisper as Hawthorn came up alongside and knelt too. He peered through the gloom and then he saw it, a ribbon of tarmacadam shining dully in the patchy moonlight. Which road it was and where it headed he had no way of knowing, but when Mumbi plunged once again into the trees, maintaining a parallel course, it seemed obvious that this was the main route out of the city to the west. To the west lay Zawutu, and Hawthorn's Hill. It could not be long now before he was reunited with his command. He felt excited at the prospect.

The road suddenly entered an area where there was forest on the other side as well, filtering out even more of the light available, but Mumbi's pace did not falter. He suddenly turned and came out of the trees onto the road proper.

"OK" he said. "Quick now."

Hawthorn sighed. Any quicker and they'd take off. He bent over to catch his breath, then straightened and set off after Mumbi at a good pace, confident that the Eshanti knew what he was about and that they were far enough from the city to be safe. He glanced back and was surprised to see the city lights not very far distant. They had clearly travelled in a huge arc to get here.

A moment later a loud, commanding voice from the trees on the left hand side of the road surprised both men. Mumbi swivelled round and dragged Hawthorn with him towards the cover of the trees on the left. Whatever the command had been, it had certainly scared the little Eshanti. But before they reached their goal a group of armed men emerged from the very spot they were aiming for. Hawthorn spun round to run in the opposite direction, but was restrained by an urgent tug on his shirt and Mumbi screaming "No!" He looked about him and saw that they were surrounded.

Mumbi did all the talking, but from the body language of the Ushkuu it was clear he was getting nowhere. The Ushkuu commander – NCO or officer, Hawthorn could not be sure – gave up arguing and snapped his fingers for the radio. A short call to New London, Hawthorn guessed, must have settled the matter, for he turned to Hawthorn and frowned.

"Englishman," he said gruffly. "And Eshanti." he struck Mumbi across the face.

Hawthorn stepped between the two men. "We'll have no more of that, if you don't mind," he said determinedly. "Civilians are not beaten up by civilised armies." This was the second time Mumbi had taken a vicious slap on his behalf and it would be the last, he promised himself.

The Ushkuu raised his fist, then let it drop. "Lucky you British," he said. "This man Eshanti. He help you. Bad man."

"You speak good English," Hawthorn said flatteringly, hoping to calm the Ushkuu down. "This man is my friend. A friend of Britain. What you did to him could make Britain very angry and I don't think Colonel Ingabe would want that."

At the mention of the supreme Ushkuu leader, the man, probably an officer from his demeanour, backed off. "This is war," he said defensively, but made no more aggressive moves towards Mumbi. "You go back now."

Hawthorn was wondering about this ambush. What were Ushkuu troops doing back here? And what a strange way to implement a road block, hiding in the trees at the side of the road. He decided to use his inquisitiveness to keep the conversation going. "Why not barbed wire or something solid across the road to stop people?" he asked ingenuously.

"Ushkuu way," the officer replied, seemingly happy and proud to explain. "Block on track is seen and Eshanti go round. Always wait and surprise."

"Ah!" Hawthorn said, making it sound as if he had just learned something profound. "How very clever. But shouldn't you be up with your army, fighting?"

The officer nodded and indicated his command. "Too young," he said, which surprised Hawthorn. That Ingabe should consider a warrior's age showed that he was not all bad.

The officer went on: "But old enough to stop Moi's Eshanti pigs. Some try to go up to Zawutu. We stop."

Hawthorn smiled. Everyone seemed to know Moi. "Brave young men," he said, sweeping the group with his eyes. "But I think Mumbi and I should be getting on now." And with that he took Mumbi's arm and began to walk away, hoping to brazen his way out.

"Stop. You go back!" the officer shouted. He spoke sharply to his men. Four of them came forward and tied Hawthorn's hands behind him, then moved on to do the same to Mumbi.

A faint glimmer of light stained the horizon in front of them as they set off to march back to the city.

"What now?" Hawthorn whispered to his fellow captive.

"Wait," Mumbi replied without turning his head.

As they rounded a bend, the trees on the left hand side petered out, leaving coarse brush country all the way to the city precincts. The sun's rim began to rise above the horizon, its light and warmth spreading over the land. Mumbi elbowed Hawthorn in the ribs. "Pee. You want pee," he whispered from the corner of his mouth.

Hawthorn nodded. "I need to go to the toilet," he complained, squeezing his knees together and pulling a face. "Pee. Piss, whatever you call it," he added for effect.

The young Ushkuu in charge shook his head. "No go," he said, at which Mumbi intervened in dialect. Hawthorn had no idea what was said, but the youngster finally gabbled something to one of the escorts, who took him by the elbow and led him into the trees beside the road.

"Hands," Hawthorn said as soon as they were out of direct sight. The young Ushkuu frowned, but obviously wasn't keen to assist with such an intimacy. He turned Hawthorn round and slipped the knot, whereupon Hawthorn hit him as hard as he could and made for the deeper forest.

The impact to his upper arm spun him round, the sound of the shot coming a microsecond later. Shock drove him to the ground, where he lay clamping the bullet wound with one hand and using the other to try and get to his feet.

Fingers gripped him roughly and heaved him to the vertical; pain ripped through his arm. He was dragged back to the road, where Mumbi and the two other Ushkuu waited.

Mumbi glanced at the blood seeping between Hawthorn's fingers and winced, but he was happy they hadn't killed him. Hawthorn's hands were re tied despite the damage to his arm. No attempt or offer was made to attend to it.

Mumbi jabbered something and waved his bound hands in the direction of his wounded companion, but all he got for his pains was another clout round the head.

Hawthorn shook his head at him. "Don't worry about me," he said. "I'm fine and you've enough to think about." He knew not much would be understood, but Mumbi would get the gist and start looking after himself, he hoped.

Nothing moved out in front except for a small herd of cows accompanied by a very young boy. The animal's bells clanged in disharmony as their wearers ambled from one source of food to the next, and neither they nor the boy could be construed as a threat.

The senior Ushkuu escort said something to Mumbi, who translated for Hawthorn. "We go. Move fast. Eshanti near."

Hawthorn nodded. His arm hurt and his sleeve and hands were wet with the blood still pumping from his open wound. He still felt strong, which should mean it wasn't too serious, that he wasn't losing too much blood. But he was thirsty, and that might be a bad sign. He took a deep breath and exhaled, then at a steady jog, assisted by a handler on each side, he covered the ground fairly well. They were soon among the mud hut slums that formed the outer perimeter of the city.

The stink grew worse as they went deeper in, deserted alleyways with only the occasional dog moving among the decaying filth. The sun was almost fully up and Hawthorn suddenly became aware that he'd been sweating for a while now. He wondered if it was the rise in temperature, the wound or his exertions causing it. He winced as perspiration oozed into damaged flesh and added a new, agonising dimension to his discomfort. He gritted his teeth, widened his shoulders and strode out stoically.

The lane they were on curved sharply at its far end and as the bend approached, four streak-faced figures suddenly appeared and with utmost efficiency took out one Ushkuu each. Hawthorn slumped against the wall, while Mumbi just watched gleefully.

A fifth camouflaged figure hurried over to Hawthorn. "Are you all right, sir?"

Hawthorn looked up and pushed himself upright. "Hullo Jimmy," he said. "Nice of you to call in."

"Captain Butler sent us," Harwell replied with a broad grin. "Reckons you've been skiving long enough." He took out his knife to cut the rope binding Hawthorn's wrists and saw the blood dripping freely from arm and hands. "What's this then?" he said anxiously, examining the wound.

The entrance hole looked bruised and angry but it had closed and was puckered up like a string purse. It was the mess where the bullet had torn its way out that worried him. There was a ragged crater which was bleeding profusely.

"This needs attention," said Harwell. He took out his field dressing, tore the shirt sleeve away at the shoulder seam and applied the gauze tightly to stem the blood flow. "That'll do until we have time to do more."

Hawthorn screwed up his face as Harwell winched up the dressing another notch, turning it into a sort of tourniquet.

"We've some transport in the edge of the Ulu. Do you think you can make it?" The SAS Subaltern asked sympathetically.

"Not across that open patch again, please," Hawthorn complained, cradling his injured arm in the other hand "That'll be the third time today."

Mumbi, a spectator now, giggled and twisted round so that Harwell could cut him free as well.

"This is Mumbi, by the way," Hawthorn announced. "He got me this far. He comes with us. And if I were you I'd let him lead you across that damned brush, he's an expert."

However Harwell wanted this done tactically with one group static while the others moved, then reversing the roles in turn, always a fire group on the ground to cover. He sliced Mumbi's bonds. "Maybe next time," he said kindly to the old man.

"Move!" he hissed to the four who had sorted the Ushkuu and were now guarding the location; one from a grubby shop doorway opposite, the other three prostrate on the ground, eyes alert, scanning the area, weapons at the ready. Responding to the command, the small action team formed up around Hawthorn and Mumbi and began the trek back; not the way they had come, but following an alternative route laid out by a fifth SAS Trooper, who met them at the next crossroads and took up the lead through dark, odorous alleyways, gradually collecting the remainder of Harwell's men, whose task had been to secure the action scene. Spread out, moving on parallel routes, the whole expedition eventually came to the slum edge of the city and dropped into cover in the deep brush that extended now to the tree line a quarter of a mile distant. From there, Harwell surveyed the open ground ahead and satisfied himself as best he could that there were no obstacles, material or human, standing in their way.

"OK, Corporal," he said to Corporal Henshaw. "You're first, followed by 2 Troop, then this group, then 4. Roll it on so that the OC can keep moving. I don't want him bobbing up and down with that arm. Sergeant, you control the advance. A minute to brief the others."

Sergeant Jackson came scuttling back. "OK sir." He gave the nod to Corporal Henshaw, who waved his team forward. They covered about fifty yards before dropping into cover, the signal for 2 Troop to move. 2 Troop advanced to Henshaw's position and hit the ground. Henshaw glanced back to check that Hawthorn and company were on the move, then rushed forward another fifty yards. This method avoided the necessity for Hawthorn to stop and take cover, making it relatively easy for him to reach the tree line in one slick, rolling movement.

Harwell paused to look back. They had arrived in one piece, and unobserved as far as he could tell. At least they hadn't been shot at.

"2 Troop rear guard," he instructed Sergeant Jackson.

The four Toyota Land Cruisers purloined from Ingabe's transport pool were where they had left them, guarded by two SAS men. They were stripped of their camouflage and pushed into line along the same track they had come in on; there were no other tracks nearby, leaving them no alternative but to retire the way they had come.

"Mount up," Sergeant Jackson repeated, moving among the SAS Troopers. "You too," he added to Mumbi when he came to him.

Mumbi's grin had been getting wider through all the excitement of the day, reduced only momentarily by the injury done to his friend Hawthorn. He revelled in the memories of the initial escape, Hawthorn's audacious attempt to walk them both out of trouble and now the thrill of being with British troops. He leapt into the back of the nearest open backed Land Cruiser like an athlete.

Hawthorn watched, grim faced with pain, but managed a smile at Mumbi's antics.

"We'll be off as soon as we've tidied up the OC," Harwell told Jackson. "Fetch Granger." Corporal Granger, medical orderly, trained to advanced Paramedic standard, came rushing up. "OK, Granger. Quick as you can" Harwell ordered the wiry, sandy-haired Corporal, indicating the bloody dressing on Hawthorn's arm.

Granger smiled. "Soon have you fixed up, sir," he said comfortingly, unslinging his medical haversack.

The dressing had soaked up the output from the wound, but it was saturated and now leaked profusely. Granger removed the sodden pad gently and used it to mop up the surplus before passing the bloody mass to another SAS man for burial; nothing was ever left for an enemy to find.

"It needs a stitch or two at the back," Granger informed Hawthorn, "to stop the bleeding." And with no more ado he plunged a pre-loaded syringe into Hawthorn's arm, twice. "Local, sir," he said succinctly.

The sewing took only a minute or two more and another dressing was applied to cover it all.

"There we are sir," Granger said, repacking his bag. "Should be OK until we get back and the MO can look at it."

"Not that butcher," Hawthorn complained wryly, a pale attempt at humour.

Harwell called in the sentries. "I'll lead, sir," he informed

Hawthorn. "You and Mumbi in the second vehicle. Sergeant, you're in the third and the remainder in the last."

"What about the Ushkuu road block? The one that caught me and Mumbi?" Hawthorn cautioned. "Some of them are still there, I guess."

"We'll go round, but if we can't then we'll take them out. I'd rather not though. Too noisy."

"OK. Let's motor, then." Hawthorn shouted above the roar of starting engines. He walked stiffly over to the second Toyota, where a restless Mumbi bounced up and down irrepressibly among five amused SAS troopers crushed into the back. He climbed in carefully so as not to jog his arm. It still pained him where the local anaesthetic had not been applied.

"When you're ready, soldier," he said, wincing. They pulled away behind Lieutenant Harwell's lead four by four.

Harwell did well to circumnavigate the Ushkuu ambush position through primary Ulu, but there were difficulties. He bottomed his Toyota on a particularly sharp hump and had to be towed off. A steep stream bank held them up while he recced further downstream for a crossing place, and then the third Land Cruiser ran out of fuel and had to be rescued by a siphon job from Hawthorn's vehicle. But gradually they worked their way westwards and finally took a chance on the road ahead being clear. The hills recently evacuated by Zawutu hove into view and not far behind them was Hawthorn's Hill. Hawthorn could feel the excitement mount, despite the onset of a deep throbbing pain as the anaesthetic in his arm wore off.

Up front, Harwell slowed, then pulled into a forest track and stopped. He got out and walked back to Hawthorn.

"Sir, I forgot to mention, there are Ushkuu on the hill. Captain Butler did a deal with Ingabe. No interference in exchange for your safety. Ingabe insisted on leaving a few officers behind to police the arrangement."

"Did he go over the hill?" Hawthorn asked sharply.

"No sir. He found a way round."

"But he's gone into the valley after the President?"

"Yes, sir."

"Very well. Why have we stopped?"

"We walk from here, sir," Harwell replied, casting a glance at Hawthorn's arm, which he knew must be giving him hell. "Get you back to where you're sorely needed and that arm fixed up. We'll wait until dark before going any closer, find a place to rest up and let Granger take a look at you. Another jab might let you sleep," he ended kindly.

* * *

Over the next hours everyone managed to get some sleep. Most had been active for almost twenty-four hours and needed to recharge batteries before continuing on to what promised to be a tricky piece of soldiering. Sentries were relieved every hour to ensure maximum alertness, the SAS Troops handling the rotation between themselves, each Troop responsible for turning out the next guard. Jackson and Harwell shared walking the rounds. Even though it was unnecessary, the SOP for this situation required it.

The unwritten active service rule – when you have nothing to do, sleep – was in full effect. It was a maxim honed to perfection by the SAS, all of whom seemed able to drop off within seconds and awaken fully primed for immediate action. Hawthorn, older and not so intensely trained, found sleep difficult with his sore arm. Granger had shot a phial of morphine into it, but even that had not brought him the rest he needed. Nevertheless, he had left strict instructions to be woken at sunset so as to allow time for him and Harwell to discuss tactics for when they reached the Hill.

The voice was insistent and the hand across his mouth rough and firm. "Sir!" he heard whispered repeatedly in his ear. "Sir!"

He opened his eyes to see the Sergeant Jackson bending over him.

"You fully awake, sir?" the sergeant enquired.

Hawthorn nodded and blinked to show he was. Sergeant Jackson slowly raised his hand from Hawthorn's mouth.

"I must have been asleep," he said, surprised.

Jackson nodded. "Miles away, sir. Anyway, it's nearly sunset."

Hawthorn sat up. "Thank you Sergeant. Where's Lieutenant Harwell?"

Jackson pointed through the trees. "With the transport, sir. Shall I get him?"

"No. I'll find him, and thanks again."

The sergeant nodded and walked slowly away with hardly a sound. He was soon lost in the dense foliage of secondary forest, chosen by Harwell for its better concealment.

Hawthorn climbed to his feet and stretched. "Ouch!" he hissed as a stab of pain shot down his injured arm and resolved itself into a steady throb. "I'd forgotten about you." He glanced respectfully at the offending appendage. Oh for a cuppa," he muttered to himself.

He pulled himself together and set off in the direction indicated by the Sergeant. Every twig and fallen leaf seemed to end up under his feet; the resultant noise sounded like a nest of machine guns. He nodded to the rare SAS men he encountered on the way, all of whom seemed to be extremely busy at something. "Mornin' sir," said in hushed tones, was the most common greeting, accompanied by a controlled smile.

"Watch it!" hissed an anxious voice from under a large bush which Hawthorn had almost blundered into.

"Sorry soldier," Hawthorn replied automatically as he moved on, without actually seeing the man he had exchanged words with.

Where the hell was Harwell? In a normal camp site, even in the jungle, there would be activity, a centre, people milling around. But here there were only trees. The SAS men were so integrated with the flora that you had to walk right over them to find them. Those damned Land Cruisers couldn't be that well hidden, he cursed impatiently. He asked the next SAS soldier he trod on.

"You've missed them sir," was the reply. "Over there." He pointed back the way Hawthorn had come. "And off to the right."

"Bloody trees," Hawthorn said. "Thank you, trooper."

"Over here, sir," Harwell called softly after Hawthorn had been wandering around in the failing light for another minute, totally disoriented.

"Thank God!" Hawthorn exclaimed as he came up with the subaltern. "Another few minutes and it would have been totally black in here and I'd never have found you."

"We'd have found you, sir," Harwell responded quite naturally, with not a trace of arrogance or bravado. A simple truth.

"Well, that won't be necessary 'cos I'm here. Where can we talk?"

Harwell led him between what appeared to be a pair of trees, but which were actually two large branches bent down and somehow staked to the ground. Inside was one of the Land Cruisers.

"I think it may be more comfortable in here," Harwell suggested, opening the driver's door and gently closing it after them with hardly a click. "How's the arm?"

"Sore, but handleable. Tell me again about the position on the Hill?"

"As far as I know there are four, maybe five, Ushkuu officers up there. I've no personal knowledge, of course."

"I understand that. Did you open comms with UK?"

"Yup. Apparently 1st Para is due to drop near the airport some time in the next few days. There's a major panic going on about something, but no one tells me anything," he complained light-heartedly, hoping for a clue.

Hawthorn looked hard at him. Time to be open with this bright young man, he decided.

"The Foreign Office reckons there's a Russian plane, purported to be carrying an atomic bomb, landed at the airport. We didn't see any such plane when we were down there, did we?" Harwell shook his head. "So, if one did land, where is it? That's what everyone's so het up about. The story here is that Major Moi has his hands on it, but with this bloody silly civil war raging no one has been able to do anything about it yet. Hence 1 Para."

"My god! A nuclear bomb, here in Zawanda!" Harwell exclaimed. "Doesn't bear thinking about. Whose is it?"

"That's the fifty million dollar question. The theory is that President Zawutu ordered it for someone else. London fears that might be Saddam Hussein."

Harwell frowned. "So, putting two and two together, that little episode when we cratered the airport runway had no local strategic significance at all?"

Hawthorn nodded. "I couldn't say anything then. Eyes and ears only, you understand. But things have got out of hand and it's better you know."

"Thank you sir. But what next?"

"Next we take back our Hill, then we try to drum some sense into both Ingabe and Zawutu. With the Paras on the way this silly bloody war has nowhere left to go. Lives are being lost unnecessarily now. Even if Ingabe wins he won't be allowed to hold on to the Presidency once our people get here, so he might just as well pack it in at once."

"So, first take Hill, is that right sir?" Harwell asked, getting things into order in his mind.

"That is exactly right, young Harwell," Hawthorn replied. "So let's get there and take a look at what we must do." His arm didn't seem so bad now he was back in charge.

CHAPTER TWENTY

The carefully choreographed progress to Hawthorn's Hill took about three hours. The recce group took another one and a half hours to secure a route to the rear, and another one and a half for the main party to reach the same spot. A similar intermittent moon to the one the night before made movement round the base of the hill rather tricky, but by 4 am Hawthorn and the SAS team were comfortably established on the valley side. From there the hillside towered like a cliff in the pre-dawn light, moon shadows casting strange shapes among the thick undergrowth. Here and there clumps of spiky bushes dotted the slopes like dark monsters. The going would be arduous, Hawthorn realised, and he had a sore arm.

"We need to know exactly the situation up there before we do anything else," he told Harwell, who lay alongside him in a deep patch of prickly brush with the SAS teams spread out around them. Mumbi was there too, excitement occupying his imagination to the exclusion of everything else.

"I agree, sir," the subaltern replied, adjusting his position slightly to prevent a particularly insistent thorn from penetrating his backside. "Pity we don't have Haldeman with us. He's been out and back again on the other side. Sergeant," he hissed to Jackson a short distance away, "fetch Fisher."

"Sir," Fisher reported as he appeared out of a clump of elephant grass not a yard away. Harwell twisted his head round to face him.

"Up on top is Captain Butler and some Ushkuu. I want you to find the 2ic without the Ushkuu finding you. Understood?"

"Sir." Fisher nodded.

Tell him we're here with the OC and get from him as much as he knows about the routine of the Ushkuu up there, then come back here with it. OK?"

"Sir" Fisher said, as unconcerned as if he had just been invited out for a drink.

"Anything else, sir?" Harwell enquired of Hawthorn.

Hawthorn thought for a moment. "I thought perhaps Mumbi might go, but on reflection he'd probably knock off all the Ushkuu soon as blink. Better send Fisher. No, I've nothing to add."

Harwell nodded. "Off you go, Fisher."

They waited almost an hour before Mumbi picked up a faint rustling sound over to the left. He shook his head at what to him was a clumsy approach, and nudged Hawthorn on his good side.

"Your man, I think," Hawthorn passed on to Harwell.

Trooper Fisher, moving flat over the ground on splayed elbows and knees, got himself within whispering distance. Hawthorn almost asked whether he'd made it all right, but that was a puerile question to ask an SAS man, or any soldier for that matter. He felt angry with himself for nearly falling into the trap, and put it down to the debilitating pain in his arm.

"Well?" Harwell prompted.

"Couldn't get close to the 2ic, sir," Fisher reported. "So I spoke to Mr Granby. Joined him for a pee in the latrine trench. A bit naughty, but the Ushkuu guards weren't looking at the time, idle buggers. If there are any more up there, they're asleep, cos I saw none of them. I managed to have a chat with a few of the Light Infantry boys as well, sir. They've got their weapons still, and ammo too."

"That's all very well, Fisher, but what did Mr Granby say about the Ushkuu?" said Harwell.

Hawthorn smiled to himself. Poor Fisher, he thought. He'd done a grand job even by SAS standards and all Jimmy could do was rollock him.

"Right," Fisher said, apparently undisturbed by his Lieutenant's impatience. "Mr Granby said he'd try to get free of his minder and meet you half way down this side of the hill in –" there was a pause, while he observed his watch "– half an hour from now. He says the Ushkuu have been lulled into a sloppy routine and aren't looking for trouble."

"Well done lad," Harwell said at last. "Wait where you are. I might need you as messenger to the rest."

"I'm surprised the Ushkuu didn't disarm our lads, or at least take their ammunition," Hawthorn muttered reflectively. "But that's their mistake, and one they'll live to regret if I have anything to do with it."

Harwell shrugged. "With you in their hands I suppose the Ushkuu thought they were safe enough without getting heavy handed and upsetting everyone."

"Perhaps," Hawthorn said, "Keep an eye on the time." He adjusted his position among the prickly undergrowth, trying to relieve the pain in his arm.

"You all right, sir?" Harwell asked solicitously.

Hawthorn managed a smile. "I'm fine, Jimmy."

"How do you want to do this?" Harwell continued. "Just you, me, both or all of us up the hill to meet Dickie?"

Hawthorn glanced at the sky. The hill stood between him and the eastern horizon, providing no clue as to light conditions from that direction. He looked down at his watch. "What time do you have?"

"Just after six," Harwell confirmed. "Should already be some light on the forward slope."

Hawthorn nodded. "I want to be in control of the hill again before the Ushkuu can react. They should be at breakfast about now, so now's a good time to move."

"What about Dickie?"

"Can't wait for him," Hawthorn decided. "If we're going to do it, let's go now."

★ ★ ★

In the event Hawthorn heard and saw nothing of the SAS men during the climb. It seemed to him that only he, Jimmy Harwell and Mumbi were on the hill, and both Jimmy and the elderly Eshanti were a damn sight fitter than he was feeling. His breath became laboured and his heart pounded as he drove one knee in front of the other. He'd lost a lot of blood and God, but this hill was steep! His knees hurt and his good hand was throbbing from the thorns implanted in it, but he pushed on, striving not to slow down the other two, both of whom kept glancing back towards him in sympathy and offering a helping hand.

A voice from somewhere above them hissed: "Is that you, Alistair?"

Hawthorn felt relieved that he need go no further for now.

"Who else do you think would be stupid enough to climb this bloody mountain?" he complained grumpily, sucking in air to satisfy his oxygen debt. By this time he could just discern a deeper shadow in the brush a few paces away. "Got you," he said.

"Mumbi, you old dog!" Granby whispered with pleasure on sighting his old friend of Palace days. He reached out. Mumbi grinned widely.

"Mr Granby. Good." He took the proffered hand and held it the Eshanti way, elbows bent, held close together, hands clasped.

"Saved my bacon, did Mumbi," Hawthorn confessed.

Granby nodded, as if that were a perfectly natural thing for Mumbi to have done.

"Now, what's the form on the hill?" Hawthorn went on, taking instant control.

"Not much has changed," Granby said. "But what's with the arm?" He came closer and spied the bloody dressing just above Hawthorn's elbow. "Looks serious."

"It's nothing," Hawthorn replied, dismissing Granby's concern. "What about the hill?"

Granby glanced at Harwell, who shook his head in a "leave it alone" gesture.

"The hill, Dickie?" Hawthorn demanded gruffly. "We don't have all day."

Granby apologised and explained the situation. "Gordon has done a brilliant job," he said. "Conned the Ushkuu left and right."

Hawthorn nodded. "I'm sure. But can we get up there and disarm the Ushkuu?"

Granby looked again at Harwell. "It's on, Dickie," Harwell said. "Just say if you think it won't work."

Granby switched his gaze back to Hawthorn. He frowned for a moment.

"There'll only be the night shift awake at a guess, two of them, and they'll be wandering around at random. They're a tardy bunch. You've another hour at most before the rest surface with any degree of alertness."

"Good!" Hawthorn said, breaking into a smile. He turned to Harwell. "Jimmy, I want every Ushkuu up there disarmed and taken prisoner, and I want it done silently and swiftly so there's absolutely no opportunity for them to use their radios to warn Ingabe."

Harwell nodded. He asked no questions, just crawled away.

"See you on top," he threw over his shoulder as he disappeared into the brush.

The light was improving noticeably now and time was of the essence. Mumbi had somehow grasped what was about to take place. "Me go," he said, a wicked glint in his eyes. He began to crawl after the subaltern.

"Get hold of him, for God's sake," Hawthorn hissed to Granby. "He'll cause mayhem up there."

Granby launched himself and grasped Mumbi by the skirt. "No go. You come with us. Better," he said softly, hanging grimly on to a leg.

Mumbi kicked out, then calmed. "Go up with you?" he asked.

Granby nodded.

"OK," Mumbi said, and relaxed.

"We'd better follow on up," Hawthorn said with a sigh, dreading the climb to the top. "Is it general that the lads still have their weapons and first line ammunition with them? Fisher, he's the SAS Trooper who contacted you, believes so."

Granby smiled at the memory. "Fisher, was it? Frightened the bloody daylights out of me. There I am having a quiet pee when this black-faced figure drops in and starts having a slash alongside, mouthing at me through the corner of his mouth. The Ushkuu guard was only a few feet away. Madness! Yes, Gordon persuaded the senior guard not to disarm the chaps on pain of severe retaliation by Britain if he did."

Both the Englishmen were panting by this time. Hawthorn was nearly at the point of exhaustion, but he pushed himself up and along. He had no breath left for conversation.

The slope suddenly increased in severity, and Hawthorn could go no further.

"Leave me here with Mumbi," he gasped. "Send someone down for me once the hill is secured." He sank to the ground.

"I thought you said it was nothing," Granby said as he squatted alongside. "Mumbi and I'll give you a hand."

"It's bloody sore, if you want to know the truth." Hawthorn lifted the arm with his other hand to get it more comfortable. "It's beaten me, and I need a rest. You must go on, though. Leave Mumbi here with me."

"Are you sure?" No wonder Hawthorn was in trouble. Twenty-four hours and no proper treatment for his wound. "OK. Don't move. I'll have someone down here for you in a jif."

"I'm not going anywhere. Just be quick about it." He smiled and gave Granby a push. Mumbi made to follow, but Granby laid a hand on his shoulder. "You stay. Look after Boss."

Mumbi looked back at Hawthorn, took in the picture and nodded. He scrambled back and sat down.

Granby breasted the brow of the hill and lay low for a minute. The whole area seemed deathly quiet; a slight mist and the improving light cloaked the scene in a sort of pale, ghostly ambience. Nothing stirred. He called out Harwell's name softly, as if it made any difference.

"Here" came the reply.

Granby looked up in surprise as the SAS subaltern clambered to his feet from a patch of gorse-like foliage a few yards distant. Gordon Butler was with him.

"All done and dusted as ordered, sir," Harwell said with a wide grin. "Where's the boss?" he added on seeing Granby on his own.

"Down the slope a way. Poor bugger couldn't make it to the top. That arm of his must be worse than he's letting on."

Harwell concurred. "It's pretty bad. I'd better get him some help."

While they waited, Granby enquired of Butler about the Ushkuu.

"Piece of cake actually," Butler replied. "They weren't expecting anything and it was all over in a jiffy. Jimmy's boys were magnificent. The Ushkuu are under guard in the command dugout."

"Good," Granby said. "Alistair will be pleased."

"I'll see to breakfast if you'll wait for the OC," Butler suggested.

Just then Harwell reappeared with two SAS Troopers, who took off over the brow of the hill, crouching low as they went. Nothing was ever left to chance.

"I'll be with my chaps," Harwell said.

Granby watched the subaltern walk away, then made for the rim of the hill. He looked down to see Hawthorn, aided by two SAS Troopers and followed by Mumbi, all within reach.

"Give us your hand," he said to Hawthorn, grasping it gently and assisting him over the last hump before the plateau.

"OK, sir?" one of the two SAS men enquired.

"Yes. Thank you Troopers. You'd better join your outfit. Oh, and get Mumbi some food, will you?" Hawthorn returned the salute left-handed. "Well, Dickie, are we all shipshape up here?"

Granby nodded. "The Ushkuu are in custody, Gordon's getting breakfast organised and Jimmy's tidying up after his excursion to rescue you."

"Sounds about right," Hawthorn replied, shifting his arm slightly inside his shirt front, which was acting as a sling.

"Come on, let's get you to the doc," Granby said, taking Hawthorn's good arm and leading him to the Regimental Aid Post. As they passed between slit trenches soldiers stood to attention and the more forward welcomed their OC back. The sight of his bloody arm caused whispering after he'd gone by.

"Fix this so I can use it," Hawthorn told the MO, Captain Jack Stanley, who smiled in that superior way of a professional dealing with laymen.

"Let's take a look before we do anything else, sir."

"How's Jones's leg?" Hawthorn demanded, swivelling his shoulder out of reach until he had an answer. "I haven't had a chance to talk to him."

"He's on his feet and doing light duties. Now, will you let me look at that arm?"

The dressing had adhered to the raw flesh around and in the wound. The doctor moistened it with an antiseptic and eased it away, except for a small area in the centre which defied all attempts at loosening. "This will hurt," he said as he jerked the bandage free. It at once began to bleed profusely.

"Mmm!" Stanley murmured, using pads of cotton wool to mop up the mixture of liquids running freely from the wound. "The entry is a bit inflamed, but otherwise OK. It's the exit wound. Quite a lot of deep tissue damage and several large blood vessels ruptured. It'll need cleaning and then repairing from the inside out. It really needs hospital facilities, but beggars can't be choosers."

"Just get on with it," Hawthorn grumbled impatiently.

Stanley sighed and glanced at Granby, who shrugged. Then with the aid of local anaesthesia and the assistance of the Regimental medical orderly, Stanley went to work.

It was almost two hours before he was satisfied. He stripped off his latex gloves, dropped them into a disposable bag already laden with bloody wads, syringes and needles, and turned to Hawthorn.

"Sorry it took so long, sir," he said. He searched in one of the medical bags and came out with a packet of pills. "These are powerful antibiotics. Three a day with meals." He went back into another bag and this time emerged with a plastic container. "It'll be bloody sore when the anaesthetic wears off," he pronounced. "These will help ease the pain, but not more than one at a time and not more than six in twenty-four hours."

Hawthorn pocketed the tablets. "How long before it's back to normal?"

"If it doesn't get infected, the stitches can come out in about ten days. Meanwhile, keep it in the sling and try not knock into anything."

Hawthorn couldn't see how he could conform with the doctor's instructions with all he had to do, but he nodded just the same.

"I'll be careful, Jack, and thanks."

Once clear of the Aid Post he made his way to the Command dug out; Butler had moved the Ushkuu prisoners to another trench under guard. Granby had left the Aid Post when things got too messy for him, and he and Gordon Butler were now perched in the entrance to the dugout. Both came to their feet as Hawthorn arrived. Butler saluted.

"I'm starved," he announced, scrambling down to join them. "Is there any breakfast left?"

Butler called over Hawthorn's batman, who had been waiting anxiously for his officer to return. "Fetch Major Hawthorn a double helping of corn beef hash," Butler said to him. "That's what breakfast is these days," he said to Hawthorn apologetically.

"Love the stuff," Hawthorn responded.

Private Smith delivered the steaming plate on a tray he had purloined from somewhere. "Glad you're back sir," he said. "Sorry about your arm."

"Thank you, Smith, and it's not your fault."

Balancing the tray on his knee, he tucked in ravenously. He cleared the plate and sent for more, and Smith finally removed the tray. Hawthorn wiped his mouth. He thought about taking a plunge in the river to swill away the dust and grime, but couldn't face the trip down and up the hill again. A quick wash would have to do. Refreshed as far as it went, he called 'O' Group.

"I want the whole company standing to in five minutes," he ordered. "And be noisy about it. We don't know if there are any Ushkuu about down below, but if there are I want them to know we're awake. Where have you got our guests?"

"In the communications bunker, sir," Butler informed him. "With a couple of Riflemen to keep them company."

"OK. let them go, but wait until I'm ready. They must see me in the flesh before they leave. I want Ingabe to know I'm free and in command again. My intention is to stop the killing. The Paras will call a halt to it in a day or two anyway and restore the status quo. So saving lives, gentlemen, that's our immediate objective."

"Are you suggesting we get between the tribes, sir?" asked Lieutenant Williams anxiously.

Hawthorn shook his head. "No, I'm not, Charlie. But we will take a hand if we have to. We go to full combat readiness from midday. A meal at eleven, Gordon. Ammo check, S'nt Major. And Doc, full medical preparedness. Dickie, talk to Mumbi. I want to know if he can find Zawutu. No use trying to tackle Ingabe. He won't listen to anything I say. Any questions?"

There were none.

"Very well. Platoon commanders report to Captain Butler as soon as your platoons are at full readiness. I shall be in the valley with the President, I hope, so you, Gordon, will be in command here."

Everyone looked up at that. The MO shook his head. "No you won't," he said firmly. "That arm must have rest and regular attention."

"And so say all of us," Granby added.

"Not now Doc, nor you, Dickie. There isn't time to argue. Ask Mumbi if he knows his way round this valley, Dickie. That's all. Dismissed, gentlemen."

Stanley hesitated. "Before we leave, sir, may I know if you actually intend to ignore my professional advice?"

Hawthorn grinned. "Don't worry doc. You're in the clear. With all these officers as witnesses I repeat, I will be in the valley with President Zawutu and I note your objection. OK?"

Stanley shook his head again. "On your own head be it," he muttered as he turned to leave.

"You didn't mention my chaps, sir," Harwell said next.

"I want you all back over here, Jimmy. Bring the radio kits and open up comms with London again. Tell them I'm back and safe, but absent on temporary duty. I'll talk to them later, tell them."

Alistair has the bit between his teeth and no mistake, thought Granby as he searched among the trenches for the little Eshanti. It would be more prudent to take a couple of SAS boys along, but Hawthorn was on a buzz. Too many pills, probably.

"There you are, you little bugger," he said jocularly, squatting down on the lip of a slit trench.

Mumbi had taken up a position for himself with a couple of Light Infantrymen and was currently hefting a rocket launcher on his bare shoulder, following sign language instructions as to how to fire the thing. He was grinning from ear to ear.

"Mumbi, you old devil you," Granby shouted down to him "Come out of there."

"This big magic," Mumbi replied.

One of the riflemen took the weapon from him. "He says he wants to kill many Ushkuu with it," the soldier explained with a grin as Granby gave the old man a pull up out of the trench.

"He's an old reprobate," Granby said affectionately. "Come on, Mumbi." He took the old man by the arm. "The boss needs your help."

Mumbi understood only a few of the words, but sensed the

meaning and felt proud. He turned to Granby "Mumbi great warrior," he said.

"Indeed you are," Granby said, smiling at the old man. "Chop chop." Mumbi frowned. "It means hurry up," Granby explained.

When they reached the command post, Hawthorn was waiting. "Dickie, ask him if he can find the President" he said. "You're better at this than I am."

Granby put an arm round Mumbi's shoulders. "Mumbi, you listen good."

Mumbi nodded and cocked an ear. "Mutti gone that way." He pointed into the valley. "Impolo," he said.

"Yes, Impolo. Mutti in Impolo. You find." He parodied tracking a spoor and wondered why he was doing this. Mumbi always seemed to catch the gist without the need for all this play acting.

Mumbi danced on the spot, laughing at Granby's antics. "Me know," he said between paroxysms. He followed this by parodying Granby's thespian performance in exaggerated format and ended with, "Me find Mutti OK."

Granby brushed tears of laughter from his eyes. "You old devil," he said. "Take Major Hawthorn. Move fast. OK?"

"OK?" Hawthorn repeated patiently, moving closer and suppressing his natural urge to join in the fun. He wanted Mumbi to realise the seriousness of what he was about.

"Move now," he said, indicating the entrance to the valley. He swept his hand up towards the peaks on the right-hand side. Through binoculars earlier he had noticed a pathway about two thirds of the way up on that side which promised a quick, safe route.

Mumbi's eyes followed the direction of the hand. "I see," he said, pointing directly at the thin ribbon of sandy earth on the side of the valley.

"God, I wish I had that degree of eyesight!" Granby remarked "At my age, let alone his."

Hawthorn nodded. "Don't we all." He turned back to Mumbi. "OK. We go."

"But he can't track Zawutu's army from up there," Granby pointed out reasonably, walking alongside.

"There's only the one valley, Dickie," Hawthorn said reasonably. "Zawutu will be well into it by now and Ingabe's on his tail. I'm not likely to miss two whole bloody armies, am I old chap?"

Granby smiled. "Touché! But why go at all? What's wrong with the radio?"

"In the first place the liaison set is still over on Jimmy's hill, and in the second, radio transmissions can be overheard. What I have to say is best said face to face."

"OK," Granby conceded. "Freddie went in four days ago now, and Ingabe two days later. There've been no sounds of battle, so I assume Ingabe hasn't been hurrying. But you'll have to, and you're in no fit state, be honest. Why not let me go?"

"Not on, old son. You're a civilian, and don't suggest Jimmy Harwell or Gordon. Neither of them has the seniority or the authority. So please, can I go before Ingabe does catch your friend and do him a mischief?"

Granby glanced sideways at the sarcasm and saw only good intent.

"See you later, Alistair, and good luck."

★ ★ ★

On one of the two borders, the refugee situation had eased. The Ushkuu, fleeing into Angola, were now returning. Four fifths of Zawanda was in Ushkuu hands, so they had nothing to fear. Total victory was only a matter of days away, or so they had been told.

375

On the Zaire border crossing, where the Eshanti pressed in their thousands against an intransigent border, the situation had worsened. In fear of retribution for the Ushkuu massacre perpetrated by Major Moi, the fleeing Eshanti were full of dread that they would be forced back. Nothing the aid agencies could say or do would alter that. Thus the Zaire authorities had imposed strict controls and refused to accept Zawandan refugees without UN aid in quantities totally out of proportion to the size of the problem.

Switching personnel and resources from one border to the other was proving difficult for the UN too. Either through Zawanda, for which they had no permission, or round and through three neighbouring states who were most unenthusiastic, it was taking time. The Eshanti were really in trouble.

Unable to help his people, Zawutu really did have his back to the wall. Dug in on the forward slopes of the escarpment which formed a small part of the border with Zaire, he had nowhere else to go. He wondered ironically whether history would be as eager to record Zawutu's last stand as it had Custer's. He prayed Ingabe would come to his senses, though why should he? He had driven the Eshanti into the valley and believed, no doubt, that he would defeat them on the day. But which day? Where were the Ushkuu?

Zawutu turned to Colonel M'Nango, who shared the command dugout with him. "I wish Major Hawthorn was here, or at least on the end of a radio," he said. "Allah knows what Ingabe has done with him."

M'Nango shook his head. "He'd be a fool to hurt a British officer."

"I hope you're right," Zawutu said. He had his doubts.

"I'm more worried about Moi," M'Nango went on. "Where the hell is he, and what's he up to? Do you think he's allied himself with Ingabe?"

Zawutu chortled at that. "Moi? No chance! He'd rather be exiled to Britain."

"Still, he's a loose cannon the way things are."

"I agree. But discounting his irregulars, how do you view our prospects?"

M'Nango paused to think. "Well, so far Ingabe has succeeded mainly by default. Remember, he has yet to face us man to man. We were taken by surprise at Qurundi and took time to reorganise. Then we left the city to save lives and buildings and finally we were forced out of the hills only because he threatened our water supply. As I said, he has yet to take on the Regular Army on equal terms. Man to man, I don't think he can win."

"That's a very optimistic forecast, my friend," Zawutu said with a wry smile.

"But one I believe in, Inshallah."

"Yes. God willing. I think I'll take a walk round the defences and do a bit of morale building. Hold the fort for me."

M'Nango nodded. "Take a signaller with you, sir. Who knows when Ingabe might appear?"

Zawutu grimaced. "I wish to God it was all over one way or the other. This waiting is killing me, and the troops must be feeling it even worse." He gazed down the length of the valley, to where it curved away to the right about a mile from the Eshanti forward positions. Every tree and bush in that mile had been flattened to form a wide, clear killing ground. With the river guarding the left flank and an almost sheer cliff on the right, the enemy had to come down the middle, and there the Eshanti had laid what few mines they had carried in, laying them judiciously so as to channel the Ushkuu into prearranged killing zones.

He paused before setting off. "You know, Alistair Hawthorn bought us this time at enormous cost to himself. I pray to God he's all right."

"We all serve the same God, Mutti," M'Nango replied reverently. "Your prayer will be answered."

Zawutu faced down the valley again preparatory to making his tour.

"Ingabe's troops must negotiate that open ground under aimed fire and through the minefields before they can close," he said over his shoulder. "Surely not even Ingabe would sacrifice so many lives? Perhaps you are right to be so optimistic."

M'Nango shrugged. "We must wait and see."

CHAPTER TWENTY ONE

Mumbi moved like an animal, fast, low and surefooted, and Hawthorn was having a hell of a job keeping up with him. At least the tablets he'd taken before setting off were keeping the pain at bay for now, and he had another twenty in the container in his shirt pocket.

The little Eshanti skimmed over the ground undeterred by his advanced years. He proceeded steadily, jogging in the indefatigable way all Eshanti boys are taught and finally tested before being admitted to the most coveted status of warrior.

"Hold it a minute," Hawthorn gasped, reaching forward to rein Mumbi in.

Mumbi stopped and looked round, a quizzical expression on his face.

"No go?" he enquired, clearly puzzled by the halt.

Hawthorn wafted his good hand in front of his face to generate some movement in the still, humid air.

Mumbi grinned, pointed at Hawthorn's shirt and forage cap, then indicated his own nakedness except for the short skirt.

"I get the drift," Hawthorn said. He transferred all his personal bits and pieces from his shirt to his trouser pockets, carefully peeled off the sweat-soaked shirt, removed his uniform cap and concealed both behind a bush on the side of the path. He then stood and glanced down at his body.

"Well, I'm tanned enough not to look like a bloody beacon up here," he said contentedly. "Let's go." He waved Mumbi forward.

The relentless progress continued, with Hawthorn feeling better for having shed the excess clothing, but his arm was not taking it too well. Despite painkillers it had started to throb, and he feared it would get worse.

The flitting figure to his front seemed to be teasing him along like an escaping butterfly, always just out of reach but earnestly desired. Then a remarkable thing happened, Hawthorn found himself falling into a rhythm, one which created a trance-like state that still left his mind sharp and alert. His body no longer ached, his legs moved without pain and, best of all, the sore sensation in his wounded arm just wasn't there any more.

Mumbi noticed the change and grinned. "Warrior now," he said. That was a huge compliment, in Hawthorn's eyes. He felt elevated by the experience.

All that day and through the night, with regular short halts called by Mumbi to pace the march, the two moved along the goat track. Dawn came and went and still Mumbi pushed on inexorably. And still Hawthorn matched him; incredibly, he hadn't needed any more pills either.

Suddenly, soon after midday of the second day, Mumbi stopped, turned and pulled Hawthorn down into some shrubbery alongside the path. He pointed down into the valley.

"Ushkuu," he said ferociously.

Hawthorn lay flat and followed the pointing finger to where Ingabe's rear guard could be seen moving along the valley floor.

"Very well," he said and gestured forward. Mumbi shook his head and made an elaborate sweep with his right hand, indicating that they should go round. "Ushkuu see," he explained.

Hawthorn regretted the extra time it would take, but was not about to argue with a tracker as skilled as the one alongside him. If Mumbi said the Ushkuu would see them, then it was so.

"OK," he said in the ubiquitous vernacular.

Mumbi began to crawl deeper into the brush, leading them away from the track, higher up the valley wall. Hawthorn followed, missing his tunic now. The old nightmare of long, piercing thorns was with him once more, and without the anaesthetic effect of repetitive movement his conscious self had wakened to the pain in his arm. He swore volubly, but pushed on despite the gnawing discomfort.

After a short time, Mumbi topped a crest and rolled down into a miniature valley on the other side. Hawthorn followed more gingerly. From there progress improved only slightly, being impeded by thick undergrowth which dragged at the passing men. Hawthorn moved his good shoulder forward to protect his bad arm, but the occasional springy bush managed to catch it a whack, making him wince.

From time to time Mumbi climbed the side to observe the Ushkuu. He usually said nothing on his return. This time, however, he looked down excitedly at Hawthorn. "Mutti," he said.

Hawthorn nodded and climbed the slope. He peered down and his heart froze. He could see Zawutu's positions on the escarpment almost directly below him, but approaching tactically, as yet out of sight of Zawutu but only a few hundred yards from the last bend before the escarpment, he could see the approaching Ushkuu.

"Too bloody late. Fuck it!" Hawthorn railed. His mind raced, but he knew he could do nothing now to prevent the slaughter that was about to take place. All that was left for him was to lie there, a helpless witness to the impending tragedy, a professional soldier who was about to observe a battle as if it were being enacted on a cloth model.

Suddenly Mumbi became agitated. He had seen the situation for himself and weighed the odds. The very survival of his tribe seemed to him to be in the balance, and he turned to Hawthorn for help.

"We go" he said, gesturing violently down into the valley and throwing himself forward. Hawthorn grabbed the departing figure by his skirt and held on. Pain ripped through his arm.

"Wait!" he said in an attempt to restrain the blind courage of the old man. Mumbi fought at first, but then seemed to accept the sense of Hawthorn's single cautionary word and relaxed before wriggling back.

"Good man," Hawthorn said, nursing his arm. It had started to bleed again. Sutures not up to the strain, he figured.

Mumbi saw the blood and frowned. He wriggled around in the undergrowth and came back with a handful of green leaves. "I mend," he said, gesturing at the spreading redness in Hawthorn's dressing.

Hawthorn shook his head. "No time," he said. He fixed his gaze on events in the valley below, struggling within himself to maintain a professional detachment.

★ ★ ★

The Ushkuu advance had reached a spot behind a prominent outcrop of rock that stretched well out into the gap between river and cliff. Leading scouts rounded the bulge, saw Eshanti, pulled back and reported what they'd seen to Lieutenant Mabouti, who was commanding the advance guard. He called a halt and radioed the news back to HQ.

Ingabe sighed. "At last," he said with considerable relief. The slog along the length of the valley floor had seemed endless. His troops had been twitchy all the way, expecting to be ambushed at any time, but now that they were within striking distance, that particular fear was behind them, to be replaced by another – the certain prospect of battle. He was too good a soldier not to realise the perils of attacking uphill against prepared defences, but he was so close to victory. Casualties would be heavy, he knew that, but with luck they would be the last, and worth the sacrifice if they gained him the presidency.

"Regroup for a frontal attack," he told his immediate staff. "We kick off in two hours."

"But shouldn't we wait and attack at dawn?" his CoS cautioned. "In two hours it will be full daylight and bloody hot."

"Zawutu will expect me to do that," Ingabe explained. "Staff College doctrine. Waiting would only allow him time to recce our strength and discover our attack formation. No, we'll surprise him and bounce the escarpment. It will be late afternoon by the time we move off the start line and it should all be over by nightfall. Not too bad for the men. A short, violent action and we can all go home."

The CoS pondered how many wouldn't, but there was no arguing with a man who wanted the presidency so badly he was prepared to shed an indefinite quantity of blood for it.

A rumble of thunder in the distance heralded the approach of the first downpour of the rainy season and, like Zawutu, Ingabe wanted this thing settled before the ground turned to the kind of mud that sucked a man's boots off his feet.

Concealed behind the outcrop, the leading Ushkuu battalion arranged itself into a wedge, with one company up and two back. Behind them came the second battalion in loose formation, then the third, with two independent companies at the rear to follow up and consolidate. The 75mm mortars, Ingabe's only heavy armament, were ordered to sight on the Eshanti forward positions as best they could without firing ranging rounds. The first few live lobs would have to serve as ranging shots.

Ingabe's plan was to throw everything into this final assault. He could not be sure which way the manpower advantage lay, but he knew for definite he didn't have the three to one differential preached by the British Staff College. Nevertheless, surprise, superior morale and fighting spirit would, he felt, more than compensate for lack of numbers. And in any event, he had no other option. To outflank Zawutu, who had the river guarding one flank and a vertical cliff the other, was physically impossible. No, it had to be a frontal attack, casualties notwithstanding.

★ ★ ★

Zawutu knew they were there. His outposts on the high ground to his right had been observing the dust of the Ushkuu approach since early that morning, and as soon as Zawutu heard he curtailed his 'visibility' tour of Eshanti positions and returned to the headquarters.

"The Ushkuu know we're here, but not, I hope, our dispositions," he suggested to M'Nango.

"He's not had the time to learn how we're deployed," M'Nango concurred. "But he's certain to put out patrols as soon as it gets dark."

"And so shall we," Zawutu said. "There's not much room out there for men to swan around undetected, so maybe we can interfere with their freedom of movement."

"I'll see to it," M'Nango confirmed.

A flashing light from the nearest elevated outpost attracted their attention.

"What's he saying?" M'Nango demanded of the duty signaller.

The signals Corporal screwed up his eyes against the powerfully-reflected sunlight and scribbled letter after letter on his millboard. When he had finished he tore off the top sheet and passed it to M'Nango, who scanned it, sucked in his lower lip and silently passed the piece of paper to his President.

"Enemy deploying for attack", the message said.

"Who's up there?" Zawutu asked, doubting the accuracy of the message. No one in his right mind would attack uphill, directly into the teeth of prepared defences, in the middle of the day.

M'Nango knew what Zawutu was asking and responded accordingly. "Lieutenant Barosi of the Second. I know him, and if he says Ingabe is about to attack then we'd better believe it."

"Very well. Stand all units to. No one is to open fire until they receive the command. All fire orders will come from here through the command net." M'Nango nodded. "I want Ingabe to think we're asleep up here. He'll have figured that I'd be expecting a dawn attack, and he was damn near right, so let's keep him thinking that way for as long as we can. No movement and no noise until we open fire, make that clear."

The message went down from HQ to Battalion to Company to Platoon. A gentle clicking of rifle bolts and magazine catches rippled through the trenches, too soft to carry. Then stillness settled over the escarpment, broken only by the occasional bird cry, and a rustling from the upper slopes as wild goats moved about their business, apparently unaffected by this sudden invasion of humankind. The river was still gurgling rather than roaring. No rains for almost a year had reduced its level to normal for this time of year, but it had always been a rumbustious river and even now it raced along, fast, and deep, sufficient to render a crossing a hazardous enterprise.

Zawutu had no fears from that quarter. Apart from the impending battle itself, his only other concern centred on Josi Moi. Where the hell was he and what was he up to?

★ ★ ★

Hawthorn watched with a keen commander's eye the regrouping of Ushkuu forces. He could find no fault with Ingabe's deployments. He surveyed the open ground between Ingabe and the escarpment, cleared of all impediments by Zawutu's forces, and nodded his approval for what they had done.

He was also searching for evidence that the killing ground had been mined. He cast his mind back to a discussion he'd had with Zawutu about set-piece defence and remembered the President mentioning that he had a few anti-personnel mines with him. Although there were no visible signs, the chances were that he had laid some, and there was no better place than that open ground.

He glanced backwards and forwards between the adversaries, weighing up the odds. If he could discern a weakness, it would be Ingabe's choice of timing. The element of surprise, a key factor in warfare, might already be lost; he had seen the flashing light on the slope opposite and guessed what the signal had said. Without surprise on his side, Ingabe was heading into a scrap with one arm tied behind his back. Defenders well dug in on ground favourable to defence will always have the advantage unless the attacker has superior numbers, which in this case he did not.

He swept the battlefield once more. It promised to be a bloody engagement, and in Hawthorn's view, one which Ingabe stood every chance of losing.

★ ★ ★

Time moved inexorably towards H Hour. Start lines had been established and marked, and formations were moving up as quietly as possible and making final preparations. For an army so recently assembled, the discipline and professionalism was excellent, thought Hawthorn from his gallery position above the arena.

On the valley floor, Ingabe moved among the leading groups, instilling them with Ushkuu fighting spirit. "This battle will put the Ushkuu back on top," he told everyone. "No more Eshanti raids, no more stealing your cattle or your women. Today we finish the Eshanti once and for all. And for Allah's sake don't make a sound," he added, fearing they might cheer his words and give the game away.

More thunder echoed round the valley, as if tuning up for the clash to come. Reports of readiness were coming in as each element moved into its prescribed position. Just before three o'clock, all was ready.

Ingabe muttered a prayer to Allah as the second hand on his watch approached H Hour. On the dot, his 75mm mortars opened up, their missiles cresting the slope in front and falling short. Adjustments were made and the second salvo landed among the forward Eshanti trenches. A scream rent the air.

"Some poor bugger's caught it," Hawthorn remarked to Mumbi, whose agitation had returned. "Be still," Hawthorn said sharply, and screwed up his face as the slight movement sent a stabbing pain down his arm.

Exactly on time, the leading Company of the leading Battalion crossed its start line and began its advance. It cleared the bulge in the ravine wall some ten minutes later and spread out on the other side. The pace slowed as the leading men, anticipating defensive fire, tried to stay as far away as possible, a natural reaction, but their NCOs drove them on. Then when nothing moved up there and no fire came down upon them, the young officer in charge of the leading Platoon sighed with relief. It looked as if this would be a walkover.

Gradually, the whole mass of Ushkuu rounded the bend and spread out across the plain. It was as if the very air around them held its breath. And still no reaction from the Eshanti.

"Are they really there?" someone asked Ingabe. He had scaled the rocky outcrop and was viewing the developing drama through binoculars.

"They're there all right," he replied grimly. "Zawutu is a smart soldier, and, anyway, didn't we hear someone cry out?"

"But are the trenches fully manned?" his aide persisted. Three times Zawutu had outwitted them; was this to be a fourth?

"If he's gone, he's gone into Zaire and that's a victory for us," replied Ingabe.

"Pray that he has then," the aide came boldly back, for he dreaded the casualties this frontal assault would inflict on his fellow tribesmen.

The mortars were keeping up their bombardment, but having no obvious effect. Ingabe wondered why, and whether his aide was right, that the trenches were manned only by a skeleton force. If so, where then was Zawutu's main force?

At that precise moment, the first mine exploded. It killed the subaltern in the first Platoon and wounded the Platoon Sergeant, along with several men. Two more explosions followed in quick succession, causing more casualties among the leading group.

What was left of the Platoon, leaderless, stopped and went to ground. Second Platoon moved up gallantly on the right and found clear ground. The remnants of First Platoon, whipped up by Corporal Tombasa, who was now in command of the Platoon, joined them.

Third Platoon, on the left, hit mines a few minutes later and took several casualties. The Platoon Commander swung left again and found safe passage. The Company behind split between the two safe routes, causing severe congestion. The next Battalion concertinaed and almost came to a stop, a deadly mistake under the guns of an enemy.

Ingabe swore, but he had expected something of the sort from Zawutu. Casualties would inevitably be higher now, but there was no way of avoiding it. What surprised him was that Freddie Zawutu had not exploited the chaos and confusion. Ingabe would have swept the minefields with fire and kept the forward sections hopping about.

He glanced at the sky and at his watch. The timetable had been seriously disturbed by the effects of the minefields, and now he wished he had listened and left the attack until dawn next day. If this thing went on late into the evening, it would benefit the defenders even more.

"Tell the lead Battalion to get a move on," he ordered.

* * *

On the escarpment, Zawutu's staff watched their leader surreptitiously, with no one willing to reveal his anxiety and concern over the lack of response. For many, a robust volley of small arms fire would at least have relieved the tension of the occasion. But Zawutu stood impassively, binoculars focused on the advancing Ushkuu. The first belt of minefields negotiated, the unsuspecting enemy obviously felt safe. Officers and NCOs could be seen whipping up the advance, increasing the pace. The compressed columns streamed between the first blocks of mines, coming on as well as any soldiers expecting a rainstorm of steel would.

The first mine in the second belt exploded under the feet of Private Mungo and sent him somersaulting into the air. The blood from the end of his legs, where his feet had been, sprayed on those behind. A second mine did much the same to Corporal Inbatu, and the advance faltered.

A sideways shuffling began and a few brave souls ventured forward into clear ground, but slowly. Then gradually the pace picked up again.

The mortars had been silent now for several minutes. Zawutu guessed they had run out of ammunition.

On the hillside, Hawthorn could not help but admire Zawutu's nerve and the steadiness of his troops. He knew how compelling the urge was to shoot at men advancing threateningly towards you.

"Good soldiers, Eshanti," he confided to Mumbi, who merely blinked and kept his gaze riveted on the action below.

Then a single shot rang out from the escarpment, from a terrified soldier for whom the dam of tension had broken.

Zawutu dropped his binoculars. "Shit!" he exclaimed angrily as more took up the physiological release of squeezing their triggers.

Back in the valley, Ingabe sighed. "At last. Now perhaps we can get on with it."

Almost as he said it the pace of the attack quickened; the paradox being that the only way to stop yourself being shot at is to get at the shooters. But the last belt of mines was still causing a problem, and now men were going down from small arms fire. Screams where men were hit mingled with yells of rage as the charge began; a cocktail of excruciating fear and uncontrollable excitement.

The Ushkuu came on in dense blobs of men who had not deployed into line since leaving the minefields. They presented unmissable targets for even the worst of marksmen and were falling in their droves, but still they came.

The first few to reach the outer ring of trenches unscathed were beaten off with the bayonet, but the mass behind had a momentum which seemed unstoppable.

Zawutu frowned. "God, but they're determined," he said, a note of anxiety in his voice.

As yet the concentrated fire from layer upon layer of defensively-terraced riflemen controlled the battlefield, but not for much longer. Zawutu could see it ending in hand-to-hand combat ere long, and hoped his men had weakened the Ushkuu sufficiently to give themselves a winning chance. Why Ingabe had chosen a frontal assault in daylight he could not imagine, but he had, and the outcome of the gamble would soon be known.

★ ★ ★

Hawthorn watched with professional interest. At his side, Mumbi was becoming more and more agitated, but too much was going on for his frenetic behaviour to merit much attention. Zawutu might have underestimated the fighting spirit of Ingabe's revolutionaries, Hawthorn reflected. Indeed, he himself might be guilty of the same error. The whole bloody thing was such a damned shame anyway. Lives sacrificed for nothing. The Paras would soon put a stop to this genocide and restore the status quo, so what was the point? It mattered not which side won. He watched the Ushkuu drive hard up against Zawutu's defences and identified cracks appearing here and there.

Suddenly, out of the very air it seemed, came a spine-chilling, high-pitched ululating sound which reverberated around the valley. It rose above the sound of battle and seemed to bring a microsecond's pause to the proceedings. Mumbi instinctively reacted to it by standing up, raising his face to the sky and joining in.

Hawthorn grabbed him by the legs and pulled him down. "You bloody idiot," he complained as the pain in his arm multiplied. "Do you want them to see us?"

Mumbi wriggled and kept on making the sound in the back of the throat. "Shut up, I tell you," Hawthorn demanded, slapping his good hand over Mumbi's mouth.

The awesome animal sound rose on the air and carried in every direction. Hawthorn searched for its source and narrowed it down to a slim defile which cut into the opposite side of the valley wall just where the escarpment began to slope upwards; an area dense with Ushkuu at full stride.

The high frequency, inhuman cry grew louder and louder until suddenly a black mass of charging men debouched from the defile and cut deep into the side of the attacking Ushkuu. The Ushkuu reeled at the onslaught and lost impulsion; those closest turned to face the new threat.

Zawutu, standing in front of his command post, pistol in hand, felt the hairs bristle on the back of his neck. It was a sound he hadn't heard since he'd been a boy; the atavistic war cry of the Eshanti nation, spoken of, demonstrated, but never used in anger since the British had put a stop to tribal warfare in the 1880s. It rattled the brain, accelerated the heart, heated the blood, gave strength to hand and arm. And the fever it generated was spreading. Even M'Nango exhibited the signs; flushed cheeks, shortening of the breath, a sudden restlessness.

On the slopes, the Ushkuu were concussed by the ferocity of Moi's onslaught. All forward motion ceased, and Ingabe's officers tried gallantly to reorganise their commands to face the new threat whilst continuing to engage Zawutu. But they stood no chance. The main attack withered where it stood. The war cry could now be heard ringing right across the escarpment as more and more of the regulars took it up.

Zawutu raised his binoculars and swept the scene below. The Ushkuu were in total disarray. The primitive Eshanti war cry echoed all around, beating in his ears, raising within him a compulsion which defied logic. The tension grew as he observed for the first time Ingabe's men beginning to move slowly rearwards.

He could control himself no longer. With the devilish

resonance now issuing from his own throat, he touched the scar on his cheek, which seemed to burn with a strange fire. He hefted his side arm for a firmer grip, leapt from the dugout and charged downhill.

"With me!" he cried as he careered down the slope. M'Nango ran at his side, lips trembling with the strain of creating that awesome sound.

Under the terrible pressure of Moi on the one hand and now Zawutu's courageous charge, Ushkuu coherence wavered, then collapsed, at least in the forward area. Ingabe had no hesitation in ordering the rear Battalion, not fully committed, to block the way to the rear and so prevent a rout.

"Stop them!" he ordered over the radio. "We must manage this. Officers must take back control."

Gradually order came. Wild, terrified troops rallied to their officers as soon as they reached the comparative safety of the rocky outcrop. The rear Battalion stood firm, taking the brunt of the joint Zawutu-Moi onslaught and providing Ingabe with sufficient time to establish a second line of defence further back.

Ingabe should have surrendered there and then, but in the way of the tribes he feared massive reprisals, and would fight until he could fight no more. With a bit of luck he might even get out of this mess and live to fight another day. He had control. A phased withdrawal was on the cards. A frustrated Moi might yet turn on Zawutu, and Zawutu might make a mistake. No; all was not lost by a long way. He squared his shoulders and began to organise a withdrawal that would contest every inch of territory.

* * *

From the hillside opposite, Hawthorn watched Moi cut into the flank of the Ushkuu and saw Zawutu charge recklessly down the escarpment. He figured the combined shock would end Ingabe's ambitious uprising there and then. But as he observed, expecting a surrender, he was astonished to see the chaos and confusion in the Ushkuu ranks turned skilfully into an organised, phased withdrawal. He shook his head in admiration. In the history of warfare not many commanders had done what Ingabe was in the process of achieving right now.

It took a moment for the implications of that tactical event to hammer a path to Hawthorn's brain, slowed by severe pain barriers. If the Ushkuu were able to sustain a steady rate of withdrawal, in two or three days they would find their arses hard up against Hawthorn's Hill and wanting to get over and away.

"Mumbi. You find Mutti?"

The little Eshanti warrior nodded energetically. "Mutti. Yes."

Hawthorn felt in his trouser pockets for the letter he'd stashed in one of them when he'd shed his shirt. There was a pencil stub somewhere too. He found both. The letter was damp from his own sweat, but he managed to scrawl his message on the reverse of an inner page. "Here," he said as he handed the folded work to his little companion. "Give to Mutti."

Mumbi plucked a large leaf from a nearby bush, rolled it into a tube, made a similar tube of the note and slipped one inside the other. With a deft movement he then somehow sealed the ends and tucked the finished article into the top of his skirt.

"Go now?" he enquired.

Hawthorn nodded. "Be careful, and you stay with the President."

A frown appeared on Mumbi's brow. "I give to Mutti," he repeated, fingering the secreted message.

"Yes, and stay there."

Mumbi did not understand, and Hawthorn could not wait. "Go," he said, giving the old man a determined shove. Once with his Mutti he would probably want to stay anyway.

With a smile and an Eshanti handshake, Mumbi slipped over the edge of the slope and skidded downwards at an unbelievable rate, displacing showers of loose scree which tumbled and fell before him. Hawthorn watched for a few seconds, then turned his face towards the valley entrance. He had to get back before Ingabe got there.

CHAPTER TWENTY TWO

Hawthorn attempted to settle into the rhythmic pace he had managed on the way out, but his arm was too painful. He gritted his teeth and jogged along the path as speedily as he could, aiming as his first objective for the bush where he'd left his shirt and cap. Occasionally he inspected his arm. The dressing had absorbed all it could. The surplus blood ran freely now down his arm and dripped steadily onto the ground.

The sun was lower in the sky and he knew he must keep moving, despite a persistent, repetitive temptation to give up and rest. Then he recognised the bush he had been aiming for. He retrieved his shirt and cap, tied the shirt around his waist by the sleeves, attached the cap by its chin strap. Thus accoutred, he moved on.

The next problem hit him soon after that; thirst. Mumbi had supplied him with water from leaves and roots during the journey out, but stupidly he had failed to take note of which leaves and which roots. He hesitated to experiment in case he hit upon a poisonous plant. Remembering a jungle survival course he had once attended, he picked up a pebble to suck, hoping that would suffice until he reached the Hill. Staggering now, weaker, unable to concentrate, he stopped more frequently and found it harder each time to force himself to his feet. He felt ready to succumb.

"Bugger Zawanda and Ingabe and the bloody President," he said to himself, lowering his aching body onto a grass patch alongside the path. "I've had it."

The pain had become agony. He searched for his painkillers and popped three into his mouth, but his throat was too dry to swallow them. He chewed them, but that only made matters worse, as the powder absorbed every atom of moisture. If he left the filthy tasting stuff in his mouth, perhaps the chemicals would be ingested through his tongue, he hoped, for the pain was excruciating.

As he lay there a cold breeze passed over him and he gave an involuntary shiver. Night had drawn in. He struggled with his shirt, drawing it over his head and attempting to thread the injured arm down the correct sleeve, but he couldn't do it. Finally he settled for resting the limb inside the shirt waist, where it felt marginally more comfortable.

He lay back and stared at the sky, feeling miserable that he had not the strength to continue. If only he alone knew the truth of this humiliating moment, it would still haunt him.

The sound of the river gurgling below came to him as if someone had suddenly turned up the volume. He sat up. Water! With water he could go on.

He struggled to his feet and explored the path ahead, seeking a junction that would lead down to the valley floor and the river. He must have passed a few during his journey this far, but where was the next one?

There - right there. It was barely visible in the dim moonlight, but it was a path and it zigzagged down towards the river. He hurried forward and turned onto it, slipping and sliding on the steep slope. In the gloom he tripped over a root, lost his footing on the loose scree and hit the ground with a thump, twisting to save his arm from the impact and driving the wind from his lungs. The rest of the tumbling descent passed in rhythmic explosions of pain as he rolled over and over. His weight and the scouring of the loose, sharp-edged scree not only reopened his wound but did wide damage to bare flesh, scratching and cutting and bruising to varying degrees of severity. He thought it would never end.

Then suddenly, it did.

He lay there gathering his wits, a mass of pain, where before it had been fairly localised. The sound of the gurgling river just a few yards away came as sweet music to his ears and reminded him of his purpose. He dragged himself to the edge and into the shallows, oblivious to the damage done to his body during his precipitous tumble. He was surprised, therefore, to see red tinted water flowing away from his immersed body, but he was too weak to worry about it.

Recalling his jungle training again, he disciplined his intake of water. It would be too easy to drink and drink, but it would be extremely dangerous for someone so dehydrated. He took some water, then rested before repeating the exercise. Soon he was feeling stronger, though no less in pain.

He felt for his pill bottle. Fortunately it was waterproof, or he'd have lost the lot. Three capsules quickly swallowed, twice as much as prescribed, but that was commensurate with the degree of damage, he figured, so it was perfectly in order.

A quick examination revealed the many cuts and scrapings, some worse than others and a few requiring attention, a stitch or two even, which they wouldn't get, not for a while anyway. He had no idea how bad his back might be; it hurt, that he knew, but it would have to wait, like the rest of him.

He clambered to his feet, splashed away from the water's edge and turned his gaze downstream towards the valley entrance. The ground looked just passable on this side of the river. Estimating the time he'd been on the move plus time lost, he figured he was a day and a bit march from home.

Night had closed in fully. The only light came from a half moon in a clear sky, which extended his night vision out far enough for him to avoid any more disasters of the likes of the scree slope.

The sounds of battle had been with him throughout, distant and intermittent, but now they were getting louder. He could not be so far ahead of Ingabe that he could afford to loiter, so, setting his chin towards Hawthorn's Hill, he set off at a fast walk, following the course of the river bend by bend rather than risk losing it by cutting across.

"Fuck this for a mug's game," he muttered cynically. The painkillers were working at last and raising his spirits.

His cap, crushed beyond any wearing, flapped at his waist. He tried it on, then threw it in the river as scrap, reflecting that he must be feeling better if he had the energy to be concerned over his headgear.

With the next bend always as his target he steadily progressed, but the effect of the pills was wearing off and the slightest movement dragged his shirt excruciatingly over the lesions on his skin, causing the worst of them to start bleeding again, and his arm had never stopped hurting. He swallowed another three pills, then two more, impatient for the relief.

Closing his mind to the tortures besetting him, the stinging injuries, the aching leg muscles, the cramp coming more regularly now, he plodded on automatically, dazed and rambling, unsure of where he was and why he kept walking when all he wanted was to fall down and sleep.

Eventually he did both.

Daylight was full when he woke, driven from sleep by a soaring pain which was no longer masked by the drugs he'd taken earlier. But how much earlier?

He rolled onto his back and immediately regretted it, but it gave him a sight of the sun, low in the sky. Early then. The rattle of small arms was still some way away, but it was distinctly closer than when he'd last heard it.

He felt for his pill bottle and popped four, washed down with water from the river's edge. Then he staggered painfully to his feet, set his sights on the next bend in the river and began to force one leg in front of the other.

The sun climbed higher and hotter, and although he now had a surfeit of water available, lack of food and loss of blood was sapping the strength from his limbs and from his will. Nevertheless he forced himself forward, reduced as he was to staggering from rock to rock and bush to bush, his objectives shrinking, each a major victory. He could rest, of course, but would he ever get up again if he did? And if he rested, might not the Ushkuu overtake him?

By late afternoon he had no strength left. Desperate, he searched for berries. Poisonous or not, what did it matter now? He would die anyway if he didn't get something inside him.

He foraged among the lush foliage along the river bank and thought he recognised a particular bush favoured by Mumbi on the way out. "In for a penny" he mumbled as he broke off a number of fat seed pods and prised one open. The taste seemed familiar, at least, so he tucked in, devouring five pods' worth before belching massively and calling it a day. Two pills and a substantial drink later and he was feeling better.

He jerked awake. How long had he been sleeping? He hadn't meant to. Not long, judging by the sun's position, but the battle sounded as if it was closer.

He struggled to rise, every muscle, every joint, every sinew resisting the movement, but rise he did and begin to walk.

Night crept insidiously upon him, the darkness closing in. Thunderclouds obscured the moon, making navigation twice as difficult as the night before. Then after what seemed an infernal eternity a dark, looming shadow appeared across his path and the ground turned upwards. It took a moment for him to realise what it was; then he fell to his knees. It was Hawthorn's Hill.

"Thank God! Am I glad to see you," he said to it. "All I have to do now is climb you, you bugger!"

Cupping his hands he tried to attract attention by calling out, "Ahoy, up there!"

A nervous voice called down: "Halt, who goes there?"

"It's me, you bloody fool," he called back with maximum relief. "Major Hawthorn."

"Is that really you, sir?" the sentry asked. He'd been told to keep an eye out for the OC and not to let anyone else up the hill, so he wanted to be certain.

"Yes, it's really me lad. Get someone to give me a hand."

A rustling of undergrowth signalled movement, then several minutes later Granby and Jimmy Harwell came scrambling down to where Hawthorn knelt, unable to stand or lie down without generating agony.

"Are you all right, Alistair?" Granby said anxiously as he leant over the kneeling figure.

"Not entirely, to be honest," Hawthorn said, swaying. "Give me a hand to the top, will you."

They took an arm each, Harwell springing back as Hawthorn yelped.

"That's my bad arm, clumsy."

"I'd forgotten" said Harwell. He took a hold on Hawthorn's waistband. "That better?"

Between the two of them they hauled Hawthorn up the steep slope, under severe instructions to ignore the groans as pain ripped through him. "As quick as you can," he exhorted repeatedly.

Once at the top, they virtually carried him to the command

dugout, where a tilly lamp provided illumination, and laid him on a folding camp bed.

"My God!" Harwell exclaimed on seeing the state of Hawthorn's flesh. "You look as if you've been flayed. What on earth happened out there?"

"Never mind about that," Hawthorn said, his face crumpling under the effort of bending to sit up. "Give me a hand, someone."

Granby clicked his tongue. "Stay where you are, you old fool," he said. "Jimmy, go fetch the doc."

At that moment Gordon Butler burst in with the MO in tow.

"Good," Hawthorn said. "Now you're all here. 'O' Group in twenty minutes."

The Medical Officer took one look and began unwinding the bloody mess that had once been a clean dressing. Hawthorn winced as the last pad came away.

"Not good," the MO said to the assembly. "Torn open and infected. Bring that light closer."

Hawthorn twisted his head to take a look, but the MO had his arm in a vice like grip. "Be still," he said.

"OK, but let's get on with it, there's a good chap. There's a lot to be done in a very short time."

"There's a lot to be done here too," Gardner replied, surveying the extensive new damage to Hawthorn's skin. "We could do with a sewing machine," he added humorously.

Granby whispered to Butler: "What shall we do? He's not fit for anything."

"You heard the man. 'O' Group in twenty minutes. And a large brandy wouldn't go amiss."

"I'll get it, and pass the word," Jimmy Harwell offered, pausing in the doorway to shake his head at Hawthorn. "Can't leave you alone for a minute, can we sir?"

It required numerous stitches to close the worst of Hawthorn's cuts and a great deal of intricate work on the bullet wound, and by the time Gardner had finished sticking on adhesive strips and painting on revolting orange coloured antiseptic Hawthorn was beginning to feel more like an Egyptian mummy than a human being. He was however feeling a great deal better, thanks to a liberal dose of Napoleon brandy from the officers' store.

"That should do for now," Gardner told him. "Lots to drink and plenty to eat. You lost a lot of condition out there. Antibiotics three times a day, no more than six painkillers every twenty four hours. We'll get you sound again by hook or crook."

"I'm not a bloody horse," Hawthorn complained. "But thanks."

The MO nodded. "Do you want me at the 'O' Group?"

"No. But you might get ready to accept casualties. There's likely to be a bit of action later on."

The MO raised his eyebrows at that. "What? You mean shooting?"

"That's what I do mean, yes."

"You're all mad," Gardner declared.

The 'O' Group members waited outside the command post until the MO had finished stitching their OC together again. "He's ready for you," Gardner said as he made his way through the restless bunch, still shaking his head in wonderment at the calm way Hawthorn made life and death decisions entirely off his own bat.

"Come in, gentlemen," Butler said, ducking out from under the low, reinforced roof, only to be eased aside by Hawthorn, now wearing a borrowed shirt to hide the worst of his injuries.

"Outside, if you please, gentlemen. It smells like an operating theatre in there." He led the way to the tree trunk on which the

Union Jack would soon be hoisted. A faint glimmer to the east heralded dawn, and he wanted his command reorientated before full light.

The last moments of darkness had a balmy feel to them. A moist breeze fanned the hilltop, clearing away fine, clinging tendrils of river mist. Faint sounds of small arms fire wafted in from deep in the valley, a reminder, if he needed one, of what had to be achieved.

He lowered himself gingerly to the ground and leaned back against the tree trunk. "Ouch," he complained, sitting sharply upright again and disguising his discomfort by asking a question of Gordon Butler.

"Have the Paras arrived?"

The officers and NCOs who made up the 'O' Group were squatting in a half circle. Butler replied: "No sir. There's been a delay. Fog at Lyneham or something. Jimmy took the message."

Harwell nodded. "That's right, sir. They're to be expected today, at the latest estimate."

Scudding storm clouds, still patchy and high, moved languorously across the sky, but they were gathering in the distance and spoke up now and then in threatening language. But light to see by would not be essential to this set of orders. No map reading would be involved; it was to be a very local affair, confined as it must be to the limits of this one hill.

"Thank you Jimmy," Hawthorn said. "You heard that, gentlemen. The situation here is that the President has turned the rebels and is pursuing them down the valley towards us. I'd say that Ingabe has about fifteen hundred front line troops left, and he's manoeuvring them masterfully. His withdrawal is textbook. My appreciation of his intentions is that he will continue to withdraw until he clears the valley, when he will disperse his men into the Ushkuu villages hereabouts preparatory to regrouping and coming out to fight again.

"To achieve that aim he will have to pass over this hill. My intention, therefore, is to deny him passage. He must be beaten well if he is not to come again. I had hoped the Paras might be here in support, but since they're not it's up to us. If we stop him here and provide Colonel Zawutu with an unequivocal victory, then it's over. Disarmed and dispersed, the Ushkuu will have to cooperate with the legitimate government.

"So, gentlemen. Own forces are as we are. We hold the high ground, we're better weaponed and better trained. The exit from the valley is fairly narrow, which gives us a further advantage."

At that moment a signaller rushed up and handed a message leaf to Captain Butler.

"Anyone got a light?" Butler enquired. Jimmy Harwell passed him a slim, pocket torch.

"You'd better see this, sir," Butler said, handing the message and the torch to Hawthorn.

"Hold the torch, Gordon," Hawthorn said, his injured arm virtually paralyzed.

The message informed Hawthorn of a further twenty-four hour delay in the drop of First Para, and amended Hawthorn's Rules of Engagement in regard to the use of maximum force, if required, to prevent the suspected nuclear cargo falling into Ushkuu hands. It was signed by Beauchamp himself.

"Well, that's a turn up!" Hawthorn said to Butler. "Gentlemen," he said, addressing the assembly, "this signal tells us that the Paras are delayed for a further twenty-four hours, and because of that the powers that be at home have released me from several of their erstwhile constraints."

"As if that makes any difference," Jimmy Harwell commented quietly to his neighbour. "I for one hadn't noticed any constraints in the way he's been acting."

"What was that, Jimmy?" Hawthorn enquired sharply.

"Sorry sir. Just commenting on the mixed bag of news."

"Well don't," Hawthorn said. "We don't have much time and this Para delay makes it all the more imperative we act quickly. As I was saying, the narrowness of the valley exit means we can't be outflanked and therefore the Ushkuu must attack head on and uphill on a limited front."

A general muttering broke out when it was realized that their CO really meant to take on the whole Ushkuu army. He ignored it.

"There is a paradox here, but in the long term the relatively few losses we may inflict on the Ushkuu by doing this will save many more lives later on," he went on. "So, 1 and 2 Platoons will dig in on the forward slopes facing into the valley. 3 Platoon to the rear. Usual dispersal. It's – "He squinted at his watch. "It's 0045 now and as you can hear," he nodded towards the valley, "President Zawutu is pressing hard on Colonel Ingabe, so I reckon we only have a few hours before the Ushkuu get here. You and your lads, Jimmy, at my HQ as a flying reserve, but immediate action for you; I want everything useful brought up from the trucks down below. I leave the choices to you. Can you see to that for me?"

Harwell nodded.

"Gordon, get a meal on the go and check with the doc. And Dickie, you stay with me. You're still officially a civilian, remember. Any questions, gentlemen?"

One Platoon subaltern raised a hand. "Fire orders, sir?"

"Good point," Hawthorn conceded. "I'm hoping Ingabe has the good sense to try and do this peacefully, at least without actually shooting at us, so I don't want him incited into doing anything precipitate. All commencement fire orders by me, my personal command. Understood?"

Heads nodded. "Is there anything else?"

There was not.

"Very well. Synchronise watches." He went through the routine.

"Thank you."

As the 'O' Group broke up in gradually increasing daylight, Hawthorn sensed the urgency and determination in everyone and felt content. Training and leadership would make all the difference when the time came, he was sure of that. He swallowed three painkillers.

"Help me to my feet, please, Gordon."

★ ★ ★

Ingabe had expected a respite during the silent hours, but it was not to be. His troops were tired and despondent, which contrasted sharply with what he guessed would be the state of the Eshanti; in pursuit, their spirits high, their physical endurance bolstered by victor's adrenalin, they could not be compared with his men, who were ready to collapse where they stood. Only the loyalty and leadership qualities of his junior commanders kept the troops going. Leapfrogging rearwards had a seriously debilitating effect on any man's army, and his boys did not have the depth of training or experience to deny on their own what must by now be a compelling desire to just give in and sleep.

His mind had been well read by Hawthorn; he intended exactly what Hawthorn had assumed he would. But a doubt burned in his brain all the same. Would the British Major stand in his way?

Hawthorn had shown every intention of denying him passage coming into the valley. Would he do the same again on the way out? Could he do it, with only an augmented Company of soldiers, Ingabe asked himself?

The thought raised the question – what if Hawthorn tried to oppose him? What should be the Ushkuu response? Attack or negotiate? He played the several obvious scenarios in his head and concluded that the best solution would be to approach

Hawthorn's Hill in as neutral a way as possible, simply ignoring the British, and walk over the hill as if he had every right, which of course he had. Hawthorn would not open fire if he was not fired upon, and anyway, he hadn't the numbers to prevent determined men from pushing their way through.

The Ushkuu leader smiled to himself; so bound up in honour and gallantry, these Britishers, they were a pushover.

He felt bone weary himself. His HQ had not touched ground since the withdrawal began and he had been permanently on his feet, moving among his formations, being seen and pretending to be cheerful. It was taking its toll.

* * *

Further up the valley, Zawutu pushed hard against Ingabe's rear guards, pressing unceasingly, hoping to break through and initiate a rout. But Ingabe had the measure of him.

Zawutu smiled at M'Nango. "I always said he was a damned good officer, and here's the proof."

M'Nango agreed, adding a comment of his own. "I wish the old bastard would see sense and talk. This must be decimating his army. Just think of the dead we've overrun and the wounded we've picked up already. And to be honest, Freddie, I'm bloody tired of chasing his arse."

Zawutu laughed. "Aren't we all. But I don't know how to get it through to him other than keep rolling him back."

The President's personal guard suddenly tightened around him and Zawutu looked about him for the reason. A half-naked figure was approaching fast from the rear, kicking up a cloud of dust. Zawutu squinted in an attempt to identify the intruder. Before he could prevent it, the subaltern of the guard fired a shot over the man's head and called out for him to halt.

Zawutu raised his binoculars to his eyes and focused the lenses.

"Well, I'll be damned!" he exclaimed. "If it isn't old Mumbi. Stop firing and let him through."

CHAPTER TWENTY THREE

"Mutti!" the little old man cried as he approached at speed and fell to his knees in front of the President. He looked up at his idol. "Major Hawthorn sent me to be quick, but the river carried me away and I came to this side after much trouble and great distance. I am late and Hawthorn will be angry with me."

"You have done well," Zawutu told him kindly, helping the aged tribesman to his feet. "Major Hawthorn will not be angry with the man who tries so hard. Now what does the Major want of me?"

"A letter, Mutti," Mumbi said almost apologetically, extracting from his skirt the tubular leaf containing Hawthorn's note. The paper, wet around the edges but remarkably dry in the centre, unfolded cleanly and Zawutu was not surprised. This method of transporting all manner of foldable items had been the way of the tribes for as long as he could remember, and for many years before that according to his father, who had shown it to him when a boy. He felt the memory in his heart and shook himself free of it. This was no time for personal sadness. He unrolled the paper and perused the contents.

Colonel M'Nango hovered close by, intrigued by this apparently sudden intervention by the British officer. "Good news?" he enquired, guarding his impatience.

Zawutu looked up. "Mixed," he replied, studying again Hawthorn's scribble and screwing up his eyes in order to interpret some of the more untidy words. "Hawthorn says that the British are sending their Parachute Brigade, due here any hour according to him."

M'Nango's eyebrows shot up. "What in Allah's name for? And shouldn't they ask permission first? At the very least their arrival will be a gross interference in our internal affairs."

Zawutu nodded. "Quite," he said. In fact he knew the British were more likely to be interested in the missing aeroplane than the inter-tribal struggle. He nearly said so to M'Nango, but pulled back in time. His Chief of Staff knew nothing of the conspiracy to provide Iraq with a couple of nuclear weapons, and it would stay that way.

"Will you complain to the United Nations?" M'Nango persevered, his anger plain to see.

"By what means?" Zawutu responded, throwing out his hands in mock helplessness. "Our present communications are limited to tactical radio sets. By the time I can get to an international line, or the Palace radio room, it will be a fait accompli. Oh, I can make a fuss after the event, but prevent it happening, unfortunately not." The UN was probably in on it anyway, he conjectured, and a complaint might open a can of worms that he would prefer to remain closed.

"Major Hawthorn has satellite communications," M'Nango persisted. "Mumbi here can take your message."

"And do you imagine Hawthorn will oblige? He may be a maverick, but he's not crazy enough to use a British comms link to complain about the British. No. I'm afraid we're stuck with the situation." He chuckled. "There is, of course, an up side to this. Ingabe is licked this time and the British will prevent him coming back for more. They won't want another uprising in one of their ex-colonies with the Commonwealth conference coming up next year."

M'Nango shrugged. Unhappy, but realising nothing could be done, he prompted, "You said the news was mixed."

"Yes. Hawthorn has ideas of his own for finishing off Ingabe."

* * *

What originally had been the British Assistance Mission to the State of Zawanda had undergone a series of fairly serious metamorphoses, bringing it closer each time to actual armed intervention on the side of the President. Jimmy Harwell, for instance, had found it apposite to remark only yesterday to a Light Infantry subaltern that he reckoned the Boss had been determined from the start to get involved in the fighting despite prohibition by the MoD. "Should be in my mob," he had suggested with profound respect.

Dug in on the hillside, disposed facing into the valley as Hawthorn had ordered, the augmented Company group awaited the arrival of what was now commonly known as 'The Enemy'.

Hawthorn himself, still sore from his encounter with the jagged scree slope and with his damaged arm in a sling, stood on the hill crest with Granby and Butler, having ingested enough painkillers to dull the pain of the surgical procedures. All three had binoculars trained into the valley.

"They're not far away," Hawthorn said. "Listen to the small arms fire."

"There," Granby said loudly, pointing.

Hawthorn aimed his binoculars along Granby's extended arm and refocused. "Where?" he demanded.

"Movement to the left, beneath the cliff."

"I see it," Hawthorn said. "You?" he asked Butler.

"Got it, yes," the 2ic confirmed.

"They'll be here by morning at the latest. Warn the Platoons. Full alert from here on in."

Butler turned to the signaller standing behind them. "All stations, now," he commanded. The signaller made the call and handed over the handset.

"All stations, this is Sunray Minor," Butler began, and went on to pass down Hawthorn's orders.

The distant sound of approaching aircraft distracted the three men into glancing skywards. Several dots appeared below the gathering storm clouds, almost invisible against the dark back ground. Three pairs of binoculars swung upwards.

"C130s?" said Butler.

"I reckon," Granby replied, switching his eyes towards Hawthorn for confirmation.

"It must be the Paras, then," Butler said.

Hawthorn watched the aircraft begin their descent towards the distant airfield and reflected that Zawutu must be seeing the same thing and drawing the same conclusion, but what of Ingabe? Now there would be a puzzled man!

In fact Ingabe was in no way puzzled. His compulsive paranoia about the British had at last become a reality; they had arrived, would soon be on the ground in Zawanda. He considered his options and came up with only one; the imperative to break free from this deliberate, drawn-out withdrawal, clear the valley and disperse his men before the British reinforcements could interfere. No time now for smart tactics, he told himself. He issued immediate orders to create a minimum rear guard and the rest to go hell for leather for the hill.

Granby, sweeping the valley between watching the C130s fly in, noted a sudden acceleration in the rearward movement and alerted Hawthorn.

"Gordon, you keep an eye on the Paras," Hawthorn instructed while he himself refocused on the Ushkuu. "Hmm. Bring forward my estimate of their arrival here to late afternoon," he said. The conclusion was undeniable.

The C130s had dropped out of sight behind the hills surrounding the airfield and sounded as if they were circling. Butler made the report and joined the other two in observing the Ushkuu.

"I think we'd better stand to," Hawthorn said, and Butler disseminated the order.

★ ★ ★

A metallic clicking echoed around the positions as men chambered rounds and checked that the moving parts on their weapons ran freely.

"All ready," Butler reported following the last acknowledgment.

"Good," Hawthorn told him. "Now, get Jimmy and his pirates to join us at the command post."

The distant movement thickened as more of the Ushkuu came into long-range view, moving quickly along the valley floor. The sounds of fighting echoed more stridently in the valley.

"Better take cover, sir," Harwell cautioned his OC. "Won't be long now."

"Don't be in so much of a hurry," Hawthorn said, amused at the SAS officer's concern. "Ingabe is too smart to shoot at us until we shoot at him."

"But will we?" Harwell asked, unclear about Hawthorn's resolve. It was one thing to deter, another deliberately to resort to arms.

"Oh yes, Jimmy," Hawthorn responded firmly. "If that's the only way to halt Ingabe, then…" He shrugged.

"A bit like Rorke's Drift," Harwell said, referring to the action of the same name during the Zulu wars when a small contingent of a Welsh regiment fighting under the command of a junior officer of the Royal Engineers had defeated massed Zulu Impis.

"Not quite," Granby threw in. "The Zulus had only spears. Ingabe has modern weapons."

"Let's wait and see, shall we," Hawthorn said, closing down the discussion. "Eyes front and keep alert. I just hope the President doesn't try to smash the Ushkuu between his hammer and our anvil."

In quick time the Ushkuu pushed up against the base of the hill and hesitated. Soon they were milling around like a swarm of ants seeking a way round. Black faces looked upwards towards the crest, hands gestured and clearly identifiable officers began to urge men up the slope.

"Pass me the handset," Hawthorn instructed his signaller. "And you lot, get down," he told those clustered around him.

The SAS group spread out, forming a rough circle around the officers, and seemed to disappear into the ground. Hawthorn watched the leading Ushkuu and saw them raise their rifles above their heads in a non-aggressive gesture.

He smiled. "Trust Ingabe to think of that," he remarked to Captain Butler at his side. "He expects to walk over us at the stroll."

"But they're not doing anything," Butler said; and neither were they, except to concertina badly.

Hawthorn nodded. "No one wants to test our resolve, that's clear. But the rearguard will soon be alarmed when they find themselves hard up against that lot down there with nowhere left to go and Zawutu hard up their arses. Panic is not what we need right now."

Just then a small group of Ushkuu could be seen forcing their way through the packed ranks below. As they neared the front they began gesticulating up the hill.

"It's Ingabe himself," Granby reported.

415

"I see him," Hawthorn said.

Under Ingabe's urging, the officers below led their men forward onto the lower slopes, parodying the elevation of weapons by pumping their hands into the air.

Hawthorn swore. "The bloody fools." He raised the microphone to his lips. "All stations. This is Sunray. Two rounds overhead fire. Commence."

A rippling crash of rifle fire rent the air, followed immediately by a second, which echoed into silence; even the birds were hushed. The Ushkuu at the foot of the hill hit the deck with alacrity, peering in every direction to search out casualties, of which there were none of course. After a tense moment the leaders began exhorting their men to their feet, else they would stay clinging to the earth in mortal fear of being shot. A few rose, then more, and finally, like a disjointed black wave, the rest.

The first up was Ingabe, who stood defiantly, hands on hips, staring up the hill. He raised one clenched fist and shook it; he knew Hawthorn would be watching. And so he was.

"Game little bugger, isn't he," Granby observed.

"Stupid, if you ask me," Hawthorn responded. "Look, he's coming again. One more warning shot, then it's game time."

The Ushkuu had reformed into something resembling an attacking formation and the front few ranks advanced onto the hill.

"Two rounds overhead fire commence," Hawthorn said into the radio, shaking his head. Two volleys ripped out and bounced around the hills until the sound attenuated to nothing.

This time, but for a few of the more nervous types, the Ushkuu stayed on their feet and kept on coming, and this time they carried their weapons aggressively at the port. Behind their massed ranks, the first of the Eshanti hove into view.

"Now what?" Butler asked.

Instantaneously, obviously in response to an order, the leading group fell prone into firing position and began a steady rate of fire towards the peak. Under this cover, a second group worked their way round and advanced higher up the hill before going to ground in turn and giving covering fire to the first group.

"Here we go," Hawthorn announced, as coolly as if he were about to kick off in a football match, which might have been something like were it not for the whizzing and thudding of high-velocity small arms rounds in passage and striking earth. "Number 1 Platoon. Take out the leaders."

A single marksman, Rifleman Smith, took aim and squeezed the trigger. Below, a man collapsed to the ground.

Ingabe went to ground, along with the majority of the Ushkuu around him. Damn silly to stand like a range target.

Hawthorn took the loudspeaker as more well-aimed rounds found their mark among those around Ingabe.

"Colonel, you must know that British reinforcements are on the ground here already and that it is my intention to deny you this hill," Hawthorn bellowed, hoping that some of what he was saying would be heard by the Eshanti close behind as his voice echoed along the valley.

Ingabe rose to his feet and waved a fist up the hill, then gestured for his men to push on up.

Hawthorn shook his head. "Wait. I'm coming down," he shouted, handing the speaker to Butler and setting off down the hill.

Butler screamed at Harwell. "For God's sake look after him!"

In an instant the SAS men were there, catching and forming a defensive cordon round Hawthorn. At the same time, seeing that Hawthorn meant it, Ingabe shouted in panic, "Don't shoot. No one shoot. Hear me."

Arriving in a dust cloud at the bottom of the hill, Hawthorn brushed aside Harwell's restraining hands and approached Ingabe. The two men stood facing each other, silent for a moment, then Ingabe spoke.

"That was a foolish thing to do," he said.

Hawthorn, whose injuries were bothering him after the scramble down the hill, merely smiled. "Foolish or not, it was necessary," he replied calmly.

"I heard of your escape. Enterprising, to say the least. You know I can come over this hill? Ingabe added, nodding at the slope in front of him.

Hawthorn glanced behind him and shrugged. "It would be costly, and you would be stopped by the British 6 Airborne Brigade, which is advancing on you as we speak," he replied. "They dropped some time ago and I have apprised them of my situation and yours." He shot a glance at Harwell, who looked nonplussed at that blatant untruth, and Hawthorn shook his head slightly in warning.

"So you see, the game is up, Colonel. No point in wasting more lives. If you lay down your arms now your people will be allowed to disperse to their villages." Another warning glance at Harwell, who knew his OC had no authority for that promise.

Ingabe bowed his head in thought, then turned to the officers around him.

"What do you want me to do?" He asked them. They looked at each other and shrugged.

"There is no other way," a senior major responded. "Think of the tribe. Save what you can."

Ingabe nodded. "Very well" he told Hawthorn. "You stop Zawutu and the Eshanti and I will surrender myself to him. Pass the order," he instructed his officers. "Cease fire and lay down arms."

Hawthorn offered Ingabe his hand. "You are a true soldier," he said in admiration. "Men first."

CHAPTER
TWENTY FOUR

Ingabe found himself under house arrest. He had feared much worse, and it might yet come. His riverside conversation with President Zawutu seven days before had resulted in the unconditional surrender of the whole Ushkuu army. There had been no alternative. A few officers, and a small number of warriors, had resisted Ingabe's call, but in the absence of a coherent command to prosecute the war further they had had no option but to surrender. It was done with great reluctance and much complaining: a bad omen for the future.

Hawthorn had remained at Zawutu's side throughout the surrender process so as to ensure fair play, in so far as he was able. His only contribution was to inform the President that the Parachute Brigade had arrived; a firm warning, indirectly given.

The only other significant event at the time had been the onset of the rains. First a few drops, then a spattering, then the skies had opened, turning dry gullies and old, cracked wadis into raging torrents within minutes. The river rose alarmingly quickly, providing an additional incentive for the two armies to evacuate the valley, which they did with great alacrity.

Hawthorn had seen nothing like it. From the relative safety of his hill he watched the river swell to flood the valley from side to side and sweep trees, bushes and the detritus of war along with it. A thorough cleansing, he thought appositely.

The men's trenches then filled with water at an unbelievable rate and the downpour began to threaten everything that wasn't tied down, a danger which encouraged Hawthorn to bring forward his own evacuation of what had been home for quite the most exciting period of his time in Zawanda so far. Hasty packing and removal to the plain became the order of the day, and even there the lower areas had flooded, making it imperative to recce routes before embarking on them. A call on the radio had trucks waiting on the main road, well above flood levels, to transport the whole Light Infantry Group back to New London and the Para Company that had arrived on the hill a little too late, to the airfield. Shelter and drying out became pleasures which temporarily surpassed even thoughts of girls and sex in the minds of the soldiery.

Despite the reassuring style of arrest, Ingabe still feared execution. "I will die like the Ushkuu warrior I am, standing tall and facing the firing squad, eye to eye," he said defiantly to Hawthorn, who was paying him a friendly visit. "I'm sorry about your arm."

"There'll be no executions," Hawthorn assured him vigorously, brushing aside the apology. "Your officers are even now in the process of being released and your ORs are already back in their villages. I told you there would be no recriminations."

"But retribution is the way of the tribes," Ingabe told him, a faint glimmer of hope suddenly apparent in his voice.

"Once upon a time that may have been true. Might even have been true this time under different circumstances, but I have the President's word. There is also a strong British presence here now, with orders to monitor the rehabilitation of your people."

"There may yet be hope for Zawanda, then" Ingabe said, forcing a smile, which faded as he recalled to mind the way troublemakers in Zawanda had a habit of disappearing without trace, usually after a convenient interval for people to forget. He expected no less for himself. Hope for Zawanda did not necessarily mean hope for Ingabe, he told himself depressingly.

Hawthorn shook Ingabe's hand and wished him well. "I'm on my way to report to the Brigadier," he said with a grimace. "After being your own man it's always difficult to come back to being a subordinate."

Ingabe laughed ironically. "Even more true when you have become a prisoner after aspiring to be a president. Good luck, Major."

★ ★ ★

Brigadier John Archibald Humphries, 'Hotpants' to his contemporaries, nicknamed thus for his reputation as an energetic and driving commander, had set up his Headquarters close to the airfield. His briefing before leaving the UK had laid upon him a clear duty to find the missing aircraft and sequestrate its contents. "No need to worry President Zawutu with any of the details," he was told. Indeed, it was emphasised that apart from normal courtesy visits there would be no need to inform the President of anything. "Tell him you're there to assist in rehabilitating the tribes" had been Henright's final word before dashing off to another Cabinet meeting.

First Battalion and some support troops, essentially a Para Squadron of Royal Engineers, had dropped with Brigade HQ and set up camp close by. 'A' Company of First Battalion had been sent post-haste to assist Hawthorn, a specific task ordered by the Prime Minister personally, with the remainder of the battalion to follow if required. The rest of the brigade were due to drop two days from now, weather permitting, followed immediately by flights in of heavier vehicles and weapons, which would require the runway to be sound. This meant the Sappers working day and night to repair the damage perpetrated so dramatically by Hawthorn's SAS contingent. Another few days would see that done, according to the RE Squadron Commander, despite the rain.

Hawthorn's driver screwed up his eyes in an attempt to see through a windscreen which looked more like a cascading sheet of water than a pane of glass. The rain thundered on the roof and bounced off the bonnet, the tyres threw up great clouds of spray and the outer skin leaked like a sieve. Thank God there were very few other vehicles on the road, Hawthorn reassured himself. Ten miles per hour felt like a breakneck pace in these conditions, with the road edges obliterated by running water and only a faint sheen of tarmac aided navigation. Whether the Land Rover was on the left or right hand side of the road seemed irrelevant; enough that it was on the road at all.

But the journey had to be made. The Brigadier had insisted. "I suggest you prise yourself out of the Palace and get here pronto," the Brigade Major had advised over the radio.

The driver obeyed the sentry's challenge at the Brigade checkpoint and pulled up. With a streaming poncho draped over his head the poor sentry looked like a drowned rat as he walked round to the passenger side. Water poured from his tarpaulin headgear through the Land Rover's open window as he bent over to check Hawthorn's ID.

"Sorry sir," he said. "It's this bloody rain." He squinted at the ID card. "HQ is over there, sir." He pointed to a marquee which looked as if it was standing in the middle of a lake.

"Drive on," Hawthorn told the driver. "Thank you sentry." He wound up the window and brushed the droplets from his uniform.

At the entrance to the marquee, Hawthorn leapt from the Land Rover and made a dash for cover. "Wait for me here," he called back to the driver. He stood for a moment listening to the rain drumming on taut canvas, then searched among the desks and workers occupying the gloomy space inside, looking for someone to report to. His eyes lighted upon a Lieutenant Colonel who was engaged in scrutinising a large map tacked to a tent pole in the far corner. He walked over, saluted and reported himself: "Major Hawthorn, sir."

The officer swung round to reveal a sour expression on a face that looked as if it was unused to any other. He made a show of studying Hawthorn from head to toe before speaking. Then, in a superior tone, he said, "Ah, Hawthorn. You made it at last. The Brigadier's been getting quite wound up over you. He's through there." He pointed to the end of the tent, where a sheet of canvas divided off a small area. "Go straight in."

No welcome, or good luck, or how've you been. Hawthorn saluted, glad to get away. "Thank you sir," he said and made his way to the space indicated. He hesitated at the canvas screen, composed his features, withdrew his arm from its sling and threw the material square onto the floor. Then he lifted the canvas and walked through.

"You must be Hawthorn?" said a strong voice from the left.

Hawthorn swivelled to the sound and saw a tallish, well-muscled man rising to his feet, hand extended.

"Glad you could make it. How's the arm?"

Hawthorn glanced at the officer's epaulette badges for quick confirmation of his rank; Brigadier. He marched over, came to attention and saluted.

"Reporting as instructed, sir." he said formally before taking the proffered hand. "Arm's a bit stiff but coming along nicely according to the MO." He worked the joints to demonstrate restored flexibility.

On first impressions Brigadier Humphries seemed friendly enough. He wore a natural smile and his hand had felt cool, dry and firm. Fair, slightly wavy hair crowned a rugged but not unhandsome face and Hawthorn had the distinct feeling that they could get on.

"I'm sorry I didn't get here sooner," he said. "I've been assisting the President and moving my unit back into barracks."

"Hmm! Well, you're here now," Humphries said, exhibiting none of the impatience and spleen suggested by his Brigade Major on the radio or the peevish Lieutenant Colonel outside. "I hear only good things about your time here in Zawanda, though I understand there are certain signals elements at the MoD who would gladly skin you alive if they could." He put his head on one side and gazed quizzically at Hawthorn. An explanation was required.

"Equipment problems, sir," Hawthorn said blandly.

"Indeed! Well, be that as it may. You were informed, I trust, that you are to come under command with immediate effect? I urgently require your local knowledge and experience to assist in finding this damned Russian aircraft. I've had every man jack scouring the countryside for almost a week now, to no avail. I hope to hell you can provide a glimmer of where it might be."

"I'm afraid I can't sir. I know little more than you, as a matter of fact."

Hawthorn could see that the Brigadier did not entirely believe him.

"It's true sir. All I know is that Major Moi, you'll have been briefed about him I suppose, undoubtedly has it hidden in the bush somewhere."

"So, where is this Major Moi?" Humphries demanded. "Let's get the aircraft location out of him."

"Sorry, sir. During the urgent evacuation of the Impolo Valley ahead of the floods, Moi and his merry men disappeared into deep bush. I can assure you, no one is more anxious to find the Major than the President himself. Moi is a loose cannon until he's found."

"Amazing how complicated things can become in these small African countries," Humphries remarked, shaking his head in wonderment, but clearly satisfied with Hawthorn's reply. "Yes, I was briefed about Moi. Does the President expect trouble from him now the Ushkuu rebellion is over?"

Hawthorn shrugged. "Moi hasn't the men to pose a serious military problem, but he could well manage a terrorist campaign, and if that runs on it would suck the life out of President Zawutu's attempts to repair the human and material damage."

The Brigadier nodded, appreciative of Hawthorn's professional view of the matter. "Well, I just hope we come across him in the process of our search. My orders are to detain him if and when. Now, as to your command, Major, have a chat with Lieutenant Colonel Hastings, he's running the search. He'll allocate you a search area."

Hawthorn coughed.

"Something wrong with that?" the Brigadier enquired sharply.

"Well yes, sir. My Company Group has been constantly on the go since the war here began right up to yesterday. They're tired and I need time to reorganise for this new task. A few days, sir?"

Humphries glared. "Soldiers must work through their tiredness, Major. There'll be time enough for rest once we've found what we're looking for."

"Yes sir. I understand that. But my men have been close to combat many times in the last few weeks. I suggest that my small unit can't make a significant difference to the speed of the search or the area covered. Just a day or two is all I ask, sir?"

Humphries gazed fiercely for a moment at Hawthorn's

determined features. "I was warned about your stubborn independence, Alistair," he said, the familiar form of address revealing a deeper insight than Hawthorn had anticipated. "It's served you well so far out here, but don't push it with me. However, I take your point about the state of your command. You've two days to work it up to full operational readiness, then it's out there with the rest of us. Is that clear?"

"It is sir, and thank you." Hawthorn waited to be the dismissed, his objective achieved, but instead Humphries turned the conversation to his keen interest in the recent civil war.

"As I understand it," he said. "Both sides fought almost exclusively with small arms. Had they nothing heavier?"

Hawthorn shook his head. "Not by the time war broke out. Originally the Zawandan army had two batteries of 25-pounders, but they ran out of ammunition and spares before the war started. Both sides had a few mortars of medium calibre, but limited ammunition. As you inferred, sir, it was an untypical conflict, possibly even unique as modern warfare goes. Of course, fighting with individual weapons is a long-established practice out here. It used to be spears and bows and arrows, now it's rifles and bayonets, but the principle remains the same as far as these people are concerned. They're not accustomed to fighting from a distance, you see. Up close, hand to hand, is their preferred method. Even the Sandhurst-trained officers who know how it's done have difficulty restraining the troops from wanting to charge in and come to grips man to man. I suppose the tribes feel more comfortable fighting in that way, it's part of their culture."

"Interesting," Humphries said. "You must have had a grandstand seat when you weren't taking part."

"I suppose so," Hawthorn replied self-effacingly, noting also the casual reference to his having become involved. He wondered what the Brigadier thought of that.

Humphries seemed to sense Hawthorn's discomfort. "You'd better be on your way," he smiled, then turned serious. "I intend to find that bloody nuclear weapon if I have to arrest every man, woman and child in Zawanda until someone squeals."

"It'll turn up, sir," Hawthorn said confidently. "Wherever it is it can't easily be moved, not far anyway. It's too big and too clumsy on the ground."

"Always assuming it's still in Zawanda," Humphries said, bringing a new dimension to the problem. "And God help us if it isn't."

"It's here, sir, I'm sure of that," Hawthorn said confidently.

"I hope you're right, Alistair."

Hawthorn saluted and retired to the outer office space, where Hastings stood marking out circles on his map of Zawanda. He paused. Should he mention to the Colonel what the Brigadier had said? No. He didn't like the arrogant twerp anyway, so why should he? He marched straight for the door flap.

"Major!" the Colonel's imperious voice came from behind, rising above the sound of beating rain.

Hawthorn stopped and turned. "Sir?"

"Haven't you forgotten something?"

"I'm sorry, sir?" Hawthorn asked, feigning innocence.

"A search area for your command, man."

"Oh, that," Hawthorn replied, making it sound a paltry matter. "The Brigadier has allowed me a few days to work up. I'll be back for orders then - sir," he added late. He saluted and turned again for the doorway.

Hastings called after him. "Hold it, Major! You may have been the kingpin out here, but now you're part of this Brigade and it would be appreciated if you would remember that and act accordingly. Report to me as soon as your period of grace is over."

"I'll remember to do that, sir," Hawthorn said levelly, cursing inwardly at the turn of fate that had once again placed him under close command. The Brigadier seemed like a good chap, but this Hastings! All staff duties and no common sense. All piss and wind, as the men would say.

Even so, he'd better make a fence-mending gesture. "Sorry if we got off on the wrong foot, sir," he said. No point in alienating the officer under whom he would soon be working, he figured sensibly.

"Not we Major, you!" was Hasting's angry riposte.

Hawthorn nodded. "Probably, sir."

"You may leave," Hastings said curtly and Hawthorn sighed. He knew that from now on Hastings would go for him at every opportunity; it seemed the only recourse available to second-rate officers.

* * *

That same night, under dense, black clouds and in a deluge worthy of Noah, a native runner emerged from the bush where it ran close to the Brigade perimeter. He evaded the sentries with ease, intent as they were on keeping as dry as possible and therefore none too vigilant. The Eshanti made directly for the lights and sounds of the Officers' Mess tent. He made it unchallenged to the entrance, where his luck ran out. Not that it mattered. He had reached his goal.

The guard, two Parachutists, had been monitoring the runner's approach from their place just within the tent entrance flap, where it was dry.

"Hold on old chum," Corporal Gavin said, stepping squarely in front of the intruder. "What's your game then?"

To Gavin's surprise the drenched native spoke back in good English.

"I will speak with Brigadier Humphries urgently," he said with authority enough to make Gavin send for the Mess Sergeant. The Mess Sergeant arrived, cursing the Corporal for interrupting the smooth running of the officers' dinner. He looked the Eshanti up and down and dismissed him as a troublemaker. "Bugger off," he said in his usual vernacular.

"If you will excuse me," the native said, shocking the Mess Sergeant with his English as much as he had Corporal Gavin. "But it is imperative I speak with your Brigadier."

Sergeant Holby cocked an eyebrow at him and ruminated on whether or not to disturb old Hotpants in the middle of dinner. He took in again the almost naked, bedraggled condition of this strange tribesman who spoke with an accent close to that of the Brigade officers, and decided that maybe he'd better.

"Keep him here," he instructed Gavin firmly and disappeared into the labyrinth of canvas. He re-emerged a few minutes later, followed by an intrigued Humphries.

"That's 'im sir," said Holby.

"Thank you, Holby," Humphries said. "That will be all for now."

"But are you sure you'll be all right with this fellow?" Holby asked, hesitant to leave his Brigadier unattended.

Humphries smiled. "I've got the two door guards." He waved Holby back into the Mess. "Don't worry, Sergeant. We'll be fine here."

"Come in out of the rain," Humphries invited, but his visitor shook his head.

"Somewhere less occupied, sir?" the native suggested, indicating the two guards with a nod of his head.

Humphries had quickly taken stock and concluded that whatever this man wanted, it must be serious. He nodded.

"Let me get my waterproofs," he said. To Gavin he continued: "Corporal, if you wouldn't mind?"

Equipped with a lightweight raincoat, rubber boots and a rain hood, he led the way to his office in the administration tent. The tent was deserted, the officers at dinner and the clerks knocked off for the night. He found the light switch and switched it on.

"Now, young man. What is so important that you would interrupt a good dinner?"

"Basbu. My name is Basbu," the man said, refusing the seat offered. "I come from Major Moi."

Humphries' heart missed a beat. He nodded as if he were not surprised, and gave no reply.

"The Major would be pleased to talk with you, sir."

"About what?" Humphries questioned as calmly as his excitement would allow. This gratuitous approach by the very man whom everyone claimed held the clue to the whereabouts of the missing aircraft appeared to present a massive piece of good fortune. His pulse was racing.

"I don't think Major Moi and I have any interests in common," he said, none too invitingly.

"There is one matter," Basbu said confidently. "It is our understanding that you are searching for a certain aeroplane."

Humphries bent his head for a moment. "That might be of interest to me," he said, looking up. "But finding it is only a secondary task for this Brigade."

"But you would like to find it nevertheless," Basbu said, undeterred.

"As I say, it is of some interest. I will meet with Major Moi, but not because of any aeroplane. It is time he ceased childish things and came back into the general stream of Zawandan life. He has much to contribute."

"If you say so, Brigadier. When would be convenient?"

Humphries had done a stint as British Military Attaché at the Polish Embassy and had learned something about diplomacy, particularly how not to let his feelings show, a skill Basbu's impertinence now brought into play. With a straight face he replied: "Tomorrow evening might be suitable. A little later than tonight though. Dinner, you understand."

"Nine o'clock, then?"

"Nine would be fine," Humphries confirmed.

"But not here" Basbu demanded firmly. "Major Moi requires this to be a one-to-one discussion with no one else present."

Humphries again swallowed his temper and nodded his understanding.

"There's a clearing a little way into the bush off to the side of the track leading here. I shall be there at nine, alone."

Basbu raised his arm preparatory to shaking hands the Ushkuu way, then lowered it to meet Humphries' more conventional offering.

"Until tomorrow evening, sir," he said. At once he turned and was gone.

Thunder rumbled ominously and a brilliant flash of lightning illuminated the sky as Humphries left Headquarters to return to the Mess. He glanced upwards and hoped the elements would be less ferocious when he met Moi. His mind was awash with satisfaction and his raingear with rain. He made his way between the two tents reflecting that, with luck, his primary mission might soon meet with success. Secrecy was everything, but he would have to brief Hastings. There were to be no escorts or hidden guards. He had given his word, so Hastings must know where he was going in case something went wrong.

His brain was in overdrive as he shed his raincoat at the mess entrance. He pondered whether he shouldn't ignore his promise and simply arrest Moi on sight. Expediency made deceivers of everyone at some time. But Moi might not cough up the location of the aircraft even then. Better leave things as arranged and play it by ear, he told himself.

He entered the Officers' Mess tent and ordered himself a whisky, adding one for Colonel Hastings whom he saw hurrying over. Nosey bugger, he thought.

Hastings was an anomaly. Normally a Brigade Major would be the senior staff officer, but the MoD had insisted on a Lieutenant Colonel and had settled Hastings on him; they had not even given him a choice, and he still wondered why. He had come to dislike the chap almost at once; too pedantic, too stiff, no flair or sparkle.

Hastings raised his glass. "Cheers, sir. You seem perky tonight. Good news from somewhere?" He was fishing. The Mess Sergeant had mentioned the native caller.

Humphries replied. "Cheers. Yes. You could say that. But not tonight, Peter. See me first thing in the morning."

★ ★ ★

Next day, with Hastings briefed and another fruitless search of half a square mile of jungle reported negative, Humphries sat alone in his tent, the rain thundering down on the canvas. He had refused quarters in the Presidential Palace or in any of the other government residences, politely, of course. He could not accept hospitality with the possibility of throwing it back in their faces should circumstances warrant it. He would take dinner alone tonight, a practice he had followed since his first full command, believing his officers to be entitled to have the occasional mess evening to themselves without the constraints of a critical senior eye always upon them. It also allowed time for personal reflection, particularly relevant tonight before his meeting with that scoundrel Moi.

Sergeant Holby served dinner along with a carefully-selected claret from the Brigadier's private stock, which, according to Holby's tittle-tattle in the Sergeants' Mess later, old Hotpants ignored, taking only one glass without the usual comment on its nose and palate. "The Brigadier has other things on his mind," he said knowingly.

At precisely eight forty-five, Humphries left his tent and walked across to the mess, where he caught Hastings' eye and indicated that he was about to leave for the Moi assignation. Hastings nodded. One hour from now, if the Brigadier had not returned, Hastings would launch a search and rescue mission using a Platoon of Paras already kitted out ready to roll at a minute's notice.

The sky loomed dark and angry and dense black clouds scurried across the heavens, depositing tons of water as they passed. Humphries hunched within his raingear, head down against the wind and rain. The sentry, charged with stopping people coming in, ignored the heavily-canvassed figure going out. It was hard to recognise anyone through the sheeting downpour in this darkness.

The track leaving the camp was only just visible, making it essential to keep a careful watch for the turning that led into the clearing where the meeting had been scheduled. Humphries kept to the left-hand side, his eyes fixed on the verge of undergrowth and tree trunks.

Gradually, the lights from the camp disappeared into the mush of weather and he cursed that he had forgotten to bring a torch with him, a serious oversight which he discovered when forced to retrace his steps, thinking he had overshot the turning. He should have come upon it before this, he reckoned. Then there it was. He turned into it and entered the clearing a few strides later.

"Brigadier!" came a voice from the darkness . "I am Major Moi."

A shadow emerged and came closer until Humphries could just discern a face, broad shoulders and a short, thick body. Moi saluted. "Sir" he said.

"Major Moi," Humphries replied, returning the salute. "Can we be quick? I am expected back within the hour."

Moi nodded and led the way to cover beneath overhanging tree canopies. Not that it helped much, as the rain was so powerful that it smashed its way through the leaves and dripped upon the two men in even larger droplets.

"It is quite simple, Brigadier," Moi said once out of the direct action of the elements. "I have an aeroplane the British want, or more precisely, the contents." He watched for a reaction and caught just a flicker.

"Oh yes, I know what's inside. President Zawutu and I planned the whole thing together. So, do you want to do a deal with me or not?"

Humphries waited for more, for some idea of the kind of deal Moi expected, but when the Major remained silent he had to ask: "What deal have you in mind?"

"Straightforward really," Moi responded, giving Humphries his first sight of what passed as a grin. "I give you the aeroplane and you, the British that is, give me the Presidency."

Humphries held himself together with some difficulty. He had expected nothing like this. Money, yes, but not a whole country.

"I am not sure the British government have the power or the authority to agree to such a huge ransom," he said and waited for the compromise.

"I think they have," Moi came back positively. "It's either that or I sell the nuclear warhead to the highest bidder."

Humphries swallowed. The little bastard meant it. "Impossible!" he said. "What's to stop me arresting you now? We will find that aircraft, you know, eventually."

"No you won't," Moi said with confidence. "My people know what to do if I don't return, just as I suspect yours do in your case. I suggest you contact your government with my proposal and see what they say. The British have one week to respond."

Humphries thought hard and fast, but could add nothing. All the stuffing had been knocked out of him by the boldness and sheer magnitude of Moi's demands.

"I'll need more time," he said, falling back on basic negotiating technique.

"One week, Brigadier, to respond, not necessarily to agree."

Some sort of concession at least, Humphries told himself. A slight shift in Moi's original position.

"One week from now, here at the same time," Humphries agreed. "But I cannot guarantee the result you want."

"One week is sufficient for now," Moi conceded. "Goodnight, Brigadier." He turned and was swallowed up in the black, shadowy jungle.

★ ★ ★

The Top Secret, Eyes Only signal was received in the MoD communications centre late that night. It was deciphered at once by an officer authorised to that level, and in view of its contents and first copy addressee a duplicate was despatched by hand to the office of the Foreign Secretary.

In the master bedroom of the Foreign Secretary's residence, Mrs Beauchamp jabbed a sharp elbow into her husband's ribs. "For heaven's sake, Henry, answer the phone," she complained.

"What is it?" Beauchamp grumbled, raising himself onto one elbow.

"It's the damned phone," his wife complained "You never hear it."

He reached out, switched on the bedside lamp and took up the handset.

"Beauchamp," he snapped angrily. He listened silently, a grave expression distorting his features.

"I'd better come in," he said at the end. "Send my car round now and assemble the policy team." He turned to his wife. "Sorry, dear. Urgent business. I need to go to the office. I'll be gone all night."

"Just so long as I'm not disturbed again," she replied unsympathetically, then modified her tone to say: "Get a warm drink before you go, my dear." He noticed, though, that she didn't volunteer to make it for him.

He threw on some clothes and went downstairs to the kitchen, where he put the kettle on. He would shave at the office. The car arrived just as he sank the dregs of his second cup of tea, this one fortified with a dash of brandy. None of the house staff had arisen to see what was going on; even his personal detective he had to wake himself. "So much for security!" he muttered to himself as he waited for the Inspector to throw on some clothes. The two left the house for the car some twenty minutes after receiving the phone call.

As they approached the Cenotaph, Beauchamp could see lights springing up in the first-floor offices of the Foreign and Commonwealth building. "Someone's got their skates on," he remarked to the police officer.

"It would seem so, sir," the officer replied.

Inside, the section containing Beauchamp's office and those of his supporting staff had come to life, albeit sleepily. People were still arriving and a low murmur of querulous voices formed a background as Beauchamp swept to his office through apparent chaos. There he found his PPS, clutching a copy of Humphries' signal.

CHAPTER TWENTY FIVE

In the Palace, Freddie Zawutu fretted over the activities of the British military. Alistair Hawthorn had been as helpful as his duty allowed, but he had disappeared the day Brigadier Humphries had paid his first courtesy visit. "If he sees me here he'll get stroppy over the delay in my reporting to him. Best if I'm unfindable," he had explained, and he hadn't been seen in the Palace since.

Zawutu had expected a polite, but unequivocal warning from Humphries about the perils of venturing into the nuclear market; no use denying his involvement when Humphries' Paras were hunting high and low for the lost Russian aircraft. And what about the crew? Another nightmare, explaining their whereabouts to Byelorussia. Or maybe the Byelorussians were too embarrassed by the whole thing to worry about their men. He certainly hoped so.

He had contemplated telling the truth about Iraq's blackmail and Saddam Hussein's kidnapping of the plot, but he feared Iraqi reprisals. And anyway, excuses would carry no weight with the British; they had, after all, plenty of experience of planting heavy, punitive feet on the necks of errant former colonies.

In the event Humphries didn't raise the matter. He said his

Brigade was in Zawanda to aid stability during the rehabilitation period, a transparent lie but diplomatically unchallengeable. He asked about the British Assistance Mission and questioned the whereabouts of its OC, Major Alistair Hawthorn, all very smoothly done.

Zawutu had pleaded ignorance. "He was here for a debriefing following his magnificent intervention which ended the war between myself and Ingabe, the Ushkuu pretender. He left the Palace this morning to rejoin his command."

"That good, was he?" Humphries asked, more in a rhetorical sense than as a real question calling for an answer. But Zawutu replied anyway.

"Without Alistair there would have been great loss of life," he asserted strongly, exhibiting proudly his admiration and respect for the British Officer. "He risked his life a number of times and managed his small command like a master, and not only that, his Unit as a whole comported itself with admirable professionalism, which again reflects well on its commander."

"I take it you like Hawthorn," Humphries said with a grin.

Zawutu looked for the sarcasm, embarrassed by his own hyperbole, but Humphries seemed pleased. "He's a good man," the President had ended lamely.

Humphries had made his excuses and retired after that, leaving Zawutu free to get on with more pressing matters, the first of which was to deal with Ingabe. The meeting had been civil. Ingabe had been anxious to hear his fate and Zawutu keen to put him out of his misery. He knew what the Ushkuu rebel would be thinking – execution. Instead, Zawutu shocked the man rigid by offering him the post of Minister for Tribal Affairs; many of the old team had decided not to return to Zawanda, which left posts to fill.

Ingabe accepted the seat Zawutu offered, though he needed time to recover his composure.

"Well, Freddie," he began eventually. "That's knocked me back a bit. Are you serious?"

"Never more so, my friend. And it isn't forgiveness. I want your flesh and blood. It isn't just a job, it's a punishment. You will work your arse off helping me homogenize the tribes."

Ingabe nodded. "Makes sense," he said. "I never wanted to fight you, you know; not until greed took over from common sense anyway. In a way the chiefs made all the running, but I'm to blame for allowing myself to be the catalyst."

"Never mind the hindsight. Do you accept?"

"I swear my allegiance," Ingabe had replied. "But only if the Ushkuu and lesser tribes are made equal to the Eshanti." He had waited for Zawutu's reaction to such impertinence, but it needed saying.

"That has always been my intention," Zawutu said. "So we are in agreement on that."

Ingabe had stretched out a hand, happily taken.

★ ★ ★

Richard Granby had taken up residence back in the Palace, even though his part in the weapons drama had come to an ignominious end. He could not, or at least did not want to, return to the UK, and was hanging on in the hope that Freddie would not kick him out too soon. The day Alistair Hawthorn had fled the Palace, the two had met on the staircase.

"I enjoyed our little escapades," Granby had confessed. "Like old times, when I was a proper soldier."

Hawthorn had smiled. "Couldn't have managed without you, old boy."

"You've seen Freddie?" Granby had then enquired.

"Just."

"The poor old chap is in a terrible way, scared to death of meeting your Brigadier."

"Not so. More scared of what it might mean for Zawanda, this silly nuclear business."

"He didn't say that exactly, did he?" Granby asked anxiously, his own perilous situation rushing to mind.

"No, he didn't. But it's pretty obvious. And if I don't get out of here soon Hotpants will grab me and nothing will get done at all."

"Point taken," Granby had said. He gave Hawthorn a pat on the back. "Remember, if ever you need me again, just ask."

"I'll do that," Hawthorn assured him, joining in the rhetorical nature of the exchange. "And now I really must go."

★ ★ ★

But that had been almost a week ago. Since then Hawthorn had met the Brigadier and negotiated a stay of execution, as he saw it, the extent of which was shrinking rapidly. He wondered if he could talk Humphries into another extension. The rains were subsiding at last. The sun streaming through the odd break in the clouds reminded those on the ground that the life-giving orb still existed up there somewhere, and heralded relief from the unrelenting downpour.

Buoyed by the change, Hawthorn decided to drive himself to Brigade HQ. He parked the Land Rover outside and walked jauntily into the command tent.

"Is the Brigadier in?" he asked a Major. He glanced round for Lieutenant Colonel Hastings and saw that the place was unnaturally empty. The maps hung untended and Hastings was nowhere to be seen. Indeed, now he thought about it, the whole camp had seemed in a state of lethargy as he'd driven in, which was odd considering the urgency expressed by the Brigadier only a few days before.

He frowned as he followed the Major to Brigadier Humphries' end of the tent.

"Ah, Hawthorn!" the Brigadier said waving to a seat. "Everything all right?"

"So so, Brigadier," Hawthorn opened. "I was just wondering whether I might not have a few days' extension for my chaps. They're coming along very well, but a few days more should give them the edge you want."

Humphries gazed fixedly at his visitor. "I understand your feelings for the men," he said kindly. "After all, they did a sterling job before we got here. But this discussion is largely academic, I'm afraid. I'll be frank with you, but what I am about to say is, and will remain, top secret. Is that clear?"

Hawthorn nodded. He knew something was up.

"Very well. Your friend, President Zawutu, will likely be deposed by the British Government."

Hawthorn's eyebrows shot up. "Deposed, sir? Why?"

"Well, we can't find the nuclear device, that's number one. Number two is that the Americans are kicking up a real stink about it. And number three, Major Moi has offered us a deal – the weapon for the Presidency."

Hawthorn looked up sharply. "But we can't give in to that terrorist," he exclaimed angrily, not caring that he was railing at a Brigadier. "He'll ruin the country. Zawutu is the best hope Zawanda's got."

"It's not settled yet," Humphries said, ignoring the outburst. Inwardly he agreed with Hawthorn. From what little contact he'd had with the reigning President, he had learned to respect him.

"We've had no word back from Whitehall" he went on. "But I must assume the Government will accept the exchange. International pressure is building up to volcanic proportions."

"What a calamity if they do accept," Hawthorn said, shaking his head disbelievingly. "It's fools' gold."

"It's no longer in the military sphere, Alistair. The politicians have taken over." Humphries breathed in deeply and rolled his eyes upwards to demonstrate his own personal feelings about the interference of powerful amateurs.

"But if we find the aircraft beforehand, there'll be no reason to submit to Moi?" Hawthorn said, thinking out loud.

"That's correct, of course, but the search has been suspended pending news from the UK."

So that was it, the reason for the inactivity. Hawthorn nodded absently, his mind in overdrive.

"Well, I'll be on my way, sir," he said, too enthusiastically for Humphries' liking. "With your permission, that is."

Humphries stared hard at him. He had expected a reaction and had deliberately not informed Hawthorn until now because of that, but the Major had a right to know. Zawutu was more than just the President, more of a friend. He thought of forbidding unilateral action by Hawthorn's people, but what the hell? The very least Hawthorn could do was find the bloody missile, and that would hardly be a calamity. He decided to play it neutral.

"Whatever you think you're up to, Alistair, just you remember, what has passed between us this morning is top secret, so if you value your career you had better not speak of it outside the Brigade."

Hawthorn was already on his feet. "Only to those bound by the Official Secrets Act," he said, holding back a smile. Humphries had indicated as best he could that he was on his own and untethered by Brigade constraints.

"Need to know only," the Brigadier modified for him.

"Yes sir."

"Get on, then," Humphries said with a sly nod.

From Headquarters, Hawthorn made his way straight to the Palace and sought out Granby.

"You said to call on you if ever there was something up,"

Hawthorn said when he found him in the grounds at the rear.

Granby smiled and nodded. "Indeed I did, and I meant it."

"Good. Grab some kit and come with me, then."

★ ★ ★

Masters sat with a reduced Cabinet, his ears still ringing from the raised voice of President Clayton. The President was less than happy with the way things were going in Zawanda. The French had involved themselves, seizing this God-sent opportunity to have a go at their so-called European partners, the British. The Germans were, on the surface, more understanding; they had their sights set on the forthcoming European Finance Ministers' meeting in Bonn, but still wanted the nuclear issue resolved before then. Russia stayed relatively silent, saying only that the matter was serious, and saying that only once on midday news broadcast.

Masters was bristling with resentment, and it showed in his demeanour as he hunched over the Cabinet table and drummed his fingers on its highly-polished surface.

"Foreign Secretary," he said loudly above the hubbub, the use of the title making his anger clear to all present.

Beauchamp coughed into the sudden silence and looked down his nose at the PM. "Yes, Prime Minister?" he responded, equally formally.

"Get on with it, man," Masters said impatiently. "Our people in Zawanda are waiting on our response."

Beauchamp snorted, offended, but he opened the folder before him nevertheless and withdrew a single sheet of paper.

"Gentlemen," he began. "This signal" - he waved it - "is from our Brigade in Zawanda. I'll read it." Which he did. When he had finished the assembly remained silent, all eyes on the Prime Minister.

"I don't believe we have any alternative but to go along with Brigadier Humphries' assessment" said Masters. "If we want that damned aeroplane, and we do, desperately, then this man, Moi, must be paid his price for it. Any dissenters, gentlemen?"

There followed a long silence.

"Is that a no, gentlemen?"

Henright, Defence, leaned forward. "Not directly my aegis, Prime Minister, but can we remove one President for another, legally I mean?"

Beauchamp fielded that one.

"The law in this case is somewhat obscure. But the Prime Minister and I" – he glanced sideways for confirmation and received a nod – "believe there is international support for the course of action outlined. After all, President Zawutu alienated world opinion and threatened world peace when he attempted to become a nuclear power."

"Better get a legal opinion, though, all the same," Masters said, suddenly backing off his previous positive position. Beauchamp sighed inwardly. More delay.

★ ★ ★

The Land Rover carrying Hawthorn and Granby braked to a halt in a cloud of dust, which showed just how fast the land was drying out. It hadn't rained yet this morning and the clouds passing overhead were of a paler complexion.

"Looks better," Granby said, lifting his chin skywards.

Butler sat at the only desk and sprang to his feet on recognising Hawthorn. "Just checking incoming signals, sir," he explained.

Hawthorn nodded. "Very well, but don't bother with them for now. Fetch Jimmy Harwell and come back yourself,"

Butler glanced inquisitively at Granby, who shrugged his

shoulders. Butler lowered his gaze. He had been with Hawthorn long enough now to know when to keep quiet. He made a beeline for the door.

Granby looked at Hawthorn, trying to figure out what this hyperactivity was all about. Then the penny dropped.

"You're going after Moi!" he burst out. "You sly bugger, Alistair. And I'll bet you've told no one, not even the Brigadier?"

Hawthorn ignored him. "Grab another chair from next door, there's a good chap," he said, as if all this was just routine. "Then sit on it and wait for the others."

Granby did as he was bid, and had just got himself settled when Harwell and Butler came scurrying in. They each took one of the two remaining chairs.

"Bad news, I'm afraid," Hawthorn commenced. "The Paras can't find a certain aeroplane." He couldn't remember who among them he'd told, but receiving no questioning glances, he continued on the assumption that they all knew. "The Brigadier has hobbled me to some extent by making me swear not to divulge certain information to non-signatories of the Official Secrets Act. He also insisted I keep it on a need-to-know basis." He glanced round the three faces before him.

"Dickie, I assume you signed the Act when you served?"

Granby nodded.

"Good, well you're still, bound by it, OK? As for the need-to-know constraint, you three definitely have an urgent need if we are to succeed in what I have in mind, so I can continue with a clear conscience."

"As if that mattered!" Granby muttered and earned a smile from Harwell.

Hawthorn ignored the interplay. "That damned aircraft will be the death of Zawanda unless it's found, and quick." He paused and looked at the three. "The next bit is absolutely top secret." He shot a warning glance at each individual in turn and received a nod from each. "It seems that Major Moi…"

"I knew it," Granby interrupted.

"You know nothing," Hawthorn said peremptorily. "Just listen."

Granby turned a light shade of red. "I'm a civvy, remember."

Hawthorn smiled at him. "I know you are, Dickie, but you volunteered for this. If you want out, leave now."

Granby looked at the others. "No need for that," he said with a short laugh. "I just knew you were after Moi, that's all."

"I'm not, so will you please keep quiet and listen. We haven't much time."

"Sorry," Granby said, chastened.

"Right. Here it is then. Moi is attempting to cut a deal with the British government. He will deliver the missing aircraft in exchange for the Presidency."

Granby gasped. "They can't do that," he said angrily, forgetting Hawthorn's injunction to remain silent. "Freddie's the best President this country's ever had."

"I agree with you," Hawthorn conceded. "But unless that bloody aeroplane is found Zawutu will find himself ordering the removals van. Brig Humphries is ninety per cent certain that the Government will accept Moi's ultimatum. Apparently they're under tremendous pressure from the Yanks and others."

"So it's already fait accompli," Harwell said, wondering why all the panic if the deed was already done.

"Not when I left Brigade Headquarters it wasn't," Hawthorn said, a wicked grin on his face. "They were still awaiting a reply from London."

"So, it's the aircraft you're after, not Moi," Granby said, the true objective now clear.

"Yes, but can we do any better than a whole Brigade of Paras?" He looked hard at the SAS Subaltern. Harwell frowned in thought, considering the capabilities of his specialists.

"Not on our own" he admitted. "My men have many skills,

but tracking in this kind of country is not one of them. And anyway, the rain will have destroyed what tracks there might have been."

Hawthorn threw out his hands. "But we have to try, Jimmy. Your chaps can stay out longer, cover more ground and do it less noisily than the Paras, good as the Red Berets are. I can't think of any other way."

"I can," Granby suddenly interjected, his face brightening. "I know a couple of Eshanti trackers who could find a needle in a haystack the size of a city."

"Immediately on tap?" asked Harwell.

"Well, not entirely. I'll need to ask Freddie Zawutu."

"Well get on with it then," Hawthorn said.

"But I thought it was all being kept secret from the Palace?"

"Fuck that for a game," Hawthorn replied energetically. "If I know Freddie he'll be chuffed to know we're taking a hand. You go and find these two trackers of yours. Meanwhile, Jimmy, brief your lads. Just you me and the search teams."

"Hold on," Granby complained indignantly. "If I don't come along who's to communicate with Sam and Onjojo?"

Hawthorn sighed. "It has to be you, I suppose, Dickie," he agreed with a wry grin, admiring Granby's determination.

"Admirable!" Granby said with glee. I'll be off then."

CHAPTER TWENTY SIX

"Is there anything you need from us to make your jungle training more realistic?" Lieutenant Colonel Hastings enquired gruffly of Hawthorn the day after Hawthorn's visit to the Brigadier.

Hawthorn smiled into the phone. Humphries had guessed, and wanted to make sure that the search and find did not fail for want of anything the Brigade could provide. Whether or not he thought Hawthorn mad and the venture impossible, he had clearly spun Hastings a diversionary yarn.

"Thank you, Colonel, but I think we're OK."

"Very well, Hawthorn. And please stay on net," Hastings ended admonishingly, referring to Hawthorn's reputation for pulling communication plugs. Hawthorn agreed to do his best and waited for Hastings to hang up, which the crusty old blighter did, having nothing left to complain about.

The office was hot and humid following the rains. Amazing how quickly the clouds had dispersed and the sun come through in its searing glory, Hawthorn reflected as he went out onto the terrace and down the two steps leading to the drill square boundary. He turned left towards the SAS billets.

"Attention!" Sergeant Jackson bellowed as Hawthorn entered the basha.

"As you were," Hawthorn replied, waving the Troopers back to what they had been doing.

★ ★ ★

"Lieutenant Harwell about?" he asked Jackson.

"In the magazine, I believe, sir."

Hawthorn felt the tension in the hut as if it were a living entity. Everyone, including himself, was wound up as they awaited Granby's return with the two Eshanti trackers, not for fear of what lay ahead, but simply anxious to get on with it before Zawutu could be unseated. Hawthorn himself felt a particular determination to pre-empt Moi and scupper any expedient deal perfidious Albion might be about to perpetrate.

"Carry on, Sergeant," he said as he turned to leave.

In the magazine, one of the few concrete structures in the camp, he found Harwell and two of his Troopers sorting equipment peculiar to the SAS. It was cool inside and he paused to savour the pleasant contrast, using the moment to study with professional interest some of the more esoteric weaponry stacked near the door, before addressing the SAS Subaltern who looked up at the voice, stood up and said: "Sir?"

"Jimmy. I want to be able to move out the moment Dickie gets back. Land Rovers loaded, men kitted out, rations etc. I'll speak to Gordon about that. And as much ammunition as the lads can carry. We don't know what we'll meet out there."

"All in hand, sir" Harwell replied. "Should be ready to move in about two hours."

"Very well," Hawthorn said formally, underlining the chain of command. He would be in charge of this one, not Jimmy.

Harwell stiffened. "Sir," he said, making it equally clear that he understood. He had, in fact, never doubted that the Maverick Major, as some were now calling Hawthorn, would be with them when the search commenced, nor that he would be in command, nor that Richard Granby would be with them. The Devil's trio, he thought, unashamedly including himself.

He watched Hawthorn leave and shook his head. How a man could recover so quickly from a neglected bullet wound and prolonged exposure amazed him. Unless the Boss was being stoical about it and was still weak and in pain, in which case he would make sure no harm came to him in the jungle. And with that matter settled in his mind he jollied up his two specialist armourers and carried on where he had left off.

* * *

Next day, at close to eleven in the morning, Granby came steaming into camp in a cloud of dust and braked outside Hawthorn's office. Sharing the land Rover with him were two native men, their faces creased from long exposure to the sun, both smiling the brilliant smile so typical of the local tribesmen.

"Sam and Onjojo," Granby said proudly to Gordon Butler as he dismounted. "Trackers extraordinaire."

The two Eshanti leaped from the vehicle and smiled even more widely, which would have seemed impossible.

"I'll fetch the OC," Butler said excitedly as he turned on his heels and re-entered the attap hut. Hawthorn emerged within seconds. "Ah, Dickie. We're on then?" He surveyed Granby's companions, noted their ragged shorts, threadbare shirts and gnarled, bare feet and bade them welcome, shaking each by the hand the Eshanti way.

"Do they need anything from us?" he enquired of Granby.

"I don't believe so," Granby said. "Sam", he indicated the elder of the two, "is the hunter. We lived off the land when we were on safari together." He reached into the back of the Land Rover and produced Sam's Eshanti bow. "Using this. In Sam's hands it's just about the deadliest short-range weapon I've ever come across. Wish I could market them." He laughed with Sam.

"Onjojo here is Sam's alter ego. He's a miraculous tracker and brilliant improviser."

Onjojo chuckled, a sound which brought back a mass of nostalgia as Granby recalled the time he had asked about telescopic sights. He raised his hands in the simulation he had used then and the three of them collapsed into paroxysms.

Hawthorn watched and said nothing. A kind of bond obviously existed between the three which augured well for the task ahead, and he was not about to spoil it. Indeed, he envied Granby.

"Sorry about that, Alistair," Granby apologised eventually. "An inside joke which I'll tell you all about over a drink one day when we have more time. Now, what's the drill?"

Hawthorn waved aside the apology. "How long do Sam and Onjojo need before they're ready to go?"

Granby conferred in the mix of pidgin and sign he had perfected on safari, then turned to Hawthorn. "Sam wants to know what it is you are looking for. The spoor of a pig and that of a lion are very different, he says."

"An aeroplane," Hawthorn said succinctly.

Granby nodded. "I've told them that, but they've never tracked an aircraft before. Damaged foliage and tyre mark impressions will be long gone after the rains, and the Eshanti are past masters at camouflaging their own tracks."

Hawthorn frowned. "So what you're telling me is that after going to all this trouble to find your friends they're not even going to be able to help us?"

Granby shook his head. "I didn't say that." He turned again to Sam and Onjojo. Sounds and gestures followed and finally Granby nodded.

"Onjojo says that Major Moi is often careless and won't be

expecting Eshanti trackers out looking for his aeroplane. He asked about guards and I told him there must be some. Moi wouldn't leave such an important piece of hardware unprotected. He says men will have been supplying food and water and so much movement cannot be disguised."

Onjojo nodded and grinned. Hawthorn grinned back.

"We're looking for where the tracks converge, men's tracks. Is that it, then?" he asked directly of Onjojo who looked to Granby for an interpretation and got one.

"He says yes," Granby replied for him. "And we should leave soon."

Hawthorn turned to Butler. "Get Jimmy, would you." Then he turned back to Granby. "Will Sam and Onjojo eat before we leave?" He mimicked the spooning of food into his mouth. Both men nodded.

Hawthorn called to a passing soldier. "Take these men to the cookhouse and give them what they want. Then bring them back here."

The soldier saluted, gathered the two natives without question and began a conversation with them as only British soldiers can; a vestigial skill from days of Empire. Granby, Hawthorn and Butler retired into Hawthorn's office, to be joined by Lieutenant Harwell in a rush. He saluted, removed his cap, took the only vacant seat and leaned forward, eager for news.

"OK," Hawthorn began. "As soon as Sam and Onjojo, they're Dickie's trackers," he explained to Harwell, "are fed, we shall move out as far as the airfield in transport." He looked to Butler, who nodded confirmation. "You know, I'm astounded at how Moi did it, unless he somehow removed the wings. But if he did, where are they?"

Granby butted in. "With respect, Alistair. Where the aircraft entered the jungle and how Moi got it to wherever it are immaterial. I thought we'd established that we're looking for human tracks, a supply route, and that could start from anywhere. Indeed, I'd have thought the last place to start looking would be the airfield."

"You may be right," Hawthorn conceded. "But we have to start somewhere. The Sappers are nearly finished doing up the runway and I expect the heavy lifts to start soon. That gives us a base and a place to get lost among all the activity there'll be at the airfield about now. Don't imagine Moi isn't watching everything that's going on, and I don't want to advertise what we're up to. Onjojo can lead us in wherever he wants, but it has to be done surreptitiously. Remember, the Brigade has called off its search, so we don't want Moi to think it's started again and tighten up on security. The more relaxed he is the better chance we have of finding him."

Granby nodded. "I hadn't thought of that," he confessed.

"Why should you?" Hawthorn said. "At the airfield we blend into the background, look busy while Onjojo and Sam recce the tree line. Then as soon as they've decided where to start we move in that same night. I hope that'll be tonight or tomorrow night at the latest, because London won't hang about. They want this bloody aeroplane too badly for that and I want us to get to it first."

"Normal jungle tactics, sir?" Harwell enquired.

"Until we find something positive, yes," Hawthorn told him. "Then we play it by ear. Any further questions?"

"What do I do with the Light Infantry Company while you're away?" Butler asked.

"Jungle training somewhere in the edge of the forest, as far away from where we'll be as possible. Colonel Hastings will be expecting it, so you should be ready for a visit. If he asks about me, tell him I'm the enemy you're pursuing and haven't caught up with yet. I don't think he'll want to go too far into the Ulu." He smiled to himself. "Right, everyone. Ready to move in one hour. Go."

★ ★ ★

Zawutu felt isolated with Granby gone. The impending pre-war nuptials, his intended marriage to Uudi, was still on hold and he was having second thoughts. The idea had seemed a good one at the time, but it had inflamed the Ushkuu and alienated Josi and might even have been the catalyst that had started the fighting. Now was not the time to resurrect anything so controversial. He would miss her, of course, and perhaps they could be together from time to time, he conjectured, without knowing quite how it would be achieved.

He pushed a highly erotic thought to the back of his mind and downloaded more important matters. What were the British up to? The Parachute Brigade had ceased its search of the jungle and all had gone quiet on that front. Hawthorn had something going, or he wouldn't have kidnapped Richard. There had been no word from Josi, not even a whisper, and the whole thing was very unnerving.

Balindi, forgiven his flexible loyalties, remained Zawanda's Honorary Consul to the Court of St. James and knew nothing either. All his requests for a meeting with Beauchamp were being stonewalled, and no one seemed to know why. Junior departmental civil servants threw out their hands or shrugged their shoulders when approached, leading Balindi to the conclusion that a conspiracy of silence was the order of the day – every day.

Zawutu fumed. His telephone calls to the Foreign and Commonwealth Office were speedily put through to Beauchamp, who enquired politely about the President's health and how the rehabilitation programme was progressing, but would not be drawn on any other subject. Frustration ruled.

"I think I'll pay a visit to Alistair," he informed Ingabe. It was mid-afternoon and he was bored. Besides, Alistair might be more forthcoming about what was going on.

"Will I come with you?" Ingabe asked, his affection for the British Major undiminished, as Hawthorn had helped him so generously in so many ways.

"Of course," Zawutu replied. He knew of Ingabe's feelings, which were similar to his own. Alistair had a talent for attracting respect.

The journey to New London Barracks took only a few minutes, the escort vehicles clearing the way ahead. As the convoy entered the barracks 2nd Eshanti Regiment guard turned out, the sentry warned by the wing flags on the presidential Mercedes. A smart Present Arms honoured the visitors and the Guard Commander's call to the new CO, Lieutenant Colonel Bimbolu – M'Nango having been elevated to the post of Minister of Defence – created a minor panic. The President did not normally visit regiments without prior warning.

Even more mysterious was the Mercedes pulling up outside Major Hawthorn's Headquarters basha before Bimbolu could get there. Zawutu and Ingabe climbed out of the Mercedes and walked into Hawthorn's office.

Butler sprang to his feet. "Mr President, sir," he pronounced in a fluster. "I'm afraid Major Hawthorn isn't here. Can I help?"

At that point, Colonel Bimbolu came charging in. "Sir," he said as he saluted. "We weren't expecting you."

Zawutu smiled. "This isn't an official visit, Colonel," he explained. "I'm here to visit the British Mission, quite informally of course. Major Hawthorn, actually."

Bimbolu looked to Butler. He had no idea of Hawthorn's whereabouts himself.

"I was just explaining, sir, that Major Hawthorn is out on exercise," Butler said, remembering the cover story just in time.

Zawutu frowned. "But I noticed your men forming up on the parade ground?"

Butler felt the sweat break out. "Yes, sir. Major Hawthorn and the SAS are the enemy. They left two hours ago."

Ingabe and Zawutu exchanged glances. Something wasn't right and both men felt it. Captain Butler just wasn't comfortable.

"Very well," Zawutu said, unable to fathom the cause of his suspicions. "I'll inspect your men before they leave. And perhaps spend a little time with you, Colonel. Find out how my old Regiment is faring."

Bimbolu looked pleased at his inclusion in the President's plans, but felt differently later when Zawutu interrogated him extensively about the British and their recent activities. He felt guilty at knowing so little about what went on in his own barracks and Zawutu left feeling none the wiser. He was also frustrated, and even more worried.

* * *

By late afternoon Onjojo had identified a starting point, and just after dusk the SAS teams entered the tree line about a mile south of the airfield. The order of march was Sam and Onjojo working parallel ahead, Lieutenant Harwell and the point SAS team next, then Hawthorn and Granby and the three remaining SAS teams spread as wide as the terrain would allow. Once hidden from outside view the whole party halted and bedded down for the night; even Onjojo's magical tracking skills could not function effectively in total darkness.

Next morning, just before dawn (though the word had little meaning under a forest canopy which spread and effectively filtered the sunlight so that dawn came later and less rapidly than elsewhere), Hawthorn's determined little band began to organise for the day ahead. Sam and Onjojo struck out, quartering for the slightest sign. The rest untied the cords which attached their weapons to their wrists and checked movements and magazines. Then they ate – cold beans, from tins which they buried as soon as they were empty. All had slept fully clothed, shedding only their lightweight webbing which carried ammunition and food and had a water bottle clipped on. Now they reversed the procedure, and as the first glimmer of light percolated through the foliage above, Harwell reported to Hawthorn that they were ready to move out.

Within a few minutes Sam and Onjojo came in, jogging fluidly without seeming to make a sound. Granby listened to Onjojo's report and passed it on.

"Onjojo says there are tracks, human tracks, maybe a few days old, but they could be anyone's. His guess is that they are in fact Moi's men, simply because no one else is likely to be moving in this part of the forest."

Hawthorn nodded. "Let's go with them then."

Harwell moved ahead with his team, behind the trackers as before, with the remainder behind the SAS point. In this way they advanced slowly all that day, with occasional halts for Onjojo to cast about for alternative tracks. Food was taken on the hoof and the empties carefully returned to the relevant haversack. Nothing must be discarded which would indicate that Europeans were abroad in the jungle.

Night came early too, and by six the trackers called a stop.

"Not good now," Onjojo explained.

"How far do you think we've made today?" Hawthorn asked Harwell.

"In a straight line, not very far. I've had the compass out most of the time and we've been moving in a sort of arc. You can still hear machinery at the airfield, so we're not all that far in."

"Makes sense," Hawthorn said thoughtfully. "Moi can't have moved a bomber-sized aircraft far in this type of woodland." He indicated the primary forest, which, in contrast to his vision of interwoven, dense undergrowth and a need to hack a way through with machetes, was surprisingly uncluttered between the soaring tree trunks. Nothing can grow at ground level in the absence of direct sunlight, making the going fairly good. But even so, a modern cargo aircraft?

"Maybe tomorrow," Harwell said.

"I hope so. Let's get some sleep, eh? Where's Dickie, by the way?"

"Chinwagging with Sam and Onjojo last I saw of him. There's a real bond between those three."

"I know. It's nice to see. Now, off to sleep, young man."

Next morning the drill was the same. Weapons, breakfast, kitting up, deploying into order of march and moving out.

Early in the afternoon, Sam raised a hand. The advance halted. Sam and Onjojo conferred and waved Granby forward.

"It seems the Eshanti have laid a false trail. The tracks we've been following peter out just ahead and Onjojo says it's deliberate," Granby reported to Hawthorn.

"Bugger," Hawthorn said vehemently. "Where do we go from here?"

"Sam disagrees with Onjojo. He reckons the trail will pick up again further out. Maybe not directly ahead, but somewhere not too far distant. He claims the spoor is just interrupted, a device commonly used by the Eshanti to muddy things up for their pursuers. Onjojo says not. So, take your pick."

"Send them both out. Two arcs of thirty degrees each. Let's see what they turn up."

It was almost dark when Onjojo came back into the rest area with news. Sam had, it seemed, found where the Eshanti trail picked up again.

"It might happen like this a few more times," Granby said after speaking with Onjojo. "But now the boys know what their chums are doing they won't be fooled again."

"Very well. Thank Sam and Onjojo and tell them we'll strike

off again at dawn tomorrow." Hawthorn turned to Harwell. "You heard that Jimmy? Brief your chaps for a sparrow's start."

The two sentries changed at two-hour intervals throughout the night, the last pair charged with waking the rest. An eerie mist had formed, which seemed to undulate round and between the trees at about head height as if propelled by some unseen, mystical force. Sam said it signified that water ran nearby and that it would soon burn off when it felt the heat of the sun. Onjojo said he could follow the trail anyway.

The party organised itself as before, and with the two trackers leading it was soon moving at a reasonable pace through close country. Sam's prediction proved correct, the mist dispersing even as they watched.

Midday came and went and Onjojo cracked on, covering the ground at a punishing pace. The trail, although still obscure to the Europeans, except for a few SAS specialists who were by now beginning to notice things, was like a road map to Onjojo. The Eshanti had become careless since breaking and zigzagging the track and had now left plenty for the two trackers to follow.

Suddenly Sam raised a hand and lowered himself slowly and fluidly to the ground. Onjojo followed suit and the rest copied him on a signal from Harwell.

Hawthorn crawled forward, heeding urgent signals from Sam to slow down and reduce noise. When he came up alongside, Sam raised himself on one elbow and pointed. Hawthorn looked hard and saw nothing unusual. He lowered himself again and looked quizzically at his neighbour.

"Aeroplane," Sam whispered, mimicking the flight of one with his right hand.

Hawthorn raised himself once more and peered intently into the area Sam had indicated. This time he noticed that the undergrowth seemed denser, that there was more shadow obscuring the view between the trees.

Then, just as he was about to slip down again, something moved. He remained perfectly still. Suddenly, to his astonishment, he saw two figures leave the shadows; a woman, accompanied by a man. The pair walked some distance into another dark patch.

Sam pulled him down. "Maiden," he said with a lascivious smile.

"Moi."

Hawthorn frowned. Was Moi actually here, he asked Sam in best pidgin? The tracker shrugged.

Hawthorn waved for Granby to come forward, which he did more expertly than Hawthorn, the result of his time in the Ulu with Sam and Onjojo.

"Sam is trying to tell me something about Moi," Hawthorn whispered.

Sam and Granby exchanged hissed words and slow, easy signals, and Granby turned to Hawthorn. "He doesn't know whether Moi is here or not. What he said was that the maiden, and maybe others, are kept here for Moi's pleasure. The girl was Ushkuu, by the way, and most certainly a captive, according to Sam."

"Can Sam and Onjojo recce round the area and ascertain the number of Moi's men there are here?"

A further exchange elicited that the two trackers would do their best, but they were already mighty close and could easily spook the guards, they explained.

"We'll be ready to move in if that happens," Hawthorn assured them through Granby. He went to call Harwell forward, but was stopped by Sam.

Granby interpreted. "He says better if you go back to talk. Here is too near the Eshanti guards."

Hawthorn nodded and slithered back to where Harwell lay with his Troop Sergeant.

Following their discussion the rearmost SAS sections moved out sideways, forming a rough line facing the suspect area. Sam groaned at the noise they made, though the soldiers believed they had moved silently. They had never before been in company with two of the world's finest.

When all was ready, Hawthorn nodded to Granby, who tapped Sam on the shoulder. Sam nudged Onjojo and the two slithered into the undergrowth and disappeared.

The SAS waited for a reaction from the enemy, ready instantly to charge in and do whatever was necessary. The seconds slipped by with no sign of alarm from the men guarding the aircraft. The seconds became minutes, then an hour. Hawthorn signalled his concern to Granby, who shook his head.

"They'll be back," he mouthed.

To an Eshanti bushman, time meant nothing. A tracker would lie up all day rather than risk alerting his prey. Granby could visualise his two friends moving, pausing to look and listen, then moving again, making infinitely patient but inexorable progress.

Just after three o'clock Sam and Onjojo returned. One second there was nothing, then the two were suddenly among them, causing the nearest SAS Troopers to raise their weapons in alarm. Sam found Granby and spoke with him.

"There are no sentries out," Granby informed Hawthorn. "Onjojo believes there are at least twenty men here, and more than one Ushkuu maiden. The aircraft is without wings and the Eshanti appear to be using the fuselage as living quarters. The guards are armed but not alert. Sam reckons he and Onjojo could take them on their own if they weren't Eshanti." Granby grinned. "Typical of those two," he added affectionately.

"All that from a look see?" Hawthorn remarked, clearly impressed.

"Sam has been in and actually touched the metal skin of the plane," Granby said nonchalantly.

"And I thought our lads were good!" Hawthorn said, shaking his head in admiration. "OK. Let's get this over with before dark. We'll pull back out of hearing and sort ourselves out. Shouldn't be too difficult."

Further back down the track Hawthorn quietly briefed Harwell. "I would prefer it if there was no shooting," he said. "We don't know if there are any more Eshanti guerrillas in the vicinity and we don't want to attract attention until the job's done."

Harwell concurred. "If Sam and Onjojo can guide us in we should be able to take the plane and the guards without fuss."

Granby conferred with the trackers and came to Hawthorn with a glum look on his face. "Sam and Onjojo are leaving," he reported. "Say they won't fight Eshanti. There's the aeroplane. Their job is done, they say."

Hawthorn smiled. "And very well done, too." He crept over to where the two trackers were squatted beneath a tree. "Thank you both," he said as they rose to their feet. He shook each by the hand the Eshanti way. "Thank you again."

Granby stayed behind to say his farewells, a more emotional parting than it had been for Hawthorn. "I see you again," he said, using the Eshanti form of goodbye between friends.

Sam smiled, hanging on to Granby's hand. "Use this well," he said, handing Granby his bow and quiver full of deadly arrows, a gift of great significance. Even Onjojo was surprised by the gesture. Granby felt his eyes pricking and lowered his head to hide the tears.

Sam let go of the hand and stepped back. "Mind the lions," he said. Then the two men turned and set off in the direction of the airfield.

Granby watched until they were lost among the trees, then with a sigh he walked over to join Hawthorn and Harwell, the bow and quiver held at arm's length. Harwell noticed them and went to comment, but Hawthorn pre-empted him.

"Get your people moving," he ordered the SAS Subaltern firmly. Granby gave Hawthorn a look of gratitude. Amazing how sensitive this rash, brash, crazy soldier could be sometimes.

The advance to their previous position took a while, since Harwell had threatened death by shooting to any Trooper who alerted the Eshanti. Then, on a signal from Harwell, the SAS teams fanned out and curved in on the flanks, similar to the horns of Zulu Impis' fighting formation. Then all went still as the men awaited the final order.

Harwell watched Hawthorn raise his hand and drop it. The Subaltern jerked his balled fist in a pumping motion and the SAS moved. Within minutes the objective had changed hands, relatively silently, and certainly without gunshot.

Hawthorn studied the aircraft and admired the camouflage that had kept it concealed from a full Brigade of energetic Paratroopers. "Tie them up," he told Harwell, indicating the prisoners. "And keep the girls here. No one is to leave until this bloody plane is safely in the hands of Brigadier Humphries." He called the radio operator to his side. "Raise Brigade."

"Sunray not here," the Brigade operator replied to the call.

"Fuck!" Hawthorn said to himself. Where was he?

Hastings came on the net. "Sunray is taking delivery of an aeroplane," he said. "What do you want from him?"

"Nothing. Out," Hawthorn said abruptly. He called his people to him. "Jimmy, you and your chaps stay here and make sure no one interferes with that plane. Dickie, you and I are going to meet the Brigadier and stop him making a bloody idiot of himself."

"Take 'A' Troop with you, sir," Harwell cautioned. "You never know."

"Very well. But let's get moving."

When he looked back the scene was as it had been; no sign of men or machine, the jungle looking like jungle. He wondered whether the Brigadier had already joined up with Moi, and how he would deal with that situation, but first he had to intercept him. He could only guess the route he would be taking, from the airfield most likely. His HQ was, after all, located close by there.

Granby kept up well, Sam's bow slung on one shoulder and the quiver of arrows in his left hand. Hawthorn was setting a cracking pace, considering he was still recuperating. Granby had notice him wince once or twice; he was definitely avoiding using the injured arm, even though it should be much improved by now.

"Take it easy, Alistair," he warned. "You've had a hard couple of days and you're not exactly fighting fit yet."

Hawthorn looked back with a grin. "When we've sorted this aeroplane business maybe I'll take a spot of leave," he conceded.

A burst of small arms fire whistled overhead and Hawthorn, Granby and the SAS Troop hit the ground. "Where the hell did that come from?" Granby hissed.

The SAS Troop reacted instantly. Always attack the attacker because it demoralises him - that was the SAS dictum that controlled this kind of situation, and Corporal Todd acted on it instinctively. Moving crouched, two at a time, the Troop leapfrogged forward, firing as they went. The response from up ahead soon petered out and footsteps could be heard retreating into the trees. Then a voice.

"This is Major Moi. I'm coming out."

A rustling, then Moi appeared on the track ahead. He carried an automatic weapon loosely in one hand.

Hawthorn stood up, Granby not far behind. "OK Corporal," Hawthorn called to the SAS NCO. "Let them go."

Todd waved his men back to where Hawthorn and Granby stood, then sited them in a protective ring around the officer and the civilian, kneeling, weapons at the ready.

"Major Moi. What a surprise," Hawthorn said. "What are you doing firing on me and my party?"

"A mistake, Major. What are you doing here anyway?"

"Reclaiming a certain aeroplane," Hawthorn said casually.

Moi smiled his twisted smile. "You're too late, Hawthorn. Even as we speak Brigadier Humphries is on his way to take possession. I am within a few minutes of becoming President of Zawanda, so I'd be careful if I were you."

"If what you say were true you would have my immediate cooperation, but unfortunately for your plans I've already found the aircraft. I'm afraid all deals are off."

Moi sniggered. "You're bluffing," he said, but his tone was uncertain. "How could a honky like you find anything hidden by the Eshanti in our own forest?"

"I'm afraid we have. We have even captured your Ushkuu maidens."

Moi stared across the distance between them, and saw the truth. "Fuck you, Hawthorn," he spat. "But there's still time to take it back." He raised his weapon aggressively, but as he levelled it Hawthorn heard a humming sound and felt a subtle movement of the air beside his ear. Instinctively he snatched his head away. The next thing he heard was a sickening thud as Moi crashed into the undergrowth and collapsed backwards into it, an Eshanti arrow protruding from his chest.

Hawthorn swung round to witness Granby lowering Sam's bow from the firing position.

"He called me Honky one time too many," Granby pointed out in a perfectly reasonable tone, adding, as if it were only a secondary, minor reason: "And he was about to shoot you."

"Exactly," Hawthorn replied. "Lucky that Ushkuu killed him just in time."

Granby frowned, then his face broke into a knowing smile. "Of course. Jolly lucky," he said, going along with the charade.

"Corporal. You saw that Ushkuu warrior, didn't you?" said Hawthorn.

Corporal Todd smiled. "Of course, sir. Pity we couldn't catch him."

Hawthorn nodded. "Make sure your lads are of the same opinion."

"No problem, sir," replied Todd confidently.

★ ★ ★

Brigadier Humphries emerged into the open area around the aircraft, now cleared of camouflage by the prisoners under SAS tutelage, and cocked an eyebrow at Hawthorn. He had with him a Platoon of Paras and two of Moi's Eshanti as guides.

"Your exercise went well, I see," Humphries remarked, flicking his head towards the wingless aeroplane.

"Stumbled upon it, sir."

"Hmmm. Where's Moi?"

"Ah! I'm afraid there's bad news there," Hawthorn replied seriously. "The poor man's dead. He was killed by an Ushkuu raiding party not fifteen minutes ago." He glanced round for confirmation and heads nodded obediently. "We left his body where we found it."

"I hope the bullet is not NATO calibre?" Humphries said, flashing a warning glance at Hawthorn.

"He was killed by an arrow, as a matter of fact."

Humphries sighed with relief. "No call for a Board of Enquiry, then."

Hawthorn shook his head decisively.

The Brigadier dropped the subject of Moi's untimely demise. He didn't want to know the details of what had gone on or exactly how the rebel Major had died. In his experience too many questions and too much knowledge could create embarrassing problems.

"The Sappers will recover the aircraft to the airfield, then the area will be cleared while we investigate the cargo" he told Hawthorn. "Meanwhile, you had better make your way there and await further orders."

Hawthorn saluted. "Sir."

The return journey was quick. Led by SAS scouts, the whole group was back on the airfield by late afternoon. The runway was obviously serviceable again, as two cargo C130s had been landed and parked near the terminal. Alongside them were two lightweight helicopters, which were in the process of being unfolded and serviced by Army Air Corps ground staff under the supervision of REME NCOs, whilst other items of heavy equipment could be seen lined up along the apron.

Hawthorn sought out the local commander, a Major of the Airborne Logistics Corps. "Can my people get a meal, and perhaps a shower as well?" he enquired.

The Logistics Major surveyed the motley band gathered behind this scruffy-looking officer. Something about them caused him to desist from critical comment. "Been on ops?" was all he felt safe in asking.

"Sort of," Hawthorn said. "Now what about food and hot water?"

The Logistics Major nodded and called over one of his own NCOs.

"Sergeant. Show this party to the cookhouse and the showers."

"The showers, sir?" The NCO questioned.

"Yes, the showers, Sergeant. In the passenger terminal."

"But the Terminal's out of bounds, sir."

"Not to these men, I fancy," the Major said. "Get on with it, man."

He turned to Hawthorn. "Do you and the Lieutenant want to take your showers first? Oh, by the way, my name's Patterson. Reggie Patterson."

"Hawthorn. And this is Jimmy Harwell. Oh and Mr Granby, a new recruit. Yes, perhaps we will try and slough off some of this grime." He smiled engagingly.

"The officers are eating over there," Patterson then explained, pointing to a where a marquee had been erected on the grass verge close to the main entrance.

"Thank you," Hawthorn said as he and his companions turned and made their way towards the passenger terminal.

Patterson watched them for a moment. He'd heard of Major Hawthorn. Wasn't he the OC of the British Mission here during the civil war? If so, the stories doing the rounds about him and his command had seemed unbelievable before this, but having met the man and seen some of his troops, he was ready to believe anything. They carried an aura of threat and danger that he had never before experienced; nor would he again, he hoped. And who on earth was the civilian?

He shuddered and hastened away to sort out another problem of bad loading which had delivered extra mortars but no extra ammunition to go with them.

★ ★ ★

Showered and dressed in their old, sweaty clothes, Hawthorn and Harwell called at the cookhouse area to make sure their people were being looked after, then, speculating together on what might be the contents the Russian aircraft, they sauntered across to the Officers' Mess tent, where Granby was waiting. The Mess had been set up as a temporary feeding hole for officers either working at the airfield or for those visiting the area, of which there seemed to be many on this day.

Hawthorn walked in ahead of Harwell and Granby and saw at a glance the variety of cap badges present. He remarked in an aside to his Subaltern that it looked as if the whole bloody officer corps had turned up to see the Russian aircraft. The three found a vacant table and sat down.

"It's self-service, old boy," a Major informed Hawthorn from the next table. Hawthorn looked up and thanked him. The Major eyed the newcomers up and down.

"This is the Mess, you know. Proper dress and all that."

Harwell opened his mouth to explain, but Hawthorn laid a hand on his arm. "Thank you for the information," he said ambiguously to the critic. "Come along you two."

They followed Hawthorn to where several tables had been laid out in a contiguous line to form a serving counter.

"We've only beef left, sir," the cook said, indicating gravy-soaked meat slices lying in a heated metal tray.

"Beef it will be, then," Hawthorn said, his mouth watering at the prospect of a hot meal.

"What an awful shit, sir!" Harwell said, nodding over his shoulder at the Para Major, who was still staring at them and shaking his head admonishingly.

"Lieutenants do not call Majors shits," Hawthorn replied severely. "Majors call Majors shits, and that man's a pompous, half-witted, obnoxious shit if ever I saw one."

Harwell glanced anxiously at his OC, not knowing whether or not he had been told off. He saw Hawthorn's smile and relaxed.

"You had me going there for a moment," he said, accepting a full plate from the cook.

Half way through their meal the Brigadier, untypically, walked into the Mess and up to the counter. The cook stuttered the 'only beef' message and the Brigadier nodded.

In the interval many of the other officers exhibited a certain restlessness; more than half of them should not have been there. Caps were retrieved and hasty exits executed before the Brigadier turned from being served. He ignored the unseemly evacuation and walked directly over to Hawthorn's table.

"Anyone sitting here, Alistair?" he enquired, indicating one of the three vacant chairs. Hawthorn assured him of their availability and the Brigadier sat down. Those remaining inside the tent watched covertly and enviously, wondering who these scruffy-looking people were to be on first-name terms with the Brigade Commander. Then someone whispered, "That's Hawthorn. You know, OC the British Mission."

Rumours of Hawthorn's daring exploits during the Zawandan civil war, already manifold and exaggerated in the telling, were the envy of all glory-seeking officers. The stares were now open, and overtly more envious. Some, though, thought him irresponsible and individual, out of place in an army devoted to the team concept; Colonel Hastings was one of these.

"So that's Hawthorn," the rude Para Major whispered to his companion at the next table, regretting his earlier outburst and figuring out how he might correct that first unfortunate impression. If nothing else, the Paras considered themselves tough, bold and imbued with above average initiative, the very qualities claimed for Hawthorn.

The object of this concern looked up from his laden fork at the stares aimed at his table. Must be the Brigadier they're staring at, he told himself self-effacingly and returned with gusto to his first cooked meal in three days, having first wafted away the mass of flies circling above his plate.

Brigadier Humphries played with his meal. He wasn't here to eat. "The arrow that killed Moi was Eshanti I'm reliably told," he murmured.

Hawthorn glanced at Granby, then looked across at the Brigadier. "Is that a problem, sir?"

"It leaves questions unanswered," Humphries pointed out.

"I'm afraid I'm not able to help you there, sir. Maybe the Ushkuu were using a batch captured during the war."

Humphries gave a wry smile. "I suppose it's as good an explanation as any," he said. "One day perhaps the truth will out."

Hawthorn shrugged. "Who knows what happened out there?"

Humphries nodded. "Indeed! Who knows?" He stared significantly at Hawthorn, who concentrated even more diligently on scooping up the last shred of meat and gravy from his plate.

"How's the arm?" Humphries enquired, changing the subject.

Hawthorn wiggled it about to demonstrate its renewed flexibility. "Good as new, sir."

They both knew they were merely filling time, waiting for the Royal Engineers to extricate the fuselage of the Russian aircraft from its jungle hiding place.

"There's someone I must speak with. Walk with me, Major," Humphries finally said, placing his knife and fork parallel on a virtually untouched plate.

Harwell and Granby stood with them. "See to the boys," Hawthorn instructed Harwell. "You can get everyone back to barracks. Give Captain Butler my compliments and tell him to cancel his exercise and pull his people back as well. I'll be there as soon as I'm free here. Oh, and leave me a Land Rover. Dickie, what do you want to do?"

"I'll just hang on here."

"No you deserve to see the end of this. Come." He hurried out to fall into step with the Brigadier, who had gone on ahead.

"You've done well, Alistair," Humphries said, nodding at Granby. "Both now and during the war, and I shall say so in my reports. But there are those who will hate your independence of spirit. Be careful."

"The irony is, sir, that they train us for this, then hate us for doing it."

"It's a tough old world" Humphries said. "But you're right. Unorthodoxy is abhorred by the establishment. Take the Paras. In order to rationalise our existence a whole new set of Principles of War have been adopted in order to make the powers that be more comfortable with what we do and what we are – highly-trained killers. Even worse, no one wanted to hear about the SAS, or didn't until all the recent publicity. Now an even newer, even more lethal level of orthodoxy has been accommodated so as to ease consciences. But your kind of activities they worry about. Out of reach and out of control most of the time; not helped in your case by you cutting communications with London every time they asked you something stupid. I recommend a spell in your own Regiment away from all this special forces stuff."

"Probably a good idea, sir," Hawthorn said non-committally.

Humphries nodded and swerved right, to where a dark-haired civilian sat in the passenger seat of a Land Rover, fiddling with a piece of equipment which resembled a large flashlight.

"Ah, Dr Miller," Humphries said as he approached. "This is Major Hawthorn, the officer who located the aircraft cargo which is of interest to you."

"Major Hawthorn," Miller said, extending a hand. "I'll be with you in a mo." He adjusted a knob on the top of the strange instrument and laid the whole on the driver's seat. On the ground he stood an inch taller than Hawthorn and looked to be about fortyish with a boyish grin and dark brown eyes. "I'm the boffin they sent out from the Atomic Weapons Research Establishment to inspect the cargo," he said by way of explanation.

"Probably a good thing too," Hawthorn observed. "I shouldn't think anyone here knows much about it."

The repeated crashing of felled trees on the far airfield perimeter attracted their attention. "The Sappers," Humphries said. "How Moi got the damned aeroplane in there in the first place is a miracle. Not a mark anywhere and no room to manoeuvre I'm told."

Hawthorn heard engines start up and glanced back to where Lieutenant Harwell and the SAS teams were loaded and about to leave for New London Barracks. He waved them off and swept the airfield with inquisitive eyes before returning his attention to the forest edge. The field, he noted, no longer resembled even remotely a civilian airport. The runway glistened and shimmered from its new layer of tarmac, but elsewhere there was chaos. Military vehicles of all shapes and sizes littered the apron. The peripheral taxi way had succumbed to drifting sand and could hardly be recognised for what it was. The terminal building looked shabbier than usual and had two helicopters and one C130 parked in front of it. REME aircraft technicians were busy servicing the choppers and a team of Paras was engaged in unloading stores from the Hercules. Other groups milled around on seemingly random tasks.

He shrugged. It would be a while, he reflected, before New London Airport could be brought back into service as the nation's only civilian airstrip. Indeed only airstrip, for Zawanda never had aspired to raising an air force; it had never been able to afford one.

He concentrated on the forest edge. A rumbling and squeaking of metal tracks heralded the emergence of a lightweight tractor, guided out onto the taxi way by a Royal Engineer NCO. Attached to it was a wire rope, the other end of which was connected to the nose cone of the Russian aircraft. Finally came the fuselage, supported on a makeshift sledge knocked up by the Engineers. A few shouted instructions and the array swung round and came to a halt on hard standing parallel to the runway.

"Well, now for the terrible dénouement," Humphries said as he led the way over to the aluminium carcass. It looked more

like a torpedo than a plane, the way it lay there devoid of wings.
The sun, reflecting off the tarmac, seemed of double intensity
and bored straight into unguarded eyes.

Hawthorn squinted and mopped his face with a grubby
handkerchief; he envied the Brigadier, apparently untouched by
the vicious climate.

The Sapper major saluted. "Shall we open the doors, sir?"

Humphries hesitated and turned to Dr Miller. "Is it OK to
open the doors, or shall you go in first to check for leakage?"

"No need. If there's a significant leak in there it's too late
already. If not it won't hurt."

Humphries nodded to the Sapper OC. "Open up then."

A flurry of activity across the other side of the airport
diverted attention and Humphries signalled a hold on opening
the aircraft doors. The Officer in charge snapped an order and
the Sappers engaged in forcing the doors relaxed. A mutterer
was heard to exclaim: "Fucking officers!"

Then all attention was on the Mercedes and its
accompanying escort, which were moving in a cloud of dust
towards where Hawthorn and the others waited. The Mercedes
bore presidential flags on its wings, and as it came to a stop
Hawthorn walked over and opened the rear door.

President Zawutu emerged through the front passenger door
wearing the full dress uniform of a Lieutenant Colonel of 2nd
Eshanti Regiment. The British officers present snapped to
attention and saluted.

"Alistair," Zawutu said, addressing Hawthorn. "How nice to
see you. I called on your 2ic the other day and he said you were
out exercising." He glanced pointedly at the aircraft fuselage.
"Found it, then?"

Hawthorn smiled and stood aside to make way for the
Brigadier.

"Mr President," Humphries said, saluting again and receiving
a salute in return. "We weren't expecting you."

Zawutu smiled warmly and glanced around the airfield. "This is Zawanda, I believe, and I am its President." His reply was devoid of malice. Hawthorn smiled to himself. Zawutu had lost none of his wicked charm, he reflected. The gentle admonishment was typical of the man.

"Indeed, sir," Humphries said, equally contained but a little flushed at Zawutu's correction. "Can I be of help?"

"Yes. As a matter of fact you can. I have heard much of aeroplanes; rumours, of course. Then when I heard you'd come across one I determined to see this elusive ghost for myself. Such a mystery how it got here."

Diplomacy had never been Humphries strong point, and how he held back the sardonic smile that quivered at the corners of his mouth he never knew. Suffice to say he did.

"Indeed," he said seriously. "We are about to open the ramp and examine the contents. Would you care to wait, sir?"

Zawutu nodded. "Exciting, what?"

The assembled officers had watched the exchange in ignorance. Hawthorn, aware of the underlying nuances, had enjoyed every mild cut and every gentle thrust.

Humphries signalled for work on the ramp to recommence. Zawutu walked over to Hawthorn, choosing to await the damning revelation in company with someone who, even if he didn't know all the truth, had suspected and never been an accuser.

"I couldn't keep away," Zawutu explained guiltily.

Hawthorn nodded. He felt he knew the President well enough now to crack a joke. "Returning to the scene of the crime, eh?"

Zawutu glanced sharply at him. "Too near the truth, Alistair, my friend," he confessed and fell silent as the rear ramp swung down and came to rest a few inches above the ground. Dr Miller, poised to make the first essay into the aircraft fuselage, scrambled up the slope, Geiger counter in hand, to reappear a moment later.

"Vehicles," he said. "Lorries. Can you wheel them out for a closer look please?"

The Officer in charge nodded to his men, who clambered inside, unhitched the tie-down straps, released hand brakes and pushed five five-ton trucks down the ramp onto the tarmac. The crowd that had assembled near the tail of the aircraft shifted rearward with unseemly haste; everyone somehow knew what was supposed to be in those lorries.

"Canopies off, if you please," Miller ordered and the Sappers obliged. Miller climbed the tailboard of each lorry in turn with his counter aimed at the contents, then walked across to Humphries.

"Not a naughty neutron in sight," he said with a jolly smile. "Spares. Missile spares. Nothing at all to do with warheads. A cold scene, Brigadier. Wherever the nose cones are, they're not here. Intended for a later flight I suspect, probably the last one."

Hawthorn heard Zawutu issue a huge sigh of relief. Missile spares did not prove a nuclear connection, and Zawutu knew it. Hawthorn began to say something about good luck, then thought better of it.

"Well, that's the show over for the day," Zawutu said euphorically. "See you, Alistair. Call on me soon." He turned to Granby. "Dickie, a lift back to the Palace?" He gathered Granby and walked over to Humphries. "Interesting result, what? I wonder what anyone would want with missile spares for non-existent missiles. Moi must be mad."

"Ah." Humphries adopted a sombre expression. "I should have informed you earlier, Mr President, but I'm afraid Major Moi is dead. Killed by a marauding group of Ushkuu tribesmen just yesterday. We left his body for recovery by your people. I assumed there would be tribal requirements."

Zawutu looked genuinely sad, the joy of the day suddenly dulled by the news of Moi's demise, for no matter how much of a rebel he had been, they had always been friends, and losing a friend is a sad business.

"Yes. I will see to it," he said, and taking Granby's arm he turned for his car, flicking his swagger cane to the peak of his cap as he left. Humphries watched him go, well aware of the emotions involved. Hawthorn was at the car door and opened it as Zawutu approached.

"I'm really sorry," he said.

"He was not always on my side, but I loved him," Zawutu confessed as he climbed in. "See me soon, Alistair."

The assembled officers saluted as the presidential Mercedes swept by and left the airfield at speed.

CHAPTER TWENTY SEVEN

The signal was received in Whitehall with rejoicing. Henright rang Beauchamp, who called the PM.

"Spare parts?" the PM exclaimed. "All that for a few nuts and bolts?"

"I'm afraid so," Beauchamp replied. "But at least the matter is resolved, except for what we do about Zawanda now it's all over."

"We'd better talk about that. I'll get Defence in as well. There is the question of whether we maintain a military presence there in case Zawutu tries something else."

Beauchamp gave a cautionary cough. "May I suggest occasional training, one Company of troops, now and then? If we are to prevent any further outbursts of trouble and make it possible for Zawutu to rule the country in the way we know he is capable of, we simply must reinstate the aid programme. There'll be very little money left for military manoeuvres after that."

"We'll talk about it later, but now I must ring Orville Clayton and do a little crowing. To think he might have shot that aeroplane down. It doesn't bear thinking about, does it?"

★ ★ ★

The Parachute Brigade was scheduled to be lifted out over the next few weeks, there being too few C130s available to complete the exercise any sooner. The Byelorussians were contacted circumspectly through diplomatic channels about their aircraft, and when its condition was described in full they had no hesitation in agreeing to its destruction and disposal locally, embarrassment being the prime motivator. Brigadier Humphries, meanwhile, read the riot act to President Zawutu and the Ushkuu chieftains with regard to their future good behaviour, the script provided by the Foreign Office, and at the same time made an appointment to visit the President formally in order to say goodbye.

"I'll be sorry to see the Paras leave," Zawutu confessed to Hawthorn during their get-together in his study two days after Moi's funeral. The warship, HM The Queen and photographs of previous Governors still graced the walls, but the pictures of all the military Presidents since independence had conspicuously been removed. It was said that Zawutu had commissioned a portrait of himself, however.

"I didn't want them here at first, you know." He smiled shyly at his guest. "I had every confidence in you and your people."

Hawthorn nodded his acceptance of the compliment. "I'm flattered, sir, but if that Para Company hadn't appeared on the hill when it did I dread to think what might have transpired.".

"Hmm! I think you'd have managed somehow" Zawutu said confidently. He had developed an almost blind faith in the abilities of this British officer to handle any situation, even the virtually impossible.

Hawthorn tried not to look over-grateful for the compliment, but he couldn't resist a wry smile. If only Zawutu knew the extent of the problems he'd built up for himself with the powers at home.

"You'll be promoted, of course?" Zawutu suggested. "The MoD, indeed the whole British government, must be impressed with what you've achieved here. My God, you stopped a war, found a missing aeroplane and single-handedly brought reconciliation to the tribes."

"Not quite all of that," Hawthorn responded modestly. "No more than duty demanded, as a matter of fact."

"Be that as it may, but in my report to London – not that they've requested one, well, they wouldn't would they? – I shall tell them of your contribution and make a few suggestions about your future."

"Thank you, sir, but I'd rather you didn't. Ironically, I'm in enough trouble as it is. My bosses do not take kindly to rebellious officers doing their own thing, and that's exactly what I've been doing ever since I got here. With respect, sir, recommendations from an equally rebellious President would only serve to compound my problems."

"Well, I'll speak to your Brigadier, then." Zawutu said, huffily. "He, at least, has hands on experience of your gallantry."

Nothing more was said of the matter, the conversation turning to Richard Granby's brave efforts and Zawutu's interest in the SAS. "I might raise a Squadron here," he said. "Do you think Hereford would train a few of my best officers?"

★ ★ ★

At last the time came for Humphries to bid his half-reluctant host farewell. He invited Hawthorn to accompany him, respecting the special relationship that had obviously developed between the African and the Britisher. Major de Lancy met them on the Palace steps.

"The President will receive you at once," said de Lancy after executing a quivering salute.

Hawthorn did the honours. "You haven't met Major de Lancy, Brigadier. Once Colonel Zawutu's adjutant, then head of security. And now ?" He looked at de Lancy.

"Personal Aide to the President," de Lancy announced proudly.

"Well met," Humphries said, taking de Lancy's hand and shaking it. Swollen with pride, de Lancy ushered the two men into the palace with exaggerated politeness. "This way, sirs, if you please."

Zawutu had arranged for the meeting to take place in his new audience room. It was the old bedroom antechamber, redecorated and fitted at one end with a roughly-hewn wooden seat in the shape of a throne. The carpets were newly laid and a chandelier taken from elsewhere in the Palace hung majestically from the ceiling. The old easy chairs and leather-covered settees were now rearranged in a hollow square at the far end of the room.

As the Brigadier and Hawthorn entered, passed on, as it were, by an over attendant de Lancy, Zawutu rose to his feet and walked over to greet them.

"Welcome," he said, "Do sit down." He led the way to the cluster of chairs.

"When do you yourself depart, Brigadier?" Zawutu enquired, despite knowing already.

"Major Hawthorn and I are on the second flight tomorrow, scheduled, I believe, for ten hundred hours," said Humphries. He looked to Hawthorn for confirmation. "But the RAF is not British Airways, and schedules can change for all kinds of reasons."

"Of course," Zawutu nodded. "Operational demands and all that. Anyway, I hope you've enjoyed your stay in my country, short though it's been. I hope too you've learned a lot from training here." He smiled cynically at the cover story which pride made it necessary to maintain.

"Indeed we have," Humphries agreed, playing along. He held a guarded respect for Zawutu as a man, a fellow officer and President, the knowledge coming mostly from outside sources such as Hawthorn and that renegade Granby. But the few times he and the President had met, their exchanges had been civilised, intellectual and rewarding. Yes, he liked the man.

"Operating in such an enervating climate, for one," he added with a mock grimace.

"We're used to it," Zawutu responded. Then the conversation turned to mundane matters of logistics and in what condition the Royal Engineers were to leave New London Airport. Zawutu was pleased that the mess out there had been mostly tidied up.

Eventually, Humphries stood. "Thank you from all ranks of the Parachute Brigade, Mr President, for your excellent hospitality," he said. "I wish you and Zawanda well for the future."

"And I you," Zawutu replied formally as he and Hawthorn rose. "Maybe we shall meet again under more propitious circumstances." That was his only and last reference to the true purpose behind the Brigade's presence in Zawanda.

"I certainly hope so. I look forward to it," Humphries said genuinely.

"Goodbye Alistair," Zawutu said, turning to Hawthorn. "And thank you for everything. He looked embarrassed for a moment, then burst out with, "There's a job for you here, you know. Richard is staying on. You two would make a good team."

Hawthorn looked flustered and turned to the Brigadier. Humphries shrugged. He didn't think Alistair was asking his advice so much as absorbing the shock.

"I'm flattered, sir, of course," Hawthorn said after the short pause. "But I'm bound in my heart to serving the Queen. Patriotic nonsense, of course, but it's the way I feel." He gazed at the floor in embarrassment. Then looking up, resumed, "Dickie can do everything I could do, and more, without any help from me. I'll miss the old sod though."

Zawutu laughed. "Yes, he's been a bit of a reprobate, but not of his own choosing. Anyway, look after yourself, my friend. I'll be watching your progress." He glanced meaningfully at Humphries, who responded with an almost invisible nod.

★ ★ ★

The ten o'clock aircraft was on time and loaded. The men of the Airborne Battery RA had embarked along with other mixed elements of the Brigade; the Battery's guns had left on the previous flight. Lieutenant Harwell and the SAS Troops had flown out on the first flight, landed by night at Lyneham and spirited away to Hereford in closed trucks. Now only Brigadier Humphries and Major Hawthorn remained on the tarmac, Humphries making certain that Lieutenant Colonel Hastings was happy with arrangements for the departure of the tail end of the Brigade over the next three days.

"See you in Aldershot," Humphries said finally.

"Sir!" A voice called out from among the Military Policemen clustered close to the aircraft. "The President's car, sir."

Humphries swung round just as the Mercedes came to a stop a short distance away. Zawutu stepped out and returned the mass salutes.

"Couldn't let you go without a proper send off," he said cheerfully. "Do you know Mr Ingabe, my Minister for Tribal Affairs?" He indicated a civilian arriving at his right shoulder. "You two have met, of course," he said to Hawthorn, who nodded a greeting.

"This is an honour, sir," Humphries said, genuinely surprised by Zawutu's thoughtful gesture, and appreciative too.

"I won't hold you up," Zawutu said. "Just wanted to say goodbye once more and thank you for everything." His eyes were on Hawthorn.

"And may I add my thanks to that," Ingabe said, reaching out a hand in Hawthorn's direction.

"I'll get on board, Alistair," Humphries said sensitively. "Don't be too long. Goodbye again, Mr President, Mr Ingabe." He saluted and walked up the ramp into the aircraft.

Zawutu turned to Hawthorn. "Well, Alistair. Take care. Off you go now. Oh, by the way. I've had new maps printed and there's a certain hill guarding the entrance to the Impolo Valley which now and for always will be known after you."

Hawthorn laughed. "I just hope it never again has to fulfill the role of bottle stopper. Goodbye, sir." He saluted and turned up the ramp.

"Alistair," Zawutu called after him. "If ever I need you again, will you come?"

Hawthorn paused, turned, smiled that annoying, enigmatic smile and disappeared into the gloomy interior of the C130. Zawutu watched the tail ramp close and the aircraft taxi away. He waited until it had lifted up into the sky and turned towards home.

"The hero of Hawthorn's Hill," Zawutu murmured to himself. "And may he long be remembered."

THE END